MW01087454

Silent are the Dead

Also available by D. M. Rowell

Never Name the Dead

Silent are the Dead

A Mud Sawpole Mystery

D. M. ROWELL

Koyh Mi O Boy Dah

NEW YORK

Published in the United States by Crooked Lane Books, an imprint of The Quick Brown Fox & Company LLC.

Library of Congress Catalog-in-Publication data available upon request.

ISBN (hardcover): 978-1-63910-499-4
ISBN (ebook): 978-1-63910-500-7

Cover design by Heather VenHuizen

Printed in the United States.

www.crookedlanebooks.com

Crooked Lane Books
34 West 27th St., 10th Floor
New York, NY 10001

First Edition: November 2024

10 9 8 7 6 5 4 3 2 1

For All My Relations

Author's Note

Although this is a work of fiction, the Kiowa customs and oral traditions shared are true. They come directly from my grandfather, his brother, sisters, cousins, and many other Tribe elders sharing our oral stories and traditions to ensure future generations learn of the Kiowa people. I share the information on Kiowa customs, history, and traditions with nothing but respect for the culture my grandfather, his brother, and his sisters instilled within me.

—Ah Ho!

Koyh Mi O Boy Dah

She Is A Traditional Kiowa Woman

Prologue

Time. All I need is a little more time, thought the soon-to-be-dead man. Hearing the crowd's roar, Gerald Bean looked back at Red Buffalo Hall. The gym-style building was alight as the Kiowa people inside were learning of his treachery and a murder. He ducked into the shadows cast by the overhanging eaves on the Kiowa Nation Complex, the largest of several buildings spread across the Kiowa Nation Compound. The wall felt rough through his sweat-soaked shirt. Though cooler than the day, the Oklahoma summer night was still sticky and humid.

"Damn Indians!" Gerald spoke aloud, then peered about in fear of having been heard. He couldn't be found. Not now. *Mud Sawpole was probably revealing my crimes. Nothing that would stick, but it was a bad time to be exposed.*

Staying in the shadows, Gerald put distance between himself and the Tribe gathering taking place in Red Buffalo Hall. He moved across the gravel roadway toward a large, 1940s-era Quonset hut. Gerald watched the door of the small maintenance office attached to one side, waiting to see if anyone remained inside. He was early for a meetup; just how he liked it. There was power in watching each partner slink in.

Silent are the Dead

The plan was supposed to be quick and easy—and it was—until Mud showed up. Gerald hacked and spat on the ground, immediately regretting it. Across the roadway, two uniformed Tribal Police officers paused on their way toward the maintenance hut.

"Did you hear that, Joey?" A football-player–sized man asked a slightly smaller version of himself.

Joey stopped and peered around. "Hear what?"

Taking advantage of the noise made by the police, Gerald slipped deeper into the shadows, keeping the closed office door in sight. There were no lights on within. No sign of his partners. Gerald glanced back toward Red Buffalo Hall; he could hear a faint cheer.

The officers argued as they walked on behind the large maintenance hut to the duty vehicles parked in back. Gerald listened until the gravel-crunching footsteps faded away.

Once the officers were gone, he moved toward the office. His partners weren't going to be happy to learn the plan had to wait. But there was no choice.

Sparsely spread gravel barely covered the wet dirt. Clumps of mud left from an earlier thunderstorm clung to his boots. He dragged his booted feet through the gravel, rubbing the dirt off. He couldn't help but wish he could rid himself of that Sawpole girl as easily. *Mud has to go—on her own or with a bit of persuasion.* An ugly smile formed on his pale face as a possibility came to mind.

Making sure no one was in sight, Gerald moved quickly to the office door. He entered the small office, thinking, *The plan will work. They just have to give it more time.*

Desks lined one side of the added-on office space. On the other, a well-worn plank-floor hallway led to the cavernous maintenance hut. He slid into a nearby desk chair, rolled it to face the office door, now slightly ajar.

Gerald heard cars in the distance. *The Tribal meeting must have ended. Those Indians will be talking about the murder. . . .* He rubbed his chin. *Today's murder could be good cover. They'll all focus on that and forget about me.* He straightened, pulled his shoulders back before finishing the thought. *The partners will just have to wait. I'll tell them we're laying low. It will take a bit more time before we cash in.* He licked his lips, thinking of the payoff.

His thoughts returned to the murder earlier in the day, solved by that meddling Mud and her cousin, Denny Sawpole. A silly emotional murder that served no purpose. Nothing he would get mixed up in. Gerald's annoyance shifted to his partners. *They really weren't needed anymore. Their disappearance would solve lots of problems and. . . .* His mind went to the money to be had. Gerald thought a little longer about death. *Murder done logically had certain advantages, like keeping all the money and no one left to talk.* His twisted smile returned. *After all, silent are the dead.*

Chapter One

A hand drum sounded, reverberating off the Kiowa Complex entryway walls. Its light, steady patter pulled the impromptu group into a circle with Tribe elder Mabel Wind. Looking down, I noticed we had unconsciously formed around the Kiowa Tribe seal tiled into the floor just outside the museum's double doors. The seal showed a Kiowa of old on horseback within a circle of ten feathers. It held many symbols, which my grandpa James Sawpole had revealed to me through stories so I understood how they weaved into the soul of being Kiowa.

I breathed deeply, feeling the song of the drum and matching Mother Earth's rhythm. There were seven of us, none of whom expected to be standing in front of the Kiowa Tribe Museum after nine PM on what had been a simmering hot day, but here we were.

My cousin Denny and I had thwarted an attempted theft of the Tribe's precious Jefferson Peace Medal. The large disk was presented to the Kiowa Tribe during the historic Lewis and Clark Expedition of 1804. The medal was the Tribe's symbol of first contact with the newly formed United States of America, the people that changed our world.

Tradition demanded the priceless relic be cleansed and blessed before returning to its place of honor in the Kiowa Museum. We were the remaining few after a Tribal gathering that exposed the attempted theft and a murder. Mabel had insisted Denny and I join the cleansing circle with the three legislators. That was fine with me; it would be a relief to see the medal returned to the safety of the museum.

Denny shifted on my left while the Kiowa Tribe's chairman—our modern-day chief Wyatt Walker—slid into place at my right. Tribe Legislator Anna ManyHorse leaned in from next to Denny and eyed Wyatt, falling back into the circle as the singing drum transitioned into a soft steady beat, Mother Earth's heart song.

Staying inside the circle, Grandmother Mabel moved to Cole Stump playing the hand drum. Cole was new to the legislative branch, but not to the drum. He didn't miss a beat as Mabel washed him with the sage smudge and offered prayers. She nodded to Jeb, the Tribal Police officer standing outside the circle. His job demanded he wear gear not allowed in a cleansing circle; Jeb respected the ceremony.

Anna, the most senior of the Tribe legislators, looked regal, her black hair threaded with gray pulled back into a tight single braid. A traditional shawl rested on her shoulders over dark clothing. Anna cupped the wafting smoke, pouring it onto her head. Grandmother Mabel nodded her approval. Denny was next. Like most in the Tribe, Mabel knew Denny and I had found a body and exposed a killer earlier in the day. We needed clearing of all negative energy—and spirits.

The pungent sage smoke engulfed my five-foot-seven frame. Grandmother Mabel seemed to smile as she drowned me in the skunk smoke. I breathed the purifying smoke in deep, hoping it could wash away all my worries. I held a cough in, until I couldn't. Choking and sputtering, I abruptly twisted away from Mabel and the sage smudge as she cleansed us before preparing the Tribe's precious Jefferson Peace Medal for its return to the Kiowa Museum.

Mabel moved on to Wyatt Walker as he stood at attention wearing a solemn look, traditional *aui-pah*, wrapped braids, and shiny new cowboy boots. His nearly six-foot frame dwarfed Grandmother Mabel's barely five-foot hunch. Wyatt looked like an important man of the Tribe; to some, he was. Others resented his quick rise to the top of the Tribe's leadership.

A rattle at the locked glass front doors caught my attention. Glancing over to the building's entry, I thought I saw my little brother, but it couldn't be him; Sky was attending classes at OU. I'd sent money to help with costs. I nearly broke the circle to make sure it wasn't Sky, when Mabel's chant shifted to cleansing the Jefferson Peace Medal. I gave the front doors a last look. No one was in sight.

Grandmother Mabel feathered and prayed over the tarnished silver disk, cleansing it of all bad medicine. I controlled my impatience; it wasn't right to have negative thoughts at a cleansing. But I was anxious. My storytelling agency in Silicon Valley needed me back for a client's critical event, my grandfather needed help ridding his land of illegal fracking, and if that was Sky at the exterior door, it meant my little brother might be dropping out of OU—again. I stopped my spinning thoughts, forced my fears and doubts out with a deep exhale, and readied myself for the rest of the ceremony.

Mabel thanked those of us that stayed after the late meeting at Red Buffalo Hall. She faced Denny and me. "We cannot express the deepness of our appreciation to the Sawpole family for saving our precious Jefferson Peace Medal, keeping it safe from those that plunder our sacred items and returning it to the heart of the nation inside our museum for all to see."

Haw, Kiowa for "yes," sounded from several around the circle. I noticed Wyatt was not one of them. He looked like a stereotypical Indian: stoic and humorless, staring straight ahead without emotion.

Cole drummed on.

Grandmother Mabel clasped my hand. "Storyteller apprentice, with the return of the peace medal and revealing the killer hiding in plain sight, you have made new stories to share with our young. Adding new Kiowa stories into the fabric of the old is how we have always done it. It is how we evolve as a people. James Sawpole has taught you well. Now, it is your turn to weave stories, Storyteller. We will see you when next the Tribe gathers for stories that remind and unite our people."

A smile bubbled up from deep within me. Grandmother Mabel spoke the words I had spent my childhood dreaming of hearing. My grandfather James Sawpole was the Tribe Storyteller; the last reader of our Winter Count Chronicles. During tribe gatherings Grandpa shared stories from our history, keeping us united as a people. I had been his shadow for as long as I could remember, absorbing our history, learning the Kiowa language, customs and oral traditions. Grandpa had trained me to be next.

And just like that, the bubble burst. It was too late. I couldn't be the Tribe Storyteller. I lived in Silicon Valley, a lifetime away from Carnegie, Oklahoma. I had returned to the land of my childhood only because Grandpa had summoned me. Soon, I would return to Silicon Valley. Very soon.

Before I could protest, Mabel turned to Wyatt and asked, "Do you have the medal, Chairman?"

He pulled a flat jeweler box from a pocket within his jacket. "Yes, Grandmother, I have it here." Wyatt stepped forward, opening the case with a flick of his finger, and presented the four-inch disk to the Tribe elder.

With her feather fan and sage smudge in one hand and the medal lifted high in the other, Mabel chanted first in Kiowa then repeated in English, "*Daw' Kee*, Creator of All, bless this token of peace—let its good medicine live on. The medal was created with peaceful intentions, given in friendship. Let its good energy ignite, engulf us in goodwill. Let us all know peace today and tomorrow." She feathered the medal a final time and ended with the traditional "All My Relations," entwining our blessings with the rising smoke to touch all our relations living upon Mother Earth.

Cole's hand drum, the voice of thunder, demanded our attention as Grandmother Mabel walked the medal through the open doors into the Kiowa Museum. A stand with a glass case on top stood waiting. We followed.

Mabel led the circle as if entering a lodge, starting east and slowly stepping around to end just before the point she had started from. We shuffled behind her, making a circle in the pattern of the rising sun—east to west. In this way we honored our Creator.

Mabel placed the Jefferson Peace Medal within the glass case and shut its door as the final loud drumbeat sounded.

Cole stepped back from the case and stood at attention with his eyes focused on Anna.

After a moment, Anna stepped forward and entered a code, arming the case and securing the Jefferson Peace Medal within.

I signaled to Denny in the old Plains Indian sign language we had learned from our grandparents, expressing relief that the Jefferson Peace Medal was safe.

Denny whispered, "The medal is in danger as long as Gerald Bean is alive."

Chapter Two

I stole a glance around the circle; no one reacted to Denny's negative words. I signed, "Later," and returned my attention to the group, catching sight of Wyatt watching our exchange. Wyatt had recently won an extremely close election to be the new chairperson of Kiowa Nation. His vision would dictate the Tribe's path for the next four years. I didn't know him, but his energy felt off—pretentious. Maybe that was the way of politicians.

Grandmother Mabel ended with an old song of peace as she led the group out of the museum located in the center of the Kiowa Complex and encircled by the Nation's legislative and business offices. Cole followed immediately behind Mabel, letting the drum sing with her. We all shuffled after them.

The Tribal Police officer went last, closing the door and making a production with securing the museum's front doors. "That's that, then," Jeb declared, snapping his keys back onto his thick utility belt then trailing our group to the Complex's front doors.

Mabel faced the group and raised her fan. "Be safe on your journeys forward. Remember to think good thoughts, they spread good medicine. And we need more good in the world!" I smiled at Grandmother Mable, sending her a dose of good medicine.

Jeb moved to the front. "I'm glad the peace medal is back, safe and sound inside the museum." He held the Complex's front door open where we lingered. "The museum doors are secured, and I'll lock these right up. That's two sets of locked doors protecting the medal." Jeb looked pleased. "Y'all that parked by the Red Buffalo Hall can go out this way. It's closer to your cars."

The Kiowa Complex, which housed the museum and the Tribe's legislative offices, was the original building on the growing Kiowa Nation Compound. Red Buffalo Hall served multiple purposes for the Tribe, from Tribal gatherings to basketball games and everything in between. We had all attended a large Tribe meeting at Red Buffalo Hall earlier.

Cole turned to Mabel. "Grandmother, may I walk you out?" He offered an elbow while tucking his hand drum under his other arm. Recently retired, Cole stood ramrod straight as he had for the last twenty years as a Marine gunnery sergeant. His dark crew top was sprinkled with gray. Cole's faded jeans had a rigid crease down the center of each leg.

"*Ah ho*, Grandson. I appreciate holding the arm of a young warrior." Not yet ready to leave, Mabel asked, "Are you enjoying your role in the Tribe?" She reached for Cole's offered arm.

Anna added, "Yes, Cole, I hear you're doing well in Business Development. The position needed new energy."

Cole beamed. "Thank you. I'm excited with our progress. My work in the military has helped a lot."

Wyatt asked, "How's that?"

"Well, being organized goes a long way. But my past contacts have served me well." Chuckling, he added, "Let's just say, I know people and how to work them."

"As long as your people help our people, that's good." Mabel looked intently at Cole.

He seemed shaken for a moment before nodding. "Of course, Grandmother." Cole used the term "Grandmother" as a sign of respect for an older Kiowa woman.

Mabel had more to say to the leaders of the Tribe. "Our leadership has failed us in the past. As you saw tonight, our museum and people are losing precious artifacts to blatant theft or forced to sell family treasures to simply survive another day. As we lose our history, we lose our identity. Saving our people and culture must be a priority."

Wyatt edged Anna aside to grasp Mabel's free hand. "As chairman, I will create businesses to raise the revenues needed to start preservation programs."

Mabel examined him. "That takes too long. People need to eat, to have electricity, computers, and the internet to survive and eventually thrive." She pulled her hand free to emphasize, "And we need these things now!"

Anna spoke up, "Grandmother, I've been trying for over a decade to pull the leadership together. We voted the bad ones out, a few remain, but they will be weeded out soon. Very soon."

I was silently cheering Mabel on. She did not disappoint.

Mabel stood as straight as she could. "We need inspiration and leaders for our young." Looking at the three legislators each in turn, she demanded, "Be that for them!"

Cole squeezed her arm. "I will, Grandmother." Wyatt nodded, though I thought I heard him mutter, "Suck-up."

Anna stepped forward. "Grandmother, being a legislator is an honor and responsibility I take very seriously."

Mabel said simply, "Good."

Cole turned to Anna. "Let's meet tomorrow. There are a few things I would like to review with you." It sounded more like a command than a request.

Anna looked surprised. "Anything in particular?"

Cole insisted, "We can discuss that tomorrow."

Wyatt smiled; he seemed to enjoy the exchange. Denny and I stayed silent as we watched.

Anna's jaw clenched before she answered, "Give me a call to arrange. My priority is to do inventory and secure the rest of the Tribe's treasures."

Cole nodded. "Tomorrow then."

I slipped to the front doors for a look outside. To my relief, there was no sign of Sky. I loved him dearly, but Sky had a knack for trouble—dumb jokes that misfired. The last ended up with a car in Lake Lawtonka. Shadows must have played tricks with my eyes earlier. I hoped.

Jeb jingled his keys. "I need to get. I'm 'bout off duty. Anyone going out the front?"

"We are." Cole walked slowly with Mabel out the front doors into the sparsely lit parking lot.

Denny spoke up. "Mud and I are parked in the back. Can we go out one of the back doors?"

"You can get out, but the back doors lock automatically. Once you're out, no getting back in without a key or breaking in." Jeb laughed. "And you better not break in, 'cause I'm done for the night and the other two officers are on training detail." He stepped out and locked the front doors. He shook the doors to show us they were secure before walking into the dark.

The moment the doors closed, Wyatt said, "Satisfied, Anna." It wasn't intended as a question.

Anna seemed to know immediately what had Wyatt upset. "Yes, Wyatt, knowing the peace medal is safe and back where it belongs, yes, that makes me satisfied. I should not have had to force you to place it in the museum tonight."

"It's late! A few hours in my desk would not have mattered."

"It matters!" Anna insisted. "You know many of our artifacts have disappeared."

Wyatt stepped closer to Anna. "You're the one that endangered the medal and all our other treasures stored in the museum. You hired Gerald Bean." He practically spit the last at her.

Denny started forward. I placed my hand on his arm, halting him.

A shocked expression crossed Anna's face before she snapped back, "With the board's approval! He had the necessary credentials—"

"Gerald owns an art gallery specializing in Plains Indian works! Of course he is going to steal from us," Wyatt snarled at Anna. "You gave Gerald free rein."

Anna faced Wyatt. Standing tall with her shawl wrapped around her shoulders, she looked like a powerful woman warrior of the past. "I made a mistake, trusted who I shouldn't. What's your excuse?"

"What's that mean?" Wyatt took a step back.

"Just that. I know and others will soon." Anna turned and walked down the hall to her office.

Wyatt's face darkened as he watched Anna.

It wasn't the ideal time, but I really needed to talk with Wyatt about trouble on my grandpa's backcountry land. Before I could seize the moment, Wyatt marched off toward his corner office at the end of the hallway, where the legislator offices ended and the business of running a Tribe began. Wyatt's shoulders rode high; I couldn't tell if they were tight with stress or guilt.

Denny whispered, "What do you think Anna meant?"

"I'm not sure. Does Wyatt know anything about fracking using Jimmy Creek Spring water?" Jimmy Creek Spring was on

Grandpa's land and was being polluted by harmful chemicals used in illegal fracking.

Denny shook his head. "Not that I've heard. Wyatt is new to his role; he was in Business Development before becoming the chairman. Cole's been in charge of Bus Dev for less than a year. I know the Tribe hasn't authorized any fracking on Kiowa land."

"I don't think the two fracking guys destroying Jimmy Creek Spring and physically threatening Grandpa are working with the Tribe. Everything those two are doing stinks of opportunity and corruption."

A fracking operation had started in the remote backcountry. The two running the illegal operation had threatened our grandfather when he protested their use of his spring water for fracking.

Denny hissed, "We've got to get those little frackers away from Grandpa's land."

He was right. Grandpa needed our help. Then I could return to my life in Silicon Valley, away from Tribal traditions and obligations. A knot tightened in my stomach.

Originally, I thought Grandpa had called me back to my childhood home to help rid his land of illegal fracking, but it had been to stop the theft of the Jefferson Peace Medal. Now fracking was keeping me here.

The Tribe officials we needed to resolve the fracking were in the building with us now. Denny and I had the rare chance to talk to the Tribe chair and our legislator face-to-face about the illegal fracking operation. This opportunity may not come again for days, and I had only hours before flying back to Silicon Valley.

I made a snap decision. "Let's talk to the chairman before he leaves." Not waiting for Denny, I hurried down the hall to the far corner office, skidding to an abrupt halt in the office's doorway. Wyatt stood in the middle of the room, his back to me as he looked toward his desk and a wall of windows beyond. Drawers were open, files spread across the desk, papers tossed on the floor and a trash can emptied.

The end window blind was hitched up slightly in the lower corner. Though dark outside, I could easily make out a pair of eyes staring in. This time, I was sure. My little brother, Sky, was peeking into the office of the highest elected official in the Kiowa Tribe. And unless Wyatt was a slob, it looked like someone had recently searched his office.

Chapter Three

In a blink, the familiar eyes vanished.

Wyatt released a roar—"ANNA!"—then spun around and pushed past me to reach the hallway. Anna stood outside her office, two doors down. A crumpled paper followed Wyatt into the hall. Without thought, I picked up the paper to throw it toward the overturned trash can. Instead, I shoved it in my back pocket to toss in another, one that was upright.

I took a moment to look around Wyatt's office. It had not quite been ransacked, but someone had gone through it—quickly. It was larger than most offices in the Complex, yet felt small. An overstuffed loveseat lined one wall and directly across from it was a round table in front of the wall of windows, leaving an oversized desk to fill most of the rest of the room. Papers on the massive desk were spread across the top in a scattered mess. Behind the desk a bank of oak file cabinets drawers were slightly ajar, and several looked as if someone had gone through the files in a rush. One desk drawer hung open with a file lifted as if marking a spot.

Denny stood beside me, taking it in.

Whispering, I reminded him, "Wyatt planned on keeping the peace medal in his desk. You think Gerald knew that and came looking for it?"

Denny snarled, "That dirty dog."

Rising voices pulled me into the hallway.

Wyatt bellowed, "Was it you, Anna?"

Strands of the fifty something legislator's hair had come loose from her usually tight, gray-speckled braid, yet Anna looked fierce facing Wyatt. "What are you shouting about?"

"Someone has gone through my office. Cole told me you're going over old records, why mine?" He strode down the hall, like an arrow aimed for Anna.

Denny slipped to Anna's side. Stepping quietly, I followed behind Wyatt.

Anna straightened like a *Koitsenko* warrior, staying anchored to her spot as Wyatt came closer.

He stopped directly in front of Anna. "I know what you're doing."

"Protecting my Tribe and serving the people. That's what I'm doing, Wyatt. I have been doing that for fourteen years." She leaned toward him. "What about you, Wyatt? What are you doing?"

He huffed into Anna's unflinching face before answering, "Sour grapes, Anna. All because I'm chair and you're not *after fourteen years*." Wyatt seemed to tower over Anna.

Denny shifted. Wyatt's eyes flicked to Denny then back to Anna. "I'm taking care of Tribe business. You, just stay out of my way." He turned abruptly, pushing me to the side. "And you! You curly headed wannabe, don't expect me to support you as the next Storyteller. Cole and I have talked, we want Kiowas that look

Kiowa. We'll be blocking any Tribal Recognition Ceremony." He gave me a nasty smile before walking into his office and slamming the door.

The slam echoed around the empty hallway, while the insult played on repeat in my mind. I had heard those remarks throughout my childhood, even the day I had first stepped forward to be the next Storyteller. Unconsciously, I ran my fingers through my dark curls. They marked me an obvious mixed race. Our elders and the Old Ones never thought twice about the band of mix-race grandkids running around our Kiowa homeland. If we had Kiowa blood—no matter the dominant hair, eyes, or skin color—we were Kiowa and they made sure we knew our customs. This ensured the Kiowa would always continue in body, mind, and spirit.

Unfortunately, this wisdom was being lost with the death of each of our elders. A loud minority in the Tribe didn't think I was Kiowa enough, not because of bloodline or heart, but because I didn't look Indian enough.

"Mud, don't listen to him. Wyatt thrives on putting others down." Anna let a little laugh out. "Truth be told, you two have the same amount of Kiowa blood. He just works on looking Kiowa. The fool forgets that we have always come in different shapes, sizes, and colors. We wouldn't exist today if we depended on the Tribe being only pureblood."

"I appreciate hearing that, Anna. *Ah ho.*"

She shook her head. "I'm just glad I insisted the peace medal get put away properly. It's too precious to sit in a desk drawer."

I asked, "You think someone was after the peace medal again?"

"It is an extremely valuable piece of history. If someone thought Wyatt was going to leave it in his desk drawer, well . . ."

She shook her head slowly then turned toward her office. "It's been a long day. I'm tired." She gathered some file folders, jammed them into an Indian blanket–designed satchel and headed out a door leading directly into the back parking lot. As a senior member of the legislature, she had earned an office with an exit. It showed prestige and respect. The door also allowed her to park right outside her office.

We followed Anna to a newer model SUV. As she opened the passenger door, I said, "Denny and I wanted to talk to you about fracking on Grandpa's land."

Anna swung her colorful satchel onto the car seat. A three-cell Maglite rolled out of her bag. She shoved the metal flashlight back into the satchel before straightening to announce, "There is no fracking on James's land."

Denny, standing by the SUV taillights, jerked his head up at the sharp tone. I pushed on. "Okay, there's no actual fracking on Grandpa's land, but Jimmy Creek Spring is being drained and polluted to support the nearby illegal fracking. A crew has an operation set up on land adjoined to Grandpa's backcountry acreage." My voice got deep with emotion. "Grandpa blocked the frackers from hauling the water directly off his land, so they drilled horizontally to tap into the spring at its source. After they're done using the water mixed with all those harmful chemicals, it's pushed back into the aqueduct, ruining the water, land, and life around the area. You have to—"

Anna slid into her car. "It's nearly ten, I have to go home. We can take this up at the proper time and place during office hours." She closed the door, ending the conversation.

Denny and I watched as Anna drove off, taillights flashing when she stopped before turning onto the main road.

I faced Denny. "She's hiding something."

Chapter Four

"It was just bad timing, Mud. Anna was tired. Wyatt had accused her of searching his office, it's late . . ." Denny trailed off as we walked toward his truck.

Denny was loyal to Anna, too loyal to see clearly.

My mind filled our silence by skipping from one worry to another but kept coming back to Sky looking into the chairman's office. I tried to reassure myself that it didn't mean he searched the office. But it was Sky and if his twin was around too . . . I couldn't go down that path!

I considered telling Denny about seeing Sky, but didn't. A glance revealed he was worried, probably over Anna and fracking. Denny didn't need any more to stress about.

An owl hoot carried on the night wind. I had to stop for a moment to enjoy the cool breeze. It was refreshing; an earlier thunderstorm had left the air washed clean and the night's sky clear of clouds. Having spent the last decade in Silicon Valley, I had forgotten what a country night sky looked like. It was overwhelming. The black was deep and there were too many stars to take in. It was blinding, intense and beautiful.

I soaked in the beauty until raised voices caught my attention. One of the voices sounded familiar. I rushed toward the heated sounds. Denny followed.

A short woman with long golden hair was a hundred feet ahead, beside one of the remaining trucks in the sparsely lit parking lot. Facing her was a short, older Kiowa man. He seemed irritated and was leaning aggressively toward the woman. A chill went through me. Before I saw her face, I knew it was Georgie Crow, my high school sweetheart and heartbreak.

After being together through our high school years, Georgie had chosen to stay and marry Buck Crow, my childhood bully, instead of leaving with me for a life in California. Brokenhearted, I escaped to Silicon Valley for college and eventually to start my agency, VisualAdvantage. Leaving my first love behind forever, I had thought.

The gray-haired man in workworn overalls was demanding, "Where's that husband of yours? He stole our family eagle feather headdress!" The man pounded his cane on the damp ground, leaving deep interlocking circle imprints.

Georgie stepped back. "I don't know what you're talking about."

From behind, Denny called, "Eli Tonay, it's Denny Sawpole and my cousin Mud. Can we help?" He moved forward into a small pool of light.

Georgie spun around and caught sight of me. We'd had an unpleasant exchange earlier in the day, and she didn't look happy to see me again. She snorted. "Yeah, great, offer to help him—but what about me, huh? I need help finding my husband. He's been gone for hours. Doesn't answer my calls or texts. Buck was so mad at Gerald . . . I'm real worried what he might do."

Denny snapped, "Buck's probably off with Gerald planning their next raid for Kiowa artifacts on unsuspecting families in need."

Georgie ignored Denny and faced me. "I just want to find Buck and go home to my baby. My mom's watching my little guy right now." Speaking of her son made Georgie's face glow, and I saw a flash of the girl I once loved.

Eli jumped in. "That's who I want, Buck. He stole from my family." Using his bead-covered cane for support, Eli leaned toward Denny.

Georgie huffed out a deep breath. "I am not listening to this. I'm going to the Pigpen to see if they know anything about Buck." But she stayed put.

Eli shook his head. "There ain't nobody at the Pigpen. I just come from that a-ways. Nothin' but some lost blonde teetering around in mile-high heels." Under his breath, Eli added, "Crazy tourists."

Before I could ask, Denny said, "The Pigpen or Pen is what everyone calls the new Tribal Police office."

"You're kidding—the police department is called the Pigpen?"

Denny continued, "Yeah, the Kiowa Compound took over the adjoining farmlands. The police got the old pigpen area. The name stuck." He turned back to Eli. "Why do you want Buck?"

Eli glared at Georgie as he answered, "Buck came and took my *Kone*'s *Ah-T'aw-hoy*, my grandfather's headdress for his boss, Gerald Bean. Now it's under glass in that gallery in town." The old man's brown face wrinkled in disgust. "On display like a captive."

Georgie tossed her golden hair back. "Buck was trying to help your family. And this is how we get treated?" She turned away, repeated, "I'm going to the Pigpen." This time, she walked off.

Eli watched Georgie cross the parking lot and gravel roadway going toward the dark maintenance hut and the Pigpen beyond it.

Denny moved to get Eli's attention. "Tell us what happened?"

Eli shifted his weight on the cane. "My grandson was tryin' to do good. He thought we needed that money more 'n those feathers." He looked up at Denny. "It's my fault Sonny don't know the importance, the value of our *Ah-T'aw-hoy*. My *Kone*, my grandpa, earned each one of those forty-four feathers." Eli's brown eyes held mine. "People call it a war bonnet, they got it wrong. You don't earn eagle feathers just for warring. They're earned for showing you cared for your people. Each eagle feather was a reward for an act of bravery, kindness, wisdom, strength . . . my *Kone* was a respected leader. I gotta get it back." He reached into his front pocket. "I got Gerald's money right here. All thousand dollars. I just want the family's *Ah-T'aw-hoy* back." Eli fanned out ten hundred-dollar bills.

Even in the dark, I could see Denny's face turn red with suppressed anger. He closed his eyes and took a deep breath. "Eli, you best go home. Mud and I will find Buck and see about getting your headdress back."

The old man pushed his handful of bills toward Denny. "Boy, take this. Tell 'em that headdress needs to be back with the family."

Denny pushed the bills away.

I reached forward, touched Eli's hand. "You hold on to the money. We will find Buck and Gerald. We'll see what we can do."

Eli looked from Denny to me. He nodded his head. "*Haw*. I've seen you with your grandfather, James Sawpole. You're the Storyteller's apprentice."

I didn't deny it.

Eli shoved the loose bills into his pocket, then grasped my hand. "My *Ah-T'aw-hoy* is part of the Tribe. It's got stories to share, it connects us. Y'all got to bring it back." He squeezed my hand hard before releasing it. I gave him a single nod in reply.

Eli thanked Denny and got into his truck. The engine sputtered to life. Eli did not look back as he drove out of the Compound.

Denny stood watching the exiting truck's taillights fade away. He turned to me. "We gotta find Buck and Gerald. They have been stealing from the Tribe under the guise of helping for long enough!" His jaw clenched.

Nodding, I agreed. "Georgie will lead us to one of them."

Denny made a face. "You're right. Where did she get off to?"

I nodded toward the dark maintenance hut just as a woman's scream pierced the night.

Chapter Five

For a moment, I stood rooted to the spot, eyes locked with Denny, I heard him say, "Where . . ." but didn't answer. I was already running toward the scream.

The arched maintenance hut loomed ahead. The steel hut's large central opening was closed. Coming out of the shadows from its far side, Georgie barreled toward me. Her eyes were wide and her mouth wider, locked in a silent scream.

I caught her before she ran blindly past. "Georgie, what's wrong?"

She collapsed into me; Georgie's head dropped to my shoulder. I felt her shake in my arms. "Are you all right?" I asked. Gripped by fear that she might be hurt, I pushed her away and tried to look her over in the dim light. One denim knee of her unnaturally distressed jeans looked torn, but I couldn't tell if that was style or caused by a fall.

"What is going on?" Denny pushed forward.

Georgie cowered, buried her head deeper into my shoulder. I spoke softly, "Georgie, what happened?" I reached to hold Georgie's face, make eye contact with her. I felt her body settling as she took a breath.

Denny demanded, "Why did you scream?"

I scanned the area. Puddles of light were sprinkled on the lightly graveled roadway and the front of the maintenance hut. The field beyond was dark except for a solitary light at the Pigpen.

Georgie was muttering a low, "Oh my god, ohmygod, ohmygod."

I held her face, forced Georgie to look at me as I asked again, "What happened?"

Her eyes landed on mine and held. "He's dead." Her voice was flat and cold.

Denny stood still next to me, silent now. I stayed focused on Georgie and kept my question simple. "Who is dead . . . where?"

Denny shook his head. "What are you talking about?"

Georgie answered, "Gerald Bean. He's dead in the hut's office."

Her words hung in the air. Then Georgie broke. She gasped and tears fell. I held her tight.

I sensed Denny was about to speak and signaled "Quiet" in the old sign language. When together, our grandparents talked with their hands accompanying their Kiowa and English words, a habit they learned from their Kiowa grandparents and never forgot. As kids, we watched and picked up the silent language, which had served us well at play, on adventures with Grandpa . . . and on occasional school tests.

Georgie's tear-streaked face turned to me. "Oh, Mud, I think Buck killed Gerald." She moaned, "What am I and my baby going to do now? My poor baby boy."

I held back my shock, kept my voice low, but loud enough for Denny to hear. "Did you *see* Buck kill Gerald? Are you sure Gerald is dead?" This was taking too long, and someone might need help. "Georgie, where did it happen?" I tried not to spook her. Tried to keep my voice low, but it rose with my last question.

She looked back at the maintenance hut. My eyes followed hers to the old WWII-era Quonset hut that had been transformed into the Tribe's maintenance workshop, vehicle garage, and storage decades ago. Though faint, there was enough light to confirm the hut's large central rolling door was down and secured.

Georgie whispered, "I fell on his body."

My eyes whipped back to Georgie's face. "What?" I couldn't get any more words out. I glanced back at the arched hut, looking sinister sitting in the dark.

Georgie took a breath and let it out, slowly. "I thought I heard something, so I went into the maintenance office and," she swallowed, started again, "and I fell over his boots . . . pointy-toed boots, right there in the office." A sob escaped.

Denny moved forward. "The maintenance hut has been closed for hours. No way you fell on a body in there." He looked at the large hut. "Especially Gerald's body. He's too darn mean to die."

Georgie shook her head. "Denny, I know it was Gerald, I recognized those ugly snakeskin boots he wears. Dyed red." She shivered in the night's warm air.

I flashed back to seeing Gerald onstage earlier in the evening. He had indeed been decked out in red boots, with a matching belt and tie. I scanned the sparsely graveled roadway leading to the maintenance hut. It was well used; vehicles had left deep ruts leading to its arched opening and ending at the closed overhead roller door. A damp dirt path led to the far south side of the hut. A single bulb by the arched roller door cast enough light to make out the attached office at the hut's side. I pointed. "Is that where the body is?"

Georgie whispered, "Yes." Her eyes withdrew.

I nodded and turned toward the dark office. "I'll go look before we call the Tribal Police." This was said with more confidence than I felt. Denny gave a nod of support. He was going with me.

As we drew near, I kept my eyes on the doorway. Shadows seemed to swirl around the office entry. I focused, tried to define modulating shapes. "Denny, you see any—" Before I finished, my ankle twisted on the hard lip of a tire rut, dropping me to the damp ground.

Too late, Denny warned, "You gotta watch those ruts."

I pushed myself up, brushed gravel and dirt from my jeans and palms, and refused to look at Denny. Instead, I focused on the ground. Lots of vehicle tread marks mixed with work boot tracks, an occasional cowboy boot toe, scuffed marks, what looked to be a pointed cane leaving piercing holes, and one well-defined Georgie tennis shoe print. Her shoe was branded expensive with its maker's name stamped repeatedly across its shape.

I shook my head. If I owned shoes that expensive, I would never wear them on dirt—heck, who was I kidding? I would never buy them in the first place. A memory of sixteen-year-old Georgie, delighted with her latest must-have jeans, flashed across my mind. Somehow, I had forgotten Georgie's need of brand-name clothing.

Her quivering voice pulled me back to the present.

"There." Georgie pointed to the office door, which stood slightly ajar. "It was just like that when I was walking by. You could see it wasn't closed, kinda opened like. I thought I heard something. So, I looked in. But it was too dark to see anything. Then I heard it again, so I pushed that door open and called for Buck." Georgie's lip quivered. "I took a few steps in and fell on those snakeskin boots of Gerald's." She stood staring at the dark door.

I took a deep breath, looked at the door again. A nearby tree's shadow shifted in the light breeze.

"You going in?" Denny whispered.

"Yeah, yeah, I'm going." I found myself whispering back. I stepped toward the door but stayed to the side of the path's damp dirt. Looking down, I could make out more work boot prints coming and going, the cane puncture marks, and another Georgie tennis shoe track. This one a sliding, smudged mess with only the branded toe clearly defined as she left the office. It had to be Georgie on the run.

Before I could change my mind, I stepped over the tracks and to the doorway. For a moment I didn't breathe as I stood directly in front of the door. Denny's eyes on my back pushed me forward. Suddenly the door seemed to huff open, as if caught in a draft. My imagination took hold—could someone, somewhere inside, close another door causing the sudden billowing? I dismissed the thought as quickly as it had crossed my mind.

In a loud whisper, Georgie asked, "What do you see?"

I shook my head. "Nothing yet. Gotta get closer." I took a deep breath, moved to the partially opened doorway, and peered inside. Fumbling a bit, I pulled my phone out and turned on the flashlight feature. I couldn't make out anything but gray shapes, yet the building seemed to have a presence. I called out, "Hello, anyone here?"

Silence answered me.

From behind, Georgie whispered, "Dead men don't talk."

Her words sent a chill down my spine.

I hesitated, then forced myself to step into the office. My foot thumped on the worn, wooden planked floor. Inside was dark gray, but light enough to make out several desks and a door-size cutout going into the cavernous maintenance hut. An AC hummed from above; the indoor air had a chill to it.

I pushed the door wider, took another step. Georgie had said she took a few steps in and fell on a body. Using the phone's light, I slowly scanned the floor in front of me.

I let out the breath I didn't realize I had been holding.

There was no body.

Chapter Six

Scraping sounds behind me announced Denny. Then a click, and bright white flooded the small room. The sudden light blinded me. I squeezed my eyes closed, watched white blobs dancing before a black background.

Denny announced, "Well, just as I thought, there's no body here."

I opened my eyes to confirm, saw only Denny standing in the doorway looking at the dirty wood floor. I turned my phone's light off, shoved it into my back pocket, and took in the room. Four desks lined the outside wall, leaving one side as a walkway. Uneven patterns were worn into the floor leading into the maintenance hut. Though heavy with grime and dirt, there was no body on the floor.

From outside the door, Georgie called, "You see, there's Gerald, just like I told you."

Denny barked out a laugh and stepped out of the office. Georgie came to the doorway. She glanced at me, then scanned the floor. Her head jerked up to me again, then back to the floor. "He was here, right here." She cocked her head. "I came in, fell right here, across his boots." Georgie pointed to the floor between us. "I was so scared. I didn't want to look at him. I just stared over at that desk." Georgie pointed to the third desk along the wall. "You can't see it from up here"—her eyes stayed on mine—"but on the floor in that desk's well, there's going to be a pair of fluffy house shoes." Georgie set her jaw.

Denny burst into laughter.

Georgie kept her eyes on me. "Mud, you go look."

I shrugged at Denny and moved toward the desk. Georgie added, "You gotta pull the chair out, but you'll see those fluffy slippers right there. I stared at them when I fell across the boots."

Two pairs of eyes watched me go to the desk and roll its chair out. I bent down and pulled out a pair of pink, fluffy house shoes. I stood holding them for Denny and Georgie to see. They were vibrant and fluffy.

"Those slippers prove I was on the floor. Why else would I be down there?" Georgie's nose wrinkled in disgust at the dirty flooring.

I bent closer to the floor, scanning the planks covered in work grime, dirt with dark stains everywhere. "I don't see fresh blood."

I moved past Georgie to the opening into the maintenance hut, pulling my phone out again and turning the flashlight on. Only the office had wood flooring; the hut's floor was decades-old packed dirt throughout a large open interior space. I could make out a garage setup on one side, tools and equipment storage taking up the rest of the space.

I turned back to the two. "Georgie, I believe you tripped over something, but I don't see any signs of a body."

Georgie said, "Maybe the killer dragged him away." She moved to peer into the hut's dim interior. "Maybe the body's in there."

A chill shot down my neck. I shook off the eerie feeling.

I tried to see through the grayness. Across the hut I could make out another doorway to the paint shed, and at the end was a back door that led to the parked vans and trucks used by the Tribe for grounds maintenance, shuttle services, and patrol.

I asked Denny, "Do you have any idea how to turn a light on in there?" I motioned toward the interior of the dark hut. "Maybe Gerald got up and stumbled off. He could be hurt and disoriented."

Denny shook his head. "I don't know the lighting setup for the hut." Denny added his phone light to mine to scan the dark cavern.

I ventured two steps in. Peering through the gray lighting, the shop seemed cluttered but orderly, tools in place and the general walk areas cleared. No obvious drag marks in sight. "Georgie, if there's a body in there, we aren't going to find it." I moved back to the office, returning my phone to my pocket.

Georgie wrinkled her forehead in concentration. Once, I had found that adorable. No more. I straightened. "I seriously doubt Gerald is dead. There is nothing out of the ordinary here—"

Denny interrupted, "You're forgetting one thing." He looked at me. "You look pretty out of the ordinary holding those pink slippers." His face broke out in a grin.

I'd forgotten I was holding the silly things. I dropped the slippers on top of a desk.

"You two keep joking around. This is serious. I did fall on Gerald's legs, and he was dead." Georgie stomped on the wooden planks.

Denny asked, "What makes you so sure he was dead?"

Georgie glared at Denny before she answered, "He was absolutely still." Her glare shifted inward, as if reliving the moment. "There was no breath. I fell right on him, and no breath came out. Nothing."

I took a deep breath before telling Georgie, "I believe you fell over something. But there is no body here. If you want to find Buck, your best bet is at the Pigpen. Let's see if the police know where he is."

"But Gerald's body has to be someplace," Georgie complained as she followed Denny out of the office.

"We'll keep an eye out for the walkin' dead," Denny retorted. "But finding Buck and getting Eli's headdress is my priority."

I moved to catch up with Denny, glad to leave the maintenance hut and office behind. The night seemed darker. Shadows shifted around every corner. I wasn't sure what a walking dead body would sound like, but I was listening intently. All I heard was the whine of a departing engine and a distant hoot.

The front of the police office had a yellow glow from a solitary bulb above its door. Denny took the entry's two steps in a single bound, landing with a loud thump on a small porch. Georgie and I stayed at the bottom of the steps. He reached and twisted an unmoving doorknob. The door rattled as Denny pulled, but it didn't open.

I stepped up and peered through the front window. "Looks pretty empty in there." Colorful pinprick lights glowed from various electronic devices within. Nothing moved.

Denny stepped back, spotted a handwritten notice. "Yeah, this note says the police are on special training tonight. I'm dialing the number on the bottom of the note."

A phone rang in the office, a red light turned green and flashed on a dark machine front.

Denny pulled the phone from his ear to look at it. "Straight to voicemail."

I laughed. "Straight to voicemail inside the empty office."

From below Georgie asked, "What now?" She looked ghostly in the yellow lighting.

"Have you tried calling Buck lately?" I asked.

In response Georgie lifted her phone and thumbed the redial button. "Constantly. It just goes to voicemail." A tinny *Leave a message* came from the cell.

I glanced over to Denny. "Let's go back to your truck and decide what to do next."

Denny took a last glance through the Pigpen's window. "All right, but let's cut across the parking lots this time."

I started across the gravel roadway. "Gerald and Buck could be at the gallery." Denny and Georgie's steps crunched behind me.

Denny moved to my side. "Gallery's a good place to get Eli's headdress back."

I nodded in silent agreement.

From behind, Georgie said, "Nope, the gallery's closed by now."

Impatient, Denny declared, "Hey, you want to stay here, stay. Mud and I are going to the gallery to find Buck and Gerald." Denny planted his hands on his hips.

Georgie caught up. "Okay, I'll go with y'all."

Denny shook his head. "Don't do me any favors." He turned and started across the parking lot. Georgie fell in step behind him.

I lingered, keeping an eye out for Sky. A body that's not really a body was exactly the kind of prank he would pull. If Sky was involved, hopefully this was the end of his fun. There wasn't time for any childish games. We had a headdress to retrieve and fracking to stop before I returned to VisualAdvantage.

I hurried to join Denny and Georgie standing at his truck.

Denny's lean frame was rigid. "You're up to something, I know it. You purposely distracted us with a body that's not there."

I interrupted, "Why would Georgie distract us?"

Georgie avoided my eyes.

Denny pressed on. "I think Georgie, Buck, and Gerald are after the peace medal. They get hold of it, sell to a private collector, and they'll be set up for life. No more stealing pieces one by one from needy families."

Georgie shook her head. "You know, I've been thinking about that peace medal." She leaned toward Denny with a little smile. "Your hero Anna is the one up to something. She was working with Gerald. If that medal goes missing, she's the one that's got explaining to do."

Denny shook his head. "I'm not worried about the medal because *Anna* made sure it was safe in the museum. What's important right now is getting Eli's headdress back from your thievin' husband and Gerald." Before Georgie could reply, he slammed the truck door and started the engine.

Denny never gave me a chance to mention seeing Sky and that the missing body could be one of his practical jokes. I rushed to the passenger side. As I opened the door, Georgie slipped in, leaving room in the bucket seat for me to join. Denny revved the engine, I jumped in and shut the door.

Warning bells chimed. Denny looked over to Georgie and me sharing the passenger seat. "No, you don't. Georgie, get in the backseat and buckle up."

Georgie reached across me for the belt. She pulled it and buckled us into the seat. The annoying chimes stopped. A whiff of sweet almonds floated my way. A scent I knew well, once enjoyed, and now dreaded.

"This is fine." Georgie wiggled in the seat. "Isn't it, Mud?"

Denny wasn't amused. "Get in the back."

I took a deep breath and Georgie's perfume, the same scent that she had worn in high school, rushed over me, through me.

My head spun. Memories swirled, the past merged with the present, and Georgie so close felt so right, but so wrong. Her breath was hot on my neck as she wiggled closer, waiting for my answer.

I choked out, "It's not safe," and moved nearer to the door to escape the nostalgic perfume's scent.

Georgie leaned toward me to whisper, "You don't trust yourself with me?"

My dark curls bounced as I shook my head, clearing it of the too-sweet almond vapor. Georgie had started wearing the perfume Poison our junior year in high school, the year I had fallen completely in love with the girl who shattered my heart. I exhaled the perfume's scent, reached across her and unclicked the belt. "Georgie, get in the back."

She stared at me, her mouth slightly open before replying, "I am not sitting back there all the way to Lawton."

Being reminded of the gallery jogged a memory. I reached across Georgie to touch Denny. "You know Denny, when I was at Gerald's gallery earlier today"—was it still today? I glanced at my watch, couldn't believe it was only eleven—"his assistant was packing up a display that contained two Jefferson Peace Medals." I recalled the blonde in tight clothing and towering heels. "She went on about how she was waiting to get the last of the set to finish packaging and mail off to a very special client."

Georgie jumped in. "Oh, those are fakes. Buck told me the gallery had a big client buy some medals, but they were just castings." She flipped her hair, whipping strands across my face. "Of course, the gallery can't sell a set of original peace medals, the Kiowa own one of the medals."

"I'm surprised that the Tribal Council would allow a casting of the peace medal." I pushed her hair off my face. "Any idea who Gerald got permission from for the casting?"

Georgie shifted in the crowded seat. "I don't know, but Buck said Gerald had permission for the original casting and then got a big-dollar buyer all lined up for that one-of-a-kind replica set." Sweat beaded on her forehead.

Denny shook his head. "I haven't heard anything about casting the Kiowa's peace medal. I'm sure Anna or Wyatt would have said something in a meeting."

"I may not be Kiowa, but even I know there's a reason Anna isn't the Tribe chairman," Georgie retorted before crawling across the console to settle into the back's jumper seat. "The peace medal's got nothin' to do with me or Buck. I'll take a ride to my car by the arena. I'll find Buck on my own and get home to our baby boy. Thank you very much." Her seatbelt clicked.

"Not before you get us into the gallery. Thank you very much." Denny threw the truck into gear and the wheels squealed as they gained traction onto the road.

"She's going to call Buck. He'll come looking for us."

"That's what I'm counting on. I want him to find us at the gallery."

"Good plan. Georgie may not have a key into the gallery, but Buck will."

"With or without a key, I'm getting Eli's family *Ah-T'aw-hoy.*"

Chapter Seven

Carnegie didn't get much traffic at the height of day, and at night there was only a single set of taillights in sight.

From the small seat in back, Georgie shoved Denny's seat, causing him to jolt forward and back. "I can't hear or see anything back here."

Denny grinned. "Good. Try being quiet so the adults can talk."

I heard continued mutterings from the back of the "King" section of Denny's truck but couldn't make out Georgie's complaints. Denny just smiled.

I found myself rubbing my deerskin medicine bundle. I had always kept my medicine bag near, but had stopped wearing it when I started working in Silicon Valley. Earlier in the day, Grandfather Buffalo had revealed himself as my spirit guide. To remind me of his attributes, the great buffalo had gifted me a tuft of hair. Grandfather Buffalo's wiry fur now nested within my medicine bag, once again hanging around my neck. I tucked the bag under my shirt and turned to Denny. "Why do you let Georgie bring out the worst in you?"

His jaw clenched. Denny took a moment before answering me in a low voice. "I get so angry every time I look at her." His hands tightened on the steering wheel. “Gerald and Buck have been raiding the poorest of Kiowa families, paying but really stealing treasured artifacts that have been held in families for generations. Just like what happened to Eli.” His face twisted with disgust. “Buck gave Eli’s son a thousand dollars for his family’s headdress. Gerald will sell it for easily twenty times that, and Buck gets his cut from every treasure sold.” Denny kept his eyes on the road. In a voice I barely heard, he added, “And Georgie gets something new.” Anguish and frustration played out across Denny’s face.

There was a pit in my stomach. “But how can this happen?”

Denny barked out a laugh. “Gerald’s been to our *Goom Maws* and sees all our regalia.” He used the Kiowa word for “dances,” which early white men had called powwows. Denny continued, “Buck knows which families have treasures and need cash. Gerald buys at a steal from the needy and sells for many times what he paid. And we all lose a bit more of our history, our culture.”

An SUV pulled out from one of the graveled side roads. Denny slowed. The SUV turned onto 115 toward Meers, a one-store gold mining town founded after the Jerome Agreement had stolen more land from the Kiowas to make the State of Oklahoma possible. The road was lit only by the stars and moon above. A coyote yapped in the distance; an owl responded.

A push from behind made Denny’s head jerk forward. “I know you’re talking about me.”

Denny gave me a half smile. “Georgie’s guessing; she can’t hear nothing. I’ve sat back there.” His head jerked forward, then back again. Denny ignored her.

His attention seemed to be on the rear of the SUV ahead of us. I followed his gaze. It was a dark newer-looking SUV, but I couldn’t make out anything unusual about it.

I'd just decided to tell Denny about seeing Sky when my phone buzzed. Only one person would call this late: Bernie at my agency in Silicon Valley. She was holding an important client's project together after I had left abruptly to answer my grandpa's call for help. Had that all been today? I glanced at my watch; it was nearing midnight here. With the two-hour time difference, it would be approaching ten o'clock in California.

Rapid-fire computer keys rat-a-tat-tatted across the phone line when I answered. Bernie greeted me with, "Hey, the second shift is ending soon. Really pushed through a lot of graphic work without the hindrance of Thomas."

Thomas, my soon-to-be ex-partner in the agency, and I worked well together in the beginning. Until he stopped working and took up spending all our profits. Now I had to deal with operation details while also doing what I did best, bringing in the clients and developing messages for startup businesses in Silicon Valley. In just three days, our newest client, Richard, was moving his company from private to public ownership. The stock market was buzzing in anticipation. I had worked months crafting the client's company story, then condensing it into executive presentations with compelling visuals that would define the company at its first press event. The client's successful public launch would also propel my small agency to national attention.

Bernie continued, "We're all set for the executives' rehearsal tomorrow afternoon. Richard's expecting to do a final walk-through with you." Bernie stopped typing for emphasis. "That means you're on a flight out of Oklahoma by high noon tomorrow. It's booked." Papers shuffled in the distance.

"Thanks for juggling everything, and I will be on that flight." The agency's success depended on me getting back in time for a final rehearsal with the executives before the big press event. The client needed to feel secure before stepping on stage. I had to be there.

The truck slowed. I glanced over at Denny. He was watching the SUV as it turned left onto a heavily rutted dirt road.

"Bernie, hold on a minute." I moved the phone away. "Denny, what's wrong?"

He slowed to a crawl. "Did you see that SUV? Sure looked like Anna's." Denny stretched forward over the steering wheel to watch the SUV's taillights bouncing down the dirt road. "That road leads to where the frackers are set up."

"Don't turn down that road. We need to get Eli's headdress."

A tinny voice from my phone shouted, "What is going on?"

Denny's head was jerked forward as Georgie demanded, "What's happening up there? I can't even get reception back here. How are you getting any?"

"Bernie, one minute." I pressed the phone to my chest. "Denny, we're helping Eli first. Fracking can wait."

From the phone pressed to my chest a voice shouted, "Mae, what are you doing?"

Denny hesitated, peered down the dark rutted road as the SUV taillights disappeared.

I pushed. "Denny, we can come back and check it out later." I caught his eyes. "We have got to go to the gallery. Eli needs the headdress, and we have Georgie to get us inside."

Another shove from behind sent Denny's head forward. "All right, I'm going," he said. The truck screeched forward, taking the upcoming curve too fast. I squeezed his upper arm. The truck's speed lowered to a steady clip.

Georgie complained, "What is happening?"

Bernie spoke loudly enough so her words carried clearly from California to all in the truck cab. "Mae—Mud. Whatever name you're going by, you have to be on that noon flight tomorrow. *Do you hear me?*"

My jaw tightened. "Everyone hears you, Bernie." I turned toward the passenger door for privacy. "I will be on the flight." I couldn't help it, I added, "Bernie, you do remember, I started VisualAdvantage. I've been working with Richard and his company executives for months honing the story for each presentation announcing their newly public company and products. I do know the importance of this launch." I regretted my words and tone immediately.

Bernie went silent on the other end. She had been with me almost from the beginning. The agency thrived under her whip cracking—success is never a solo effort.

Now I felt ashamed of my outburst. "Bernie, I am sorry. Without you, the agency wouldn't be able to create the show needed for Richard's national press event or be poised for the attention that will follow his announcement. We each have our role in the agency's success."

Across the air waves, Bernie took in a deep breath and slowly let it out. "Mae, I don't know what you're doing there when you should be here, but I've got everything handled on my end. I'll get the presentation and graphic files sent before I leave tonight. You review them and give me notes as soon as possible. I'll get everything scheduled after that and make sure the walk-through is smooth for everyone." Bernie wasn't warm, but there was no chill to her words.

I calculated. "All right, I'll get all notes back to you no later than five in the morning, your time." That gave me until seven AM here. Plenty of time to review the presentation files and catch the noon flight back to Silicon Valley.

Bernie ended with a simple, "The sooner the better." Computer keys clacking resumed before the connection abruptly ended.

Denny glanced over as I stored my phone. "You're leaving tomorrow? You just got here."

I shoved the phone into my pocket as I answered, "This wasn't a planned visit. Grandpa called yesterday, said he needed help and I was to come home—now. So, I did." That was twenty-four hours ago. Since the call, I had not eaten or slept, yet I felt strangely energized.

Denny nodded. "You've not said much about finding Grandpa on Ghost Mountain. You did talk with him after hiking all that way, right?"

I shook my head. "Not really. He was all about a quest—one I'm supposedly in the midst of and in need of." A laugh slipped out.

To my surprise, Denny didn't laugh with me. "He's right. About time you stopped running and take time to find your way." His glance revealed a smile in his eyes.

Denny was playing with my true name, my Kiowa name, *Ahn Tsah Hye-gyah-daw*, She Knows The Way. It was during my Kiowa Naming Ceremony that an ill-timed joke from a young Denny led to my family, Tribe, and everyone in the surrounding area calling me Mud. Only in California did I reclaim my birth name, Mae.

I made sure Denny saw me glaring at him before I answered, "I've been meaning to talk to you about that." I had his attention. "You stole my moment. Grandpa gave me an important name and"—I shook my head—"you declared me 'Mud'."

Denny seemed to think before answering. "I've always felt bad about that. When Grandpa said"—Denny took on Grandpa's accented rhythmic tones—"you would find the balancing point between earth and water." He returned to his own voice: "All I could see was you falling into a mud puddle. You know, water and earth blending . . ." He faced me with a grin. "But you gotta admit, 'Mud' fits."

I couldn't resist that grin and the truth. "'Mud' fits."

Chapter Eight

Humming tires were the only sound inside the truck. The silence was a relief. My mind drifted from nonexisting bodies to the peace medal, my grandpa's trouble with illegal fracking, Sky outside Wyatt's office, Eli's headdress then Anna's SUV going toward the fracking setup.

Denny snapped his fingers. "Wake up, Mud."

"Not sleeping," I insisted. "Just thinking that Anna," I eyed Denny and added, "or someone in the Tribal government that could be bought is exactly what anyone fracking in Kiowa country needs. It gets them a lot of info."

"How?"

"That I don't know, exactly, but I'm sure before fracking the operators need to know where to frack. They can get that kind of land mineral info from the Tribe. Someone in Anna's position could find that info, push paperwork through—"

Denny jumped to Anna's defense. "Mud, you've not been here for the last ten years. Anna has made a difference for the Kiowas. Kids are getting good lunches all year long, seniors get activities, meals, and rides. Anna's even bringing the young and old together for Kiowa storytelling times." Denny spoke from his heart. "And language preservation. Because of her, many in our next generation will know Kiowa ways."

From close behind, Georgie asked, "If Anna's done so much, why isn't she the chairman?"

Denny and the truck jerked, surprised that Georgie had crawled forward between the seats to join the conversation. He pulled the truck back to its lane before answering, "Like I said, Anna's been working within the system, helping people directly."

Georgie pushed back. "Yeah, she's done good. But that's not the same as the kind of money Wyatt Walker brings to the Tribe. I can see why most Kiowas voted for him to be the chairman."

Denny looked at Georgie leaning in across the console. "You're not even Kiowa, what do you know?"

Ignoring Denny, Georgie glanced at me. "Buck voted for him, said Wyatt was real good for the Tribe. Buck said Wyatt knows business and has already brought a lot of opportunities to the Tribe."

I looked across to Denny. "What do you think about Wyatt Walker?"

Denny answered, "He didn't grow up around here; recently connected with his mom's Kiowa relatives. First I heard of Wyatt, he was with the Tribe's business development group. He was in charge of finding new ways to help the economy of the Kiowa Nation. Everyone credits Wyatt with getting the casino started and the new Cultural Center planned in Anadarko. Lots of people worked on the projects, including Cole, but Wyatt was front and center." Denny looked like he had a bad taste in his mouth. There had to be more that he wasn't saying.

Georgie pushed. "Just like I said, that's why he got voted in, look at all the business and money he's bringing into your Tribe. I hear Cole Stump has lots happening too."

Denny shook his head. “Yeah, but I don’t see much more money for Kiowa programs. Truth is, money is tighter than ever for the people.”

“Denny Sawpole, you’re just upset Anna is not the chairman. Buck said Wyatt has done a lot for the Tribe’s infrastructure. It’s just lots of stuff you don’t see or know anything about.”

“Is it real if you don’t see it?” Denny demanded then added, “and get in your seat.”

Georgie leaned back but stayed close.

“So, you don’t like the new chairman?” I shifted to look at Denny.

“Wyatt talks a good story.”

I pushed Denny. “Come on, what do you think of the man?”

In a lowered voice, Denny said, “Wyatt’s dad was Osage.”

With the mention of the Osage Tribe, I knew why Denny instinctually distrusted Wyatt. I hated to admit that I still carried bad feelings for the tribe that had been responsible for the slaughter of 150 Kiowa women, children, and elders at Cut Throat Gap.

“What did you say?” Georgie demanded.

Denny repeated, “I said Wyatt Walker is part Osage.”

Before Denny said more, I turned to Georgie to explain. “In the spring of 1833, a group of Osage warriors watched Kiowa Chief A’date’s, also known as Island Man, band from afar. The Osage waited for the Kiowa camp’s warriors to leave on a hunting expedition, and once the camp was empty of all armed warriors, the Osage attacked the sleeping camp. They killed everyone in sight using their recent gifts of *Hanpoko* rifles and sabers.” I noted Georgie’s confused look. I clarified, “American-supplied rifles and sabers.”

Through a clenched jaw, Denny added, "Those 'brave' Osage used the sabers to decapitate the dead Kiowas, mostly women, children, and the very old. So proud of raiding an unarmed camp, they placed the heads in cooking pots and circled the burning camp with their trophies."

I added, "Never before had a Plains tribe done such a cowardly deed to another tribe."

Georgie shook her head. "That's . . . that's disgusting. Why would the Osage do that?"

I answered, "They slaughtered the Kiowa camp because the United States wanted it done."

Denny nodded in agreement.

"Why! What do you mean?"

I continued, "Prior to that point, the Kiowas had avoided all attempts at diplomacy with the Americans. The U.S. was desperate to form a treaty with the Kiowas—so they armed the Osage and sent them to attack the Kiowas."

Denny added, "An American form of diplomacy."

"I don't understand how getting a tribe to attack a Kiowa band is going to get y'all to sign a treaty."

I explained, "The Osage also took two children as captives and a sacred spiritual bundle. The U.S. volunteered to mediate between the two tribes. Which led to the opening the U.S. had been wanting for years, and ultimately to the Kiowas living on reservation land." Here I left it, I didn't want to get into the far-reaching repercussions of Cut Throat Gap, the tragedy that had been the turning point for Kiowa life as they had known it.

"That was so long ago." Georgie pushed hair from her eyes. "Y'all need to move on."

Denny watched the road ahead as he answered, "Some things are easier to forget than others. Chief A'date was Grandpa's great-great grandfather. Many in that camp were our ancestors. A'date was stripped of leadership after the massacre. He spent the rest of his life trying to redeem himself—which he did—fighting and ultimately dying to keep Kiowas free."

Georgie shook her head. "You're holding a grudge against Wyatt Walker for being part Osage. That's why you won't consider that your precious Anna might be working with art thieves or involved in fracking." She shook her head. "Hate to hear whatcha think of Cole Stump, he's more Navajo than Kiowa." In silence she sat back and buckled her seatbelt.

"Anna's not working with thieves or frackers," Denny shouted so Georgie could hear in the back.

The rest of the way, we sat in silence. I hated to admit it, but Georgie had a point.

It was late, and we seemed to be the only vehicle on the road. In town, Denny signaled a turn into a dark business strip. We entered a parking lot facing the back doors of the strip's retail shops. Gerald's gallery was toward the end of the strip.

I spoke loud enough for Georgie to hear, "Any sign of Buck's van?"

Georgie leaned forward in her seat. "Nothing, and I haven't been able to reach him. There's no lights on in the gallery either. I think y'all should just take me back to my car in Carnegie. Buck's probably at my mom's with the baby."

"If Buck's not here, we still want to get Eli's headdress," Denny said. He parked near a row of back doors, one marking the gallery as "TribalVision" in gold script stylizing the *T* and *V*.

I looked over to the gallery's back door. There were no windows facing the back parking area, which meant there was no way Georgie could tell if lights were on or off inside the gallery.

Before I could question Georgie, Denny pointed toward a dark section at the end of the strip. "There's a small, low-slung sports car back in that corner by the dumpsters."

As we watched, the sports car's brake lights flashed three times.

Denny glanced at me, shrugged, and flashed his bright lights three times in answer.

Georgie unbuckled and moved between the two front bucket seats. She looked toward the car. "That's not Buck. He drives the van or his truck. He wouldn't be in something that small." She tapped the back of Denny's seat. "Let's go. I want my car and to get home to my baby boy."

"Just hold on. I want to see who that is," Denny answered.

I leaned forward to try and see the car type or license plate. It was too dark to make out either.

Georgie raised her voice, "I've had enough of you two tonight." She shook the driver's seatback, jerking Denny forward and back. "Take me back to my car—now!"

The sports car driver's door swung open. No interior light showed. A tall dark shape rose from the low-slung seat, standing at the open door. And waited.

From the back, Georgie snapped her seat buckle in place. "Time to go. Take me to the Complex now."

Denny shook his head. "Nooo, I'm going to step out and see who that is."

"Come on, it's late. I want to get back to my car and be rid of y'all."

Denny pulled the latch on his door.

The dark figure bent and reached back into the sports car.

Across the console, I grabbed Denny's arm. "Let's see what they pull out of the car first."

Georgie loudly announced, "This is none of our business. I want to go." Denny's seat was pushed abruptly forward and back. "Now!"

Denny stayed focused on the dark shape.

The figure rose with a large flat rectangle—a large envelope—in one hand.

Denny opened the door and stepped out. I followed.

The dark figure started to move forward, then stopped. A high-pitched voice called, "Hey, you're not—who are you?"

The dark figure moved into a dim puddle of light cast by a nearby light post. The light revealed a shapely woman wearing a snug-fitting business jacket, short skirt, and alarmingly high stiletto heels. I wasn't sure how she balanced on the narrow sharp points of her appropriately named shoes. I barely maintained my balance on the simple leather flats I wore with business attire or for that matter, just wearing my typical sneakers. "Klutz" should have been my middle name: Mud Klutz Sawpole, perfect. I reined in my thoughts.

The woman placed her hands on her hips before demanding, "Who are you? What do you want?"

Denny released a low whistle. I wasn't sure if it was in appreciation of the shapely body in tight clothes or in response to the sharp demand. I gave him a shove.

There was something familiar about the woman. I thought I recognized her from my earlier visit to the gallery. I moved toward her. "Hi, we met earlier . . . well, yesterday actually, in the afternoon. I was looking for my black rolling suitcase. You let me in the gallery to check."

The woman cocked her head. "Yeeaahh, Gerald had it by mistake. Did he get it to you?"

"Yep." I indicated the back of Denny's truck. "Got it in the truck bed." I smiled, though the woman probably couldn't see it in the dark. "That's my cousin Denny. We're looking for Gerald. Are you headed into the gallery?"

The woman let out a huff before answering, "I've been waiting for Gerald all night. I thought you were him."

"Do you have a key to the gallery?" Denny asked. "Can you let us in?"

She looked back and forth between Denny and me. "Do you know how late it is? I'm placing this inside and going home." She waved the thick envelope at us.

Denny moved into the puddle of light. "Perfect, we'll go in with you. We won't take a minute."

The woman stepped back, wobbled on her stiletto heels. "Are you robbing me or the gallery? Get away from me!" Her volume increased to a near screech.

I stayed where I stood, with my hands up. "No, no. We are not going to hurt you." I took a tentative step forward. "Denny is anxious. Sorry. We're looking for a friend's artifact that Gerald got by . . . accident."

Denny had stopped when the woman raised her voice. He copied me and put his hands up, palms forward. "Mud's right. We're just after a friend's headdress. Can you let us in to get it?"

She looked between us, both with our hands up, trying to appear nonthreatening, then declared, "No. I don't know what you two are up to, but there is nothing in that gallery that doesn't belong in the gallery." She tried to stride toward the gallery's back door, but stepped into a pothole, losing her balance on her heel's deadly narrow tip. Instead, she turned around and took careful steps back toward her car. She opened its door and dropped into the low seat. The woman placed the envelope on the seat at her side.

I caught Denny's attention, signaled for him to fall back. As another woman, I thought I would be less threatening. I moved to the sports car door. "I'm sorry, I forgot your name." I left the implied question hanging there, hoping the woman would answer. She didn't.

But she did have a question. "Did I hear right? Your name is Mud?"

I let her hear the smile in my voice. "Yes, thanks to my cousin over there." I indicated Denny. "Everyone calls me Mud."

She gave me a long look.

"I probably told you Mae before. That's my real name."

Denny let out a laugh. "Don't let her fool with you. Her real name is Mud. I kinda messed up her Kiowa Naming Ceremony when we were kids, and it stuck. She's Mud and I'm Denny." He moved to the car.

The woman leaned to the side and pulled out a pair of daisy print high-top sneakers from the passenger footwell. She dropped them to the blacktop and kicked off her four-inch heels. One dusty leather shoe landed at my feet. I picked it up and examined the shoe in absolute awe that anyone could walk in such a modern torture device. I handed it to her.

She took it without expressing any thanks, scooped its mate from the ground, and tossed both toward the back of the car. She reached into a dark bag in the footwell and pulled out a pair of black workout pants. Without leaving her seat, she wiggled into the pants, pulling them up under the short skirt. The woman bent forward to put her high-top sneakers on. She purposely ignored Denny and me through her wiggling and shoe-lacing process.

Finished, she stood up. Without heels, the woman wasn't as tall as I had thought. She was close to my height of five feet seven. But she wore it better. Even off the towering heels, the woman was a shapely bombshell, and knew it. She undid and slid the tight skirt down her warm-up–clad legs, then bent to toss the skirt in with the heels somewhere in the back of her car. The tight jacket went next, leaving her in a dark silk shell and tight warmup pants.

The woman watched me, watching her. She smiled with no sign of humor. "Had to get out of those heels and skirt. You know how it is." She looked me up and down. "Well, maybe you don't." This time a smile reached her cool eyes.

I bit back my first response and struggled to keep a smile in my voice. "Sorry for showing up so late. But it is urgent that Denny and I get Eli Tonay's family headdress—"

"No Indian givers allowed." The woman flipped a hank of hair over her shoulder. "We run a business, not a pawn shop." She turned back to the car and retrieved the large envelope from the car seat.

I lost my smile and made my face blank, going for unreadable after the insult rolled from her pink lips.

Envelope in hand, the woman added, "Man, if I had a nickel for every time one of you all tried this. Sell it and want it back. Classic." She laughed. "I would be rich. Especially if it was Indian head nickels." This thought seemed to amuse the woman, who chuckled aloud.

I bristled. It had been a lifetime ago since I had heard such prejudice for being who and what I was—a Kiowa mixed race. I pushed the anger and disappointment down. In a low, controlled voice, I said, "Let's give the police a call. Let them sort it out."

All humor dropped from the blonde woman's face. "All sales are final." The woman placed hands on her hips and glared at me.

Denny shifted forward, started to speak. With an unseen gesture, I signaled "Hold."

I looked directly into the blonde's eyes. "I'm sure all sales are final"—her smile turned to a smirk as I added—"but this was not a sale." I leaned forward. "This was grand theft. I think the police, especially the Kiowa Tribal Police, will be interested to hear how a Kiowa elder, the owner of a valuable family headdress, discovered his heirloom missing." I smiled. "And how that missing treasure ended up in this gallery."

Denny pitched in, "Yep, Eli's son had no right to sell the headdress to Buck and Gerald. And they knew it!"

Before the blonde could respond, a truck door slammed behind me. We all paused and turned toward the sound. From the front of Denny's truck, Georgie called, "Brenda Lee, just let them have the headdress back. Buck took it by mistake."

The woman's rigid posture softened. She leaned forward, trying to see through the gloom. "Georgie? Is that you, Georgie?"

"Yeah, Bren. It's me." Georgie took a deep breath. "These two won't stop until they get Eli's headdress back to him tonight. We've been looking all over for Buck to straighten the mess out. But haven't found him anywhere. Have you seen him?"

The blonde moved toward Georgie. In the dim light, I could see her high-top sneakers covered in the unexpected yellow daisy pattern. Brenda answered Georgie, "Buck's not here. I've been waiting for Gerald and that—anyways, I had to go home to get my key." Brenda stopped in front of Georgie. "I've just been trying to decide whether to go in or go home for the night, when you all drove up. I thought you were Gerald." Her eyes never left Georgie's face. Denny and I were forgotten.

Georgie moved forward, gave Brenda a hug. "So glad you're here to let us in. My car's over at the Complex. I have been stuck with these two all night. You don't mind giving me a ride out to Carnegie, do you?" Not waiting for an answer, she locked arms with Brenda and moved with her across to the gallery's back door. Georgie leaned close to her friend. She seemed to whisper to Brenda, but with the shadows, I couldn't be sure.

Brenda Lee pulled loose. "Wait, I gotta get the key. I usually don't need it. Gerald and Buck are always here first thing and last ones out at night." She shook her blonde head. "Me, I've got a life."

Georgie called to Brenda, "So this is where Buck's hiding while I deal with the baby all day and night."

Brenda turned back toward her car. A flash of surprise washed across her face at the sight of Denny and me still there. Denny bent to open the car door. "Here you go, Brenda Lee."

She stared at Denny. "My friends call me Brenda Lee, it's Brenda to you." Brenda flipped her blonde hair back, whipping it across Denny's face. She leaned into her car, pulled a key on a long ribbon from the console. Brenda looked over to where Georgie stood at the gallery back door. "Got it."

Brenda moved Denny aside to shut the car door. A short beep announced the car was locked and alarmed. Brenda moved back toward the gallery and Georgie. We followed closely behind. At the door, Brenda turned to face Denny and me. "Good thing you know Georgie, or I wouldn't be giving y'all the war bonnet back. This is an exception." Convinced she made her point, Brenda slid the key into the lock and pushed the door inward. Frigid cold air rushed from the building. Somewhere inside, an AC had gone rogue.

Brenda muttered, "Those two!" She flipped a hall light on and rushed to a nearby thermostat. "Someone set it to the lowest temp." Brenda moved the dial. "That should do it." A rapid fan slowed, then stopped.

We moved inside and closed the door.

Brenda blocked the hallway. "That's it. You go no farther. I will get the war bonnet from the front display." She stared at us. "But you two, stay put."

Georgie stepped to Brenda's side. I noticed that their hands brushed. Georgie announced, "I'll help Brenda get the headdress." They walked down the hall together.

Ignoring Brenda's command to stay put, Denny moved to examine the art that lined the hallway. Even in the limited lighting, the collection of Kiowa Five flat-style depictions of Kiowa ceremonies, dance, and life were captivating. I had seen the collection earlier and understood Denny's intense focus on the paintings. The watercolor paintings were intentionally flat, no shading used to add depth. The art was simple, colorful, primitive, and powerful, each painting a window into the vanishing culture.

Denny slowly moved down the hall, looking at the paintings. He reached the last one at the end of the hallway across from Gerald's closed office door and waited. I stood at Denny's side. Georgie and Brenda were huddled together a few steps beyond in the central room of the gallery.

Georgie glanced over at Gerald's office door. "Brenda Lee, you get the headdress. I'm going to take a quick detour to look at the day's logbook. See if Buck noted where he went this evening. I want to know where that man is!"

"You know Buck, he hates to follow orders. But Gerald did get on to him last week when no one knew where he was for hours. The log should be on the desk." Brenda shook her head, watching Georgie walk to the office. "Buck is so irresponsible. Well, you know what a selfish man he is."

I stood by Denny, watching the interaction. Georgie opened the golden oak office door while Brenda continued on to the front of the gallery. Brenda flicked a switch to turn on another set of lights in the main room. She went around a partial wall, out of sight. Almost immediately Brenda cried out, "The case is empty!"

Denny reached Brenda first. His eyes moved quickly from the empty display case with a shattered side to the undisturbed cases, artifacts, and paintings nearby then faced Brenda. "What are you trying to pull? Is this a trick to keep the headdress?"

Brenda raised her voice. "No, someone broke into the case and took it. See, the casing is shattered on this side. It must have happened when I left to get my key at home."

I moved closer to examine the area. Shards were scattered inside the case, a few on the floor surrounding the stand and case. Also on the floor was a torn price tag—even at a distance, I could see it was high—and a few steps away, a chunk of petroglyph stone. The stone was slightly larger than a fist, one end jagged. The perfect size and shape for an etched camp scene and to break a glass display. I pointed the stone out to Denny.

He stepped closer to the stone. "This could be staged." Denny turned to Brenda. "Why are you here so late?"

As Brenda stepped back from Denny, she lifted the large envelope. "I had . . . an important delivery to take care of." She looked around. "Georgie knew about it. Georgie—where are you?"

Georgie didn't answer.

Brenda crossed the room back toward Gerald's office. I stayed close behind her, leaving Denny to examine the shattered case.

Georgie stood at the open doorway into the office, one hand on the interior light switch, staring at something in the office.

I pushed past Brenda to reach Georgie's side. Her face was frozen. I asked, "What's wrong?"

At the sound of my words, she turned into my arms. Georgie shook. I gave her a reassuring hug then looked over her head into the office and stiffened.

We had found Gerald.

Stretched out on his back, boots pointed skyward, eyes staring blankly.

Chapter Nine

For a moment, I just stared at those red snakeskin boots, uncomprehending. Georgie started muttering, "No, no, no." The sound jarred me into reality. I released Georgie and moved to Gerald. I knew before I lifted the clammy wrist for a pulse, there would be none. Gerald's heartless soul had vacated its shell.

I had mixed emotions over the man's death; he was greedy, stole from and cheated the needy, put money ahead of all else—but these were not reasons to kill him.

I pushed the negative thoughts away, and mentally recited a silent prayer wishing Gerald a safe crossing.

Only then did noise from behind make me aware that the other three had entered the office. Brenda, wide eyed, leaned back against the wood-paneled wall, her fist at her mouth, biting down to keep a scream inside. Her envelope laid at her feet, forgotten.

Georgie grabbed Brenda's shoulders to keep her from sliding onto the floor.

Denny stood just inside the doorway, shaking his head. Eyes locked on the red, pointy-toed snakeskin boots.

Realizing that I was still holding the dead man's wrist, I dropped the near-stiff arm. It made a soft *plop* upon landing. This was too much for Brenda. She let out a scream that was muffled as Georgie pulled Brenda's head down onto her shoulder. She began rocking and patting Brenda's back, speaking in a low voice as if comforting a baby.

Still squatting beside the body, I forced myself to look at the dead man's gray face. His features were contorted in such a way that it looked like death came as a surprise.

His wide-eyed stare held me.

"Now, that's what you call a blank stare." Denny tried to smile at me. I knew his heart wasn't in the joke, but his voice freed me from Gerald's death gaze.

I gave Denny a half smile. "That's morbid, Denny."

"Morbid is touching a dead body. Mud, we know Gerald's dead. Come up away from the body." Denny reached to lift me up.

I pulled away. "Wait, I want to know what killed him. There's no blood anywhere. Except for the death stare, he looks . . . okay." I didn't touch the body again. Instead, I shifted around and saw something wrong with the left side of his temple.

I leaned in closer. A single spot, that's all it was. A small circular indent, the sunken mark looked like a little hammer had nailed the most vulnerable spot on a human head, a small trickle of dry blood marking the wound.

I rocked back on my heels, avoided Gerald's eyes, and looked at the rest of the duded-up cowboy. Gerald didn't appear to have struggled before death. There were no bruises on his knuckles. His clothing was ruffled a bit, but everything was clean and in place. The only flaw was the dribble of blood running from the small, round indent at Gerald's temple, ending on his cheek.

Finally, I stood, and moved to Denny's side. "It looks like a single blow to his head brought him down, instantly. Maybe a small hammer." I glanced around the office for a weapon.

Denny eyed the head wound. "Who would know how to do that . . . in just one blow?"

"Could have been a lucky hit." I shook my head slowly. "Or very unlucky, for both of them."

Brenda choked back a sob. Georgie made more soothing sounds.

I stepped back from the body; only then did I notice the folded hundred-dollar bills stuffed in Gerald's cowboy shirt front pocket. *Eli had been here.* "No, not him," slipped out.

Denny followed my eyes, took in the scene. He announced, "Nope. He did not do this. Eli would not take a life. Never. Not even for his headdress. It would bring shame to the feathers." In a softer voice Denny added, "You know that, Mud."

"Denny, I don't want to think Eli killed him." I tilted my head indicating the body. "But Eli had plenty of time to get here before us, he wanted his headdress back and those hundreds." My eyes traveled back to the folded bills in the front shirt pocket of the dead man. It looked like there were ten hundred-dollar bills in the folded wad—the same amount Eli had fanned in front of us back at the Compound.

Denny pointed at the body and raised his voice. "Gerald carried money around like that all the time. He had to have cash to flash in front of the needy."

The room was quiet. The sobs and murmuring had stopped. Brenda was still wrapped in Georgie's arms, but no longer looked stricken. She wiped her face, squeezed Georgie's waist and stepped forward. In a voice stronger than I expected, Brenda announced,

"Looks pretty obvious your friend Eli did this while I was out fetching the gallery key. I missed Gerald's return; he must have caught Eli stealing the war bonnet." Brenda pointed through the office door toward the shattered case in the gallery. "Eli probably used the same petroglyph rock to kill Gerald. One side of that rock has a jagged edge. That's what broke the case and. . . ." She had to swallow before adding, "Gerald's temple." She stole a glance at Gerald's wound and went pale under her sunlamp tan.

I shook my head. "The petroglyph rock couldn't cause that injury. The wound is perfectly round."

Denny moved to face Brenda. "See! Eli did not do this. It was most likely Buck. A falling out with his partner in crime." Denny looked over to Georgie.

Georgie stepped to Brenda's side. "Buck didn't do this. You're not going to put the blame on him." She placed two fists on her hips.

Denny looked confused. "You said it yourself, Buck was real mad at Gerald and you were afraid of what he might do."

"My husband was always complaining about his boss, but that's not a reason to kill him." Georgie shook her head. Brenda squeezed her arm in support.

Denny glanced between the two before he settled back on Georgie. "You saw Gerald's body at the Complex. Said you tripped over his red snakeskin boots. Buck was searching for Gerald. Makes sense that he hauled Gerald's body here." Denny looked to me. "Tell them, Mud."

Before I could answer, Georgie did. "I'm not so sure it was Gerald's body in the maintenance office, now that I think about it."

Color rose in Denny's face. "You were sure at the Compound, claimed you recognized the boots." Denny stepped back and clenched the edge of Gerald's mahogany desk.

Georgie snapped, "That was before I saw the real thing." She took a deep breath, let it out slowly. "I don't know what I tripped over . . . I could have imagined it all and now it just happens Gerald got killed here . . . by Eli, probably used that cane he was swinging around." She lowered her head. Georgie never could look you in the eye when she lied.

Denny's jaw clenched. He vibrated with contained anger.

Brenda put her arm around Georgie's waist and pulled her in. "Had to be Eli. Only thing missing is the war bonnet he wanted. That old Indian stuck a thousand dollars in a dead man's pocket." Brenda shook her head in disbelief. "Waste of good money."

I stepped forward. "That's not the only thing missing." All three turned to me. I pointed to a five-foot-tall case just inside the office door. The case was all glass, and empty.

"That had an original *Koitsenko* sash and lance in it when I was here yesterday. It's empty now." I moved to the empty case. "Only the ten bravest in the Kiowa Tribe carried the *Koitsenko* sash and lance. They vowed to protect the Kiowa people from all invaders. Those warriors staked themselves to the ground wearing the sash around their necks like a collar while the feathered lance pierced the sash's other end, anchoring the *Koitsenko* warrior firmly. They were a human barrier, protector of the people. The *Koitsenko* warriors fought to the death if necessary."

"Oh, stop the history lesson." Brenda had followed me to the case.

"Just giving background on the importance and emotional value Kiowa families have with Tribal artifacts. There's only two sets left in the Tribe. It's an honor to have one in a family." I looked over to Georgie. "But you know that, don't you, Georgie?"

Georgie gave a grudging nod.

"The *Koitsenko* sash and lance that was in the display case once belonged to the Crow family. That's your husband, your son's family, Georgie."

She avoided my eyes but answered, "Buck sold it to Gerald without his grandfather's knowledge. When his grandfather learned of the sale, he told Buck he brought dishonor to the Crow family."

I moved directly in front of Georgie, but she still refused to meet my eyes. "I know Buck wanted the sash and lance back from Gerald."

Denny jumped in. "Yeah, and obviously Buck took it right over Gerald's dead body."

Brenda glanced at Georgie, then said, "How do you know Buck took the sash and lance? Most likely it was Eli. He obviously broke in for the war bonnet."

I faced the tall glass case sitting empty by the office's door. I pulled on the case's closed door. It rattled but held. "This case wasn't broken into. Someone had a key to open and close it."

Georgie shot back, "Buck took all that stuff earlier. Way before Gerald was onstage—*still alive* at Red Buffalo Hall."

Brenda and Georgie exchanged a quick look; they seemed to come to a silent agreement. Bolstered, Georgie continued, "Buck said Gerald poisoned his soul with greed. When his grandpa died, Buck knew the sash and lance had to come home. Buck told me before—"

"Before you found Gerald dead at the Kiowa Complex," Denny interrupted. He strode over to the display case, examined its locked door.

Georgie glared at Denny. "I must have fallen and imagined Gerald dead. I mean, he's here . . . dead." Georgie flipped her hair off her shoulder. "I had Gerald on my mind. So scared Buck was going to—"

"Kill Gerald," Denny finished. "Looks like Buck succeeded." Denny looked toward the body.

Brenda pushed between Georgie and Denny. Her lip curled into a snarl. "Dead bodies don't get up and move."

Denny leaned forward. "This one did." He glared back at Brenda.

I broke their stare-down with a question. "Is anything else missing in here or the gallery?" I knew we should call the police, get out of the office, stop destroying evidence, but a display case sitting on the large desk lured me deeper into the office. Sparkles within caught my eye; inside the case, two large Jefferson Peace Medals dangled by silver chains. The glass case had an empty slot waiting for a third peace medal.

Brenda hurried forward, blocked me from going farther. "There's nothing else missing. Just the feather war bonnet." Brenda looked to Georgie. "Like she said, Buck took the lance and sash thing earlier. Except for the hour I went home for the key and a snack, I was here waiting for a delivery before I could ship out a client's order. I didn't get the last piece until—" A panicked expression washed over Brenda's face. Her eyes wildly scanned the room, skimmed across the body, and stopped at the envelope on the floor by the office door. She let out a deep breath.

A few feet closer to the door, I got there first and bent to retrieve the envelope. From behind, Brenda shouted, "Don't touch it!"

The envelope was in my hand when an unexpected push knocked me to a knee. I went down, the envelope banging into the wall and its contents falling onto the blue carpet. I dropped to the other knee to look closely at what had fallen out. A sulfur scent wafted upward. I leaned forward, couldn't believe what I was seeing.

Brenda shoved at me from behind. "Move!"

I ignored her, bent closer to confirm.

Nestled in the plush blue carpeting was a large four-inch Jefferson Peace Medal.

Chapter Ten

I reached to touch it, to hold the large disk in my palm. Its silver chain snaked down my open hand. The patina was a dull, tarnished gray going to black around the worn lines of Thomas Jefferson's profile. Around the silver disk, gray wood peeked through the thin edging, revealing its wood core, just like the peace medal on display at the Kiowa Museum. If I had not seen the original recently, I would have believed this was the Kiowa's Jefferson Peace Medal.

Having seen both within hours, the differences stood out, the wood centers were the obvious tell. The original Kiowa Jefferson Peace Medal's exposed center consisted of ragged, gray flakes of old, extremely dry wood. While the disk in my hand's wood center was a similar gray but instead of dry flakes, the edges looked blunted . . . like the wood had been soaked in water to age fast, leaving no flakes.

Brenda reached over my shoulder. I shrugged her off and stood, keeping the medal out of reach. I needed a moment more.

Denny sputtered, "Is that . . . is that the Kiowa's Jefferson Peace Medal?" Before an answer came, he asked, "How did you get it?" Denny moved closer. Georgie followed.

Brenda turned toward Denny. "It's an exquisite casting of the original." She said it as if well practiced.

"How did you get a casting of the original?" Denny demanded. "The Tribe never approved it."

Georgie piped in, "You don't know that for sure, Denny." She moved closer to Brenda.

"Gerald has—had his ways." Brenda stopped a smile from forming, glanced over at the pointy-toe red boots and away.

Denny filled in, "Yeah, stealing was one of Gerald's ways."

Georgie made a face at the mention of Gerald's name. "Brenda Lee doesn't know Gerald's inner workings. She's . . ." Georgie glanced at Brenda. "She's just a sales assistant."

I registered the conversation, but my mind remained focused on the peace medal. While Denny had Brenda and Georgie's attention, I moved over to the other two peace medals suspended in the glass case sitting on Gerald's large mahogany desk. The two medals were also gray with tarnish, but with a richer tone to their gray. Each medal had its wooden center exposed in different wear patterns. I bent to examine the encased disks—in both the exposed wood was crumbled and worn from age. They looked like originals. I peered closer at the medal in my hand; its gray wood splinters though swollen and blunted rather than crumbling, could pass for the real thing.

I was so focused on the three peace medals I didn't hear Brenda's approach.

She swept the medal from my hand. "I'll take that." In a single motion, Brenda slid the medal back into the envelope. She seemed to look down her nose at me as she talked. "The medal is a replica, but still valuable. Made from the first-ever casting of the original. It goes perfectly with the other two. I'll send them off to the customer tomorrow, get final payment for the set." Brenda glanced at the body and back to me. "It's the least I can do, to wrap up Gerald's business." Her eyes snuck back toward the red rattlesnake-skin boots and away.

Brenda lifted the clear case. The suspended medals within tilted to one side. "I'll take these to finish packaging."

I stepped forward, blocked Brenda. "I don't think you should take anything from the office. We've contaminated the crime scene enough already. We all need to leave. I'll call the police and report—"

Brenda shook her head, jiggling the medals within the case. "My customer has paid for this set, he owns it. It doesn't belong in here." Brenda bumped me as she turned toward the open door. My feet remained planted, I refused to move out of her way. From within the case, a muffled tinkle sounded.

Denny and Georgie were watching the scene play out between Brenda and me, the body forgotten.

I reminded them.

"There's a dead man in this room. Someone killed him." I locked eyes with the blonde. "Put the case down."

Her eyes stayed hard, but I could see different emotions play across her face until she landed on sales mode. "You don't understand the significance and value of this set." She placed the case on the desk, keeping a possessive hand resting on its top before continuing, "This is the first time all three peace medals will be together since Thomas Jefferson presented them to Lewis and Clark before the start of their historical expedition."

Georgie cleared her throat.

Brenda Lee's fake smile faltered. She corrected herself. "I mean of course the first time these *original castings* of the three medals are together." Her blonde head bounced up and down.

Denny moved toward Brenda and the medals.

"My customer deserves to have his property delivered to him." She bent to lift the case again.

I placed my hand on its top, pressed downward. "It stays."

Brenda glared at me. I returned the glare.

She huffed out, "This is my office. I call the shots here."

My hand stayed on top of the glass case. Brenda tried to push the case free. It stayed put.

Brenda turned to appeal to Georgie. "Tell her the medals need to come with me."

Georgie moved closer. The scent of Poison reached me first. Keeping my hand in place, I shifted to look at Georgie. She saw it in my eyes. There was nothing she could say or do to change my mind. We all needed to leave this office. There was a dead man in the room.

Before Georgie could speak, I announced, "We all need to not touch anything more, and step out of the office. Now." I watched Brenda.

Georgie and Brenda Lee exchanged looks before Georgie moved forward and pulled Brenda by her arm. Both avoided the body as they edged toward the open office door.

Denny nodded and followed Georgie out the door.

Brenda lingered in the doorway; she needed a bit more urging before I was able to close the office door. I leaned back against the oak door and took out my phone. "Time to call the police, let them figure out what happened here."

Denny reached forward to grasp my dialing hand while saying, "Whoa. Wait." At the same time, both Georgie and Brenda surged toward me.

Georgie let out, "Don't! What are you doing?"

Denny squeezed then released my wrist. "Hold up, Mud."

Brenda agreed with Denny for the first time that night. "Yeah. Just hold up. Let's think about this."

I looked at the three circled around me. "There is nothing to think about. We have to call the police." I shook my head. "What's wrong with you all? This is murder and probably grand theft."

Denny jumped in. "Mud, you can't call yet. We need to talk to Eli first, before the police jump to conclusions."

"Denny, there is a dead man in there." I tipped my head toward the door at my back.

"He doesn't get any more dead waiting until we clear Eli."

Georgie and Brenda watched, waiting for my response.

"The police will be able to solve this faster without us messing things up any further. We need to call." I raised my phone.

Denny spoke softly. "Mud, you ain't been gone that long. You know the police are going to see one suspect in this mess. *The Indian.* They'll arrest Eli and never look for the true killer. Case closed."

Brenda piped in, "Pretty obvious that is what happened here."

Denny snapped back, "Pretty obvious Buck did this, here or at the Complex. We know he was at Red Buffalo Hall earlier looking for Gerald."

"You're throwing one Indian over for the other. Is that right?" Georgie protested.

Denny shook his head. "I'm not doing that. I'm just stating the truth. Buck did it and took his family artifacts; may have done it with the *Koitsenko* lance. It ends in a sharp point."

Georgie raised her voice, "The father of my baby did not kill Gerald!"

"Then why do you want Mud to keep the murder quiet?" Denny shifted to confront Georgie.

Georgie leaned toward him. "To prove Buck didn't do it." She stared at Denny for a moment before turning to me. "Mud, you can't report this yet. Y'all go see Eli. Hear what he has to say about killing Gerald—."

Denny cut her off. "Eli did not do this."

Georgie tightened her hands into fists. "Fine. Go hear his story. I'll find Buck." She looked at me for confirmation.

I took in the three: Brenda white faced, Georgie with clenched fists, and Denny locked-jaw silent. They all watched me.

I shifted to face Brenda. "How do I know you won't go back in the office for the medals or to change things?"

Georgie jumped in, "I'll stay with Brenda Lee. She'll help me find Buck, and we will bring him here to prove his innocence." She took hold of Brenda's arm and squeezed.

Brenda glanced down at Georgie, then nodded in agreement. Color eased back into her face.

She looked too confident for my comfort. I told Brenda, "I'm not sure I can trust you."

Denny added, "Or Georgie."

Georgie spun toward Denny. "You want to prove Eli's innocent; I'm doing the same for Buck."

The two stared at each other until Denny gave a slight nod and shifted his attention back to me. "Mud, we talk to Eli, they get Buck and bring him here then we call the police with what we know." Denny's eyes silently pleaded.

Georgie and Brenda nodded their agreement.

I raked my fingers through my curly mess. If we proved Eli didn't murder Gerald, that would help the police as well as Eli. Denny was right, in the past the police had tended to arrest a convenient Indian for most crimes in the area, often as not shooting before waiting for answers. Few knew that Indians—Native Americans—were killed in police encounters at a higher rate than any other racial or ethnic group. Indians have been massacred throughout United States history, with today's police continuing the tradition.

I pictured the older man in his worn overalls trying to explain the hundred-dollar bills on Gerald's body to an overworked, judgmental police officer. As I thought, I rubbed my medicine bundle. Within it nestled a tuft of Grandfather Buffalo hair to remind me that I, too, was a guardian. I knew what I had to do. I tucked the leather bundle back into my shirt and faced the three. "I keep the key to the gallery. If we leave, no one goes in until I return."

Denny reinforced his immediate "*Haw*" with a rapid nod.

But Brenda backed away, shaking her head. "No! There's valuable inventory in here. I'm not handing over my key!"

I folded my arms. "There's a dead man in there." Lifting my chin, I indicated the office behind me.

Denny moved to my side. "A dead man trumps inventory any day."

I nodded, then turned my attention to Brenda. "The only way we do this is my way." Georgie and Brenda exchanged looks. I went on, "You two get Buck, bring him here. Denny and I will talk with Eli, find out what he knows about this . . . murder." The word hung in the air for a moment.

Georgie pulled Brenda to the side. They tried to have a private conversation, but Georgie never could keep her voice low. Georgie tugged Brenda's head down and loudly whispered, "You have what matters."

Brenda pulled away. "Do I?" She stared intently at Georgie.

Georgie moved closer to her. This time I didn't hear what she said, but Brenda seemed to melt.

Impatient, Denny cleared his throat. "Are we doing this? Time's a-ticking."

Brenda stood straight, clasped her envelope. "Okay. We don't tell yet. You go to Eli, get his story. We'll find Buck."

"And I get the key to the gallery."

Georgie answered, "Yes. You get the key to the gallery." She assured Brenda, "Mud will return it when we meet back here."

Brenda turned to me, her face flushed. "I get the key back." It was a demand.

I gave a slight nod.

Denny rocked to his toes. "All settled. Mud, let's get going." He walked down the hall without looking back.

Georgie followed, pulling Brenda along. I brought up the rear.

Brenda held the gallery back door open, waited for me to move past before closing it. She used the key on the ribbon to lock the dead bolt. "This is the only key I have." It dangled from her hand.

"Good to know." I reached and took the swinging key.

She let it go easier than I expected.

I stepped forward and pulled on the locked door, making sure it was secured. Brenda and Georgie watched my every move. Denny was across the parking lot by Brenda's car.

I wasn't sure this was a good idea, but we needed to try to keep an innocent man out of jail.

Chapter Eleven

A short horn blast shattered the dark, making me jump. Denny was inside his truck, engine running, ready to go. An orange glow from the instrument panel illuminated his face as he gestured at me to hurry. I lingered.

Georgie and Brenda Lee stood outside the gallery door, huddled together. The unexpected sharp beep had brought both heads up in unison. I felt their eyes on me as I got into Denny's truck. Before my belt was buckled, Denny was off and rolling away from the dark parking lot. I turned to look out the rear window to watch Georgie and Brenda watch us leave. My stomach tightened. Was leaving the dead man a mistake?

Denny in the driver's seat had no such worries and headed out of town toward the nearest highway leading to Eli's house. He was on a mission.

Denny started repeating himself. "We gotta hear what Eli has to say. Prove he didn't do it. That old man couldn't kill Gerald. They're covering for Buck . . ."

I only half listened to Denny's chatter. I was still watching. I twisted in the passenger seat, to get a better view out the back window. The seatbelt cut across my extended neck. I saw nothing: the night remained black.

Denny tapped my upper arm to get my attention. "You have ants in your pants?"

"There's no headlights behind us."

Denny slid into a lecture voice. "Lawton is a much smaller town than what you have in California. I'd be surprised to see any headlights behind us at . . ." He glanced at the clock on the dashboard. "My gosh! It's nearly two."

I didn't respond, just pulled the strap from my neck and moved in my seat to find a better view out the rear window.

"Mud, what are you doing?"

"Georgie and Brenda have not come out of the parking lot," I answered as I sat forward to watch for headlights through the rearview mirror. The street remained a dark swath in the darker night. I glanced over to Denny. "Circle back. Let's see what they are up to."

Denny continued to the on-ramp for I-44 east out of Lawton. I took another glance through the mirror before shifting my attention to Denny. "Hey, I want to go back."

Denny turned toward me with a grin. "Those two are still at the gallery parking lot. They'll be there for a few hours. Plenty of time for us to get back before they can get up to no good." I didn't think his grin could get bigger, but it seemed to double in size as he finished.

"Denny, what did you do?"

"Bought us time to figure out this murder."

"Are you *mawbane*?" I'd not used the word much in years, yet it slipped out. It fit. Denny was acting crazy, not thinking. He was *mawbane*!

Denny laughed at my question. "Maybe so. But you solved that other murder. We get enough info, you'll be able to prove

Buck did this one." He sped down the road, eyes forward, head nodding in agreement with himself.

"Denny, what did you do?" I asked again.

"No need to worry, Mud. I didn't harm no one. Just let a bit of air out of that little sports car's tires. Those two will be sitting right there when we get back. They can't get in the gallery 'cause you have the key—so the evidence is safe and they can't work an alibi out with Buck, because Georgie and Brenda *Lee* are stuck in that parking lot with no reception. I checked." He leaned back in his seat, satisfied.

I couldn't help but smile at him. His glee was contagious. I hated to make him face reality, but had to say, "You bought us half an hour at most. There's probably a spare tire in the trunk."

Denny answered. "I thought of that. So, I let the air out of two tires." His fingers seemed to tap-dance on the steering wheel. "They might have one spare, but not two." His fingers danced on. "That side of town at this time of night, well, morning, they're not going to get help anytime soon. Nope, they are stuck for quite a while."

He glanced from the road to me. "We just gotta prove Eli didn't do this before going back and calling in the police. I know you can figure this out. You always were the smart one."

I had one word for him. I repeated, "*Mawbane*!"

Denny was crazy, thinking we could solve this. I wanted to hear Eli's story, help him explain to the police, then we had to let the professionals handle it. We had fracking on Grandpa's land to deal with, and I still needed to find an internet connection to view the files Bernie had sent. My business depended on it. Denny was right about one thing: time was ticking away—fast.

After a few minutes of silence, Denny asked, "What do you think happened?"

"Happened?"

"You know, to Gerald?"

I cocked my head, looked at Denny's profile lit by the orange glow from the instrument panel. "Why do you say this dead man's name?" Before he could answer, I went on, "We both intentionally avoid saying Buck's dead grandfather's name, yet we say this one." I reminded Denny of the Kiowa taboo of speaking the dead's name in fear of holding their soul back from moving on.

Denny seemed to think about my question. His fingers slowed. "Must be because Gerald's *TD'aukoy*." Denny used the Kiowa word for "White People." "They don't think about death the same way." After a bit, Denny added, "I'm not sure Gerald even had a soul. Might be best to not let a soulless spirit out wandering. Saying his name anchors him to the here and now."

I shook my head. "We shouldn't speak ill of the dead, even Gerald."

"Kinda have to."

"Why?" I looked at Denny's flexing jawline highlighted in orange. It took a while for him to answer.

"Gerald was heartless and cruel. He stole from the needy to line his pockets. He's been stealing Kiowa artifacts and selling for huge profits, and he tried to steal the Jefferson Peace Medal. Gerald chose his life path . . . and death."

"That's harsh."

Denny took his eyes from the road to look at me. "Looks like someone killed Gerald to get their family treasure or money back. That makes Gerald's death his own fault." He returned his attention to the road. His fingers kept dancing.

I thought on that. "You said 'someone.' So, you don't think it was Buck?"

"I still think Buck did it. He had plenty of reasons, not just wanting his family's *Koitsenko* sash and lance back. Remember, those two worked together to steal treasures from Tribe members. I think Buck and Gerald argued over money, Buck lost control and hit Gerald with the sharp end of the lance. You just got to find all the pieces to prove it before the police decide Eli killed Gerald."

I shook my head. "That's not how it works. We can't decide Buck did it, then find ways to prove it."

Denny's fingers stopped their happy dance. He slowed for the Medicine Park—Carnegie exit. A stretch of bright lights announced the last chance for fast food delights before leaving civilization for the dark backcountry.

Denny didn't respond.

Finally, I added, "You do realize that there's a lot of evidence pointing to Eli as the killer." Before Denny protested, I went on, "Eli was desperate to get his headdress back, he was at the Compound earlier looking for Gerald, and he had a handful of crisp hundred-dollar bills just like those left in Gerald's pocket." I reached to touch Denny's arm. "It really doesn't look good for Eli."

"Maybe, but that doesn't prove he did it. Gerald could have been alive when Eli gave the money back."

I just shook my head.

Denny repeated, "I think Buck killed Gerald and moved him for some reason. Maybe Buck needed the key to the art gallery to get his sash and lance back."

I turned toward Denny. "So, Buck took the body instead of just the key. Come on, Denny, you're forcing pieces to fit."

Denny's fingers tapped slowly. "Okay, Mud, you're right. We need to find the murderer, whoever it is." Denny glanced at me.

"I know it won't be Eli. And I tell ya, Mud, we can't let him suffer while the police take their time catching the real killer. The man's reputation will be ruined. The stain will last the rest of his life. We gotta find the killer." His gaze lingered before returning to the road.

I didn't respond. Denny let the silence grow. Through the rearview mirror, I noticed dim yellow dots for headlights turn out of the Burger Barn onto the highway behind us.

I understood Denny's desire to protect Eli, but I wasn't so sure we could figure this murder out. There were too many questions and too few hours to get answers before I had to be on a plane. I found myself rubbing my medicine bundle, hoping for direction.

Denny slowed to the speed limit. Medicine Park Police patrolled this stretch of the highway and strongly enforced the speed limits: it was a top revenue generator for the small town. Two pairs of car headlights, including the dim yellow ones, slowed behind us. Obviously, locals in-the-know.

I cranked the window down and the night's fresh air rushed into the cab. The coolness washed across my face, leaving me feeling refreshed. I took a deep breath of the crisp air, filled my lungs, and slowly exhaled. It was over twenty-four hours since I had slept; this trip to Oklahoma was beginning to feel like a vision quest of old.

When the Kiowa young reached the right age, they were encouraged to take a four-day quest of introspection. There was no eating or sleeping, just water, thoughts, and prayers for insights or a vision showing your road forward. I had tried several times to seek a vision, but none had ever come to me. Instead, I forged a path ahead in Silicon Valley. It had felt right, but now I wasn't so sure of my chosen path.

I sensed it before spotting a dark shadow gliding daringly low toward us. I watched transfixed, expecting the large form to pull up and away from our headlights. Instead, it seemed to adjust and align with our windshield. Denny seemed oblivious to the silent winged barn owl coming straight at us.

Orange orbs came into sight first. The owl's eyes held mine, seemed to bore deep within me before swooping up and away. I watched the owl disappear into the night. It took a moment before I could get out, "Did you see that?"

My question jarred Denny from his silent thoughts. "What—a deer?" His whole body seemed focused on the road ahead.

My head hung out the open window looking up into the sky, hoping for another sighting, finding only the silver moon and rivers of stars. I explained, "An owl just swooped past. He looked into the windshield at . . . us." I settled back into the seat.

Denny laughed. "You're tired, Mud."

"No! I'm wide awake. Its piercing eyes stared right at me." Really it had felt like the stare had gone into me. Found what it needed and moved on. But I wasn't going to say that to Denny.

"You know the Kiowa believe that hearing an owl hoot means there will be a death."

I tried to squish my windblown curls back into shape. Gave up before answering, "This owl never made a sound. Besides, it would be pretty late with its warning. Gerald's been dead for hours."

In a soft voice, Denny said, "Maybe there's another death coming."

"Not funny, Denny." I rolled the window up, missed the fresh air almost immediately. "Besides, owl hoots aren't just death omens. You know that."

"I know. Can't be a Sawpole without knowing about Owl Talkers."

Our last name, *Sawpole*, was Kiowa for "owl." Our shared last name came from Grandpa's grandmother, *Sawpole Gyah*, Owl Talker. She was descended from one of the Tribe's greatest Medicine Men, *Mamanti*, SkyWalker, the first Medicine Man to fly and talk with owls. His visions benefited and even saved the Kiowas on many occasions, from ensuring the Tribe had a successful raid to warning of a planned predawn attack. Owls have always served as messengers for our family. As kids, Denny and I had used an owl hoot to signal each other during nighttime adventures.

"Not sure what your owl was up to, but sure glad I didn't hit him." Denny looked over. "That would be a bad sign."

I started to laugh until I saw his face. Denny was serious.

We dropped into a comfortable silence. Both contemplating omens of death.

Seeing Mount Scott woke me from my thoughts of death. The mountain rose above Lake Lawtonka. The Kiowa called Mount Scott *K'Hop'Ale*, the Big Old Mountain. *K'Hop'Ale* was one of the largest in the surrounding Wichita Mountains gnawed low by time. Kiowa spiritual leaders felt power within the oldest range of mountains in North America. It's one of the reasons the Kiowa chose this land for their home generations ago, before Manifest Destiny was conceived.

The mountains and lake calmed me. My family belonged to the *Kop-adle-gya*, People of the Mountain, or the less formal, *Kop-gya*, Mountain People Band of the Kiowa Tribe. This land was home.

"Where does Eli live?"

"He's out by the Slick Hills going toward Carnegie."

Back to where we started. The Kiowa Complex was in Carnegie, and the fracking operation was in the Slick Hills.

"Mud, I'm going to make a quick stop." Denny hurried with his explanation. "That fracking setup's on the way to Eli's place. I just want to take a look around." Seeing my reaction, he quickly added, "Won't be but five minutes extra . . . maybe ten."

"Denny, we left a dead man in town—"

He cut me off, "I know, I know." Denny took his eyes from the road to look at me. "Mud, I gotta see what Anna was doing down that road." Denny shook his head. "Just makes no sense. Why would Anna go to the fracking office?" His focus returned to the winding road.

"You're not even sure it was Anna's SUV," I reminded Denny. "It's dark—"

Denny interrupted, "It was Anna's. She had a small crack on her taillight covered with red tape. I got close enough to tell it was her SUV." He looked at me before returning his attention to the highway.

"But you trust her, Denny."

"Yeah, but you don't." He looked at me for a moment before admitting, "And things creep into my head after what Wyatt implied and Georgie said . . . making me wonder, and I don't like wonderin'. I gotta know." He stared at the road, his fingers no longer danced.

"I admit, I don't think Anna has been completely honest."

"Stop soft-footing around and just talk to me, Mud."

"All right. It seems like she's hiding something."

Denny looked at me. "Like what?"

"I don't know." I turned away to look out at the starlit night.

"Well, that sure gives me plenty of reason to have doubts about a woman that's done lots of good for the Tribe."

How could I explain something that was just a feeling? I drifted off into thought. The constant tire thrum on the road lulled me deeper into twisting thoughts. I didn't say anything, but I watched Denny. He must have felt my eyes on him.

"I won't believe Anna is behind illegal fracking or trying to steal the peace medal with Gerald. Anna wouldn't do that to our people." Denny slowed the truck for the upcoming turn.

I looked out the window. "Then why are we here?"

Denny turned onto the deeply rutted dirt road that led to the fracking office and pumps. "Answers. I'm just looking for answers." He pushed a knob and the truck's headlights went off. A blanket of darkness descended. As my eyes adjusted, gray fields of raw chopped earth stood out of the blackness. Denny followed two deep parallel ruts leading to the fracking operations. I pitched forward as the truck crossed a deep rut. Sweat beaded on Denny's forehead as he strained to watch the road. His attention stayed focused on the road ahead—a trail, really.

I rolled the passenger window down. The night's fresh breath rushed in. It felt cool across my face, welcoming.

Denny traveled slowly on the rutted dirt road, using only the partial moon's light to show the way. The deep ruts were evidence of heavy loads being transported in and out of the area. Despite Denny's caution, the truck dropped into another rut.

It was after two in the morning, and maybe seventy-five degrees. I took a deep breath in, enjoyed the fresh air. The night was quiet, other than the steady thrum of the truck's engine.

"Denny, you hear that?" I cocked my head, listening.

"I don't hear nothin', Mud." His attention remained on the road.

"That's what I mean. Listen, nothing's running. No pump motors going." I hung out the window. The slight breeze generated from the truck's movement whipped my hair up and off my neck.

Denny lowered his window. Silence flowed in with the refreshing breeze. "You're right." He slowed to a near stop.

I turned to Denny. "When we were here before, there was a constant thumping that was deafening just from a single pump." I looked around the silent dirt field. "The frackers were planning on having the other pumps up and going by now. It shouldn't be this quiet." I squinted into the darkness.

Denny and I had had a run-in with the frackers, Gene and Wayne, when we demanded they stop stealing and polluting our grandfather's water at Jimmy Creek Spring. The spring water was critical to the area's farmers, natural habitat, and wildlife. Gene had laughed at us and said their boss wanted all pumps going full steam by end of day—yesterday. Gene made clear nothing was going to stop that from happening.

But something had.

Denny's truck rolled to a stop, facing a line of pumps frozen in their last act like kids playing red light, green light. There were six in total, each in a different position from the others, all waiting to be released back into action.

Denny stared toward the pumps. "Those two fracker boys were going to keep the pumps running twenty-four hours a day. That's how they make their money and get in and out of a location so fast."

"This is eerie." I twisted around in my seat. "Don't see anyone out here. Strange . . ." A water truck, small bobcat, and a dump truck were parked haphazardly around the field. I appealed to Denny, "I don't like this. It's too quiet . . . dead quiet."

Denny continued toward a dull orange light coming from the fracking office a football field away. A pickup truck at the back of the office was parked under a large, solitary oak, the only life in sight for acres.

We approached the rear of the small metal trailer that acted as an office. Denny drove toward the oak tree. The amber light spilling from the office windows made the truck sparkle and glisten. An overhanging branch scraped the top of Denny's truck. We watched the back of the trailer for a few long minutes. No one looked out either of the two back windows.

Denny unbuckled his seatbelt. "I'm going to peek inside. I'll be right back."

I released my belt and opened the door. "Not without me." I walked to Denny's side and glanced over to the other truck parked under the tree. It was an unusual sight for this area: a new, loaded Ford pickup with chrome trim, lights, and running boards shining in the moonlight.

Denny peered through its side window, let out a small whistle. "This is one sweet truck. It's got everything." He moved away from it. "That truck's probably smart enough to drive itself, but will never do a single day of real work in its life." Denny patted the hood of his old Dodge with appreciation.

The adoring look Denny gave his truck brought a real smile to my face, but the feeling was fleeting—the night's silence was heavy. Only Denny's beloved truck made a sound, a steady tick as the engine cooled.

I moved to the back side of the trailer office, under one of the windows. "I don't hear anyone moving around, no TV or radio. There doesn't seem to be anyone in the office."

Denny eyed one of the two windows. A dark yellow glow came through an opening in the curtains. "Looks like a night security light is the only thing on."

I nodded at the two windows. "We're not going to see anything through those windows. They're too high."

Denny looked upward, calculating. "I think you're right. Plus, the curtains block seeing anything inside. Let's go to the front. There was a big window by the front door." He crouched low and walked softly around the trailer to its front.

The trailer sat in a barren yard of rutted dirt. An uneven cement block path and steps led to the trailer's front door with a large window to its right. From somewhere, a lonely owl hooted.

Denny stopped at the side of the front window. I grabbed the back of his shirt and tugged. When I got his attention, I whispered, "I really don't like this."

He shook loose and turned to approach the window.

"Wait, just listen. There's no crickets, no cicadas, nothing. There's something wrong here."

Denny answered in a whisper, "This whole setup is wrong. It's against nature. That's why it's so quiet. Animals have enough sense to get away from this poison."

"I'm not sure we should be here either." I scanned the surrounding area. Found nothing moving in the dark nightscape.

"I'm going to see if anyone's inside. If they are, then I have a few questions for those fracker boys." Denny set his jaw. "I'm gonna find out if they know Anna and why." Denny stayed low as he moved toward the front window.

Amber light spilled from a dust-covered window, turning its silverplated framing gold. Curtains hung loose at the window's sides, leaving the middle open. Denny stooped low to stay out of sight, just beneath the window. Once in position, he slowly eased up to peek in. I was happy to see Denny had a twig from the oak tree in his hand. Denny used this as he moved into position to look inside the trailer. The twig was raised first, then his head and eyes. This placed the branch between him and the glass pane. Anyone inside looking out the window would notice the oak branch and not the eyes peering into the trailer. Something my brother Sky should have remembered when he was looking into the chairman's office.

Denny shifted, tossed the small branch aside, then stood upright. He wiped a swath of window clear of the collected dust with his palm, placed a hand above his eyes to block the orange glare, and stared inside.

I edged closer to Denny and hissed, "Get down! You're going to be seen."

Denny answered, "I don't think so."

The silence screamed.

Suddenly, I felt chilled. I stayed below the window in a squat. "What's going on?" The quiet was seeping into my bones, made me uncomfortable . . . on alert.

"You gotta see this, Mud." Denny urged me up to look through the window. He rubbed a spot clean for me.

I eased my head up slowly and peeked into the amber-lit room. Directly in front of a desk to the side, someone laid flat on his back, unmoving. Pointy-toed cowboy boots aimed skyward.

Chapter Twelve

I stepped back in disbelief—another body.

Denny watched my reaction. "Yep, that's 'bout how it hit me."

I moved to the window. From the corner of my eye, a motion inside caught my attention. "Someone is waving." I kept my eye on the large hand gesturing for attention. "See, on the desk, by the front door."

Denny returned to the window to peer through the amber glow, dust, and darkness inside.

"It's Wayne." Denny named the hefty-size fracker we had met the day before. "That must be Gene lying on the floor." The two men ran the onsite operations, but from our earlier discussions it had been obvious that someone else was the brains of the outfit. Of the two men, Gene was the boss. He was small, lean, and yes, mean. Like the unmoving leg inside, when we had last seen Gene, he had on jeans with a crease as sharp as him.

"Why's Wayne sitting on the desk?" I leaned closer to the window, trying to see more.

Denny moved to the uneven cement-block walkway. "This is silly. I'm going in, find out what's going on." He went to the door, pulled it open and stepped inside.

I raised my voice. "Denny, don't go in. Something's wrong here." He didn't listen to my warning. Denny was already inside at the front desk when I got to the doorway. I reached to flip the light switch on. Nothing. I flipped it up and down again, just to make sure. I ventured a few tentative steps inside, letting the door close behind me.

Denny was at the front desk, facing an aggravated Wayne squatting on the desktop. Wayne was in a rumpled T-shirt and dirty jeans. The pointy-toed boots on the other side of the office were motionless. Everything was washed in an amber glow from a security light mounted to the ceiling. I wrinkled my nose at an unpleasant musky smell. A soft hiss escaped from somewhere.

Wayne, still waving his hands, was repeating in a hushed voice, "Stop! Stop! Stop!"

A flicker across the room caught my eye, something moved by the pointy-toed boots. Maybe Gene was alive. I kicked a burlap bag to the side, moved toward him, intending to check for a pulse.

Wayne waved wildly, making the desk creak in protest. "You. Gotta. Stop. Now!"

I stopped. Returned my attention to Denny and Wayne.

Wayne looked around the room with eyes wide, the whites turned yellow under the security light. In a loud whisper, Wayne cried, "Don't move. They're everywhere!" The desk complained under the large man's weight. Wayne's work boots had dropped red dirt clods on the desktop.

I watched Wayne but spoke to Denny. "Maybe you should back away from Wayne." The big man on top of the desk worried me.

I caught sight of a slight shift in shadows on the floor near Denny, but wasn't sure what caused it. Denny must have spotted the movement too; he kept his feet in place while he looked around the room. Denny asked, "What's that?"

Nothing moved in the room. Wayne hissed, "Snakes! And not just any snakes, rattlesnakes! Everywhere!"

A wave of cold washed over me. I froze in place, too terror-stricken to move anything but my eyes. I scanned the floor searching for movement, any sign of a rattlesnake, anywhere, everywhere.

While they may not want to bite humans, rattlesnake bites kill more people in the U.S. than any other snake bite. I knew this fact because I was petrified of rattlesnakes, so of course I read all I could find on them.

The office had plenty of crevices and junk to hide a snake. Large pipes were stacked haphazardly around the office along with outsized bolts and nuts and other gear needed to keep pumps pumping. Shapes were distorted, washed in dark yellow from the security light. My mind began imagining snakes at every glance.

Slowly, Denny raised a foot to turn in my direction. Immediately, a *brrr* came from under the desk Wayne sat upon. Denny froze, foot in the air. The sound raised the hair on my neck. I felt the chill to my bones. Everything in me screamed, *Run!*

Wayne declared, "Now ya done it, ya stirred them up again." He shifted on the desk to look around. The desk complained, the snake below rattled. "They'd just settled down after you stopped our pumps. Those rattlesnakes hated the constant vibration the pumps was making. Made 'em mad."

What did he mean, *stopped our pumps*? I put the thought aside as I looked around again, frantic to spot the snakes.

Denny slowly lowered his foot. From beneath the desk another *brrr* sounded. He twisted at the waist to face me. His eyes locked on mine, speaking volumes.

Denny was trapped. A rattler was at his feet, and neither was happy about it.

Denny's situation forced me into action. I signaled "Stay," looked to Wayne and in a calm, hushed voice asked, "How many and where?" My heart raced.

A triangular head peeked out from under Wayne's desk, its forked tongue flicking toward Denny a foot away. We both watched it slide out, its body thick, yet sleek in motion. The amber light didn't hide the distinct dark brown diamond-shaped blotches.

Wayne stared at the snake and repeated, "Everywhere, just everywhere!"

Slowly, I slid a foot forward and a *brrr* went off at my side. I stayed still and scanned the floor. Another snake slid by my foot. I forced myself to look beyond the snake; this time I spotted a wastebasket and an idea started to form.

The rattlesnake close to me was beginning to coil, getting into the prime strike position. Another handy tidbit I knew: rattlesnakes can bite from any position; coiling allowed them to propel about two thirds of their length. I was easily within this one's strike zone.

I asked again, in a low voice, "How many?" I had seen two, one under Wayne's desk by Denny and the other to my left. The snake at my side shook its raised tail. The sound chilled me.

Wayne waved madly and said, "I don't know. They're everywhere!"

Disturbed by Wayne's movements, the snake by the front desk turned its head, flicked its tongue upward toward the man squatting on the desk. Wayne's mouth opened in a silent scream.

I tried to catch Wayne's eyes, finally got his attention. In a voice calmer than I felt, I said, "Wayne, you're safe up there. Just breathe." He seemed to listen, but moved away from the front of the desk. The snake hissed below. The desk moaned.

"Denny, I see two. One at the desk by you and this one at my side." To confirm my count, both snakes shook their rattles in a harmony of spine-chilling *brrrs*. I forced my feet to stay put.

The snake close to me looked huge. I reminded myself that rattlesnakes are not aggressive, and only strike when threatened or deliberately provoked—if given enough room, snakes tend to retreat. Unfortunately, there was no room to give.

I thought of the metal wastebasket—there was no other choice. I had to reach the basket steps away and trap the nearby snake, all without provoking it into biting me.

"What are we going to do, Mud?" Denny whispered.

While thinking, I unconsciously rubbed the leather medicine bundle I kept around my neck. I dropped it as I made a decision. "You got to stay still for a bit longer. I'm . . ." I faltered before continuing. "I'm going to take care of the one by me, then help with yours."

"How?" Denny asked.

Wayne shifted on top of the desk.

A loud *brrr* was followed by a slithering movement as the desk snake formed a loose coil and lifted its tail to shake another warning. It was getting serious.

Wayne's eyes got big.

In a low voice, I ordered, "Wayne, don't move."

"I . . . I can't. I won't." Wayne's eyes were fastened on the amber-colored snake rattling intensely.

The desk rattlesnake's warning set off rattles from the snake at my side. Then yet another snake revealed itself, slithering by the motionless man on the floor.

I choked back a scream when I saw the third snake. Wayne was right, they were everywhere! My heart missed a beat then raced. I looked around through the deep yellow lighting, trying to locate more rattlesnakes. Large metal washers for the pumps appeared to be coiled rattlers, buckets looked like twisted masses of snakes, varying lengths of pipe were slithering rattlesnakes. I wanted to run out of the office, but I couldn't leave Denny or Wayne behind.

Denny's watching eyes settled me. He needed me to think.

Beads of sweat broke out, dripped down my long Kiowa nose and off the tip. I took a breath, caught my racing heart, and searched for my center. I needed to be in control. I needed to be slow and steady. I needed to think clearly to trap the deadly snakes—without anyone getting bitten.

I searched for calm and found it in thoughts of my grandfather's morning ritual. With the first ray of sunrise, Grandpa and his drum sang. Always the drum had the same slow, steady beat. Soon Grandpa's heart and drum would beat in unison, matching the rhythm of Mother Earth as she woke to another glorious day. Grandpa's drumming seemed to travel across the air and time. I cocked my head to listen, the slow beat steadied my heart and mind.

I closed my eyes. Grandfather Buffalo, my totem, appeared and filled my being with courage to do what must be done . . . despite my frantic fear.

I eyed the metal wastebasket three short steps away, yet so far.

I took another deep breath, my fourth, and was settled, ready. I signaled my intent to Denny in the silent language of our ancestors. He shot me both acknowledgment and faith with a single look.

I took a small step to the side, checked for other snakes around the wastebasket, and listened to the nearby coiled snake sound its displeasure. My fear rose with the rattlesnake's frantic rattle. I fought the instinct to freeze and stole another step.

In my peripheral vision, I saw the rattlesnake use its belly scales like treads on a tire, providing traction as its muscles pulled it up and forward into a deadly raised *S*. For a moment I admired the beauty of the snake's design, its undulating pattern that became fluid and seamlessly enabled quick movements—then my focus returned to survival.

In slow motion, I picked up the wastebasket and slid toward the coiled snake. Back to where I did not want to go, but had to.

Wayne sucked in a breath sounding like a large serpent's hiss. The nearby snake followed with a louder hiss. Denny stayed motionless, only his brown eyes moving, following me, encouraging me.

The snake by the front desk, closest to Denny, remained in a loose coil but stopped rattling. The snake's head swayed side to side, flicked its tongue, noting our positions.

I lowered my eyes, focused on the rattlesnake closest to me. Its head was pulled back, cocked and ready. The snake opened its mouth wide and bared its fangs. The sight stopped me. Even in the amber-lit room, the snake's pink mouth stood out in contrast to its long white curved fangs. In my mind's eye, the glistening fangs drooled yellow venom in anticipation of striking me.

Finally, I forced my gaze away from the fangs, only to find the rattlesnake's deadly cold vertical pupils locked on me. Waiting for a reason to launch. Any reason.

A chill rushed through me. I lost my center. I wanted to escape, *now*. I tried to steady myself, but felt my panic rise.

From somewhere Grandfather Buffalo bellowed his support. It bolstered me, slowed my racing heart, and set me on my path once again.

Without thought, I found myself chanting to the snake now raised in an *S* at knee level, "Old Man Snake, I see you. I've heard many stories of Grandfather Stony Road." I named the snake featured in early Kiowa legends.

I took a slow step forward. The rattlesnake cocked its triangular head farther back. Its slitted eyes locked on me. From somewhere another snake rattled, and by the pointy-toed boots a large snake slithered over the still legs. The sight sent shivers down my spine.

I shook it off.

I focused on the rattler by my side. Looking at the serpent, I told it, "Kiowas sang the first Mourning Song at Grandfather Stony Road's death." The rattlesnake did not seem interested, but I continued, "Now most Kiowas have Family Mourning Songs used at funerals. We have one in our family."

I lifted the wastebasket to shoulder height. The snake gave me a loud warning.

Denny whispered, "Mud." And nothing more.

"But you, young snake, do not need a Mourning Song. I do not want to harm you." Without giving away my intent, I slammed the wastebasket over the coiled snake. A thump followed as the snake struck the side of the metal wastebasket. Frantic rattling within the metal wastebasket reverberated through the room. I pulled an oversized bolt over and put it on top, holding the wastebasket in place.

Then I breathed.

The rattlesnake by Denny started its warning in earnest. It was coiled between Denny and the front of the desk where Wayne still sat on top. The rattlesnake raised itself off the floor and faced Wayne. It swayed from side to side.

Wayne, near tears, choked out, "It's looking at me. It's looking at me!"

Denny stayed still but watched the snake at his knees. Through tight lips, he squeezed out, "I can grab its head from the back."

The snake turned its head and disagreed with Denny.

Wayne squealed, "Nonoo!" He shrunk farther back on the desk. The desk squeaked its protest. A wrong move would tip the desk over and put Wayne on the ground, with the snakes.

I slid a foot forward, very slowly, and caught Wayne's eyes. In a soft voice, I urged, "Wayne, be still. Just be still." I made another slow move toward the desk. "We will get that snake."

Wayne focused on the snake. "It's coming up here!"

The snake shifted its attention back to Wayne, lifted its tail high, and rattled. Its head weaved side to side, flicked its tongue to locate Wayne.

In a calm voice that seemed to belong to someone else, I told Wayne, "You have got to stay still. The snake thinks you're dangerous—"

Wayne shifted on the creaky desk. The snake cocked its head back.

"Wayne. Stop!" I caught his eyes and spoke softly but with urgency. "I'm getting a bucket, and you need to be absolutely still. I'll get the snake's attention and Denny will put the bucket on it."

Wayne stopped moving. The snake returned to its side-to-side motion, watching him.

"Okay, I'm moving to my right for the closest bucket. Do you see any snakes in that direction?"

Wayne whispered, "No." But his eyes stayed on the snake facing him. In response, the snake hissed.

Over by the pointy-toed boots, a tail slithered out of sight. The rattlesnake trapped under the wastebasket seemed calm; no rattles came from it. There were no other snakes in sight. I wasn't sure if that was good or bad.

I glanced at Denny. The amber light highlighted the sweat beading on his forehead. "Denny, I'm getting a bucket, then we will trap the one in front of you."

Denny squeezed out, "Mud, get out while you can. We have no idea how many rattlesnakes are in here, maybe more by that bucket."

Before I could protest, a voice from the floor said, "Three."

Denny stayed frozen, but Wayne cried, "Gene, you're alive!" His accompanying movement brought rapid rattles from the snake by the desk. Wayne added in a horrified whisper, "No, no, no!"

Gene, on the floor, had no further response. His pointy-toed boots remained aimed upward, unmoving. I shivered thinking of the rattlesnake crawling across his legs earlier and hoped Gene had been unconscious. I would not have been able to handle a snake on me. Being in this room with rattlesnakes was my worst nightmare. A rattle from the front desk area reminded me that this horror was reality.

Gene's one-word, "*Three*," encouraged me. I had to believe Gene was telling us how many rattlesnakes were in the room; he was in the position to know.

"Denny, we have this." I hoped my words sounded stronger than I really felt. "You two stay absolutely still—and quiet." I shot a look at Wayne, held his eyes until I saw him calm, and said, "I'm going to get that bucket."

Still watchful, I stepped toward a five-gallon bucket. I made sure my move was not toward either snake. After my first step, I stopped, waited to hear any warning rattles, just in case.

Denny and Wayne watched me intently. With Wayne settled, the rattlesnake lowered to a coil at Denny's feet. Its tail remained upright but silent, at the ready for rattling or launching.

In four steps I was at the bucket, a five-gallon hard plastic bucket. Upended, it should safely contain the snake at Denny's feet.

I stepped soft and slowly back toward the coiled rattlesnake. Everything in me again screamed, *Run!* I resisted, reminding myself that each step brought me closer to Denny and out of here.

Keeping my eyes on the coiled snake, I stopped before it felt the need to act in defense. "Okay, guys, we're going to get this one covered." I looked around. "Is the other snake in sight?"

Denny, in a soft voice, answered, "It's under the other desk on the far wall over by Gene."

Knowing where the third rattlesnake was made me more comfortable. I looked over the situation at the front desk and did not like the setup. Denny was too close to the snake to get the bucket over it. He needed a couple steps back, some space for maneuvering.

As if he knew what I was thinking, Denny slid one foot back. The snake went ballistic. Machine gun *brrrs* rattled through the room. The other snake under the far desk slithered out to investigate.

Denny froze.

Before Wayne could panic, I spoke. "All righty then, Denny, stay where you are. I'll get the bucket on the snake." I didn't give Denny a chance to protest. "Wayne, you're going to get the snake's attention when I get in position. No protesting. This is the way we all get out of here. Got it?" I waited for Wayne to give a single nod, hefted the bucket upside down, then took a slow step closer.

"Wayne, just lean toward the snake." I wanted the snake's fangs facing away from Denny's leg before I got closer.

An internal struggle played out across Wayne's face before he leaned ever so slightly toward the rattlesnake. The snake turned to Wayne and hissed with fangs bared. Wayne jerked back quickly, too quickly. The sudden move startled the snake, which raised upward toward Wayne and launched a strike.

Without thought, I slammed the bucket down onto the striking snake. I captured its bottom half, pulling the airborne snake down but not capturing the deadly head. It writhed, turned, and struck at me. The first strike hit the bucket's side. The second strike had me in sight. To keep the thrashing serpent pinned with the bucket, I was bent over, face to face with the angry rattlesnake. As if in slow motion, I watched the snake's cold eyes focus on me. It pulled its head back and thrust forward at my face.

I jerked back, but not enough.

I closed my eyes and waited.

Chapter Thirteen

A knee pushed me to the side as Denny's foot came down on the rattlesnake's head, trapping it on the floor. Thumping erupted from the bucket I held down with the rattler's lower third trapped inside.

Denny shouted, "Move the bucket now. Get it over the head."

On automatic, I did as he commanded. I lifted the bucket scoop-like so the rest of the thrashing snake's body remained inside. I slammed the bucket down to cover the trapped head as Denny removed his foot, shoving a wayward coil back under the bucket.

I leaned across the bucket feeling and hearing the angry rattler as it struck again and again at the bucket's side. Each thud stopped my racing heart. I couldn't move, yet I did not want to stay on the bucket, so close to the snake.

From the desktop, Wayne handed an oversized wrench to Denny. The unexpected weight of it pulled Denny's arm down. He gave a slight smile, urged me off the bucket as he placed the heavy wrench on top. The snake struck the side another time; the bucket stayed in place. I stepped away and bent at the waist to take a deep breath. My whole body trembled. I felt sick.

Breathing hard, Denny commented, "Two down, one to go." He wiped the sweat from his face.

Wayne stayed atop the desk. "I'm not moving till they're all gone."

Denny eyed Wayne. "You better stop moving, or you're going to tip over right on top of the next rattler." The desk creaked in agreement.

I fought for control. Found my voice. "Anyone see the third snake?" I looked across the room toward the other desk. Everyone went silent as we looked.

I edged toward the man lying flat on his back on the floor. "Gene, do you know where the rattler is?"

Gene didn't answer, but his right boot tipped slightly toward the other desk against the far wall. In the amber light, I made out a yellow mass that might be the snake. It stuck its tongue out to confirm.

I released a deep breath. I did not want to deal with another snake but could not leave it loose in the office. Denny stood by the front desk with Wayne on top of it. I turned to him. "Any ideas?"

"Well, now," Denny said *now* nice and slow before continuing with a sly smile. "It's pretty safe for you and me to get to the door. We can slide right on out of here, lickety-split. Just leave these two with their last snake." Denny took a step toward the front door.

Gene's eyes popped open; he looked around the room and settled on me. His eyes seemed to be pleading.

Wayne moved to the middle of the desk. "No, no. Don't go. Just get that last one." He watched Denny and added, "Please."

Denny nodded at Wayne. "Then answer a few questions for me."

Wayne nodded in agreement. "Yes, whatever you want!" The desk shook.

A low voice demanded, "Snake first." Gene's wide-open eyes looked toward the snake stretched out beneath the desk a few feet away. The snake flicked its tongue our way.

Denny took in Gene on his back on the floor, and the terror-stricken Wayne squatting on top of the desk. "All right. We get that snake all taken care of, and you two answer my questions. Deal?" Denny focused on Gene, waiting for his answer, although Wayne had yelped, "Yes, yes," before Denny had finished talking.

Gene gave a slight nod.

Denny demanded, "I want to hear a yes."

Wayne's repeated "Yes!" almost drowned out Gene's soft "Yes." The snake hissed.

Denny reached to one of the stacks of piping and pulled out a four-foot pipe. He hefted it before declaring, "This should work," and handed it to me.

I took the pipe but had no idea what Denny expected me to do with it.

"This one we're going to bag." Denny picked up the burlap bag I had kicked to the side earlier. He moved past Gene on the floor and laid the bag on the ground by the short end of the desk, away from the rattlesnake. Using a small pipe segment, he propped the mouth of the bag open.

I watched, still not understanding what Denny planned.

Wayne said, "We can't stay here waiting for it to crawl into your bag."

Denny waved him off, found another four-foot length of pipe.

"Now that's more like it. Beat it to death!" Squatting on top of the desk, Wayne looked like an overweight shaggy dog excited for treats. If he had a tail, it would be wagging.

"We are not going to hurt the rattlesnake . . . if we don't have to." Denny watched the snake push forward and poke its head from under the desk. It flicked its forked tongue toward Denny, appraising the situation. "Okay, Mud, this here what we're going to do. Nice and slow, you're going to push that snake out the other side of the desk." Denny moved to the far wall. "And then together we'll get it into that bag."

I shook my head. "The snake can bite through that burlap bag. If it doesn't get us before that."

"We'll make it nice and snug inside the bag so it can't move or bite," Denny assured me.

"Just what do you think I'm going to do, reach under there and pull it out?"

Denny laughed. "Naw, I'll be the one grabbing this guy. We got the advantage of having space to work with this time."

I'm sure my face said it, but in case Denny couldn't make out my expression, I told him, "You're crazy."

Wayne nodded in absolute agreement. Gene kept his hard eyes on Denny. I didn't trust the guy, even lying flat on his back.

Denny watched the rattlesnake. "I do this all the time when I come across snakes around my cattle. Don't worry, Mud, like you said, we got this." Denny looked to me for a moment with the smile that had always led me into trouble.

As I have done as long as I could remember, I gave in. "All right, Denny, what do you need me to do?"

Denny nodded. "This here's what we're going to do, Mud. Using the pipe, you're going to urge, maybe push that snake out the short side of the desk. Just get over by the knee well behind the snake."

I took a deep breath before giving a nod to Denny. I really did not want to push a rattlesnake anywhere.

"Once it's out from under the desk," he went on, "what I want you to do is get your pipe under the snake 'bout its middle point and lift it a bit." Denny watched me. "You hear me, Mud?"

I must have looked faint. I felt it. I swallowed hard. "Yeah."

Denny went on, "Then I'm going to get its tail. Once I have its tail, that snake can't lunge or twist and turn." He looked intently at me. "But I got to get its tail, and you've got to keep its head away from me."

"You just said it can't twist and turn, so why do I need to keep its head away from you?" I protested.

"Well, it'll still twist and strike, but I'll get control of it." Denny moved to the middle of the office. "'Course you gotta stay out of its range." The snake moved its head, flicked its tongue toward Denny.

"Okay, Mud, you got it?" Denny watched the snake. "You know what we're going to do?"

"Yeeaaaahh," I stretched out my answer as I moved to the other side of the desk. "Denny, that bag opening is awfully small. You sure about this?"

Denny spared me a quick reassuring glance. "Mud, it's good. That snake likes dark, small spaces. It will go in with a just little bit of help." He set his feet. "Ready?"

I thought, *Now or never*, took another deep breath before answering, "Ready."

I didn't move.

Denny pushed his sweat-damp hair from his face. "Mud, you got to urge it out this way." He stood between the burlap bag and the end of the desk.

I stood with my pipe at the ready. "Yeah, I'm urging me first."

Denny smiled at my response. "Mud, we got this." He kept his eyes on the snake. "Darn, I've missed our adventures."

"Misadventures is what I remember." I moved to the other side of the desk.

Wayne from atop the desk urged, "Do it already!"

I took a deep breath. "All right, I'm doing it now." I stepped toward the desk's knee well, directly behind the coiled snake. Before I could change my mind, I pushed a thick midsection of the snake out from under the desk.

The rattlesnake hissed before it formed into a loose coil with its head pointed at me. The snake raised its tail high and rattled its displeasure.

"That's perfect, Mud." Denny slowly slid closer to the snake. "Exactly what we want."

"Yeah, perfect for you." The snake's attention stayed on me. I needed to lift the midsection of that angry snake so Denny could grab the tail from behind. This really was *mawbane.*

Staying a safe distance back, I forced the pipe between the snake's coils, lifting its midsection slightly upward. The snake twisted and struck out. I jumped back but kept hold of the pipe. The snake was off the ground, supported by the pipe in my hand. In a flash, I realized the snake was crawling up the pipe toward me with deadly intent. Its cold, dead eyes locked on me as the snake's body scales modulated forward on the pipe; the snake seemed to smile as it advanced.

Before I could panic and drop the pipe, Denny grabbed the snake's tail just past the rattles and gently pulled the snake back away from me. Using the length of pipe he held, Denny moved the snake toward the propped-open burlap bag.

"Just got to go real slow and gentle like," Denny talked as he maneuvered the snake. The rattlesnake had other plans and twisted and struck at Denny. He jerked his midsection in, avoiding the bared fangs. "Gotta keep my distance, as I lift this tail up." Denny lifted the tail to waist level, the rest of the snake stretched out before him.

He used his length of pipe to direct the snake's head toward the bag. "Gotcha now. See, it can't lunge much without its tail for leverage." The snake's front third disagreed as it whipped toward him. Denny used the pipe to keep the thrashing snake at a safe distance and slowly moved it toward the propped-open burlap bag. I cringed, watching Denny and the rattlesnake. I didn't want to watch, yet I couldn't take my eyes away.

With one hand holding the snake's tail, Denny directed the head into the bag's opening. The snake twisted, tried to escape to the side. Denny used the pipe to gently push it in. The snake's triangular head poked into the bag, then out, until finally it entered the bag's dark recesses.

Once the head was inside the bag, Denny, with the rattlesnake's tail still in one hand, dropped the pipe, freeing his other hand to lift the bag. With practiced ease, Denny allowed gravity to force the rest of the snake into the bag's depth, then released the tail. Once freed, the snake's tail whipped across Denny's hand before following the rest of its body into the bag.

In a single motion, Denny had the discarded pipe laid straight across the width of the bag, driving the snake deeper into the bag's furthest corner. Once a large snake lump formed at the bottom, Denny lifted the bag and twirled it several times to secure the bag around the snake trapped within.

Denny talked as he worked on the bag. "Gotta get the bag tied up tight so the snake can't move and bite. 'Cause it will bite right through that burlap." He tied the end into a knot. Looked about, then placed the securely bagged snake into a plastic bucket partially filled with metal screws.

Wayne knelt on top of the desk while watching Denny bag the rattlesnake. "You gotta put a lid on that bucket." Wayne shifted and pulled a saucer-like plastic lid from a nearby pile. "This will do." He frisbeed the bucket's lid to Denny.

Denny nabbed the lid in flight and popped it onto the bucket with the bagged snake within. He pulled a knife from his hip, used it to carefully punch several holes through the lid. Satisfied, he holstered the knife back into its belt case. Denny wiped the sweat from his brow and moved to stand above Gene still on the floor. "Now I want some answers."

Wayne clumped off the desk, nearly tipping it in the process—again. "Man, oh man. I cannot thank you enough." He rushed toward Denny with an outstretched hand. "I thought I was a goner." Wayne pumped Denny's hand.

Denny pulled loose.

Wayne went on, "Yep, when Gene dropped, I was sure I was next." Wayne bent over the man on the floor. "Gene, where'd you git bit?"

"I didn't." Gene picked himself up from the floor. He carefully brushed off his sharply creased jeans, adjusted his huge silver belt buckle, and tucked in his sweat-drenched button-up shirt before he settled his mean eyes on Wayne. "I stayed still, 'cause those snakes were all around me when they came slithering out of that bag."

I shivered at the image.

Wayne wasn't buying it. "You did that on purpose, just dropped straight down and never flicked an eye . . . for hours?" Wayne seemed disappointed Gene had no snake bite. "I was all alone with those . . . things." Wayne's voice trembled. "All around me rattling like crazy."

"I was tryin' to keep the snakes calm, to help us both."

Shaking his head, Wayne moved away from Gene. "Didn't know how to get away with all those snakes rattling everywhere." He turned to face Denny. "See, we had all six pumps going, and the ground was jumping. The vibration just made those snakes mad when they come crawling out of that bag." Wayne's body trembled with the memory. "Man, I was so glad when y'all stopped the pumps. The snakes settled right down after that. That is, until y'all came in. That got them all riled up again. I tried to warn you." Wayne broke into a big grin. "But I'm sure glad you showed up." Then his eyes glazed over. "All those rattlers rattling everywhere . . ."

"You okay, Wayne?" Denny took a step toward the big man.

Wayne blinked, cleared his thoughts before he nodded at Denny. "I'm okay now." He shifted his attention back to Gene. "You just dropped to the floor, left me to deal with them rattlers."

Gene turned away from Wayne. "Oh, stop being a crybaby."

Before Wayne could respond, Denny stepped in with, "Enough, you two owe me answers, remember?" He didn't wait for either to respond. "Let's start with who left you a bag of snakes." Denny looked directly at Gene.

It took Gene a moment before he turned from Wayne to face Denny. "I'm guessin' we got rattlesnakes instead of this week's cut." He shot a quick glance toward the bagged snake in the sealed bucket.

"Go on." Denny urged.

Wayne jumped in with, "See, our cut is a couple weeks late. The boss got mad, and our pay hasn't shown up like usual. I saw the burlap bag in the corner." He pointed behind Gene's desk. "And thought the boss musta come while we went out to eat." Wayne glanced toward me. "We got burgers, over at Meers. Those burgers are pretty fillin'." He licked his lips. "Anyways, we haven't got our payout. That ain't right."

Satisfied, he looked to Gene and was met with a glare. "Wayne, you talk too much."

Wayne stepped back, surprised. "They rescued us, Gene." Wayne pointed to Denny. "And we agreed to tell him the truth."

"We can give them the truth without our life story," growled Gene.

Denny moved to face Gene. "Then give it. Why are you here, and who set this operation up?" He leaned closer to Gene. "Who are you working for?"

"All right, already, don't get an attitude." Gene moved to his desk by the far wall, settled into a chair, and kicked his boots up on the desk.

From somewhere nearby one of the snakes rattled. We all froze for a moment. I looked to Gene. "You sure there was only three?"

Gene looked around the floor carefully before putting his tough guy act back on. "Oh, yeah. I saw all three come out, one after another." He couldn't hide a slight tremble. "They all went right over me to scatter around the room."

Denny pushed Gene's feet off the desk. "Keep talking before I let one of the three out on top of your desk."

Gene stared up at Denny for a moment before he answered, "We were supposed to make some fast money here. Everything looked right. This land got lots of nearby subsurface formations where oil and gas are usually holed up in pockets. We could get to all those pockets without being on the land over them 'cause we're drilling horizontal and spiral." Gene let a cold smile form. "Yep, with our drills, the boss just finds land with enough nearby pockets and a water source, don't matter who owns the land above, we just octopus out from a small base and suck it all up." His eyes looked off in the distance. "We pump them all at once, get out fast and rich. Usually with the landowners none the wiser." His smile was chilling.

Denny looked down at Gene in the office chair. "How much you pumping out, what do you make out of here?"

"We're just getting started here." Not able to resist bragging, Gene went on, "From this twenty-acre base, we got six pumps. One pump usually does about sixty barrels a day, times that by thirty days," Gene calculated, "comes to eighteen hundred barrels times the usual forty dollars a barrel, and we get roughly seventy-two thousand dollars per pump each month." Gene's thumb and index finger unconsciously rubbed together. "Man, when we get all six pumps going, that's over four hundred thousand a month. Wayne and me get a cut of what we pump each week." His beady eyes shone.

Wayne nodded in agreement as he listened to Gene. My eyes glazed over, thinking of the dollar signs.

Gene added, "Usually that's how it worked."

Wayne added, "We were supposed to have the sweet life after this one. We're tired always being in the middle of nowhere. This was the last time."

Gene nodded in agreement. "This plot looked real promising on all the reports. Told the boss, we were done after this take."

"Is that why you got a bag of snakes?" Denny asked.

"Could be," Gene affirmed. He put his boots up on the desk and leaned back in thought. "Someone sure left those snakes on purpose."

Wayne nodded. "They wanted us dead."

"Who wants you two dead?" I asked.

Gene answered, "Everyone around here wants us gone."

"Gone is different than dead," I pressed.

Wayne looked upset. "It had to be the boss. He said we had to be here night and day. Got real mad when he found out we went to town and the pumps got sugar in the motors."

Gene agreed, "Boss was not happy that we're down to one pump. He wanted us to be out of here by now. Said things were getting too hot at the Complex. All thanks to Sawpole."

This of course was our grandfather, James Sawpole. Grandpa had reported the fracking and illegal use of Jimmy Creek Spring water. When that didn't stop the fracking, Grandpa found other sweet ways to slow them down.

Denny pushed. "So, you're working with someone in the Kiowa legislature?"

Wayne nodded. "He makes all the land deals, tells us where to set up, where's the water source, everything."

Denny shifted to look at both Gene and Wayne. "Who's your boss?"

Gene muttered, "I don't know."

"You don't know!" Denny's voice rose. "You work with someone you've never met." He knocked Gene's boots off the desktop again.

Gene snarled at Denny, started to reply, but Wayne cut in, "We've never met, he just calls."

Denny looked between the two. "But your boss is a man, not a woman?" I knew he wanted it to be a man involved with illegal fracking on Kiowa land—not Anna.

Gene answered before Wayne. "Don't know if the boss is man or woman. We just get orders over the phone and our cut every week. The voice is disguised."

Wayne, anxious to be helpful, added, "Once I answered the call and he—it had this robot-like voice."

I asked, "You always get your cut of the money delivered in burlap bags?"

Wayne shook his head. "No, that was different. The money's usually in an envelope left on Gene's desk." Wayne moved to stand in front of the desk. "Show 'em, Gene. He's got all the envelopes and notes in the top drawer." Wayne glanced over to Denny, missing the dark look Gene shot him. Denny didn't.

"Yeah, Gene. Let's see the envelopes and notes. Everything you got from the boss." Denny moved the bucket with the bagged rattlesnake closer to Gene's desk. A muted rattle sounded.

Gene clenched his jaw before he scooted forward then pulled the top right drawer, which jammed, partially open. Gene pushed the drawer back in and jerked it out abruptly. The drawer jammed again. Gene bent to look through the crack, to see what prevented the drawer from opening completely. With Gene's face inches away from the opening, we all heard it: a rapid, bone-chilling rattle from within the drawer. Gene jumped away from the desk, knocking his chair over. A forked tongue flicked out from the drawer's opening. Gene stared at the opening, eyes wide with fear. In a choked voice, he exclaimed, "There's a rattlesnake in my drawer!" Gene backed up to the wall, looked like he needed it to stay upright. The rattlesnake's blunt nose poked out of the slightly open drawer. Gene waved toward the desk. "Everything from the boss is in there. You can have it all."

Wayne scrambled away from the desk. "There's more snakes!" The whites of his eyes were a deep yellow in the amber lighting. "Get it, get it!" His wild eyes pleaded with Denny.

Denny stayed where he was. "You two aren't being straight with me. You gotta know who your boss is, or at least if it's a man or woman. Something." He took the lid off the bagged snake's bucket. Denny and the bucket moved closer to Gene pressed against the wall, ramrod straight.

It was Wayne that spoke, nearly crying. "I swear, we really don't know who it is. We play with guessin' who sometimes. But we don't know. We just get this mechanical voice that tells us what and where to go. The voice tells us where to set up and start pumping, when the trucks for pickups are coming, we do what it says, then we get our cut each week. Until now." Wayne took a deep breath.

Denny looked at Gene for verification.

"Yeah, that how it's been," Gene growled, "until now."

"You have no idea who the boss is?" Denny demanded. He set the open bucket on the floor close to Gene. The burlap shifted.

Gene stayed focused on the moving burlap bag holding the snake. Denny slid the bucket closer and the bagged snake found room to rattle. Gene's eyes rolled to Denny, terror and fury obvious.

"We been doing this about a year with the boss. Different locations, in and out. No. Idea. Who. The. Boss. Is." He set his jaw. "We get phone calls or notes. The phone number never works again after we get a call. And you are welcome to any notes left in that drawer." He looked to the partially opened desk drawer. The snake's tongue flicked from within the drawer, tasting freedom.

Denny walked to Gene's desk, gently closed the drawer, and placed the lid back on the bucket with the bagged rattlesnake. "I believe you two. But I think it's time you pack up and get out of Kiowa Country."

Wayne nodded. "I'm gone first thing tomorrow. I'm not even staying in here tonight. It creeps me out." He shuddered. "Snakes."

Gene's eyes narrowed at Denny before finally giving a slight nod.

The nod wasn't enough. Denny demanded, "I want to hear it."

Gene hissed, "We're leaving."

I moved to the door, more than ready to leave myself. Denny followed. At the last, I glanced back to catch Gene sending us a look that sent a chill down my back.

In that moment, I realized Gene had snake eyes: cold and dead.

Chapter Fourteen

Outside the office trailer, I raked my fingers through my hair damp with sweat. I had survived a nightmare. A slight night breeze washed over me, cool and crisp. It felt so good.

From behind, Denny grabbed me into a bear hug. "Man, that was something." He released me. "Thanks for not running. Three rattlers may have been too many to handle without you."

"I never want to do that again." I shivered thinking of rattlesnakes, then gave Denny's shoulder a slight push with my own. "But I am glad you were trapped with me. I would not have kept it together without you." I felt the hair raise on my neck, shivered again.

Denny turned me toward the back of the trailer. "Enough. Let's get out of here before more snakes show up."

I agreed but had to add, "Your quick peek sure turned into a mess. No more side trips. We need to chat with Eli, then go back to call the police."

"Yeah, but we can't ignore this." Denny stood under the oak tree, the only remaining tree on the ravaged twenty acres. He continued, "I figure you're right. The fracking boss has to be in the Tribe's government. They're the only ones that have access to

Kiowa water and mineral reports, lease info, land development—heck, Tribe leaders are the only ones that would know the right people to contact to make all this happen." He waved toward the frozen pumps, scattered equipment, and gray, barren land. Denny's face struggled to hide his disgust. It was hard to believe that a Kiowa leader would intentionally do so much harm to the people and land—for money. This level of greed was contrary to the Kiowa Way. We took pride in achievements, but not at the cost of another and not through shameful deeds.

I hesitated before asking, "Someone in the Tribal Legislature is making a lot of money—but who?" I looked to Denny. "I've been gone. You know these people, who would do this?"

"You know them too. Most of the legislators we grew up knowing or someone we know knows them . . . 'cept . . ."

I waited, but finally had to prompt Denny. "Except who?"

"Don't seem right to accuse anyone."

"We're not accusing, just talking possibilities." I waited out a long silence before adding, "Like Anna." I hurried on, talking over Denny's protests. "You saw her come down this road. It leads only to one place." I took in the fracking office, equipment, and pumps. "Anna is up to something." I waited for Denny's sputtering protests to wane, for him to be open to possibilities. I found myself rubbing my leather medicine bag again as I thought about Anna, artifact thefts, fracking, and a dead man.

"Put the bag away, Mud. I'm settled."

Embarrassed, I tucked the bag under my shirt.

Denny pulled me from my thoughts. "You're gonna have to share what got you wearing your medicine bundle again. Not that I'm complaining. Everyone needs good medicine in their lives. And our medicine bags are a reminder of what's important and positive." Denny pulled his worn leather pouch from beneath his shirt. "And I tell ya, Anna is a positive force for the Kiowas." His eyes brightened. "Maybe Anna stopped the pumps." Denny placed his medicine bundle back under his shirt and moved toward his truck. "That's why she drove here."

I bit the inside of my lip. "Okay."

Denny surprised, stuttered, "O—okay. Okay?"

"Yes. If you say Anna's helping, okay." I resisted reminding Denny that we had seen a large flashlight roll out of Anna's bag earlier, perfect for dropping off rattlesnakes in a dark trailer. Instead, I glanced at him on the other side of his pickup. "Who else could be the boss? Who has access to the necessary information?"

Denny looked thoughtful as he slid into the driver's seat and started the truck. "Well, anyone on the legislature has access to land info, so does Busdev and the chairman, of course." He twisted his mouth in thought. "Not all the legislators would have access to land and lease info out in this area, only District Four's rep."

"Who's that?"

In a low voice, Denny said, "Anna." Rushing he added, "Business Development and the chair would have all the details, too, as well as signing power to lease out Kiowa land in all the districts." Denny looked triumphant. "It's gotta be the chair, Wyatt Walker, or Cole Stump in Business Development. Stump's new to the position. Cole took over from Wyatt when he got elected chairman." Denny drove slowly down the rutted road. "Cole is ex-military; he could easily organize the operation. He oozes military precision and he 'knows people.'"

"Sounds like we've got good suspects." I smiled. "We'll talk to Eli, help him with the police, and then, we follow the money.

Track down which Tribe official is spending lots more money than they should. That will lead us to the boss."

Denny added, "*Haw*, yes. Wyatt or Cole, one of them has got to be the boss of those little frackers. We'll get Anna's help to figure out which one."

My smile tightened but stayed in place. I wasn't convinced of Anna's innocence, but I let it go for now. I glanced at my watch and did a double take. I could swear hours had gone by while we were trapped inside that office with the rattlesnakes, but it was less than an hour.

Denny went on, "Wonder if Gene and Wayne will leave tomorrow. Their boss still owes them money, that may be reason enough to stay."

"Yeah, but they're not getting any money now. The boss stopped making payments," I reminded him. "You know, Denny, it was probably the last straw for the fracking boss." He shot me a questioning look, and I went on, "Gene and Wayne have been going into town instead of staying put, they're flashing money around, they're driving a new truck, all while the pumps are producing less than expected."

Denny added, "Thank Grandpa and maybe Anna for that."

I nodded in thought. "Yeah. Grandpa slowed them down, but you're right, there was someone else helping. Whoever stopped the pumps tonight wasn't Grandpa." I thought of Sky. Could that be what my brother was doing, helping Grandpa fight the frackers? Then I remembered, Denny didn't know that I had spotted Sky earlier. I faced Denny. "I've got to te—"

Denny cut in, "Yep, had to be Anna. Grandpa couldn't have done it. He started his vision quest yesterday morning." He looked at me. "Same as you, but Grandpa's doing his traditionally. Staying put on the ledge for another two days."

Ignoring Denny's implication that I was in the midst of my own vision quest, I abruptly changed the subject. "Denny, I saw Sky earlier."

The truck stopped, front end down in a rut, back end up on the dirt road. Gravity pulled me forward in the cab. My seatbelt tightened its hold.

"Are you talking about the Troublesome Two?" Denny used the family's nickname for my younger brothers.

"Only Sky. I spotted him at the Complex looking into the chairman's office. Well, maybe I saw him a bit earlier at its front door, but I really thought Sky was at OU, this is his final semester, so I didn't think it was him at first. Sky should be at school." The words rushed out then stopped. I waited for Denny to catch up.

It didn't take long. "If the brothers left those snakes—"

Before he got too worked up, I interrupted, "I don't think Sky left the snakes." I held up my hand. "Let me finish. Yes, planting a tied bag of rattlesnakes is something the brothers would do, but they would not hide a rattlesnake in a desk drawer. That's like pointing a loaded gun. Something's bound to happen." I still didn't let Denny speak. "The brothers do outrageous pranks, constantly get in trouble, but they have never endangered someone. I do not believe Sky put a rattlesnake in that drawer."

"Why is he here?" Denny demanded as if I should know.

"No idea, I sent a text a bit ago." I glanced at my phone. "No answer yet." Before Denny could suggest it, I told him, "I'm not calling our parents to find out about Sky. I shouldn't be this close to home without visiting."

We both took a moment to breathe. Denny put the truck in gear, and it crawled forward. My seatbelt slackened, and I took another deep breath. "I think the frackers had two visitors tonight.

One that dropped off a bag of snakes—not Sky," I emphasized before going on, "and another that sabotaged the pumps." The truck dipped sharply in and out of an unseen rut.

"It could be the same person doing both."

"I thought of that, but . . ." I shook my head. "I don't think so. Leaving rattlesnakes is an attack on the frackers; stopping the pumps doesn't threaten a life. Seems like two different types of people and reasons. Sky or Anna could have stopped the pumps, but I don't see either leaving a rattlesnake in the drawer." I gripped the armrest as the truck lurched back onto the relatively smooth gravel road. "Especially, the drawer that held all correspondence from the boss. Bet there's no envelopes or notes in that drawer anymore."

Denny bit his lip in thought. "You're probably right about that. Still, I don't think Gene and Wayne will do any more fracking out here. Those two were scared. That snake in Gene's drawer about did him in." Denny glanced at me. "I think those two are hitting the road first thing. Once they're gone, we'll go through that office. See what we can learn about their boss."

"You weren't going to hurt those frackers, were you?" I didn't think he would purposely injure another person, but. . . .

"You do realize those two have done a lot of harm to all the land around their fracking operation." Denny locked eyes with me. "Their *illegal* operation."

"I know that, yes." I returned. "But—"

"No buts, Mud. Those two should be in prison for what they've done here, and you heard them, they've done this before." He broke eye contact. "I know I'm not judge and jury. I wanted some answers and got what I could. I wasn't going to do them no real harm. But—" Denny smiled, a hard little grin. "I don't mind scaring them a bit."

We drove the rest of the way to the highway in silence. I was glad for the quiet. For the first time since I left California, I was feeling tired. The adrenaline rush from the experience with the snakes had left me drained. Suddenly it was hard to keep my eyes open, and when I did, the world drifted and became blurry. The engine hum lulled me, urged me to let go.

Drums tapped a steady beat. Grandfather Buffalo stood before me. He huffed a blast of hot breath my way. In the wave of heat came a message, *"You are not seeing."*

I faced Grandfather Buffalo. My eyes questioned, "What was I not seeing?"

In a snort Grandfather Buffalo threw back, *"Your calling."*

"What do you mean? What calling?"

There was no answer. Grandfather Buffalo was gone.

Something buzzed. I leapt to attention and was pulled back by my seat belt.

Denny looked at me with a strange expression. "You going to get that, see who's calling?"

My mind was muddled. "What calling?"

Something *brrr'ed* again, so like the earlier rattlesnake that my body jerked, my heart raced.

Denny made a turn. "Mud, that's your phone."

I fumbled with the phone, one more jarring *brr* before I got it to my face and croaked out, "Hello." I cleared my throat and tried again. "Hello."

"Mae? You there, Mae?"

Again, I shook my head to clear it. "Yep, Bernie, what's up?"

"You okay?" I heard concern in Bernie's voice.

"Yes, I'm with my cousin, working on family business still." I rambled a bit, saying nothing.

Bernie hesitated, seemed to want to question more but didn't. Instead, she launched into an update on agency business. "Wanted to let you know that all files have been sent and are ready for your once-over. Marcus has the new company logo 3-D treatment ready as well." She sounded tired, but pleased.

"Bernie, that's great!" I smiled into the phone. "I'll look over everything and get revisions noted on each presentation back to you by the morning shift. That will give the crew plenty of time to make any necessary changes before your review with the executives." I glanced at my watch and automatically subtracted two hours—it was just after 1:30 in California. "Thanks for staying on these. You better head for bed. You're going to need to be sharp for the review."

Bernie would conduct the upcoming review and walk-through with Richard's top executives. Each would speak at the event. For many of the executives, this would be the first time rehearsing with the visuals for their speeches. It was a fine art getting an executive comfortable on stage, and making sure the visuals enhanced the speaker's words without distracting from the message. After this review, stage rehearsals would follow before the company launched with its big press event. I had to be there for the final rehearsals. Bernie could manage the walk-through, as long as she got my notes on the speakers and any necessary timing adjustments.

Bernie let a yawn slip. "I'm going home now. I'll get in early to make sure any changes you want are ready for production." I could hear papers shuffling and an office chair creak. "Don't forget I need your notes on the files as soon as possible. Then you have only one thing left to do." Bernie raised her voice. "Be on the noon flight so you are back in time for the final walk-through. The client wants you here. The business needs you here."

Denny heard Bernie. He immediately waved for my attention, and added in a loud whisper, "We've got to solve a murder, and follow the money to find the fracking boss. Remember?"

I moved the phone from my mouth. "We'll have time."

Denny snorted and shook his head.

I turned from Denny, answered Bernie with an abrupt, "I've got it," and shoved the phone into my pocket.

I felt Denny's eyes bore into me. As soon as I was off the phone, he asked, "How are you going to solve a murder, find the fracking boss, *and* catch a noon flight?"

"I'm not solving a murder. We're helping Eli." I ended with a lame, "We'll get it done." Fortunately, Denny didn't push the issue. I had no answers.

Again, we fell into silence. Neither felt the need to fill the void. There was no more to say until we talked to Eli.

A bump in the road brought headlights behind us to my attention. In the rearview mirror a familiar set of dim yellowed headlights went up, down, then leveled several car lengths back. It was strange to have anyone else on the road with us this far out in the country, especially this late. Most homes we passed were dark husks, occasionally a barn or a porch's pinprick light was left on as a beacon. The dim set of headlights stayed in the rearview mirror as we turned toward Carnegie.

I didn't disturb Denny, just watched. The lights also turned. The headlights didn't rush to catch us but stayed a measured distance behind.

Denny stared straight ahead, deep in thought, driving the well-known road on automatic, not noticing the dim yellowed headlights pacing us.

A few miles down Highway 19, Denny slowed and signaled a left onto a gravel road you would miss if you didn't know it was there. I snuck a peek in the rearview mirror and let out a breath. No headlights in sight.

Then they appeared—again.

Chapter Fifteen

Gravel crunched under our tires as we turned onto the road leading to Eli's house. I twisted to look back. The headlights stopped at the turn. The dim lights got smaller and smaller as we traveled farther down the road. I watched, waited for the car to turn onto the gravel road, to follow us. It didn't. The yellowed headlights sped off and disappeared into the dark.

I was glad I hadn't said anything to Denny. No reason to give him something more to tease me about. Denny leaned forward, peering through the windshield. Not sure what he saw to mark it, but he took a turn off the gravel road onto one that was more dirt path than road.

He slowed to a crawl. "Eli's place is just over that hill." Denny's chin lifted toward the road ahead. The truck came to a stop at the foot of a rise.

"Is it too late—or early—to see him?" I looked toward the clock in the dash. "It's nearly four."

"Eli will be waiting for us." Denny leaned forward, looking at the empty road.

I peered through the windshield, not sure what absorbed Denny—all I saw was a dark path weaving through overgrown bushes and trees. "What are we waiting for?"

"Just giving Eli some time. He probably heard us turning onto the road. This is the kind of night he'll be out in the *TD'oh poat*, brush arbor."

Mention of the open-sided structure brought a smile. Brush arbors were a staple of spring and summer life. They were simple structures, made from stripped pines for lodge poles and young cottonwood branches to form a roof. Our Kiowa grandparents always had *TD'oh poats* through the hot summers. They were the best way to survive Oklahoma's heat. Nights in the arbor were sleepless adventures usually spent with a gathering of cousins.

Denny gassed the truck forward, slowly easing over the hill. The dirt road ended at a small house set back in a cluster of oaks. As we crawled closer, I realized it was more cabin than house. Before getting too close, Denny turned his lights and engine off to not disturb anyone sleeping inside. He let the truck coast behind another truck parked under a detached carport off to one side of the house. With the engine off, we waited. Hot metal ticked off the seconds as the engine cooled. Finally, Denny decided the proper amount of time had elapsed and he opened the truck's door.

Stepping from the truck, we were greeted by the night's insect orchestra of cicadas' constant buzz-saw siren accompanied by katydids' rhythmic *ka-tydid*, mixed with *zitzitzitzit* chirps from crickets in the grass below. Occasionally, a frog added its defining note to the symphony.

The night had cooled to a refreshing seventyish. Stars shimmered across the sky like a lake of diamonds. A hint of sweet resin-laden smoke rode on a light breeze. Somewhere close-by a cedar bundle burned.

Cedar, the evergreen tree of life, protected against evil spirits and negative energy. The wafting smoke turned me toward a brush arbor tucked in a cluster of three oaks just beyond the carport. My eyes were drawn to a small fire at the center of the arbor. The fire wasn't used for warmth; it was the source of the sweet scent of cedar. Cedar-rich smoke rose above the fire's flickering flames, warding all evil and negative spirits away from the surrounding area and people.

Once my vision adjusted to the dark, I spotted the eagle headdress. It sat on top of a wooden staff just outside the arbor and in the direct path of the drifting smoke. The feathers fluttered in the near-dawn breeze. As we drew closer, the headdress seemed to turn to watch our approach. The moonlight splashed through the brush arbor's branched roofing, adding dappled silver light to the flickering orange hue from the small fire. Slowly, forms within the arbor took shape: a dark picnic table, spattering of lawn chairs, oversized cushions, and a large rocker moving in and out of the silver light shafts.

Eli's deep voice came from inside the arbor. "*May hay bay, gaw bay saw*, you all come in and sit down." This was a traditional Kiowa greeting, one I had heard many times through my childhood. I noted that Eli had used the inclusive *may*—meaning "all"—rather than *aim* for a single person.

Eli's voice was coming from close to the center of the arbor, by the fire. We entered from the east, stopping to wash in the swirling cedar smoke to ensure we left all negative spirits and thoughts behind.

As my eyes adjusted to the interior's charcoal murk, I spotted Eli rocking slowly back and forth on what looked like a handmade cottonwood rocking chair. His cane laid across his lap. He still wore the workworn overalls, now with one strap hanging loose, the bib corner dropped forward revealing a missing button on Eli's plaid shirt. His smile broadened at our approach. "*Ownah day aim broh*, it is good to see you."

Denny leaned forward, extended his hand to grasp Eli's. He said one word, "*Khoam*, friend."

Eli nodded. "*Haw*, we have been friends for a long time. It's good to see you both." He looked up to include me. "I see the Storyteller apprentice is still with you. That's good." Eli rocked back, waved his hands downward. "Sit, sit."

It didn't feel right towering over the gray-haired man in his rocker with the intent of questioning him about a murder, so I sat on the edge of a nearby bench seat. Denny settled beside me. I knew I shouldn't launch right into what we had come for, but I couldn't wait on custom niceties. I looked over to the headdress guarding the arbor. "I see you got your headdress back."

Denny poked me with his elbow. I slid down the bench, out of reach. Resettled and asked, "How did you get it?"

Denny didn't let Eli answer. "Eli, please forgive my cousin. She doesn't mean to be rude. Mud's been away for a long time. She forgets some of our ways."

I felt heat rise. Denny had hit a sore spot—and he knew it. I grew up as the only curly-headed Sawpole in our family of dark, straight hair. Despite my knowledge and training, my curls marked me as not Indian enough for some in the Tribe.

I stood, shifted so I faced both Denny and Eli. I kept my voice low, but loud enough to be heard. "I haven't forgotten our customs, but there is a time for customs and a time for action. Now is a time for action, we need answers." I shot a glare at Denny before turning to Eli to ask again, "Grandfather, how did you get the headdress?"

Denny set his jaw but remained silent.

Eli had leaned back with his face in partial shadow as he listened to me. At my question, he rocked forward. "My grandfather's *Ah-T'aw-hoy* is home, where it belongs." He lifted a drawstring pouch from his lap. Eli opened the bag, started a chant before he sprinkled the contents onto the fire. The flames crackled as they reached for more resin-rich cedar. The resulting smoke plumed upward and out, riding a light breeze.

Silence stretched. I held my tongue—barely.

Finally, Eli rocked into a shaft of moonlight. He planted his cane and leaned forward. "First time Buck showed up with that Gerald was to ask about oil in the Slick Hills. That's when Gerald spotted the headdress. Offered to buy it, right then and there. I told him he didn't have enough money to buy my grandfather's *Ah-T'aw-hoy*. So, Gerald got Buck to get the family headdress from my grandson. Sonny don't know it's value. He just knew we needed the power turned back on."

Eli reached for the cedar smoke wafting between us. He cupped his hand and poured smoke onto his head. I knew he was washing negative thoughts away. Letting them go.

Eli returned to his story, but not to what I wanted to hear. "I'm going to have a cleansing, make sure Sonny and all my kids understand what this headdress means to the family, and our people. They need to know what it took to earn each one of those feathers." Eli used his cane to point at the fluttering headdress.

I wanted to urge Eli on, to explain how he got the headdress and what he knew about the body at the gallery. That we didn't have time for a long story. My face must have given my impatience away.

Eli used his cane to stomp the floor four times, leaving one-inch overlapping circle prints in the dirt. He raised his hand, palm forward, and announced, "*Thigh-gyah ate thoe-dayn-mah*, I speak straight, tell the truth." He switched back to English. "But you must understand, there is value in the story rather than the quick words you think you want." The cane returned to lay across his lap. Eli rocked slowly back and forth, saying no more.

Denny kicked the side of my shoe.

I shifted where I stood and looked down at the perfect circle indents left by Eli's cane, knew I was right—but wrong. I took a breath before turning to the older man. "Eli, I am sorry for rushing you to tell us what happened. You're right. The story is important. Can you tell us now?" I sat back down on the bench, watched Eli rock in and out of the shadows, considering my request.

Finally, Eli leaned forward into a sliver of light and started, "I just couldn't rest none after I saw y'all at the Compound. I tried, even went home, but it was no good." He shook his head. "Knew I had to go get the headdress back right then and there." His head shake turned to a slow affirming nod. Eli rocked back.

I gave up any hope of Eli telling us about the dead man quickly. Eli was going to tell his tale at the pace that was right for the story. If I interrupted again, I would only delay the telling. I tried to get comfortable on the hard bench seat. Denny had already leaned back against the table, settled in to hear Eli's story.

"Y'all know eagle feathers aren't earned just for bravery. Nope, you don't get feathers just for warring. It's not like what they show on TV. Few Kiowas earned enough feathers to have a headdress like my grandfather's." He looked hard at Denny and me in turn. "My grandfather earned feathers for bravery, wisdom, leadership, compassion, generosity, fairness, and teaching." Eli looked toward the headdress. "Those feathers show a man's life lived in balance. My grandfather walked the Good Red Road." His eyes glowed with warmth and pride.

I stole a glance at Denny. He remained focused on Eli. The night's insect orchestra fell to the background. Eli's voice captured the night.

He rocked back into the shadows. "I just couldn't rest my mind with our *Ah-T'aw-hoy* under glass." Eli's fingers raked through his thick gray hair then returned to squeezing the rocker's armrests. He went on, "It was like it couldn't breathe. Those feathers need air ruffling through them."

Denny uttered, "*Haw*" under his breath. The fire crackled.

Eli went on with his story. "Anyways, I went on down to that gallery, saw my headdress through the window with a price tag for forty-two thousand dollars." Eli shook his head. "There was a light on in back, so I banged on the front door, even on the big window. But no one came." Disappointment crossed his face. "I went on around to the back door, figured I would bang on the door closest to the lights there in back. Whoever was inside was bound to hear me, and they sure weren't going to get out without talkin' to me." His hands gripped the rocker's arms.

Denny and I stayed silent.

It took a moment before Eli continued, "I banged on that back door. No one answered. So, I grabbed hold of the doorknob." Eli looked at his hand as if watching it twist the gallery's doorknob. He looked up at me. "And it turned." Eli's face showed his surprise. "I walked right in and down this long hallway. The light was coming out of an office, but I didn't care about nothing but the headdress. I went right to those feathers." Eli pointed to the headdress with his chin.

Denny leaned forward.

As Eli rocked, shadows dappled across his face. "I didn't steal nothin'. Just went and got what was mine. I'm sorry about breaking that glass case with the story rock. But that headdress needed air."

I started to ask a question, caught myself and stayed silent.

"I left Gerald his money." Eli looked intently at me. "I don't sell my heritage!" I gave a slight nod. I knew he spoke the truth. Satisfied, Eli said, "I took what was mine. Wore it right out of there. It felt right." Eli set his jaw before pushing back on the rocker.

I bit my lower lip to stay quiet, to not ask questions until I was sure Eli was done. Denny nodded in time with the slowly rocking chair.

Eli shifted forward, added a small piece of wood to the hot embers before he scattered more cedar onto the fire. "It is right and proper the *Ah-T'aw-hoy* is here. Family needs to know our history and the Tribe's history. They're braided together." Eli made a tying gesture with his hands. "Ain't that right, Storyteller?"

I ignored his question, but took advantage of the opening. "What about . . . the body?"

Denny seemed able to wait patiently for the answer. I found I was on the edge of my seat.

Eli looked directly at me. "I went toward the lights in the office to give that man his money. I found him inside, laying on the office carpet. Obvious it didn't matter to him anymore, but it did to me. I tucked his money into his shirt pocket. Told him that our dealings were done." Eli looked into the small fire. "Wish I had a bundle with me, I would have burnt cedar there for his spirit." Eli pushed back, setting the rocker in motion.

I watched him go back and forth a few times before venturing another question. "Do you know who killed him?" Denny smiled at me. I knew he was glad I didn't ask Eli if he had killed Gerald.

The rocking continued. "Can't say I do. He'd been dead about two hours. I've hunted my whole life. I know stages of death. His body still held some warmth when I placed the bills in his pocket."

"What time was that?"

"Not absolutely sure. But 'bout midnight. I'd come home for a bit after seeing y'all at the Compound." He nodded toward the dark cabin.

"Do you remember if the air conditioning was running at the gallery?"

This stopped the old man as he thought about my question. "Funny you asked that." He nodded and touched his forehead. "Yep, I wiped sweat away before I put the headdress on, but kinda felt a chill all over. It was getting cold inside." Eli went back to rocking.

I let the old man rock in silence for a bit while I tried to think what else to ask.

Denny cleared his throat. "Eli, did you see anyone around the gallery?"

Eli slowed his rocking to answer, "I didn't see anyone, but I did see a white van in the back parking lot." Eli nodded. "Yep, I forgot about that, I looked in the van first. Didn't see anyone in the front and couldn't see into the back . . ." Eli paused while thinking. "After that I went to banging on the gallery door, then went on inside." He gave a single nod, done with the night's story.

But I wasn't. "Have you seen anyone else tonight?" I was thinking of Sky and was surprised by Eli's answer.

"Sure have. Seems no one's getting much rest tonight."

My "*Haw*" prompted him to continue.

"Been no time to sleep since I got home after getting my headdress. Anna come by just as I settled in. We sat a spell, but I could tell she was worked up 'bout something. Finally, she asked about my pastureland back in the Slick Hills."

Denny piped up, "I didn't know you had land there."

"Oh, yeah. Not much, just a few acres, enough to feed the cows a bit. Not really good for much but grazing land." Eli moved forward into the moonlight. "That is until this summer."

"You're not using it for the grazing?" Denny looked surprised.

"Oh sure, I still use it for grazing, but the Tribe got me a deal." Eli grinned. "That's where I got the money to keep our power on. The Tribe's Bus Dev heard we was struggling and offered to lease the land and still let me graze on it. Don't that beat all?" Eli slapped his knee.

Denny and I exchanged a look. Bus Dev could be Wyatt Walker, the Tribe chairman, or the new business development officer, Cole Stump.

Before we could ask questions, Eli continued, "The Tribe got me a lease deal with an oil company they know. The company is just testing the ground, not even doing drilling or nothing, just want to know what's down there." Eli looked to us. "Can you believe that?" Not expecting an answer, he went on, "I'm getting a couple hundred a month. And that's after a leasing bonus." He gave his knee another happy slap. "Bunch of us are leasing out our land around the Slick Hills through the Tribe's Bus Dev. The land's not worth much, too rocky to plant. But it's sure nice getting that extra money right now." Eli smiled as he rocked.

Denny shifted on the bench seat. I could tell he had questions that wanted out, but he held them in.

Eli stopped the chair, looked thoughtful. "Don't know why, but when Anna left, she was mad as all get-out."

Denny finally burst. "I'll tell you why, Eli. You're letting them frack on your land!"

The old man stopped mid-rock. "You got it wrong, Denny. None of that's happening on my land. I don't cotton to none of that." He shook his head. "They're just taking pictures that shows 'em what's down there real deep." Eli started rocking again. "Nobody's fracking on my land. No, siree."

Denny pushed. "There's no pumps on your land?"

"Nope, nothing. I tell ya, the Tribe's Bus Dev group found some company that just wants to study the rocks and ground down deep." Eli folded his arms. "I would never agree to fracking." The topic was settled.

I asked, "Was it Wyatt that set this up for you Eli?"

"Must have been. Wyatt is the chairman, he's the one responsible for the Tribe's business." Eli looked surprised at my question.

I drilled down. "Did you talk to Wyatt?"

"Nope, just the oil company man. He had all the paperwork needed from the Tribe to get set up. Made everything quick and easy. Just signed a couple papers, and I get money every month. Just like clockwork."

Denny started to ask another question but stopped as I stood and faced Eli. "Thank you for telling us—"

Eli interrupted. "Got one more thing to say. I knew you two would come here tonight. You told me you was going to get my *Ah-T'aw-hoy* and fix things. I just couldn't wait. But I knew you would come. Y'all do what you promise." He looked at Denny then focused on me. "I'll tell you what, Storyteller Apprentice, your way is harder than it should be. We older Kiowa know the only way to honor the Creator is to be true to yourself. And you . . ." Eli rocked forward and pointed to me with his chin. "Storytelling's in your blood, not your curly hair." He rocked back, laughing at his joke.

Denny rose to stand beside me. Eli rocked forward, he had more to say. "These young Kiowa take on white society norms.

They forget our ways. If James Sawpole says you're the Storyteller, well, that's that. I know James, he don't make mistakes. You know who and what you are in here." His fist went to his chest above his heart. "Believe it and live it." He threw the last of the cedar onto the red, hot embers. "I'm sending good smoke your way."

The fire crackled; cedar smoke rose, engulfing us.

Chapter Sixteen

"You're right, Denny, we've got to help Eli. He can't get caught up in a murder charge." After hearing Eli's story, I knew—felt in my heart that Eli did not kill Gerald. He didn't have murder in him.

Denny drove slowly down the dirt road away from Eli's house. "I knew you would see he's innocent." Denny glanced at me. "You never even asked Eli if he did it. You knew he was telling the truth." His gaze returned to the road. The orange glow from the instrument panel revealed his grin.

I didn't want Denny to get over enthused; we had a nearly impossible task ahead of us if we wanted to keep Eli from being arrested for Gerald's death. "It doesn't matter what we think we know. Unfortunately, Eli will be the main suspect. He left his fingerprints on the back door, stole the headdress—"

"Took *his* headdress back," Denny asserted.

I went on as if not interrupted. "And left more prints on money stuffed in a dead man's pocket. Brenda is sure Eli did it and will make him look bad." I shook my head. "The police aren't going to believe Eli and definitely won't sit still long enough to hear the *whole* story." I stretched out the word "whole" to put the smile back on Denny's face. It worked. The grin got bigger when I added, "You're right, we are going to have to find the real killer to keep Eli out of this."

"I love hearing those words!" Denny turned onto the gravel road, heading back to the highway. "Where do we go from here?"

"I'm not sure . . ." I let my voice drop away as I tried to think things through. "We need to lay out the facts, see what that tells us."

Denny stopped in the middle of the empty gravel road, shoved the gear into neutral. It would be easy to spot any oncoming traffic from where we sat—as if there would be traffic out here at this time of night—morning. Dawn was a few hours away.

Denny shifted to face me. "Eli didn't tell us anything about the dead man, except to confirm he did not kill Gerald."

"Eli told us more than that." I thought back to Eli's words before continuing. "Like he said, there was value in the story, which I would not have heard with just the answers I wanted. Thanks to Eli's story, we have a good idea what time Gerald died."

"How you figure?" Denny's eyes reflected orange from the dashboard light.

I bit my lip as I thought it through. "According to Eli, Gerald died a little before ten. Eli said he saw the body a bit before midnight, and death had been about two hours earlier. That puts the death around ten, which fits with how the dead man's wrist felt when I grabbed it to check for a pulse." I hesitated, shivered, pushed my feelings down and went on, "The touch was clammy, not cold. Rigor had not set in, but stiffening was beginning." I shook off thoughts of the dead man's arm and returned to working out a timeline. "We came across the body at one-ish. That confirms—to me, anyway, that Gerald must have died close to ten o'clock last night." I shook my head, was it really last night?

Looking out at the dark morning, I couldn't believe his death was just hours ago.

Denny jarred me back to the present. "That doesn't help much."

"It does if Georgie really did fall over Gerald's boots at the maintenance office. That would have happened just after ten—"

Before I finished, Denny interrupted, "That would mean Gerald was dead at the maintenance office and Georgie is lying now." He leaned forward in his seat. "I knew Buck did it. That proves it."

"Wait, you lost me. How does that prove Buck did it?"

"Buck was angry at Gerald. Mad enough it scared Georgie." Denny got a distant look in his eyes as he talked on. "Betcha Buck found Gerald and knocked him upside the head with a hammer." Denny's eyes refocused on me. As if he were playing the game Clue, Denny announced, "That's it. Buck did it in the maintenance office with a hammer."

I didn't play along. "Hammer is too big, would have bashed Gerald's head in rather than dent the temple." I rubbed my forehead with two fingers as I considered the precision of the hit.

Denny's face deflated. He slumped back into his seat. "You're sure not coming up with anything."

"I'm not telling a story. I'm trying to gather facts."

"So, what do you have?"

"Gerald died just before ten. Someone hit him on the temple with a small, round object—not jagged like the rock at the gallery—it had a perfect round point." I stopped, taking a moment to think about a round surface, hard enough to kill. Eli's cane came to mind, a good possibility, but I couldn't picture the old man capable of taking a life.

Denny said, "Two facts that get us nowhere."

I ignored Denny. "Gerald was most likely killed at the maintenance hut's office, but why move the body?" I answered my own question, "To misdirect. The killer didn't want the body found at the hut's office." I looked at Denny and grinned. "That's why the gallery's air conditioning was on high."

His forehead wrinkled. "I was following, until you threw in the air conditioning. What does AC have to do with a dead man?"

"Someone moved the body from the maintenance office to the gallery then turned the AC on high to try and mess with the time of death."

Denny repeated, "That's why someone moved the body—to try and change the time and place of the murder." He turned in his seat, his face glowing orange. "Georgie did it. And she's making us her alibi."

My turn to be confused. "How? Georgie was with us all night. She found the body. There wasn't an opportunity for her to move it to the gallery."

He set his jaw. "Don't know how, but she did it. Georgie lies so smoothly." Denny slipped into a mocking voice, "*I imagined it all.*"

I shook my head. "If Georgie did it, why tell us about the body? We would never have seen a body in the maintenance office. We weren't going there."

"Georgie used us to set up her alibi. And you're falling for it. She wasn't with us all night. She went stomping off without us while we talked with Eli. She had plenty of time to kill Gerald, stash the body—heck, there may never have been a body in the office. Georgie could have killed him somewhere else and just led us to the maintenance office. Yep. She plumb played us."

I shook my head. "No, that doesn't make sense."

"It all makes sense." Denny eyed me. "Or is it you don't want it to be Georgie?"

"I want the truth!" I faced Denny. "And I'm tired of you implying I'm in love with Georgie. Enough already. I am done with her that way."

My spark of anger brought a chuckle out of Denny. "Okay, okay." He put his hands up as if blocking an attack. "Whatever you say. You are finally done being lovesick for your high school sweetheart. Great news." He dropped his hands. "Now, open your eyes and see her guilt."

"Denny, she had no time!" He frustrated me. Teasing me, then pushing where the facts refused to go.

"Think about it, Mud. Georgie was out of our sight for about twenty minutes. That's plenty of time to swing a hammer"—he gave me a look and amended his words—"a small hammer. You said it yourself: Gerald was killed with a single blow. That doesn't take any time at all. Maybe it happened in the maintenance hut and not the office like Georgie said." Denny was getting excited about his story. "Georgie met Gerald in the hut, grabbed a ball-peen hammer and nailed him." He lifted his hand grasping an invisible hammer, swinging it. "Gerald goes down. She leaves him there in the dark part of the hut, runs into the office and out its door screaming that Gerald was dead in the office."

I didn't interrupt, just let Denny get his story out. I'd learned my lesson with Eli.

He looked toward me, excitement in his voice. "That's how she did it! We couldn't see the body in the hut's dark cavern. Let's go see if there are drag marks in the hut and out its back door. Yep. Georgie thinks she pulled one over on us. But the facts are the facts."

I put my hand on his before he shifted the truck into drive. "Denny, Georgie did not have time." I squeezed his hand to silence his resistance, then released it. "You're right, Georgie probably had twenty minutes away from us and what you map out is possible, but not probable." My eyes held his. "You jump from facts and twist them to the conclusion you want. How is she going to find a ball-peen hammer in the dark? Did Gerald just stand there and let her aim before hitting him? How did the body get to the gallery? Georgie had no chance to move the body or tell anyone where or how to help her move it."

Denny sputtered, wanting to interrupt, but I talked over him. "Just listen for a moment. My turn to talk."

Denny left the truck in neutral, leaned back in his seat and told me, "Go ahead." His jaw appeared rigid.

"You have to listen, not just let me talk."

He laughed; it relieved the tension. "Go ahead. I'm listening now."

"We had Georgie with us most of the night, she didn't have a chance to call anyone for help."

"That's where Buck comes in."

I twisted in my seat to face Denny. "Then you're talking premeditated murder, and you're giving them both more credit than Georgie or Buck deserve."

Denny didn't want to give in, I could see it in his eyes. I pushed him, "Can we just get back to the facts?"

"You keep ignoring the fact that Buck wanted Gerald dead. I think together or separate, those two are behind Gerald's death." Denny pushed his hair from his face. "If we could figure out how she moved the body, we'd have her."

"You're being too single minded." I put my hand up to stop Denny from going on. "Just let me think."

"Go ahead. But I have it worked out, and it fits the facts we have."

Sharper than I should have, I answered, "You keep jumping around with who did it. First, it's Buck, then it's Georgie, then it's both of them. Who's next?"

Denny clamped his lips together and looked out the dark windshield. His headlights lit the gravel road ahead. Nothing moved outside.

I took a deep breath, let it out slowly. "Denny, I'm trying to look at the evidence and figure this out. That's what you want, right?"

He struggled for a moment before releasing his clenched jaw to announce, "We know Eli didn't kill Gerald. Now, you need to face the facts about Georgie. She's in this. No one else was around the Compound that could have killed Gerald." He folded his arms and watched me for a reaction.

"Denny, you're not looking at everything. Or everyone." He wasn't going to like what I was going to say.

"Who else was around?" Before I could, he answered, "There was Buck on the loose, you, me, Eli, and Georgie. We're out, Eli's out. It leaves those two. There was no one else around." The orange glow from the dash lit his face, showing that he genuinely looked confused.

I had one name to add. "Anna."

Denny went from confused to protective in a flash. "Oh, come on! Anna wasn't at the maintenance office."

"We don't know where Anna went after we saw her in the parking lot. Anna has to be a suspect. She was there at the right time." I quickly added, "The maintenance hut isn't that far from the legislators' offices, and she worked with Gerald reviewing the museum's stored artifacts." I ended with, "Including the peace medal."

"Come on. Now you're stretching. Why would Anna kill Gerald?"

"Maybe Gerald threatened to expose her in the plot to steal the peace medal."

Denny snorted. "Next you'll say Gerald and Anna were in on the fracking together."

"There is something going on with Anna and fracking. She brought it up with Eli." I had to admit, "Not sure how fracking fits in with Gerald's death . . . maybe Gerald was the boss—" I shook my head; now I was the one reaching and skipping the facts.

Denny threw the truck into gear. "You know what, we're going to ask her."

The truck crunched down the gravel road back toward the highway.

"Where are you going?"

"To Anna's house. She's not far from here. We're going to eliminate another suspect, so you can focus on how Buck and Georgie did it." Denny turned onto the highway's blacktop, spitting gravel in his wake.

Headlights popped on behind us.

I glanced at Denny; his jaw was locked tight and his focus forward.

The headlights got bigger.

Through the rearview mirror, I watched the lights advance on us. Growing bigger. Getting closer. Denny stared straight ahead, unseeing. The headlights were less than a car length back and coming fast. I tried to look beyond the glare to who was driving.

Brights flicked on, hitting us with a blinding flash from behind. Denny muttered, "What's that guy doing?" He slowed. "I'm going to let this guy get past us."

An engine roared as the blinding headlights shot to the next lane. A van accelerated quickly, drawing alongside and past us before it abruptly jerked back into our lane. Denny braked hard, swung right, and slid to a stop. The van seemed to scream at us as it swerved right, twisted, and came to a rocking stop, blocking our truck with its bright lights blaring directly on us.

Chapter Seventeen

The van had no windows along its side and too-dark-to-see-in driver and passenger windows in the front. Which really didn't matter at the moment, since the bright white headlights blinded us from seeing anything. I asked, without expecting Denny to know, "Who's in the van?" I squinted, trying to see into the van's interior.

"Don't know, but I'm going to find out!" Denny jerked his door open and slid out.

"Wai—" Too late. He was out of the truck. Denny hadn't changed much in the ten years I'd been gone. He still charged into every situation. I let a small smile escape as I stepped out into the bright darkness. And I was still following my big cousin, just like when we were younger.

"Turn those lights off!" Denny marched toward the van making demands. "You nearly hit my truck. You drunk or what?" Denny kept moving toward the driver side of the van. The headlights went out.

I was blind in the sudden darkness, dancing white blobs making it impossible to see where Denny was situated. I shuffled, reaching forward to find the side of the van. I closed my eyes, then squinted through them. Slowly my eyes adjusted to the dark.

I spotted Denny, who had continued moving around the rear of the van toward its driver door.

An opening door squeaked. I rushed to the front of the van. Denny was exposed, coming from the van's rear to the driver's door. The van driver had the advantage of sight and position. I hurried to get across the front of the van and to the door. If I reached the opening door from the front, I could push it closed, trapping the driver inside until we knew who and what we were dealing with. Denny's anger jet propelled him toward the van's door. He was steps ahead of me.

The door swung fully open and a gruff voice shouted, "Found you, finally!" The van's interior lights revealed Georgie's husband, Buck, sliding out of the driver seat, face red with fury. He stormed forward to confront Denny. "I've been chasing after you all night." Buck chest-bumped Denny.

Denny pushed back into Buck. "You ran me off the road! Better hope nothing is wrong with my truck."

"To hell with your truck. Who you been with all night, huh?"

I reached the van door, pushed it inward out of my way. The door let out a squeal.

Buck turned, spotted me. "Oh, that explains it. Shoulda known." In the same instant, he spun and came straight for me. His eyes locked on me, but I didn't think he saw me. The man was in a blind rage.

Denny was caught off guard by Buck's sudden turn toward me. He was two steps behind the charging Buck, but coming fast.

I stood with my hands on the van door, watching as he charged toward me.

Buck was steps away. Spittle dripped from his open mouth as he hurled insults at me. A part of my mind noticed Buck was now beardless. I flexed my knees, preparing.

A wicked grin spread across Buck's freshly shaved face. He telegraphed his intent. Still rushing toward me, Buck lowered his weight. The man was going to tackle me.

I forced myself to focus.

My eyes locked on Buck, his pink face reminiscent of the boy of my childhood. His eyes full of fury . . . and pain.

I watched the charging bull of a man.

Timed it.

And pulled the van's door open just as Buck lunged. Both screeched.

The impact pushed me back, I nearly toppled, but balanced at the last second and stayed on my feet. Buck wasn't so lucky. The van's interior light spilled out the open door and onto Buck. He was curled on the ground, his left arm grasping his right shoulder tightly. A moan escaped from him.

Denny arrived out of breath and gave me a half smile before he bent at the waist to ask Buck, "Do you need help?"

Buck glared upward and grunted, "Not from you!" He shifted, rolled to his knees, and stayed there, sucking in air. Through a grimace, he demanded, "Why'd you do that?"

"To save myself," burst out without thought. My heart beat as if I had finished a fifty-yard dash. I held onto the van's door; it steadied my shaking hands. Adrenalin rushed through me.

Buck growled, "You're going to need more than a door to save yourself from me." He used the side of the van to slowly get to his feet. His right arm hung at his side. Buck's face twisted with contempt. "I know what you've been up to all night. You messin' with what's mine. Get 'er out here."

Leveraging off the van, Buck launched at me.

Before I could react, Denny grabbed Buck's injured shoulder and pushed him back onto the side of the van. "What is your problem? You're a grown man trying to beat up a woman. Pretty pathetic." Denny shook his head in disgust. "Don't know why Georgie stays with you."

Buck pushed off the van, stepped toward Denny. "Don't be talking about my wife." His tough act ended with a groan. Buck slouched back against the van, cradling his injured shoulder.

I stepped closer but watched Buck carefully. I didn't trust the man.

Denny faced Buck. "Looks like Mud beat you up again. You going to run home to your mommy now?"

When we were growing up, Buck had been a bully to all the kids smaller than him. One afternoon, my younger brother came home with chain marks inflicted by Buck. In a rage, I brought the twelve-year-old Buck to his knees with a solid punch to his nose. He went home covered in blood and simmering in hate. The hate seemed to still consume him seventeen years later.

Buck ignored Denny's taunt. He glared at me. "Where is she, what you done with 'er? Time for her to git home to the baby."

I wanted some answers before giving any. Maybe Denny was right, and Buck was the killer. Buck had thought Gerald killed his grandfather, until I revealed the real murderer. Vengeance was strong motivation. Using Plains Indian sign language, I signaled Denny not to mention Gerald's death. I wanted to find out what Buck knew and where he was around ten last night.

I stared back at Buck. "Who are you talking about?"

His face contorted. "Don't play innocent with me. I know you two been runnin' around again." He spit on the ground. "And she's a mother now."

The venom in his voice forced me to take a step back. Buck didn't mean Denny and me running around. "Are you talking about Georgie *and me*?"

Buck's face became guarded. He took a deep breath, pushed from the van, winced but stayed upright. "Just get 'er out here."

He stood in a slip of light coming from the open van door. In addition to shaving his beard, Buck had cut his long hair. It hung in a ragged line at his neck as if gathered and chopped all at once. In the old days, Kiowas would hack their long braids off in grief or disgrace. I wondered which it had been for Buck.

A bandaged hand dangled from Buck's lifeless right arm. He'd damaged the hand hitting a tree after I told him his grandfather was dead. Now, he added a shoulder to his injury list.

Denny spoke, "Buck, you're acting crazy. Are you drunk?"

"I've not touched a bottle. Swore off it." He smacked his lips.

I wondered if this was a recent pledge.

"Then what is your problem?" Denny's anger was building. "You forced me off the road! Why?" He moved toward the unsteady Buck.

Buck teetered but stood his ground. "I've been looking for my wife all night. I know she's with you." He fumbled one-handed before he held his phone up to show a tracking app. I've been watching her phone." His lips formed a smile, his eyes rejected it. Fury seemed to give Buck strength, he straightened before shouting, "Get her out here. Now!" Buck shuffled toward Denny's truck.

I moved back to the front of the truck. "Buck, Georgie's been worried about you."

"Like I'm going to believe that."

"We have been looking for you," Denny shot back.

Buck stopped at the truck's side, leaned on it. "All week, Georgie's been sneaking away. Leaving the baby with her mom. Well, I seen where she been all night and now, I know who she's been with." Buck looked like he might charge at me again if he could summon enough power.

I shook my head. "I just got to town yesterday and tonight, Georgie's been with me *and* Denny. She asked us to help find you. Georgie was worried, she thought you were going to kill Gerald." I watched for a reaction when I said the last.

A strange look crossed Buck's face. "Sure wanted to when I thought he killed my grandpa." He pushed away from the truck's side. "But you proved Gerald didn't do it." He swayed forward. "Get Georgie out here. Y'all been in my business enough tonight."

I told him the truth. "Georgie's not with us."

Buck turned to look through the window into the truck. "I know she's in there. I've been tracking you and it shows Georgie's here."

Denny answered, "Her phone must have got left in my truck, because Georgie's at the gallery you stocked with stolen Kiowa goods."

Buck let go of the truck's door handle, turned to face Denny. "I didn't steal nuthin' from nobody." Buck puffed out his barrel chest.

Denny, leaner but taller, seemed to tower over Buck as he said, "Eli told us how you cheated his grandson, Sonny. Bought the family headdress for a thousand dollars, then Gerald was selling it for over forty thousand." He locked eyes with Buck. "You're disgusting."

Buck started huffing and spitting, but before he got words out, Denny moved closer. "You even sold your own family treasure." Denny shook his head in disgust. "Sold your son's heritage."

Sparks flared in Buck eyes. He didn't like what Denny had to say but stayed quiet.

Denny continued, "You shamed your grandpa before he died."

Buck could hold it no longer. He shouted, "That was all Gerald's fault! That man poisoned my mind. He made me forget how important the *Koitsenko* sash and lance are, made me think dollars were more valuable." Anger made Buck forget his injuries; he stood breathing hard with fists clenched. "The sash and lance are home now, where they belong."

"You stole the sash and lance back?" Denny taunted Buck.

"I didn't steal what's mine. I earned the sash and lance back. Went right over and got them, once that Tribal cop let me go." Buck stuck his jaw out.

Denny looked like he wanted to punch the extended jaw. I wanted a few more answers, so stepped forward. "Did you talk to Gerald?"

I was surprised Buck answered me. "Lucky for Gerald, I didn't see him anywhere. Or I might have—" Buck cut himself off. "I didn't get a chance to hunt the snake down. Y'all saw me get walked off Red Buffalo Hall's stage." He shot a look at me. "I didn't get away from that Tribal cop until near ten o'clock." Buck chuckled. "The cop sure was mad. Kept complaining about overtime 'cause they was shorthanded; a couple of the other cops were out for training."

I stayed silent, hoping to hear more.

Buck added to his story, "That cop was happy to let me go. Said ten was as late as he was staying. I left with the lights going out. All I wanted to do was go home to my family." As if he just remembered he was mad, Buck's face flushed red. "But you was off running around with my Georgie." At this, he turned and pulled Denny's truck door open. The dome light came on and exposed empty seats. Buck winced as he bent to look farther inside. "Where the heck . . ."

Denny stepped into the spilled light. "We told you, Georgie's not with us."

Buck straightened, jerked his phone from his pocket and checked the app. I could see the flashing light for Georgie's phone location on his screen. Buck looked from it to the truck's interior. One armed, he pulled the driver seat forward for a better look into the small back seat area. He shoved a crowbar, miscellaneous parts, and fast-food debris around, revealing my messenger bag. I felt a stab of guilt. I hadn't looked at the files from Bernie yet. Buck reached for my green bag.

I pushed past him and pulled the bag to me. "Georgie's not in my bag or in the truck."

Buck huffed a hot, sour breath at me before he pushed in for a final look inside the truck. This time he came out with a cell phone. "Like I said, you been running around with Georgie all night."

I shook my head. "She was with us earlier. The phone must have slipped out of her pocket. Georgie is not with us now."

Buck slammed the door and moved to the side of the truck. With his good hand, he reached past tools to grab the edge of a tarp and pull it. At the same time, he shouted, "I knew you was hiding!" Under the tarp was my suitcase tucked between hay bales. I had completely forgotten about Denny stowing my case there yesterday.

Denny tugged the tarp from Buck's hands. "Enough! Georgie's not here." Instead of anger, a strange smile crossed Denny's face. "Last we saw Georgie, she was with that hot blonde at Gerald's gallery."

Buck stiffened.

Denny saw it. His smile got bigger. "Yep, they was all nice and cozy." He leaned over the pickup's side to adjust the tarp, making sure it covered my suitcase and the bales. Finished, Denny turned to Buck. "Mud just got here yesterday. If Georgie's running around with someone, I bet it's Brenda Lee." He shook his head. "We did see them holding onto each other, real tight like." Denny's grin brightened the morning darkness.

Buck moved toward Denny. "I oughta wipe—"

Denny shifted, squared off with Buck. "You wanted info on Georgie, I'm just tellin' you what I saw." His eyes dared Buck to make a move.

Buck clenched his jaw and shoved past Denny back toward his van. Pain shot across Buck's face as he pulled himself into the van. Buck reached across to start the engine with his left hand, shoved the van in reverse and gunned it so the tires spit dirt as he rushed off to pursue Georgie. Denny and I watched the van fishtail down the dark highway toward Lawton and probably Gerald's gallery.

When the taillights disappeared from view, I turned to Denny. "Why did you make Buck think something's going on with Georgie and Brenda?"

Denny answered as he moved toward his truck, "Because there is. Brenda Lee brightened at the sight of Georgie." He stopped to look at me. "You saw them, Mud. Just a bit too close, held on to each other just a bit too long."

He was right. They had seemed . . . close. "Maybe, but why tell Buck?"

Denny wasn't listening, he was jumping to his next conclusion. "Hmm . . . maybe they did it together. Georgie killed Gerald, and Brenda Lee moved the body."

I walked to the passenger side of the truck. "Yeah, Brenda moved Gerald's body to the gallery—that's why she nearly collapsed seeing it in Gerald's office. Just add Brenda to your revolving list of suspects."

Denny slid into the driver seat. "Georgie's always looking for her next step up." He pulled the door closed before going on, "I think Brenda Lee is it." He looked across as I settled into the seat. "Can't believe I feel sorry for Buck. That poor man does love her."

My phone went off, ringing and vibrating. A sigh of relief escaped as I hurried to answer it. Blissfully unaware that I was exchanging one uncomfortable discussion for a far worse confrontation.

Bernie's voice was loud and clear. "Mae, I'm pretty frustrated, and worried. It's after two in the morning here. Gotta be near four-thirty there. The files have been available for quite a while. Why haven't you downloaded them?" She gave me no opportunity to answer. Bernie's voice rose as she continued, "This may be your business, but it's my livelihood. It's make it or break it time."

Denny turned away, pretending to not hear Bernie's rant.

I lowered my voice. "Bernie, there's plenty of time for me to get the files and notes back to you. I am going to get to them." I looked at my watch, then to Denny waiting for me to solve a murder. I added, "Soon."

"Get to them soon! Are you forgetting this client's success will launch your agency? All the years of our long days and late nights paying off. This IPO will make a huge difference to my career." Bernie took a breath, returned with her voice lowered. "Pull it together, Ma—Mud. I'm beginning to understand why everyone there calls you Mud."

"What do you mean?" Her tone stung.

"You're acting like a mess. It's like you're deliberately sabotaging the agency's success." I tried to interrupt, but Bernie spoke over my protests. "You suddenly fly to Oklahoma—over twenty-four hours ago—because of a phone call. Leaving the client just days before their IPO and our biggest event. You don't ask me how any of the reviews with the executive speakers went, you haven't downloaded the files or looked over any of the graphics.

The first walk-through with nervous executives onstage using the recently created graphics on-screen is coming up in *just* a few hours—without you. You're not paying attention to the most important event of your career. I'm worried!"

I stayed quiet, letting Bernie say all she needed before I replied, "You don't need to worry." She scoffed. I continued, "Bernie, we have spent over six months preparing for this event. I have spent those months not just putting Richard's company story together for the IPO, I've spent time with each of the executives. They know their parts. And I know the graphics will stun onstage, because of you and Marcus and the team we've built. We are good at making others look good." I put a smile in my voice at the end. This outburst wasn't like Bernie. I needed to reassure, not react.

She was silent.

I went on, "I know Richard's IPO is important. I will go over the files and have them back to you with notes before the morning shift starts. I'll also check in with Richard. Is he worried?"

Bernie admitted, "No, Richard is okay," but had to add, "as long as you're here for final rehearsals."

"I will be. And you should go to bed. Stop stressing."

"You want me to stop stressing? Review the files and be on the flight back here at noon."

I hesitated, thought of fracking, Eli, and the dead man. I glanced over at Denny, who was pretending to be absorbed with something on the dashboard. I waited too long to reassure Bernie.

She announced, "Mud. Get with it. Don't blow what you've worked so hard for."

On that, my dearest friend ended the call.

Chapter Eighteen

I stared at the phone.

"Ready?"

"What?" Denny's question jarred me back to the moment.

"We were going to Anna's. You've got to start figuring out how Georgie did it."

I clenched my jaw. Denny had heard Bernie on the phone, knew my agency was in trouble. I was under pressure and time constraints, but his only focus was proving Georgie guilty of murder. My first response was to snap at him. Instead, I consciously relaxed my jaw and took a deep breath. I was on the verge of taking out my frustrations on Denny, who was really only concerned about making sure Eli was not arrested for a crime he didn't do. Once again, I found myself rubbing my medicine pouch while in thought. I let my breath out slowly. There was time; there had to be.

I relaxed. Dropped the deerskin pouch back under my shirt and turned to Denny. "I'm ready. Let's go."

"Good. We've got to get a move on if you're going to wrap this murder up in time to make your flight."

"I *have* to be on that flight."

"I know; I heard." Denny added a faint smile to take the sting from his words.

I added, "Besides, if we don't have Eli cleared of the murder before noon, we need to call in the police."

He looked at the truck's clock. "We've got near seven hours to get this murder all wrapped up. We better get a move on." He threw the truck into gear and eased onto the road.

Almost immediately, dim yellowed headlights appeared directly behind us. Its brights flashed on and off. I turned in the seat, looked at the approaching lights. "Uh, Denny . . ."

"Yeah, I see them. Buck must be back. I'm pulling over in that patch there. Enough of this foolishness with him."

In a rush I said, "It's not Buck. These headlights are aged yellow, not bright like Buck's van. I've seen those headlights following us through the night."

"And you're telling me this now?" Denny threw me a look as he eased off the road, putting the truck into park.

An old farm truck with a single spear for hay rolled in behind Denny. The truck's brights and engine were left on.

We both tried to see through the glare to spot the driver; we had no luck.

Denny said, "I don't recognize the truck; it's just another patched-together farm truck. Thoughts?"

Before I could answer, the engine and lights went out and a screech sounded as the rusted truck's mismatched door swung open. I glanced at Denny. "Time to find out." I stepped out of Denny's truck and called, "Who's there?"

It was too dark to see who was standing by the old truck, but the voice that answered was unmistakable. "Mud, that you?"

In quick strides I rushed to my little brother, pulling him into a tight hug. "Sky! So glad to see you." A dam of worry and fear burst, flooding me with anger. I pushed out of the hug to yell at Sky, "Why aren't you at OU? Why were you at the Complex? What—"

Denny stepped up to fist bump Sky. I was surprised to note my brother was slightly taller than Denny and much fuller. Denny said to me, "Give the kid a chance to answer." He then slapped the back of Sky's buzzed head. "What the heck have you been up to tonight?"

Sky responded to the head slap with a scowl at Denny. "I'm not a kid. Knock it off!" He moved toward me, looking anxious. "I'm looking for Grandpa. Where is he?"

Denny answered, "You heard what happened today, uh, I mean yesterday, right?"

"Yeah, yeah, I went to Grandpa's house first and saw the cleansing ceremony underway. I heard all about your and Mud's adventures, but no one had seen Grandpa. I've been everywhere searching for him and been hearing about you two all night. So, I figure y'all know where he is."

Sky's question was for both of us, but he had his eyes on me. I kicked into big sister mode. "What do you need Grandpa for, what is going on, Sky?" Both of my little brothers, six years younger, had always confided their childhood traumas to me.

Sky's eyes pleaded and he started to answer, "We need to kno—"

Hearing the "we," Denny interrupted, "You got Kohn stashed somewhere?" he asked about Sky's minutes-younger twin.

Kohn was Kiowa for "water" and my youngest brother's name. Sky and Kohn were named for two sacred beings from one of the earliest Kiowa legends. After heroic sacrifices made for our people, one returned to the sky and the other to water. Most Kiowas never realized the significance of the twins' names. So much was being forgotten.

Sky shifted from vulnerable to guarded in a blink. "I'm looking for Grandpa, that's all I'm asking of you." His tone made clear that he did not want Denny and me in his business.

Denny prepared to slap the young pup down, but I stepped in. "Sky, Grandpa's on the second day of a four-day quest." I knew Sky would understand that Grandpa sat on a ledge in the Wichita Wildlife Refuge seeking answers and giving thanks.

His shoulders sagged. "I was hoping he would have answers for me."

"What kind of answers?" At the moment, wiping the misery from Sky's face was all that mattered.

He looked at me, hopeful. "I really need some info from years ago about old property lines and records."

Before I could voice not having that kind of historical knowledge, Denny demanded, "Is that why you searched Wyatt's office at the Complex? You've gone too far messing with Tribal records."

Sky stepped back. He looked like he wanted to escape but was trapped between the front of the old truck and us. "Nope, not me! I want property info from really old records. I was searching for Grandpa, not going through any office."

Denny pressed on, "Why'd you run? You saw Mud. You could have asked her about Grandpa then."

"Y'all were in the middle of heavy sh—stuff. I didn't have time to get involved, and . . ." Sky stopped.

"And what?" Denny demanded.

Sky leaned toward Denny. "Why do you expect me to answer your questions, huh? What are you two doing? I've seen you running around all over. You seem in a rush to get places, but you don't stay long. What's down that deep-rutted road, huh? What are you looking for?"

I gave Denny a hard look and signaled, "Silence." No way were we getting Sky involved with fracking or a murder. I gave Sky part of the truth, enough for now. "We're looking for who all was planning to steal the Jefferson Peace Medal."

Sky seemed satisfied with my answer. "Closure, huh. Fair. You round up all the snakes?"

Denny sprung onto Sky, pushing him hard against the farm truck's rusted hood. "You did that! You left those rattlesnakes—"

Sky sputtered out, "Rattlesnakes? I'm talking about the snakes that planned to steal from the Tribe."

I pulled on Denny. "Let him go. Now!"

Reluctantly, Denny stepped back.

Sky pulled his T-shirt back into place. "What is wrong with you?!" He stood and pushed past Denny.

Fists tight at his side, Denny squeezed out his question, "Did you leave a burlap bag of rattlesnakes at the fracking office?"

Obviously bewildered, Sky answered, "What fracking office?"

I explained to Sky, "Someone set up fracking in the back-country, and someone else left a bag of rattlesnakes for the guys running the operation. Unfortunately, we stumbled onto the snakes." I didn't have to ask if he did it, his face said it all. Sky had no idea fracking was going on so close to home. Denny saw it too and relaxed his fists.

"So, that's what you were doing down all the dirt roads. I kept losing you, just when I was close enough to flash my brights at y'all." Sky ended with a small smile.

"Sky, tell me what you saw at the Compound?"

He cocked his head, seemed to be considering something before answering, "I only went where I thought Grandpa might be: Red Buffalo Hall, the Complex." Sky rushed to add, "Only because the museum's in the middle and Grandpa goes there a lot." Denny gave him a slight nod. Sky continued, "Then 'cause I wanted to see things and not be seen, I went over to the maintenance hut. It's up on a rise, and you can see most of the Compound from there."

Exactly what I wanted to hear. "Who did you see, where and when?" I gave Sky an encouraging look.

He responded, "Just you all at the museum and then at Wyatt's office. Man, I could hear Wyatt yelling at Anna even though I was outside." He shook his head.

I urged, "Do you know who searched Wyatt's office?"

Denny moved closer.

Sky shifted, offering room for Denny. "Naw, I got there when you spotted me at the front doors. You got tracking on me or something? How'd you look up right then?" He gave me a crooked grin. I knew we both were remembering when as boys, I usually stopped the brothers in the midst of planning an escapade. Neither ever caught on to the obvious cues they leaked trying to keep a secret.

I returned the smile, then got back on track. "After watching Wyatt and Anna argue, who did you see?"

Denny stayed quiet, giving Sky time to answer.

Sky rolled his eyes upward, seeking memories. "Saw Buck and one of the Tribal cops. The cop was at the Pigpen and Buck was leaving it, coming toward me. I was hiding in the shadows by the hut. Buck walked right past me, never even saw me."

Denny asked, "What about when Georgie screamed?"

"Scream? Didn't hear a scream. After seeing Buck, I went down to Red Buffalo Hall. There was no one there, so I decided to find you again." Sky looked at me. "I came back to the Complex, thinking you and Denny were still around. Didn't see you . . ." Sky seemed to drift in thought, then returned with a nugget, "I did see Anna."

Denny responded, "We know that. You already said you saw her fighting with Wyatt."

"No, I mean after that."

I quickly asked, "When?"

Sky answered, "It was after I came back from Red Buffalo Hall. I checked at the Complex then went back to the maintenance hut for a last look about the Compound."

Denny jumped in, "Couldn't have been Anna, she left the Compound before Buck got let loose at the Pigpen." His dark hair swung as Denny shook his head. "We watched her drive away."

Sky took his time before declaring, "I know what I saw and when. I saw Anna ManyHorse after seeing Buck leave the Pen. She was dressed all in black and sneaking around."

"Sneaking around! What do you mean?" Denny tried to control his rising voice.

"Just that. She was dressed all in black, walking in the shadows like me, so I figured, like me, she didn't want to be seen."

"I don't believe it." Denny looked confused then determined.

Sky set his jaw. Only then did I notice that Sky was dressed in black jeans and a black T-shirt.

I faced Denny. "Let Sky talk. Stop interrupting."

"He shouldn't be talking like that about Anna!"

Sky piped in, "I know you're all protective of Anna because she's your girlfriend's mom and you're afraid of telling her about you and Becca."

Denny pushed toward Sky. I stood in his way. "Denny!" Then I saw Sky wearing a self-satisfied grin. "Both of you. *Ohdayhah!* Enough!"

Sky's grin dropped. "Man, I've really got to roll." He turned toward the hay truck.

I called, "Wait, Sky."

He kept walking.

Denny muttered, "Let him go."

An owl let a double hoot out, scaring its prey into a final scramble through the nearby field.

I reached Sky before he got into the old truck. "Sky, I need your help." I locked eyes with him.

He leaned back on the rusted door. "What do you need, Mud?" he sounded guarded.

"Are you alright?"

My question surprised him. His eyes softened. "Yep, just got to settle some old property lines. Grandpa will figure it out." He took a deep breath. "Really nice knowing you're home. The parental unit will be happy to see you here. It's only been a couple months since they visited you, but it's not the same as having you home."

I shook my head. "I'll have to call them and explain later, but I would prefer Mom and Dad not know I'm here right now."

This got Sky to smile. "You don't tell them I'm here, and I won't say anything about you being here. Deal?"

"Deal." I pulled my not-so-little brother into a hug and held him. He squeezed back before letting go.

Giving me an impish grin, Sky said, "I gotta admit, Mom and Dad probably know you're around, or they will by sunup. You and Denny solving a murder yesterday is the talk of the countryside. Like I said, that's all I heard about while I've been searching for Grandpa." He looked thoughtful before finishing, "Guess if I want answers, I'll have to find them on the vision quest ledge with Grandpa." Sky got into the old truck.

I leaned on the open truck door. “You’re going there, not back to OU?”

“Mud, you got secrets to keep and so do I, and right now, Grandpa’s got the answers I need.”

Sky grinned like the little boy I so remembered. I had to smile back at him.

“Alright, I won’t push.” Before closing the driver’s door, I threw at him, “Last question, you’re sure about seeing Anna *after* Buck left the Pigpen?” I noticed Denny moved closer to hear the answer.

“Absolutely! Not sure where she came from, I suddenly caught a glimpse when she ran from one shadow spot to another. Obviously, Anna didn’t have Grandpa for a teacher. I moved slow and steady away from her. Anna never saw me.”

I reached in, rubbed Sky’s buzzcut head. “Let me know if I can help. Okay?”

Denny suddenly stood next to me. “That goes for me too.” As close to an apology as he would give.

Sky smiled; it looked real. “Y’all stay safe. I’m heading to the Refuge.” With that, Sky turned the patched-together truck around and left Denny and me.

I felt a heavy weight lift; I was relieved Sky was going to the Refuge. It would be best if he returned to OU, but anywhere far away from murder, theft, and fracking made me happy.

Chapter Nineteen

I gave Denny a shove. "Becca, huh? How long has that been going on?"

Denny seemed to blush. "It's fresh. Becca hasn't checked family connections with Anna yet." The Kiowa Tribe was small. So small that when meeting another Kiowa, most found familial connections within a few generations.

"I'm pretty sure you two are good to go. I don't recall any connections."

"That's what I said, but Becca wants to talk to her mom before we go public." Denny shook his head. "No idea how Sky knew. Becca's going to have to hurry up with telling Anna." He gave me a stern look. "No saying anything. Got it?"

"Got it," I confirmed with a smile as I slid into Denny's truck. I leaned back and buckled up. "Let's go see what Anna has to say."

He side-eyed me. "What does that mean?" Denny edged the truck back onto the road.

"Just that. We now know Anna was around the maintenance hut after we thought she'd left. We need to know where she was from nine-fortyish to midnight. If Gerald was killed at the maintenance office and then moved, that's the time span it all happened within."

"Couldn't be her, and I'm not saying that because I respect Anna as a legislator or that she's my girlfriend's mother. Anna just didn't have the time. So what if she went back to the Compound, we know it was close to midnight when we saw Anna going to the frackers' office, and that was before the body was found in Lawton. That pretty much clears her."

"You're right about when we saw her, but from before ten to midnight is plenty of time to circle back, kill Gerald, and move the body." I pushed my fingers through my curls, freeing them to spring in wild discord. "I also want to hear what Anna was doing at the fracking operation."

Denny shook his head. "Why don't you like Anna?"

"That's the problem, I do like her!" I leaned toward Denny. "But Anna's not being upfront with us. Something is going on with her."

Denny protested, "Anna's a legislator; she's busy!"

I ignored Denny and went on, "If Anna is involved with illegal fracking, then it opens the real possibility she was stealing artifacts with Gerald. I can't let your feelings about Anna or Becca influence finding the facts."

"Oh, come on!" He took his eyes from the road to look over at me.

"Just saying, if Anna is involved with illegal fracking for money, it's a small step to stealing stored artifacts from the museum for extra cash. Anna does have easy access to museum items."

"Oh, now she's guilty of stealing artifacts." The truck slowed.

"Not saying she is." I touched his arm. "Denny, can you just keep an open mind?"

"I am open-minded"

"Not about Anna."

Denny shook his head but said nothing. He flicked the truck's brights on as he strained to look for a turnoff in the dark. He finally spotted it and turned onto a sparsely graveled road.

I broke the heavy silence. "We don't want to tell Anna about Gerald."

"I know. The fewer people that know we left a dead man without reporting it, the better. I didn't say anything to Buck or Sky, I won't mention it to Anna either." Denny turned his brights off. "I tell ya, I'm sure she won't know anything about Gerald's death."

"I hope she knows something."

Denny stopped the truck and turned to me. "Sounds like you want her to be guilty! Who doesn't have an open mind now?"

"I don't want Anna to be guilty." I leaned toward him. "I'm hoping she knows something or saw something that leads us to the killer. 'Cause we've got nothing right now."

Denny slid into an exasperated tone, "You're forgetting Georgie and Buck."

"Buck didn't kill Gerald." I didn't repeat that Georgie didn't have time to do the deed either.

"How you figure?"

"We think Gerald was killed just before ten o'clock."

Denny nodded.

"That clears Buck. Sky confirmed Buck was leaving the Pigpen and the Tribal cop was closing the office at ten. Buck didn't have enough time to kill Gerald before Georgie found the body."

"Unless they were in it together." Denny rushed on, "See, I think the three of them were planning to steal the peace medal and had a falling out. That's why Georgie and Buck planned on killing Gerald in the maintenance office with one of those small ball-peen hammers. It all works. Gerald gets there, Georgie takes off screaming, Buck kills Gerald, and drags him off. There was a good ten minutes or so before we got into the office." He looked satisfied with his latest story.

I wasn't. I stayed quiet, but my face gave me away.

Denny threw in another piece of proof. "That explains all the fuss over the fluffy slippers."

"You lost me, Denny."

He twisted in his seat to face me. "Georgie used the detail of the pink, fluffy slippers to prove she fell over a body. No reason to mention the slippers, except to try and prove there was a body."

"Denny, stop. I need to figure this out without twisting facts to fit the way you want them to." I squeezed Denny's forearm to soften the comment. "Let's finish getting information from the people we know were at the Compound. Like I said, let's see what Anna has to say. She may know something that solves this whole thing."

"Going to be hard to get details without telling Anna what's going on."

"Denn—"

"I know, I know, we are not telling Anna about Gerald. I'm just saying, it's going to be hard to get info without telling her everything."

"We didn't tell Buck about Gerald and were still able to get quite a bit of information."

Denny nodded. "True. But Anna's no dummy. She's not going to be so easy to get info from."

"I've been thinking about that. We'll lead with fracking." I didn't really know how we were going to get Anna to tell us what she had done since we last saw her at the Complex, but fracking seemed to be a good starting point. "We'll see where that gets us." I gave Denny a reassuring smile.

He shook his head and put the truck in gear. "Her house is just up here a bit."

We moved slowly down the road. Denny leaned forward, looking for the right house. As we came around a curve, I immediately knew which house was Anna's. There was only one house on the hill that had all the interior lights blazing. Anna must be staying up all night too.

Denny left his headlights on when he rolled to the front of Anna's home. Her house looked like all the other seventies-era HUD Indian houses—a simple rectangle with the front situated on one long side, and a side door into the kitchen on a short side with a carport across from it. The layout was the same as my grandfather's house. To the side of the kitchen door was a small dinette room window.

The truck's headlights swept past Anna's SUV sitting in the carport. We pulled in behind it. As we had done at Eli's house, we waited a bit before switching the engine off and getting out of the truck. Instead of marching up to the front door, Denny headed for the rear of Anna's SUV. I followed.

He fingered a line of tape over one of the taillights and nodded. Denny straightened, glanced at me. "That's what caught my attention with the SUV when it turned at the fracking operations' road earlier. I knew it had to be Anna's SUV." His forehead wrinkled. "Just can't figure why she would be going there."

"Let's find out." I moved toward the front door, displaying more confidence than I felt. Anna's house looked well-kept for its age. The four-foot brick façade was recently caulked, and the wood siding had a new paint job.

Denny called me back. "Where you headed?" He motioned toward the side door by the carport. "You know, no one uses the front door around here. You'll scare her ringing the front doorbell." He shook his head in disbelief. "Sometimes, it's like you never lived here."

I ignored Denny and walked to the side door. He was right. My grandparents and several aunts and uncles had the same house style offered by the government for low-income Indians. The front door was seldom used. Family and friends all came through the convenient side door that led into a small dinette and kitchen, the true center of every Indian home.

There were a couple of cement steps leading to a small porch at the door. Really more a perch, just room enough to set groceries down while retrieving keys to get inside.

Denny pushed past me. "Maybe I should knock and do the talking." He looked back. "Anna knows me. It won't freak her out seeing me before dawn."

I moved to the side and peeked into the dinette window. Anna was sitting at her dining table, head flopped down in a midst of papers—everywhere. Like Sky described, she was dressed all in black.

Chapter Twenty

I hadn't thought much of Anna's all-black outfit covered by her traditional shawl when we saw her earlier at the Complex, but knowing what Sky saw and now with her surrounded by files and papers, Anna looked guilty of searching the chairman's office. Was it to cover up illegal fracking or stolen artifacts? Did it all lead to murder?

Denny nudged me aside to look through the window. Without comment he turned and knocked briskly on the door.

I saw Anna's head jerk up; her panicked eyes moved to the door. She swept papers together as Denny rapped a second time. Anna stood, grabbed a dance shawl draped over a dining chair, then covered a corner of the table with the shawl and shoved more papers under it. I took a last glance through the window before I moved to Denny's side in front of the door.

A slightly muffled-sounding Anna called, "Who's there?"

"It's Denny . . ." Hearing no response, he added, "Denny Sawpole and my cousin Mud."

The silence stretched until Anna answered, closer but still through the closed door, "It's awfully late, well, early."

"Sorry, but we need to talk with you. It's important." Denny shuffled on the cement landing.

Again, a long silence before Anna opened the door just enough to peek out. "This really isn't a good time. Can we just meet in a few hours at the Complex?"

"I'm sorry, Anna, but this can't wait." Denny's voice had an edge to it.

Anna opened the door a bit wider. "Why? What's going on?"

"Seems that—"

Thinking fast, I cut Denny off. "We're worried someone might have searched the chairman's office to get a key to the museum to steal the peace medal." Hearing her reaction to Wyatt's office search could be revealing.

Anna seemed to relax a bit. "You don't need to worry about our Jefferson Peace Medal. It's safe in the museum. It's sitting in the only spot in the Complex with an alarm." Anna let the door open wider as she continued, "After the Red Buffalo Hall meeting, Wyatt had a harebrained idea he could leave the peace medal in his office all night. Can you believe it? After almost losing the medal once." She shook her head. "Really appreciate the concern, but y'all do not have to worry about the Jefferson Peace Medal." Anna moved to close the door.

Before the door closed completely, I asked, "How many people have the disarm code for the alarm?"

The closing door halted, opened slightly. Anna answered, "Just three. Wyatt didn't even have it. There's me, Floyd Redpine—he tends the museum during visiting hours. And of course, Gerald Bean, but he doesn't have keys to get into the Complex. We were using Gerald to help appraise stored museum pieces. I will change the alarm code and we won't be using him anymore." Anna's face twisted with disgust.

Denny shifted on the porch, but before he could say anything, Anna continued, "After last night meeting's revelations, there's enough evidence to charge Gerald with theft of Kiowa artifacts. I will make sure that man does not get his hands on any more Kiowa treasures." Anna looked determined. "If that's all you came for, I really have to get my day happening." She stepped back to close the door.

Just before Anna disappeared completely behind the door, I announced, "The person who searched Wyatt's office wasn't after the peace medal. But you know that, don't you, Anna?"

The door stopped its inward motion. Through a small opening, two dark-as-coal eyes landed on me. I went on, "Anna, what did you do after we saw you at the Complex?"

Anna gave no answer. The door remained barely opened.

Denny pleaded, "Let us in to talk." He edged closer to the door.

Anna didn't move; the door didn't open. We waited.

Finally, she announced, "The house is a mess, best talk here." She opened the door a bit wider, staying behind it like a shield. "I don't have much time. There's chores to do before I head into the Complex."

I got to the point. "You aren't worried about the office search because you did it."

This got a reaction from both Denny and Anna. Denny turned to stare at me. Anna went on the defense. "I have been doing my best for the Kiowa people, and you accuse me—" She stopped, got control. "I have to go."

Denny stepped forward. "Anna, we can help."

Anna stared at Denny for a long beat before bursting into laughter. "You, help. That's good." She snorted. "Yeah, help 'bout as much as James has. You two just go away. I've got work to do before my day even begins." Anna went inside muttering to herself, forgetting to close the door. Forgetting us on her porch.

Denny and I exchanged a glance, silently coming to agreement before taking the slightly open door as an invitation and following Anna into her house.

Anna stood beside the dining table. She picked up a paper and skimmed the document. Finished with it, Anna balled the paper, then threw it across the table toward the lumpy dance shawl. It bounced off and slowly rolled across the bright material to the wood-like tabletop.

Denny and I watched Anna from just inside the doorway. The small dining table was directly to our right. Papers were scattered on the floor, a few across the tabletop, most in piles under the shawl.

Denny moved to Anna's side. He implored, "What is going on here?" He looked from the floor with strewn documents to the lumpy shawl covering the far corner of the table.

Anna's head whipped up at the sound of Denny's voice. "Wha—don't know what you mean."

I bent and picked up a handful of documents—most seemed to have the Kiowa Tribal seal. On the top one, I glimpsed the words "Mineral & Oil Lease" before Anna grabbed the papers from my hand. "Those are private, official documents."

"You have a lot of them." I pointed to the lumpy shawl.

Anna faced us. "Y'all have to leave. I worked real late and lost track of time. Don't want to be rude, but it's not even dawn yet." She tried to herd us toward the door. We stayed put.

Denny pushed his hair back and stood straighter. "Anna, your behavior makes it look like you're involved with fracking—illegal fracking. I gotta ask straight up, are you?"

Anna clenched her fists, glared at Denny. "You know me better than that!"

"I thought I did, but you've got me worried." Denny's eyes begged her to prove us wrong.

Anna took a deep breath. "Your grandfather trusts me."

I responded, "That means a lot. But he's not here."

Anna turned to face me. "That's the problem! That man was supposed to be here, helping. But James decided a quest was calling." Her face got red. "He shouldn't have answered until this mess got took care of."

What mess was she talking about: the dead body at the gallery, illegal fracking, or the near-theft of the peace medal?

"You see this—this mess." Anna lifted the shawl from the table, papers took flight. "That's what I've been doing. Your grandpa claimed his water was being stolen for fracking. I started looking into how it could be happening. Had to do it all on the sly. Just me and James, then just me." She shot me an angry glare. "And what did I get? Piles of nothing—nothing illegal, anyways." Anna collapsed into the dining chair.

Denny insisted, "The Tribe hasn't approved fracking. How could it happen legally?"

Anna took in Denny's earnest expression. Her shoulders sagged. "It's a loophole, that's how." She sighed and leaned forward to shift through the mounds of documents until she found a yellow-lined tablet with scrawled notes. Anna flipped a few pages, turned the tablet sideways, and placed it on the table in front of Denny and me. "James sketched this." The simple line drawing showed the Slick Hills with owner names and property lines. I didn't need Anna to tell me that Grandpa had created the sketch, I could see his artistic style in the lines and occasional landmark noted. I leaned closer to the diagram. Grandpa had drawn gasping fish in murky water to mark Jimmy Creek Spring.

Denny settled into a chair and said, "*Haw.*" Encouraging Anna to tell her story.

"James told me about the fracking operations set up just over the hill alongside his one hundred-sixty acres." Anna stood to point at the leaking oil derrick in the drawing on a corner of Kiowa Tribe acreage.

I noted the location and the wavy lines indicating nearby Jimmy Creek. Glancing up at Anna, I gave a single nod.

She dropped into her chair. "It's a bit of a checkerboard of land ownership out in the Slick Hills. What used to be all Kiowa land is now checkered with multifamily Kiowa-owned, Tribe-owned, and a spattering of non-Indian–owned small parcels."

Denny spoke up, "Been that way since the state got formed."

"Thanks to the Jerome Agreement," I said. That document had dissolved the Kiowa reservation land, giving allotments of 160 acres to all Kiowas born before 1905. The remaining millions of Kiowa-owned acres went to the Sooners, the Oklahoma settlers.

Denny added, "The government had to get land from somewhere to offer the incoming hordes."

Anna nodded. "An agreement no Kiowa official agreed to or signed. That's one of many injustices nicely forgotten in American history." She looked off into the distance, then returned with a shake of her head. "I'm tired, been at this for a few days now." She looked over the scattered papers. "Wasn't easy finding how it's being done."

Denny and I stayed quiet; we didn't want to interrupt Anna now that she was telling her story.

Anna leaned forward. "This company, Strider Inc., is leasing ten- to fifteen-acre parcels, always on or close to a water source and adjacent to oil-rich land owned by others. Then the frackers horizontal drill the oil from the adjacent lands. As needed, they use the natural water source for the fracking. Just like those two boys are doing at Jimmy Creek Spring. The fracking office and pump operation is on that spot legally, but everything else is stolen, from water to oil."

Denny leaned toward Anna. "How can Strider get these strategic leases—even know about them?"

Anna sat back in her chair. "Someone inside the Kiowa government is helping Strider find these small-acreage leases and get them real cheap. I checked around to learn what the going rate for mineral leases are and these leases," Anna pointed to a nearby spilled pile, "are getting pennies on the dollar for the lease and nothing for the gas or oil." Disgusted, Anna pushed the pile of papers away. "Landowners think they're getting a good deal on a grass lease for grazing cattle, so they stay away from the back-country while Strider's sucking that land and its neighbors dry through strategically placed fracking pumps." She looked frustrated.

We waited. When Anna remained silent, I asked, "How is this legal if the Tribe doesn't approve fracking on Kiowa land?"

"That's the thing, it's all illegal but they're doing it legally."

Anna's story was getting confusing.

I asked again, "How can this be legal?"

Anna pointed at another pile of papers. "All these documents are legal leases through the Tribe. They are all under twenty acres. That's the loophole." She flipped through the tablet. "Took me a while to figure out how it was being done. Then I found a rarely used provision that allowed for leases of under twenty acres to be automatically granted. Under twenty acres of rough land isn't enough to do much with. It usually sits around growing weeds, so if a lease opportunity comes up, the Tribe wanted to simplify it getting approved. The provision was supposed to automate and improve use of the small parcels Kiowas own dotting the countryside. The intent was to make grazing leases easy and get dollars into needy pockets." Anna showed a burst of anger. "Mind you, this was never meant for fracking, but that's how it's getting used by Strider. No one verifies the land's use is for grazing. The lease just gets approved if it's under twenty acres." Anna's anger flamed out.

Denny got excited. "That should be easy to track. Who requests the lease? That's who is partners with Strider."

Anna's shoulders drooped. "We, your grandpa and I, think we know, but we have nothing to prove it." She lifted her hand palm out to stop Denny's next question. "They're smart. Whoever is doing it uses a computer in the Complex's central room to enter the lease request. All leases less than twenty acres get automatically approved. No requestor, no approver listed, no signatures to track. That computer's even available to the public." Anna sounded defeated.

"All this paper and nothing proves who is behind it all?" Denny's face expressed disbelief.

"Believe me, I want to expose Strider and any legislator behind allowing fracking on our lands. Like I said, James and I have a good idea who it is, but no proof." Anna shook her head. "Really thought I had the proof I needed when I was making these copies."

"Is that what this is, copies of records?" I looked at the papers strewn everywhere.

Anna bit her lower lip and nodded.

I didn't ask; I stated it, "You searched Wyatt's office."

Anna let out a sigh. "I admit I did it and a lot more." She set her jaw. "I did what needed to be done."

Chapter Twenty-One

Denny's brown eyes got big. "You don't mean you kil—"

I grabbed Denny's arm and squeezed. "Let Anna tell us what she did." I looked intently at Denny until he gave me a quick nod.

Anna watched our exchange, gave a questioning look that dissolved into a shrug. She slowly answered my question, "Yeah . . . you're right, Mud. I did go back to the Complex. I needed to get records to figure the fracking out." She looked sheepish. "I 'bout died when my flashlight rolled out of my bag in front of y'all. Thought you would figure out what I was planning. Y'all asked about fracking yesterday, but I couldn't tell you anything. I have no proof." Anna ended with a whispered, "I was so close."

Before I could ask another question, Anna pounded the table. "I stashed a lot of the records I had been gathering so I could come back to copy them after everyone left. I won't take original documents out of the building. Copies made sense, but I missed one, somehow. I think I saw a document tying him to Strider but, well . . . a coyote's call scared me off. After all I did, setting up a police training session to get the night shift out of the way." Anna shook her head. "Who can plan for a random coyote howl in the night at just the wrong time. So close, it scared me."

I was glad Denny didn't reveal that it had been Georgie's scream, not a coyote. Instead, he bent to pick up a paper from the floor. Holding it up, Denny asked, "Why do you have Wyatt Walker's expense report?"

I interjected, "That's who you think is working with Strider—Wyatt, the Kiowa Tribe chairman?"

Anna sucked in a cheek as she thought. "You're James's grandkids, guess I can tell you. . . I found an early deal, maybe the first lease agreement made with Strider, before he figured out no signature was needed for under twenty acres." Anna looked excited, proud even. She announced, "That first lease with Strider was authorized by Wyatt Walker. He got smart after that and only used public systems and no names. But that first lease had his signature connecting him to Strider!"

Denny said, "So you do have evidence!"

Anna shook her head. "No. What I have here is all circumstantial evidence that suggests Wyatt doing wrong through the years. That expense report is one of many." She slouched in her chair, continued her story in a tired voice. "The Tribe was looking for ways to develop revenue. After Wyatt brought in investors for the Red River Casino, he could do no wrong. No one looked over his shoulder, checked his expense reports or any of his contracts." She pointed at the report Denny held. "Wyatt has a long history of expensive lunches with casino and oil people, all on his expense account. He *and his family* stayed at hotels in vacation hot spots all over the nation, all on the Kiowa Tribe's dime." Anna looked disgusted. "Wyatt always claimed he was exploring new business opportunities, and no one questioned him." She glared at the table covered in papers. "If I had that first document with Wyatt's signature, that with the expense reports I got from his Business Development years, that would tie all my other evidence together enough for a full-fledged investigation." Excited for battle, Anna had sat up straight, but with her last words, she slowly deflated. "But I lost the document because old *Saynday*, our trickster coyote's night call scared me." In old Kiowa myths, Saynday was a semigod that created mischief for all creatures on Mother Earth. He often took the shape of a coyote.

I took a moment reviewing what Anna had shared. I thought I saw another way. "Denny and I have had a couple run-ins with the two frackers polluting Grandpa's spring water. They may have lease rights for the land they're operating on, but what Earl and Wayne are doing at Jimmy Creek Spring isn't legal. They don't have rights to Grandpa's water source. They are trespassing, and we can prove it." Thinking of the surrounding land, I added, "There's got to be a slew of broken environmental laws to add to what they are doing illegally around the Slick Hills. Let's get them stopped on that too."

Denny agreed, "All you have to do is look at the contaminated creek to know what's happening!"

Anna was nodding but didn't look like she agreed. "You're right, we stop them at Jimmy Creek Spring and even arrest those two fools running the pumps, *but* we don't get Strider. And they won't give up the main man, he's got the money." Anna looked thoughtful. "Unless there's paperwork in that fracking office that directly implicates Wyatt."

"Denny convinced Earl and Wayne to talk a bit." This brought the snakes immediately to mind—both kinds—I had to take a cleansing breath before continuing, "They claim they don't know who the boss is."

Denny nodded. "The big one, Wayne has no idea. Earl's the boss of the two and I'm pretty sure he doesn't know either."

I turned to Anna, "Don't forget it could be Cole; he's in the right department and '*knows people.*'"

Anna shook her head. "I just don't think it's Cole. He has a warrior's heart, wants to serve his people." She thought on it a beat longer. "No, Wyatt is greedy. Greedy for recognition and money. It has to be him."

I wasn't convinced Anna was telling the whole truth. I prodded her, "Gene and Wayne made it sound like the boss might be you."

She let out a short bark of a laugh. "I went to the fracking operation yesterday. Twice."

Neither of us spoke into the silence; we waited for Anna to go on.

Anna explained, "I tried to get those two boys to reveal who they were working for. I first pretended I was there looking over things for the boss. You know, tried to get them to say the name. I wanted to hear it was Wyatt Walker—not because he beat me for chairperson of the Tribe, but because he's dirty. I know it." Anna stopped to glare out the window. "But they wouldn't or couldn't flip." In a lowered voice, she repeated, "I blew my chance losing that document with Wyatt's signature."

Denny and I looked at each other, neither wanting to admit it was Georgie that disrupted her late-night document copying. That would lead to too many questions that ended with a dead man.

Anna's story explained a lot but still didn't account for where she had been through the evening—specifically the time period during Gerald's death and move to the gallery. I had to ask, "You've been here all night after going back to the Complex?"

Anna reacted to the suspicion in my voice. She slapped a nearby pile of papers, sending them flying across the table. Her voice became tight with controlled anger. "You want to know what I've been doing all night? Huh?" Anna leaned across the table toward me. "I left the Complex after seeing y'all and parked blocks away. Couldn't have my car seen after leaving, so I walked back and let myself into the office."

"How did you get in?"

Anna huffed out, "I have a key. I wasn't breaking in."

I didn't comment.

Anna continued, "I gathered all the files I had stashed, started making copies and putting the originals back, but I got interrupted." Anna's eyes flared with suppressed anger. "After the trickster's screech, I rushed to put everything back before sneaking out. I was afraid of getting caught by Wyatt or the Tribal Police." She leaned back in her chair. "How would that look?" Anna didn't expect an answer. She went on, "Got myself right out of there before finishing the copies. In my rush, I must have lost that one document that ties Wyatt to Strider and fracking."

I asked, "You've been home all night after leaving the Compound the second time?"

Anna straightened. "Didn't realize this *was* an interrogation. You want details about my night? Well, alrighty then. Let me tell you. After being scared out of the Complex, I hiked back to my car and because of James—I told him I would take care of those pumps—I went out to that fracking operation again. I drove down this deeply rutted road, parked and hiked what felt like a mile to the pumps. I promised James I would stop them one way or another, so I did." Anna crossed her arms at the end of her tale.

"You were the one who stopped the pumps last night?" Denny looked surprised.

Anna stood. "James and I wanted to slow the fracking down until we could find proof of what the chairman was doing. After being interrupted getting the evidence last night, I went to stop the pumps. Someone had to while James is off on his vision quest." She said the last with a sigh.

I asked, "What about the snakes? You do those too?" I really couldn't see Anna collecting rattlesnakes to toss into the fracking office, but I couldn't see her sneaking around or sabotaging oil pumps either.

Anna's "What?" was more scream than question. "Nope, I have nothing to do with any snakes." She shivered. "If someone brought snakes to the Complex or those pumps, it wasn't my doing. I just stopped the pumps and got out of there. Saw a friend for some guidance and came home to sort out these copies." She glanced at the mess of papers. "I thought I had that signed lease. Looks like my night was a bust. They'll get the pumps running again in no time because I have no evidence to stop them—permanently."

Denny could hold the truth in no longer. "We're the ones who scared you in the Complex. Or really, Georgie Crow, Mud's old girlfriend."

"What?"

Denny continued, "It was Georgie that screamed because—"

I cut in, "She got scared going to the Pigpen by herself." I did not want Anna to know about Georgie falling over a body that moved. It was way too much information.

Denny sputtered to a halt and looked guilty at the end of my explanation.

Anna's hands went to her hips. "That's obviously not all of the story. What's going on?"

I answered, "We're trying to stop the fracking too."

"Then spill. What are you two not saying?"

I shook my head, refusing to lie.

Denny looked down. "Really sorry."

Anna stared at Denny then me. Her eyes went black. "I think it's time y'all leave."

Denny offered, "We can help with the frack—"

Anna cut him off with a sharp tone, "But not tell me everything, no thanks. I really don't want to see y'all right now. I was close to getting all I needed to shut the fracking down—you won't explain, but you're behind me losing my only chance to get proof on Wyatt Walker." She held tight to the table edge, eyed Denny still holding Wyatt's expense report. "Leave the papers. Leave me alone."

Somehow, we had moved from the table to the door.

Anna announced in a tight voice, "Y'all have done enough."

She closed and locked the door.

Chapter Twenty-Two

Denny faced the closed door, head downcast. I didn't say anything, just stayed at his side. He sucked in a breath, turned, and shuffled to the truck, his earlier energy and confidence gone. I followed, slid into the passenger seat as Denny turned the engine over. He didn't speak, I didn't push. We drove down the gravel road back toward Highway 115.

I felt at a loss, not sure what to say or how to help Denny, and worst of all, I had no idea who killed Gerald. Everyone's ins and outs through the night spun my head around. I hadn't slept for over twenty-four hours; I was losing focus.

The thought that I had no way to do the one thing Denny asked me to do—prove Eli's innocence, save the old man from the disgrace of being painted guilty for murder—haunted me. The truck's tires seemed to mock my failure with each rotation on the gravel road, chanting *Loser, loser, loser. . . .*

Denny's low voice jarred me back. "Well, that leaves Georgie. She really must have killed Gerald." His eyes stayed on the road.

I shook my head. "This is a big mess. It's like a fishline tangle—the more I pull, the tighter the knot gets. All this running around, and we're no closer to proving who did it than when we found the body. Someone's lying, but I don't know who."

"Georgie—"

"Denny, don't start. I've heard all your Georgie theories. Maybe you're right. Georgie doesn't have a solid alibi, but I gotta be honest, Anna doesn't have one either." My mind wandered to Buck, who had wanted Gerald dead, and Eli desperate to get his headdress. "No one has a good alibi."

Denny's voice rose. "How can you say Anna's not clear of the murder? She may be mad at us right now, but she's been busy dealing with fracking all night. Anna didn't have time to commit murder and move the body." Denny stated it as truth.

I didn't want to hurt Denny. Anna was his hero, his girlfriend's mother; but he had to hear it. "She did have time to kill Gerald and move him. Anna has it all: motive, opportunity, and means."

"How you figure?" Denny said it as a demand more than question. His truck hit a pothole, jarring us forward. Denny slowed.

I shifted in the seat to look at him. "I'm not saying she did it, I'm just pointing out she could have done it."

"I'm not seeing that. I don't think you should say anything against Anna." He stared at the road. The truck creeped down the gravel strip toward the highway.

"Denny, we have only Anna's word on what she's been doing all night." I held my hand up to stop his protests. "I'm talking supported facts. All we know for sure about Anna is that she drove out of the Compound around nine thirty, was at the maintenance hut after ten, and was going down the turnoff leading to the fracking office just before midnight." Denny didn't interrupt, so I delivered the blow, "That leaves plenty of time to kill Gerald, move the body to the gallery, and stop the pumps."

Denny stomped on the brakes and threw the truck into neutral. He faced me. "Anna told us what she had been doing *all night*. You're forgetting the time used up walking between her car and the Complex, then she hiked back and forth to the pumps." He shook his head. "*Hawnay!* Anna has been too busy dealing with fracking to kill and move Gerald."

We sat on the gravel road, no other vehicles in sight. An owl hooted off in the distance. I really didn't think Anna was guilty. But I went on, "Just because Anna said she left her car and walked back doesn't mean she did." I spun a possibility. "Anna could have gone out that driveway waving goodbye to us, turned around and come in one of the other entries that goes right to the maintenance office to meet Gerald in secret."

"Why would she do that?" Denny eyes hardened.

"For the peace medal or another artifact. Something goes wrong between Anna and Gerald. Anna hits him with the first hammer that came to hand." I glanced at Denny; his jaw was clenched, but he was listening. I kept going. "Anna's SUV is right there behind the hut; she has plenty of time to move the body after Georgie stumbles over it. All she has to do is stay quiet in the back and we wouldn't know anyone was there."

"You're forgetting Anna was in the Complex making copies of records."

"No, in my story Anna's SUV is behind the maintenance hut. No walking necessary, which gives her plenty of time for copies before driving to the gallery to dump the body."

I could see Denny forming a protest. I went on before he could speak, "Anna could have used Gerald's own key to get in the gallery. Not wanting the body to be found until the morning, she turned the AC on high to hide the time of death. Anna's all done before eleven. That leaves plenty of time for her to be seen stopping the pumps, visit Eli, get home, and scatter the stolen records around her kitchen." I was surprised Denny let me get this far without an interruption. I rushed to finish, "Anna stopped the pumps and Eli to create her alibi. No one would ever suspect her of Gerald's death."

"You can't really believe all that!" finally exploded from Denny. "Anna would never partner with Gerald to steal Kiowa relics. You saw how disgusted she was with Gerald and the way he had been acquiring Kiowa artifacts."

Pain crossed Denny's face. I reached across the console. "I'm sorry. I don't really think Anna killed Gerald." I took in a deep breath, let it out slowly. "I just . . . I don't know . . . wanted to show you any of them could have done it."

"But only one did." His words hung in the air.

I had no response.

Denny broke the long silence. "I know you'll figure out who did it." He grasped my hand. "You'll find the way." Denny played with my Kiowa name, *Ahn Tsah Hye-gyah-daw*, to lighten the moment. To express belief in me.

I didn't react. I was too tired. Silence stretched as Denny waited, waited for my reassuring smile. I didn't have it to give. What could I say? I just didn't know anymore who did what, when.

I lowered the window, let the crisp, early morning air wash over me. Settled back in my seat. Looked out into the still-dark morning sky.

"What do we do now?" Denny looked at me, expecting an answer.

"Denny, I don't know." I continued to gaze into the darkness. "I just don't know."

He surprised me with his response, "We need food." His eyes got a sparkle in them. "I know just where to go. She's always got something on the stove, and it's not far from here."

"I'm not hungry." I wasn't. I felt empty inside.

"A bit of food will get the brain working again."

"You're recovering from Anna's snub well." The moment it was out, I regretted saying it.

Denny forced a smile. "Anna doesn't know about the body. She'll understand our behavior tomorrow after the murder and killer are revealed." His smile amped up a bit more. He still had hope.

I wasn't sure I had any. "Denny, I'm not—"

"Don't worry, we've still got time to solve this and make your flight."

"Denny, we don't. It'll be dawn in a little more than an hour." I looked out at the inky sky. The earlier sparkling stars were fading. I turned to Denny. "We have to go back to the art gallery. Georgie and Brenda might still be there . . ." I stopped to think about that possibility, realized it was unrealistic. Went on, "Anyway, we've got to call the police, report the death." I slowly shook my head. "Everything still points to Eli, because of the stolen headdress, and those darn hundreds! Maybe we can stay with Eli while the police question him—"

"No! Eli cannot go through an interrogation and arrest. We still have time to figure this out." Denny's eyes pleaded. "Mud, we just need a bit of food. If we don't know what to do after eating, we'll go back to the gallery and report the death."

I looked at Denny, knew it was time to call the police, but melted under his dark chocolate gaze. After all, what difference would another hour make? I made a soft protest, "No idea where you think you're going to get a meal at this time. It's just going on five. That's AM. The sun not's even up."

"I know exactly where to go." His stomach growled.

"Where?" I demanded.

"*Tsi yee* Cora." This was our great-aunt, Grandpa's older and, according to her, much wiser sister. *Tsi yee* was Kiowa for paternal aunt. It became the term of respect and affection we all used for Grandpa's four sisters, our great-aunts.

I smiled for the first time in a long night. It lightened the load. "Isn't it too early for her?"

Denny actually chuckled—music to my ears. "Does Aunt Cora ever sleep? She'll have something on the stove."

"She always does," I agreed. The truck thumped from the gravel road onto the highway's blacktop.

"Yeah, something good." Denny's eyes gleamed with anticipation. For the moment, concerns over a dead body, Eli, fracking, and Anna were wiped away with the prospect of food.

My phone buzzed. I should have listened to my first instinct and not answered the call. Instead, I rolled the window up, stopped the wind blowing through my hair, and immediately missed the fresh air. But it was time to deal with reality.

My hand went to the medicine bundle around my neck. My fingers kneaded the soft leather. Tired, I stared at the phone, forced myself to answer Bernie's call.

She didn't wait for a hello, just started right up, "Mae, I really hated the way we left things. I know you've worked harder than anyone. I'm just worried." The phone shifted to another ear. "You there, Mud? I'm real sorry I pushed. It's just, well, I'm not sure I'm ready to be solo with the execs. I'm really glad you'll be on the noon flight. Just couldn't sleep until I got that out."

I let the silence stretch. I shouldn't have answered the phone; I didn't see any hope of being on that flight. There was the murder, facing the police at Eli's side, fracking to stop, and Kiowa families who were still being swindled out of artifacts. I couldn't leave Denny, Grandpa, my people, now. I was disappointing everyone here, and there.

Bernie broke the prolonged silence, "Mud, you there?" Strange, it didn't bother me hearing her use my nickname; it seemed to roll off her tongue naturally.

I released my medicine bag before answering, "There's a good chance I'm not going to make the flight back."

Absolute silence rang out from the other side of the call.

I rushed to fill it. "I would if I could, but there really is an emergency here." I looked to Denny for support. His eyes stared straight ahead. I think he saw a cheeseburger through the windshield.

I returned to the phone. "Bernie, I hate doing this, but it doesn't seem likely I'll make the flight and it's better you know now."

When she answered, Bernie sounded wide awake. She was direct. "Have you reviewed the files?"

I had to be honest. "Not yet." Then I rushed to add, "I'm headed to an internet connection." I looked to Denny for confirmation.

He replied loud enough for Bernie's ears, "Oh yeah, Aunt Cora is with it. She's connected." He gave me a thumbs-up.

I shook my head—the goofus wasn't helping. I turned back to the phone. "I'll get the files reviewed before you arrive at the office."

There was no answer.

"I'm really sorry."

Again, no answer, just silence that screamed.

With what could only be called a sigh, Bernie said, "I'm going to sleep. Good night, Mud."

Maybe I didn't like her using my nickname after all. I shoved the phone into my pocket.

Denny looked over. "We do have time to wrap this all up before you get on your flight."

I shook my head but said nothing. I was tired.

Denny continued, "While we eat, we can tell *Tsi yee* everything." Relief crossed his face. "She may see something we don't. Aunt Cora has always been the practical one of the great-aunts."

The words were scarcely out his mouth as we came around a curve to see a glow at Aunt Cora's. The house was dark, but flames rose above the roofline in back.

Denny gunned the engine, racing past her house toward the back. We both were out before the truck rocked to a full stop. I followed Denny toward the flames, broke through some bushes and bounced off an abruptly stopped Denny. From my sprawled spot on the ground, I took in the scene that had stopped Denny cold. Flames reached for the sky while a dark figure danced naked around a rip-roaring campfire.

Chapter Twenty-Three

Laughter crackled in the night. Just past the back of the house, in front of a circular collection of oak trees, a fire roared and my great-aunt danced, naked.

Denny turned around. "You deal with this."

"Laughter is good medicine!" shouted our frolicking aunt.

Denny whispered, "I don't want to laugh at my naked great-aunt even if it makes me feel better." He shouldered past me toward the house, ignoring the dancing woman.

Another crackle of delight came from Aunt Cora. Her dark form danced to the side where a cotton dress hung over a webbed lawn chair. She pulled it over her head. "We've been waiting for you, *Ahn Tsah Hye-gyah-daw*."

I looked around to find the others in Aunt Cora's "we," but spotted no one.

An owl hooted nearby. Flames continued to dance, lighting the dark morning.

Aunt Cora moved toward me, I closed the gap and pulled the small woman into a hug. "*Tsi yee!*" The Kiowa word for "paternal aunt" slipped out as I squeezed the old woman. She looked just as she had ten years earlier, threads of black woven through her long, flowing white hair framing a face full of laugh lines leading to dark brown eyes that sparkled.

She chuckled, pushed from my arms to see me better in the flickering firelight. "So, the Seeker comes home for a spell. *Ownah day aim poroh*, it is good to see you, Granddaughter."

Aunt Cora, as with all traditional Kiowas, viewed children and grandchildren of a sibling the same as one of her own. We were of her flesh, no different than her own children. There was no Kiowa word for "cousin." The relationship did not exist; we were all brothers and sisters.

Aunt Cora scolded, "You took much longer than expected." Not waiting for my reply, she looked up to the sky. "And you didn't tell me they were so close." An owl hooted as if in response.

I looked up, only saw floating sparks from the nearby fire. Cora grabbed my arm and urged me toward a log acting as a bench and single stumps that ringed the fire. "Let's get Denny settled before we start."

I pulled back. "Start?"

She slid her arm in mine. "You didn't think your quest ended coming off the vision ledge yesterday, did you?" Cora chuckled. "It's not traditional, but traditions must evolve to exist. As they have always done." Aunt Cora looked up into my eyes. "My granddaughter, you have a calling. The time is approaching for you to see clearly, to find your way, *Ahn Tsah Hye-gyah-daw*. That's the purpose of a quest: time to settle your mind, introspection; you must understand yourself to find your best way forward."

"*Tsi yee*, I don't have time for a four-day quest to find myself."

"She really doesn't, Aunt," came from behind. Denny walked to the fire, which had calmed to a blazing campfire, and sat on the log bench. In his hand he balanced a bowl atop a plate piled high with golden pieces of fry bread. From the bowl rose the aroma of stew beef and corn. A family favorite. My stomach growled.

Flour-based fry bread was a reservation-era staple that filled starving bellies and evolved to comfort food status for most Plains Indian families. Fry bread—never fried bread or fry breads—was served with stews and soups, or when palmed larger and dropped into boiling oil, the dough plumped to plate size, making the perfect base for Indian tacos. Seasoned beef, beans, tomatoes, onions, and cheese piled on top of fry bread was a meal intended for special occasions. The thick, soft, and bubbly bread was also enjoyed as desserts or breakfasts by topping with butter, honey, or cinnamon sugar. While of little nutritional value, the bread got the Tribe through the starving years of early captivity.

Denny sat with the plate balanced on his knees. He tore a chunk of fry bread and used it as a spoon to shovel the stew into his mouth. Denny hummed with delight. "This is so good, *Tsi yee*!"

My stomach gurgled. I couldn't remember when I had last eaten.

Denny grinned as he tore another strip from the fry bread. "I always say your fry bread is the best, Auntie."

Cora stood in front of Denny, backlit by the firelight. "I know you, Denny Sawpole, and you say that to anyone that has a plate full of warm fry bread." She smiled, obviously pleased, watching Denny enjoy the food.

I moved to Denny and reached for a fist-size piece of fry bread. Denny shifted and swatted my hand away. I protested, "Come on, Denny, I'm hungry."

Mouth full, Denny sputtered, "Get your own."

"Sit, sit. I'll get yours." Cora moved to a table outside the fire's circle. A bucket and bowl with a cotton rag over its top sat on the table. Cora lifted an old, long-handled dipper into its matching white enamel bucket. She filled a glass with water and placed it in front of me. "You need to drink deeply."

She was right; I didn't realize how parched I was. I downed the glass. Cora used the dipper to refill it. She reached into the large bowl and pulled out a slice of watermelon in the shape of a smile. "This melon's been creek cooled all day." Cora handed me the slice, giving a smile of her own.

I bit in the middle of the slice. Watermelon-sweet coolness exploded in my mouth. The slice disappeared quickly. Cora handed me another, before trotting off to the house.

Denny slurped loudly, then grinned at me. My stomach growled in anticipation of the stew.

As Aunt Cora refilled Denny's bowl of beef and corn, she gave him a stern look. "You filled the hole. Now slow down, try to enjoy this bowl."

I looked at her, expecting my own bowl of stew. She offered none; instead, Cora moved to the table to refill my glass of water. "Aunt, are you eating? I'll get bowls for us." I moved off the stump.

Cora let her tinkle of a giggle out. "You can't have heavy food, *Ahn Tsah Hye-gyah-daw*, it would weigh your spirit down. We have a sweat to prepare for." She handed me the glass. "Drink up."

"Denny's eating!"

Through a mouth full of bread and beef, Denny said, "Don't drag me into your quest. I'm eating 'cause my spirit needs to be grounded." He swallowed a large mouthful, turned to Cora. "We do need answers, Auntie. Has Mud told you what's been happening through the night?" Not waiting for an answer, Denny revealed, "We found a body. It was the yellow-haired *td'aukoy* that owned *that gallery* in Lawton."

Denny said "that gallery" as if he and Cora had discussed it many times. I glanced at her, now sitting on a nearby stump. She sat unfazed, head tilted, taking in Denny's words.

Denny continued, "Eli looks guilty." He hurried to add, "Though he's not. Eli just picked the wrong night and time to get his grandpa's headdress back from the gallery. But it'll be okay." He assured Aunt Cora, "Mud's going to find who really did it before the police arrest Eli."

I just stood there, shaking my head in disbelief.

"That's good." Aunt Cora looked up to give me a grin. The firelight made her eyes sparkle.

I sputtered on the water I'd just swallowed. "It's not that simp—"

Denny interrupted, "We've been talking to everyone around at the time of death." He used his chin to indicate me. "Mud figured the timing out from the body's condition and when Eli saw it and probably from when Georgie fell over it the first time, not when she found it again in the gallery and pretended that was the first time."

Cora nodded, listening intently as if this all made sense.

I had to interrupt, "I'm not really sure . . . just trying to figure out a timeline." My protest trailed away. Denny jumped into the silence to continue his story. I returned to the stump and drank my water. I was never going to solve this murder. Listening to Denny explain our night adventures to Aunt Cora only confused me more.

Denny ended his tale with, "Mud's going to figure it all out from everyone's comings and goings." Denny looked around. "Is there any more watermelon?"

Cora used her chin to point at the bowl on the table. Denny went to it, pulled the cover away and took a slice of cool watermelon. "What do you think, Auntie?"

"Seems to me, y'all been taking a shotgun approach. Time to focus, take aim."

My head jerked up. "Aim at what?" I wanted directions. If someone had an idea, I was happy to focus on it because I really was lost on who killed Gerald.

"Aim on the details you've seen, heard, and felt."

Denny nodded as he thought over Cora's words. Still chewing, Denny asked, "Have the owls told you anything?"

"Just that you all have been going from one end of the country to the other and back again. Says it looks like you're going nowhere when you already have the answers you seek." Cora looked up to the sky and announced, "Guess you were right. Sounds like they're lost. Not seeing what's in front of their noses."

Denny stopped chewing. "What do you mean we already have the answers?"

"Just what I said, Grandson."

Denny tilted his head to look to me. "Mud, you know who killed Gerald?"

He acted like I really should know because Aunt Cora and her owls said so. "Are you crazy, Denny? I don't know anything more than you do." I felt frustrated, ready to be done with the conversation. I asked Aunt Cora, "I need to do some work for my agency. Denny says you have internet. Can I get online for a bit?"

"Sure. Right after our sweat." Cora gathered the dirty dishes and handed them to Denny. "Make sure to clean these and put them inside."

Denny stood holding the dirty dishes with a confused expression. "Wait!" he looked from me to Cora. "Does Mud know who murdered Gerald or not?"

I shook my head and stated a quick, "No," as Aunt Cora nodded with a grin and said, "She doesn't yet know what she knows, but she knows." This was followed by her laughter.

Denny nodded, satisfied. "Excellent." Without a backward glance, he walked to the house with his arms full of dirty dishes.

I protested, "Aunt, what do you think I know? I really want to know!"

Cora came to my side and patted my arm. "Don't worry. All will be revealed. What James started on the ledge now needs the woman's touch." She handed me another glass of water.

I pulled back. "Aunt, what I need is to use your internet. I have work—"

"You're right. We have work to do. First a sweat." Cora spoke over my protests, "Can't do the usual four rounds, but it's time to blend old with new traditions. One sweat round will do, for now." Aunt Cora looked up at me with an impish grin.

There was no saying no to her. But I tried. "Aunt, I can't do a sweat." I automatically took the offered glass, but protested, "I have too much to do."

"That's why you need the sweat, to seek insights that lead you to the right path." Cora motioned upward. "Drink your water. We need to prepare."

Denny returning from the house, asked, "Have you looked at her, Auntie? She's a typical muddy mess. You'll need to hose her down before crawling into the sweat lodge with her." Denny laughed at his jab.

Cora looked me up and down in the flickering firelight as if it were the first time she was seeing my physical self. She *tssked* at my mud-stained jeans, wrinkled her long nose at my sweat-stained, smelly blouse, and laughed when her dark brown eyes settled on my curl-sprung hair. Self-conscious, I patted down the wayward curls, but knew it was no use. My hair had a mind of its own.

Aunt Cora reached for my hands and held them between her two brown ones. "It is wonderful to have you home." She squeezed my hands. "Go to the creek first, get out of those dirty things, take a cool dip and put on the cotton tunic I left on a branch for you. You know the way to prepare, just the tunic. Don't bring anything else with you."

I pulled away. "Aunt, you don't understand, we have to go to the gallery and report the death. There's no time for a sweat."

Cora nodded. "Yes, I understand. You need this sweat to move forward."

I turned to Denny. "We have to get back. Ready?"

Denny stood between us. Aunt Cora held his gaze for several beats before releasing him to me. Denny said, "I'm not returning to the gallery, until *Tsi yee* says it's time." His eyes found mine, seemed to plead. "Besides, Auntie says you need the sweat to see clearly. That sounds good. It'll give you a chance to figure out who the killer is."

I shook my head. I'm sure my mouth even dropped open. Denny knew better. I turned back to my aunt, tried to protest once more, "*Tsi yee*, there is no time."

She shushed me with waving hands. "Didn't you listen? One round, not the normal four; that's what the spirits want this time. One round in the sweat lodge to remind you of who you were born to be."

"I know who I am. Living in California has not made me forget that I am Mae Sawpole."

"No, but it has made you forget you are *Ahn Tsah Hye-gyah-daw*, She Knows The Way, called to be a Storyteller, Keeper of our Sacred Stories."

"*Tsi yee*, I have not forgotten. It's just . . ." I stumbled to offer an excuse Cora would accept, that I would understand.

But she was done listening.

"Come, Granddaughter. We have a sweat to do."

Chapter Twenty-Four

Aunt Cora trotted down a well-worn path leading to a creek. Before she disappeared down the twisting trail, I called after her, "Can I use your internet first?"

Her voice carried on the wind, "Don't be silly. First things first. To the sweat!"

I moved down the path following the dancing steps ahead. While my aunt easily trotted down the narrow path in the dark, I had to watch my steps. Roots seemed intent on tripping me, branches slapped at me, and a cloud of gnats buzzed around my eyes. I swatted them away.

I came to the trail's end, stopping at a short drop to a small beach leading to a creek. Water moved quickly, splashing around rocks in its rush downstream. A loud splash sounded to my right; Cora stood in the water calf deep, smiling.

"Your tunic is around the bend at the Deep-end." Aunt Cora named a well-used swim hole. "Take a dip, clean a bit. Prepare. Then come back to me."

I slid down the bank to the beach. Watched my great-aunt play. She splashed and kicked water, giggling as she got wet. I thought again of my agency's files waiting for me, Bernie's anger, and a dead man. *Always the dead man.* Aunt Cora edged closer to the beach, bent, took aim and sent a splash of water that covered me from head to foot.

I leapt back, dripping, slipped on the wet ground and landed on my knees. "Watch what you're doing!"

Chuckling, she said, "I did."

Before I could sputter out a response, Aunt Cora commanded, "Get a move on. Prepare. Properly." She said the last with emphasis.

I pushed wet curls from my face, took in Aunt Cora. There was no smile, she was serious. I set my jaw. All right, I would go ahead and get this sweat over with so I could review the files and get them back to the agency. Then to the art gallery to report a dead man.

I stood and went down the beach around the bend to where a tunic waved in the breeze and the creek widened to create the Deep-end, a natural pool. Just beneath the tunic, Aunt Cora had left roots of young yucca plants. The crushed root created a soap mild enough for skin and hair. Aunt Cora said that her land was once a favorite Kiowa summer camp. Generations of our family had used the Deep-end as I was now: for summer swimming and bathing.

I sat on the gravel beach, removed my shoes and left the rest of my clothes and belongings in a pile to the side, out of reach of the creek. I made sure my cell phone, my connection to the agency, was secure in my jeans pocket. Carefully, I removed my medicine bag and placed it inside my shoe for safekeeping. I tried to leave my worries, but they lingered.

Washing, after the last thirty-plus hours I'd had, really did sound good. I just didn't want Aunt Cora to know I appreciated the drenching.

As children, we had run barefoot into the creek, oblivious to sharp rocks or possible snapping turtles. Those days were definitely in my past. I made my way to the creek slowly, avoiding sharp-edged rocks until making it to the round-pebble bottom of the flowing water. I splashed on toward the deeper end and dived, immersing myself in the cool water, losing sense of up or down, until air bubbles pointed the way. I surfaced for a breath, then propelled downward again, enjoying the freedom of movement enveloped in the crisp cool water.

I took Aunt's "prepare properly" command seriously. I knew she meant I needed to be free of negative thoughts, and return in a state of balance, or as close as I could get. I tried to let go of my bad energy: worries for Eli, doubts of my ability to help, concerns over my agency's big event, and anger at thieves and killers. I floated; pushed worries, concerns, and doubts from my mind. As they sneaked back, I exhaled the negative thoughts away. Remembered that there was only room for positive energy, good medicine, in a sweat and in life. If any drop of negative came in, it polluted all. I drifted a bit. Enjoyed the cool water on my skin. Tried not to worry about a dead man or a potentially bankrupt agency.

Consciously, I breathed in deeply and slowly released each breath, tried to find balance. My eyes slowly grew accustomed to the sky lit only by the half moon and the fading stars above. I lost myself in the dark depth between stars while forcing worries over the dead man out of my mind. Night sounds emerged; a frog croaked and crickets sang. In the distance, I heard the fire pop and crackle as it settled into a small campfire. Water kissed rocks gently. Cora sang an old song, the words too faint to make out, but the energy of the song entranced. I floated. The night's events played like a movie across my mind's eye. I watched and thought—nothing.

When it was the right time, I cleaned with the crushed yucca roots, washed the sweat of the day and night from my skin. I dove deep to rinse. It felt like flying, free of gravity, of constraints. I worked the gentle yucca foam through my hair; I rinsed and repeated. Welcomed the cool water against my skin that left goosebumps.

Slowly, I moved from the creek to the branch that held a towel and tunic. I squeezed water from my hair, shook it out and set an explosion of curls free. Wind rushed through them, removed any lingering bad energy. After drying, I pulled the tunic over my head and slipped my arms through the large openings. I glanced to where I had left my shoes and clothes, and found none. Didn't worry about it.

Body and mind cleansed, I was ready.

Barefoot, I picked my way around the bend back to my aunt on the beach. Her form perched on the bank with her feet resting on the carved dirt step below. As I got closer, I could see that she had braided a red strip of cloth into her silver-white hair.

Aunt Cora gestured. "Come, let me prepare you." She indicated for me to sit at her knees at the edge of the bank. She sat above, with me using the step as a seat and scooting my back in close to my aunt, between her knees. We faced the creek, listened to the water rush to join Lake Lawtonka, to fulfill its purpose.

Tsi yee, my great-aunt, talked as her fingers worked through my hair. "Your grandpa thinks he knows it all. Well, there is much he does know and shares with you, as it should be. But women have power, too, and secrets. Buffalo Spirit is strong medicine—you may be a Sawpole, but the Buffalo Spirit has come to you." She grabbed my hair in both hands, tugged and let it go. "You were born to it, just look at that buffalo hair." We laughed together, as we had done since my childhood. Aunt Cora always celebrated the good in the world.

Cora pushed at my shoulder, wanting me to turn. I twisted to face her. She dangled my medicine bag. "I cleansed this for you. This is your spirit bundle, inside is medicine for your soul. The items inside help you remember, give focus, guide you along life's journey so you are walking a good path."

She waited to hear my "*Haw*"—my acknowledgment that I was not just listening, but that I understood her words.

Tsi yee continued, "I've added two special feathers to your medicine. The first is an owl's bristle." She held a small dark feather carefully between her thumb and finger. "These little feathers are strong. Bristle feathers have a stiff shaft, they encircle an owl's eyes, serve like eyelashes clearing its sight in flight. This feather is for you *boen own knee*, to see clearly." She slipped the small stiff feather into my leather bag. "There is one more." Cora showed me a puff of a feather. "This is an ear tuft feather. Owls watch and listen before acting. Be like an owl, Granddaughter: watch, listen, see clearly before acting." She placed the feather inside the bag, squeezed it four times with her eyes cast upward. "You need to wear your spirit bag to feel the strengths offered, to understand them and remember to embrace them. Let your totems guide you to a better you." She placed the leather bag over my head and released it. The bag rested above my heart. My creek-chilled body warmed.

I knew not to speak yet. *Tsi yee* would let me know when it was the proper time.

Cora pulled me back to rest between her knees as she talked. "I took a small tuft from the buffalo hair you had in your spirit bag." From behind she showed me a mat of brown fur that she had wrapped around a brown-striped feather, with a single red strand binding them together. "I'm blending the buffalo medicine with this owl tail feather. All owl feathers are specially designed.

Tail feathers are used to steer in turbulent times. This tail feather will help you find your way." I drifted as she talked, flowing with the rhythm of her words. Enjoying her warm hands in my hair. Hearing her words but not listening deeply.

She pulled a hank of hair sharply. "Remember, you're supposed to be finding your way, not fighting your way. You hear me?"

I jerked alert. "*Haw, Tsi yee!*" squeaked out of me.

Cora pulled me back, gently. "Many call me a Medicine Woman, but I'm a Spirit Woman. Like my mother and grandmother before me, I talk to owls. They tell and show me much, and through them I send messages."

She waited to hear my "*Haw,*" to make sure I was listening. I was.

Aunt Cora went on, "You, Granddaughter, do not always listen. You may have a buffalo guide, but you are a Sawpole. We have always talked with the owls. Before you can talk, you must first learn to watch, and listen. Remember, the owl is our messenger bird. The owl has been calling you here all night, and you refused to see or hear. That is the first step to being an owl talker—you must first listen to see."

I nodded, carried by her intensity.

Tsi yee lifted a chunk of hair at the crown of my head, at the start of my life spiral. Kiowas believed that our spirit entered and exited a chosen body through the natural spiral we all have atop our heads. At her touch, I saw a flash of blue, felt a tingle.

Cora's deft fingers began braiding the buffalo hair and owl feather into my scalp lock. Every touch sent a jolt of electricity through my body. My senses seemed hypersensitive. I heard Denny, off at a distance, wrestle my suitcase into Aunt Cora's house. Sweet cedar smoke sailed on a light breeze. I sensed an owl swoop low and land out of sight by the now sedate campfire.

Aunt Cora chanted as she weaved my hair with the feather and buffalo tuft. My breathing seemed to match the rhythm of her words. She put the final touches to my scalp lock and gave it a little tug that made my body vibrate. Wind rustled the leaves above, whispering secrets while the moon's light exposed small animals scampering into hiding beneath the tangled brush around the creek.

"Look at me, child."

I kneeled in front of my great-aunt. She took my face in one hand; with the other, she swiped beneath each of my eyes. "When a Kiowa is seeking, you wear red beneath your eyes or on your hair part. It opens the way to answers." Cora stood, brushed the dirt from her dress. "Come, time to return to the fire."

I followed her back toward the fire. She led me deeper into the circle of oaks, where a small domed hut wrapped in buffalo hides stood.

Aunt Cora threw a buffalo-hide flap to the side, opening the sweat lodge. She signaled for me to sit on a tree stump, this one closer to the lodge than the fire. Aunt Cora moved to a tree and took a long branch in hand. A large elk pelvis bone was strapped to the end of the long wooden handle. Aunt Cora used the device like a shovel and dug into the depths of the fire.

She looked over to me. "We don't want any metal or modern things in the sweat. When you're seeking answers, you must do it right, focus on your inner light." Cora shifted ashes around the still burning fire, stopping as she unearthed several large lumps. "Aw, yes. You're the right two." She lifted the shovel, cradling two round cobblestones glowing red with intense heat. Aunt Cora moved to the sweat lodge, bent low at the small entrance to gently place the rocks inside the lodge. "It's warm in there already. Good."

She returned to the fire for more rocks. Cora laughed at the expression on my face as I watched her wrestle two more large stones from the fire and place them inside the lodge with her elk pelvis shovel. "We're going in with eight cobblestones tonight. I had four in already, warming things up. It's going to be a hot one. You need a good sweat," Cora declared, looking at me.

I moved to leave the stump, but she halted me with a hand signal. I sat back, waited. From a bag at the side of the sweat lodge, she took out a deer bladder water container and a buffalo horn shaped into a large dipper. "Gotta get everything ready. This bladder is full of Medicine Creek water. I carried it from Medicine Bluff for tonight's sweat."

Kiowa and many of the early Plains tribes believed that Medicine Bluff was a spiritual place, touched by the Creator, *Daw'Kee*. It sat on the rolling plains, a towering rock dome cleaved in half, with no sign of its other half anywhere. A spring-fed creek flowed from atop Medicine Bluff; it was believed that the water carried special healing properties. My great-aunt had hiked miles through the day's heat for the special water—for me.

I said a heartfelt "*Ah ho*"—thank you.

After placing the water and horn dipper inside the lodge, Cora retrieved a cedar box from her large bag. From the box, she took an eagle feather and a leather pouch. "We're ready to start, but first you listen. When I was young, they still did it as the *Bn'ee daw,* Old Ones, instructed." Her smile brightened, thinking of the days of her youth. "When it was time to take you into the sweats, they took you up in the mountains, you fasted for two to four days. And if lucky, you got a vision, sort of an insight into the life path best for you. When you're inside the sweat, you take time to sit in silence, let introspection guide you to your true heart, your purpose." Her eyes found mine. "We honor the

Creator when we find our way, live our potential. Being true to yourself is the greatest way to honor *Daw'Kee*."

I answered with "*Haw*," the Kiowa "yes." I urged my *Tsi yee* to tell me more of the Old Ones and days past.

Cora didn't want to linger in the past; her focus was on today. "Our traditions must evolve to stay alive. A proper sweat has four rounds. We go in four times." She used her chin to point to the sweat lodge. "First time in is for prayers. When you finish your prayers, we don't say 'Amen.'" Shaking her head, she said, "Nope, we always end with, 'All My Relations.' That's how we acknowledge that we are all connected, all dependent on Mother Earth and Father Sun. We are kin with all that travels this world. *Daw'Kee* has created everything on heaven and earth. So, we're all related. No matter what the color of our skins, or if we walk, fly, or slither, we are all related to one another. That's why we say, 'All My Relations,' to share our blessing with all our brothers and sisters."

I nodded to show I understood. I'd heard these words at the end of all prayers throughout my life. I understood why we said them; tonight, Aunt Cora made me feel the words.

Cora went on, "A sweat's second round isn't always the same, it changes based on the need." *Tsi yee*'s brown eyes focused on me as she continued, "That's the round you're on. Your first round was with your grandpa James up there on the vision quest ledge yesterday. Your second round, we're doing together in the sweat lodge. Your last two rounds will follow in the coming days."

It was hard to stay silent. I had no time for two more days of a quest. I needed to help Eli, catch a plane, save my business . . . find my way.

Tsi yee seemed to focus on something far away as she added, "Tomorrow will be your third round, you'll heal, see a glimmer of your way forward. And on your fourth day, that will be your final day of this quest. You will *boen own knee* and give thanks. That's the four rounds."

I nodded as I said, "*Haw*" to let my aunt know I was listening. I heard her, yet didn't understand what she was telling me.

Cora seemed to shake herself out of a trance. Her eyes focused on me as she announced, "Come, Granddaughter. There is much to see, much to think, much to do." Taking her eagle feather and pouch, Cora crawled into the sweat lodge.

Not knowing what else to do, I followed her into the dark sweat lodge. Aunt Cora seemed to make less sense than normal, and yet, made too much sense to ignore.

Chapter Twenty-Five

It was dark and hot. So hot, it took my breath away. I took a moment to refill my lungs before crawling toward the east, around the edges of the lodge's circle until I sat across from my aunt. Having crawled completely around the lodge's circle, she sat back at our entry point. Moonlight peeking in from the small opening lit her face. *Tsi yee* sat with her eagle feather in hand, water and dipper to one side and her leather pouch to the other. In the center of the sweat lodge was a hole piled with hot rocks. A wavy ring of heat radiated from the rock pile.

Sweat ran down my forehead, dropping into my eyes. I wiped it away, settled and sat cross-legged, like my aunt. She didn't seem bothered by the rising heat. Cora flashed me a smile full of white teeth as she reached, closed the flap and plunged us into total darkness. A black so deep, you don't remember light. The rocks had a faint glow. I could make out the pile of hot rocks and nothing more.

My aunt's voice cut through the darkness, "The Old Ones say where you build your sweat lodge, that's the center of the universe. And there"—a feather brushed the rocks in the hole in the center of the sweat lodge—"that hole is the absolute center of our universe." Cora's feather whisked across the rocks as she spoke.

"The world is round, our sweat lodge is round, wherever you put the sweat lodge, it's the center of the universe." As she talked, Cora sprinkled special grasses, cedar, and sage on the hot rocks. The rocks sparked in response. Smoke rose. "If it's the right time, you'll look in those rocks and a blue flame will show. Then you go deeper, look inside the center of self."

She threw another handful of grasses; the hut filled with resin-rich skunk smoke. Breathing became difficult. I took each precious breath in deeply as I looked within the center of the universe. All I saw was black emptiness.

I'd never had a vision during quests. I went searching but never found answers. On my first quest at eleven with my grandfather, I had sat on the ledge for four days, chanting, hoping, praying, seeking a sign that I was Kiowa enough. Even then, nothing had come to me. Though, Grandpa claimed my name, *Ahn Tsah Hye-gyah-daw*—She Knows The Way—had come to him. I wasn't sure the right name had come; I seemed to have lost my way. I was successful in Silicon Valley, I thought that had been enough, but now, I had doubts.

Sweat trickled down my long Kiowa nose. The light tunic clung to me, already soaked in my sweat.

Aunt Cora shifted in the dark. "I'm going to pour life-giving water onto the hot cobblestones. Their life breath will rise as steam." I sensed the dipper hovering over the burning hot rocks. She continued, "It will take your breath away as the cobblestones' first breath goes through your body. Be ready."

I nodded, realized she couldn't see me, and said, "*Haw.*" But I wasn't ready. A blast of heat hit like a rogue ocean wave, smashed down on me. Every pore leaked. Cora splashed more water onto the rocks. It popped and snapped like hot oil, releasing another thick cloud of hot steam. I had no more to sweat, yet I did.

The air became so thick with hot moisture, I couldn't take in a breath. I felt lightheaded. Finally, thinking to pull the tunic up over my nose, I sucked in hot air cooled just enough to breathe through the sweat-damp cloth. I couldn't voice that I was choking.

Through it all, Cora chanted an old prayer thanking Mother Earth for all her gifts. She settled back, and must have exchanged the water dipper for her pouch of a special mixture of cedar, sweet grasses, and sage because the rocks crackled and added more pungent smoke to the thick steam.

Aunt Cora reminded me, "We're not praying to those rocks or Mother Earth, we're respecting them. It is the Creator we pray to. *Daw'Kee* made all on our world and beyond. We are all connected, related."

I felt Cora waiting for my acknowledgment. The heat was so thick, I still had the cloth covering my nose and mouth. I choked out a *"Haw"* that was more cough than assent.

Aunt Cora must have thought I would live. She went on, "This is a whistle made from the leg bone of a brown eagle. The brown eagle flies highest of all birds, he carries our words up to *Daw'Kee*. I'm going to blow it four times. Four times for the four directions . . . four times calling spirit power to come in, be with us tonight."

A whistle so piercing I could barely hear it, sounded and was repeated three more times. At the end of the fourth, Cora said, "*Daw'Kee,* we come to you in a good way. My granddaughter is seeking her life path. She walks in two worlds. Show her the way to blend her worlds. Start her on the path for her heart to be happy."

Cora tossed a handful of her quest blend onto the red, hot rocks. Sparks flew upward, dancing in the thick rope of smoke. "When the Old Ones prayed, they just talked directly to *Daw'Kee*.

Discussed what was needed, then took time to look within for answers." The cobblestones crackled in response. My aunt waited a moment to emphasize, "Remember, introspection is necessary to truly know yourself, for you to be *Ahn Tsah Hye-gyah-daw*."

From the rustling sounds in the dark, I knew that Aunt Cora was preparing another dipper full of Medicine Creek water for the rocks. This time I got ready for the rush of intense steam heat. Well, as ready as I could be. I sucked in air as deeply as possible, knowing the hot steam would take my breath away, then covered my mouth and nose with my tunic before the steam wave hit.

Cora poured the water onto the rocks, releasing a storm of billowing steam. She announced, "Feel that steam going through, taking our prayers up to *Daw'Kee*."

A blast of heat hit, coming in hard and thick. I kept my mouth covered. Took short desperate breaths through the fabric as I tried to survive my aunt's cleansing and prayers.

Aunt Cora, sounding like true happiness, sang, "Our medicine came in. Our words will be heard." A feather whisked across the rocks as Aunt Cora said, "See how the cobblestones look. They've gone blue. This sweat is going to be powerful." She chuckled and tossed a handful of her quest mix onto the rocks. "This is a good sign." Pungent smoke joined billowing steam.

Outside an owl called; nearby, another answered.

Tsi yee hooted, "Owls have come to you. Owls will talk to another generation of Sawpoles! Grandfather Buffalo knows you need two guides to find one path for both worlds. Grandfather Buffalo's guardian spirit and strength will meld with the All-Seeing Owl's stealth and wisdom. This is good."

An owl, sounding like it was just above the lodge, announced his approval. *Tsi yee* returned the hoot. A drum beat started in the distance—faint, but persistent.

I looked at the cobblestones, watched a spark emerge from a crackle or maybe a pop. It floated upward. Midflight, the spark turned blue and drifted toward me. The blue spark defied gravity as it danced in front of my face. I stretched to touch the gyrating blue light. It glowed and buzzed, staying just out of reach.

"Granddaughter, be ready; the fourth dipper of water is coming." *Tsi yee* chanted before pouring the water onto the burning rocks. The steam wrapped me in a thick blanket, it was suffocating. I thought the inside of the sweat lodge could get no darker. I was wrong. With the blackness came intense heat. I couldn't breathe, there was no air. The blue spark danced to the drum beat, slow, steady, and calling.

Heat sucked the remaining air from my lungs; the blue spark beckoned to me. I was faint; the blue light danced and the drums called. I floated upward into a spiral, following the blue spark into inky blackness. Round and round, the blue light spun out of the lodge, answering the drum's call.

I hesitated before leaving the sweat lodge. I seemed to exist in two worlds: in one, sitting, sweating in the lodge while also above, in the dark, floating. From above, I watched the back of my head drop forward. My motionless body remained seated across from my aunt. As my head below dropped, tethers released, I drifted upward, out and above the sweat lodge, floating on the breeze, flowing as the wind.

The blue light led me ever higher and deeper into the black void. The drum beat called, louder and louder. My heartbeat answered, matching the steady drumming, melding into one, together.

Clouds shifted and formed memories, images: a young me, crawling closer to a group as I listened to my grandfather and his friends tell stories of the Old Ones and days forgotten. Clouds moved; others blow forward to form me, hiding in my grandfather's workroom as he painted, watching a Kiowa story emerge from a blank canvas. Later an older me sharing the stories of our Tribe with a group of young. Smiling, enjoying the telling and knowing the stories will continue. I am a link, passing knowledge to the next generation. As it should be, as it has always been.

Clouds shifted and reshaped, forming Grandpa at my Naming Ceremony, the day I was named *Ahn Tsah Hye-gyah-daw*, and called Mud. Floating above, I listened to my grandfather explain how my name had come to be. The name had been whispered the night of my birth but demanded to be given after my first quest. I heard Grandpa's words again: "This one must find her balance in two worlds. She must find the point where air and fire meet, that balancing point between earth and water. She will find the path, not lost in or between her worlds but at the balancing point where the worlds come together. That is her way. Her Kiowa name is *Ahn Tsah Hye-gyah-daw*, She Knows The Way."

My soul quivered upon hearing my true name spoken aloud. The truth resonated throughout my being. I am *Ahn Tsah Hye-gyah-daw*.

Then a young Denny in his high-pitched voice announced, "Water and earth come together—her name is Mud!" And just like that, once slung, the nickname stuck. For the first time, I smiled hearing the name. It, too, was me.

Clouds reformed; late nights with numerous clients evolving to my current client, Richard, flowed by until it was me, Mae Sawpole, presenting the new company's story, its identity to an excited Richard and executives. Words formed pictures showing Richard's company initial public offering preparations; Bernie, Marcus, my agency's employees working hard on the press event.

Then it's just me, Mae Sawpole, professional storyteller for start-ups at the computer, long after all have left, alone.

Images float by, I watch, and think; from deep within, I call out, "*Daw'Kee*, please give me knowledge and wisdom to see clearly." I don't know if I spoke the words or sent them in thought, but I felt them lift from me and take flight.

An owl's call pulled me out of the clouds. Flying together, we swooped low over the Kiowa Compound's maintenance hut. The owl had a message; I knew I should see something, hear something. His piercing yellow eyes cast downward; my gaze followed. The owl dipped a silent wing toward the day's tracks going to the maintenance office, leading to a death. I dived down closer to see clearly, but a cold wind hit. Shivers shake my soul . . . I'm falling . . . I'm engulfed in the confusion of sudden death as a spirit passes. Then heat and darkness . . . and laughter.

Laughter lifts me, gives me hope.

The laughter of my *Tsi yee* calls me back to the sweat lodge. It fills me with warmth. All traces of the death chill vanished. Cora's voice comes out of the dark, "Live life happy."

I slowly shook my head, trying to clear the clouds around my mind. "Auntie, I don't understand."

Aunt Cora answers, "Whatever you do, do it with a happy heart. That makes what you create full of good medicine." I sensed her lean toward me in the dark. "Spread good medicine to the world." Cora laughed again as she sang out, "Live life with a happy heart. It fills the world with good medicine."

Tsi yee's words made sense. In my mind, a spiral of happy hearts spun out into the world, wrapping it with good medicine. I smiled watching the swinging, happy hearts.

"That's right, spread smiles! They're contagious." I felt my aunt's smile through the pitch black of the sweat lodge. It bolstered me. Good medicine filled me with each breath. I gave a big grin to my great-aunt. She giggled.

"Do you know you?" came from the dark.

Images from earlier flashed through my mind. All versions of me. I answered with the truth, "Not yet, but I'm listening and watching, Auntie."

I felt her nod through the dark. "That's good, Granddaughter." Cora sprinkled something onto the cobblestones. They sparked and snapped. The pure, sweet smell of cedar filled the lodge. "Before we go, we gotta end with, 'All My Rlations.' We want to spread the good medicine outward to All My Relations! Feel it when you close the round, Granddaughter."

I did.

Chapter Twenty-Six

For a bit, I forgot. I forgot about a dead man and an unknown killer, about my agency's pending demise, the threat of illegal fracking destroying Kiowa country, and the horror that Eli, an innocent man, was going to endure once accused of murder.

It was so nice to forget.

Aunt Cora left me on the creek's beach with water and the creek-cooled watermelon. The slices, as promised, were chilled and refreshing. Just what my body craved after the sweat.

I lifted a watermelon smile to my mouth and let the sweet juices flow. The slice's upper edges left sticky spots on my cheeks. I tossed the rind into the cooler Aunt Cora had left. Using the back of my hand, I wiped the sticky juice from my cheeks. Reached for another slice, bit and felt the juices revive my senses. Rather than drained from the sweat, I was buzzing, full of energy.

Denny shuffled into view. He had my lime-green messenger bag slung over one shoulder; his steps dragged kicking pebbles up from the dirt path.

"What's weighing you down, Denny? I know it's not my messenger bag." I reached for the bag as he plopped down beside me.

It became immediately obvious that the nearby cooler was what Denny truly wanted to sit next to; he pulled a slice of watermelon from it. The slice en route to Denny's mouth slung red juice across my messenger bag.

"Hey!" Wiping it, I moved the bag to my other side, away from Denny.

"No worries, that bag is an awful color already. A splash of Oklahoma watermelon pink is exactly what it needed."

I pulled my bright lime-green bag closer. "This bag has been with me since I started my agency, VisualAdvantage."

"Is it your lucky bag?" Denny teased.

"Nooo." I let out an elongated denial that said it all.

Denny chuckled and grabbed another slice of melon. "I've been thinkin' while you've been with Auntie." Denny made it sound as if I had been visiting our elderly aunt, not forced into a sweat that I hadn't wanted . . . at first.

"We don't need to be running around chasing people. You need to stay put and think so you can figure out what happened, who did it and how."

Denny's words pulled my drifting mind back to the moment. "What? What did you say?"

He shook his head, frustrated with my inattention, before repeating, "We've been rushing from one place to another all night. You just need to sit here and think a bit to sort it all out. Aunt Cora says you know who killed Gerald. You just need to see clearly." Denny stated this as a simple truth I had yet to grasp.

"Oh, that's what I need." My sarcasm went right over Denny's head. He smiled and nodded as he got up. "Yep, that's it. You just haven't sat and thought about everything enough." Denny brushed the damp creek gravel from his jeans. "I'm gonna let you alone for a bit. Then we'll go wherever you say." He kept smiling.

I could feel the hope and expectation in the smile. Denny added, "It's not even dawn yet, still plenty of time to make your flight to California after you figure out what you know."

I refused to look up, just shook my head. "Denny, I don't know—"

He let out a gag-cough. This made me look up, just in time to catch Denny wrinkle his long nose in disgust as he announced, "You smell like a wet skunk. You better clean up. I left your suitcase at the Deep-end, just like *Tsi yee* instructed." He walked off, back to the path leading to the house, his feet nearly skipping. It looked like all had gone as Denny had hoped. I was to sit and see clearly.

I laughed, what else could I do? After all, laughter was good medicine.

I refused to ruin my sweat lodge buzz with thoughts of murder. I picked up my messenger bag and slid my computer out. I didn't bother with the notes I had on Richard's company. I knew the client's story—I'd created it, formed it, and told it many times already. I just needed to make sure each of the executives told their part properly to build to Richard's ending announcement. And, of course, that our graphics enhanced the telling and did not overshadow the message.

Getting on Aunt Cora's internet connection was no problem, the password, *digital_moccasin*, was printed on a note left inside my computer. Her password brought a smile. Aunt Cora was moving the Tribe's telegraph moccasin to the computer age. I loved that in her eighties, my aunt embraced technology rather than avoided it. As she had told me many times, "To save traditions, we must evolve."

My mind drifted . . . what did a traditional storyteller evolve to? Me? A storyteller using digital tools. No, not me, I do it for corporations . . . what was traditional storytelling in the digital age?

I pulled my focus back to my computer. Bernie's files were downloading faster than expected. I could start opening and reviewing them. From start to finish I seemed to flow with the story—saw each presenter in my mind's eye doing the telling with the showing. I sensed the needed adjustments, wrote asides to Bernie with hints and tips, and noted necessary tweaks for presenter, graphic elements, and timing.

At the end, I viewed the last-minute, animated company logo created by Marcus, the agency's creative director, for the event's opening. It was near perfect. The ten-second piece introduced the company's new identity with a light flourish—just the right touch. I offered a few suggestions, then congratulated Marcus on making a quality piece happen in such a short turnaround.

I sent the last of my notes off to Bernie, imagined hearing a slight buzz as the files magically returned to Silicon Valley. I slid the computer back into its nest inside my lucky bag. It felt good to get one thing done. Bernie would be happy to see the reviewed files when she arrived at the office . . . and relieved. Though she of all people should know that the agency was my livelihood, too, I needed Richard's IPO to be successful. VisualAdvantage would be a nationally known agency—maybe worldwide—with his company's successful launch. Only an emergency like this would keep me away.

It had been nice to forget. To focus only on Richard's company's story, to feel competent again, yet the dead body haunted my thoughts. Memories from the night's adventures flashed to the forefront at unexpected moments, each time sending a jolt through me. I knew something, but what? Sit here and see clearly wasn't as easy as Denny thought. How do you see clearly when you have no idea where to focus?

I slung my messenger bag over my shoulder and headed down the path toward the Deep-end. A swim in the chilled water sounded like a perfect way to wash the residues of the sweat from my body, and maybe, the presence of a ghost demanding answers.

I left my messenger bag by my suitcase, waiting for me as Denny had promised. On impulse I dropped to sit on a slight rise at the creek's edge under the tree that held another towel for me.

I stared out into the dark sky. Dawn was approaching. The morning was at its darkest; the stars and moon retreating, making way for the start of the day.

A motion, one I sensed more than saw, skimmed the top of my head, lifting the owl tailfeather tethered to my scalp lock with a tuft of buffalo hair. The touch ignited fireworks through the spiral at the top of my head all the way down to my toes curled in the damp creek bed. I shivered.

My eyes followed a silent owl as it landed on an old cottonwood branch directly across from me. The owl took its time to look around, literally. It turned its head completely, until the piercing yellow eyes landed on me. Its gaze cut through me—saw me. I felt connected.

I leaned toward the owl. "My aunt says I'm supposed to listen to you. You've got the answers." I waited, half expecting to hear the All-Seeing Owl talk, but it said nothing.

I returned the owl's silence, waiting to hear its wisdom as a Kiowa asking an Elder for direction should. The silence stretched, until All-Seeing Owl broke it with a, "Whoo?"

I kept my eyes on the owl's round ones. "That's the question, who? Who killed Gerald? Who is behind fracking? Who?" I asked, hoped the owl truly had answers. Because I didn't.

The owl swiveled its head to examine the creek bed. I followed the gaze. All I saw were my barefoot tracks from earlier, still in the mud at the creek's edge and another showing my toes digging in and slipping where I had climbed the bank to the path.

I spoke aloud, "All-Seeing Owl, I'm trying to listen and see clearly, but I don't understand what you're telling me." I watched the owl closely. It shifted on the branch, adjusting its wings. Once settled, its head turned back toward me. It seemed ready to speak, but didn't.

I let a snort out and laughed at myself. I was expecting an owl to tell me who murdered Gerald—maybe it would also know who was behind the illegal fracking. I chuckled.

The owl hooted another, "Whoo?"

I looked up at it. Tried again, "Yes, who is the who?" As expected, All-Seeing Owl had no answer. Instead, as if frustrated with me, it turned its back, lifted from the branch, and silently disappeared into the blackness.

A laugh escaped; I was sure glad Denny wasn't around to see me talking to an owl and then worse, get snubbed by it. I got up, pulled the tunic off, and walked into the creek. Reaching the Deep-end, I dove, going down, then twisted around and slowly kicked back up until I broke through the surface. I shifted to my back and floated, looking up into the dark sky, not quite admitting that I was looking for the All-Seeing Owl.

Uncalled thoughts flooded my mind, floating from one to another. Georgie coming to me in a cloud of Poison perfume, begging us to find Buck before he killed Gerald. Sky's eyes staring, Anna dressed in black sneaking around the maintenance hut, Eli leaving interlocking circles on the ground as he banged his cane with fury over Gerald, Brenda's yellow daisy-covered Converses, and Georgie screaming at finding a body and screaming again but then there was no body, until there was.

I flipped over and dove, trying to wash the images away. But thoughts waited for me once I surfaced. Something was niggling at me; something I saw, heard that would solve it all. The thought, the memory came close to the surface then seemed to take a quick dive, just out of reach.

I wished I could believe like Denny, that I had the answers within. That I was just not seeing clearly, or listening to what I'd heard . . . that I knew.

But I didn't.

I was floating when it started behind me, just before dawn. I'd heard it once before, as a child out early with my grandfather. It was stunning, almost spiritual: a cacophony of bird calls greeting the day. A blue jay was first, followed by crows, then from large to small, all the birds pitched in. My grandpa had said, "The birds do it just moments before sunrise. They like to announce the new day before Father Sun is even up." Grandpa always chuckled at the end. It amused him that the early bird sang before the hunt for worms.

As quickly as it started, the bird songfest stopped. We all stopped to watch a miracle—the dawning of a new day. Night meeting day: they touched, joined for a stolen moment before one gave way to the other. Very slowly, morning light peeked through the trees. The surrounding landscape took form. The day burst forth.

I emerged from the water, enjoyed the feel of waterdrops running like little rivers down my body as I left the creek behind. I wrapped myself in the towel, drying off the morning chill.

Stacked next to my suitcase were my freshly cleaned and folded jeans, shirt, and shoes. I gave my hair a last towel dry scrub before putting on undergarments, then kicking into my clean jeans and shirt. I folded the towel, placed it on the damp ground to use as a seat. I finally had clean jeans again; I didn't want the wet gravel to dirty them while I sat to put my shoes on.

A rustling crackle sounded when I bent to sit and when I wiggled to get a sock onto my damp foot. Something rustled in my jean pocket. I put my hand into the rear pocket of my jeans, touched a paper edge, and in a flash, remembered. When Wyatt rushed from his office, a crumpled wad had followed, and I'd shoved it into my pocket to toss later. I'd never looked at it, had forgotten the sheet almost immediately watching the heated argument between Wyatt and Anna then after that it had been nonstop hunting, finding, and running, and something . . .

How could I have forgotten?

I pulled my phone from my shoe and used the light from the screen to look at the crumpled sheet. *Kiowa Nation Mineral and Oil Rights Lease Agreement* was at the top of the page. It showed twenty acres leased by Wyatt Walker. It *was* the lost document! The first lease, before Wyatt learned about the under twenty-acre automation the Tribe had in place. Before he learned to hide in plain sight.

I grabbed my other shoe—time to go back to Anna's house. This document was Anna's alibi. It proved that Anna was truly searching for the link showing Wyatt Walker was the fracking boss, and that Anna didn't have time to kill Gerald. This document cleared Anna of all doubt. Denny would be thrilled.

I jammed my foot in the other shoe, hit a blockage and pulled my foot out. Nested inside the shoe was my white leather medicine bundle. I edged it out, didn't want to take the time, but knew I had to. I cleared my mind, filled it with positive thoughts and held my medicine bag—or spirit bundle as *Tsi yee* called it—to the four directions to give thanks. I put the bundle on, resting at my breast, close to my heart. It warmed me.

Again, I jammed my foot into the shoe then grabbed the towel, shoved it in my messenger bag, placed the bag on the roller case, and headed up the bank to Cora and Denny. Hurrying up the muddy bank, my foot slid out of my untied shoe. I pressed hard with my toes, trying to keep the shoe on and my footing on the slick bank. Instead, I did a slow-motion split, with one foot sliding down the creek bank, still in a flopping shoe, and the other foot solidly planted at the top of the bank. Finally, I sacrificed a sock to save my clean jeans. I pulled my foot loose from the sliding shoe and planted my stocking toes firmly into the side of the bank then bent down and pulled my shoe from the mud. It left a distinct elongated waffle-style footprint.

With no place to sit without getting my jeans dirty, I carried the shoe, reclaimed the cases, and hopped-walked on the path back to the fire. Denny and I had to go. Anna needed to see this document. Prove the truth of her story. Get the fracking stopped.

Chapter Twenty-Seven

The bags fought me the whole way down the path toward Aunt Cora's house. Wheels jammed, refused to roll on the mud, then the gravel. The messenger bag kept jumping off its perch on the roller case and the towel flapped wildly.

With one shoe on, the other in hand, and dragging a wobbly roller case with my lime-green messenger bag flopping off the side, I burst from the path to face Aunt Cora and Denny sitting at the fire. "We've got to go!" They both seemed to freeze, staring at the crazed-looking me.

Then Denny jumped to his feet. "You figured it out! You know who killed Gerald?"

For a moment I was lost, I'd forgotten, again. I'd been so excited about the document, all else had slipped my mind. I let out a slow, "No."

Denny dropped back onto the stump he used as a chair, deflated.

"But I think I've got *the* paper." I let go of my case handle to hold up my muddy shoe. The roller case with my messenger bag resting on top toppled over. I looked at the shoe. It wasn't the document.

Aunt Cora snickered.

Denny pushed his dark hair out of his face. "You were in the sweat too long. We wanted a killer, not a piece of paper." He turned to Cora. "I think her mind is slipping."

Aunt Cora quipped, "That's good. The best thoughts are fluid."

Denny cocked his head to think on it.

I searched my pockets. No paper. "Just wait, I have it here." I patted myself down, listened for the crackle only a sheet of paper makes. Nothing.

Denny watched me do a self-body search. "So, where's this proof?"

Panic built. I took a breath, pushed it out. I thought back to having the document in hand.

As if in the distance, I heard Aunt Cora say, "Good, she's thinking."

Then I remembered.

My great-aunt exclaimed, "And now she sees clearly."

"I put it in my messenger bag, because my shoe came off and it was handy to shove everything in the center pocket." I looked at the shoe still in my hand and tossed it toward a nearby stump.

Denny was running out of patience. "So where is this paper—now?"

I turned back to my fallen bags. Around the baggage heap, papers and loose items laid strewn about, spilled from the open messenger bag. I scanned the surrounding ground and spotted the document, grabbed it and uncrumpled the paper to confirm. It was the right document. I sent a silent *ah ho* skyward, turned back to Denny and walked toward him with a wet smacking sound. My muddy sock slapped the ground with each step. I ignored his taunting expression and handed the crumpled document to him. I slap-walked back to my cases, gathered my belongings, and rolled them to a nearby stump. Sitting, I pulled the dirty sock off then used the upper part of the sock to clean my foot before retrieving a clean one from my roller case.

Neither Denny or Aunt Cora spoke. Denny held the crumpled paper, his eyes moving from line to line. I reached for my shoe, slid my foot in, and tied it securely before Denny finished and handed the document to Aunt Cora. He faced me and questions tumbled out, "How—where did you get it?" Denny looked hopeful. "Is this really *it*?"

I nodded. "When I followed Wyatt out of his office, this blew out and . . . I guess, automatically, I stuck that paper in my pocket and forgot about it. It was transferred into my clean jeans with all my other stuff."

Denny took the document from Cora. He bounced on his toes. "If I'm reading this right, Wyatt leased those twenty acres in his own name. Mud, the fracking setup near Jimmy Creek is at that location." Vibrating, he announced, "This is it!" Denny beamed, looking at the sheet and back to me. "Let's go to Anna's house!"

The paper shook in his hand. I reached over to pull it loose. "I'm putting this in a safe place."

Denny shot out a worried, "Where? We can't lose it now."

I returned to the cases and pulled my messenger bag to me, unzipped an inner pocket and slid the folded document in, zipped the pocket, and secured its center section. The messenger bag was sealed tight. My eyes went to Denny. "Okay?" He gave a slight nod. I slung the bag over my shoulder and patted it against my side. "Auntie, sorry to sweat and run, but—"

"Yes, yes, I know, the quest continues. Remember, you have the answers within you. Just believe in yourself and let them out." She chuckled as she reached up to kiss my cheek.

Denny bent and gave her a quick hug. "I'll be back soon, Aunt." He grabbed the handle of my roller case and carried it to his truck. Denny swung the bag into the truck's bed, latched and secured it beneath the tarp. I placed the messenger bag behind my seat, tucked out of sight.

I buckled up before turning to Denny. "Anna is going to be so happy to see us."

Denny bit his lip. "If we can get her to open the door."

I settled into the seat as Denny drove down the road back toward Anna's house. "Oh, she'll open."

"What makes you so sure?" Denny's voice sounded hopeful.

I reached to squeeze his arm. "We'll lead with, '*We've got the document.*'" I let a laugh out. It felt good. This paper was the solution to illegal fracking. I felt it.

Then Denny asked, "So, who killed Gerald?"

In an instant, the glow was gone; I realized that I had forgotten again, just for the moment. The murder never really left my thoughts, but at times Gerald's death got pushed from the forefront of my mind. When the memory returned, it hit hard.

Denny sensed the change. "You were so happy, I just thought. . . ." He dropped it there.

"I got carried away . . . and forgot." I admitted, then tried to explain, "I just got so thrilled about the fracking document."

Denny tried to make me feel better. "Don't worry, you're right, you should be happy." He glanced at me, then back to the road. "The answer to the murder is on Indian time."

I couldn't help it. I laughed. "*Indian time*. You know, most think that just means always late—Indians are never on time."

Denny explained, "Naw, Grandpa says when it happens, it's meant to be. That's Indian time—when it happens, that's the right time. You'll figure out who the killer is at the right time." He flashed a smile at me.

I tried to recapture some of the glee of discovering the paper Anna sought, but Denny's expectations of having all the answers made the murder the only thing on my mind.

There was more traffic on the roads now. Farmers out tending fields, ranchers caring for cattle, kids getting early morning chores done, and small animals that skittered and slithered.

Denny turned into the driveway at Anna's house, parked behind the empty carport. Anna's SUV was gone.

He glanced at the clock on his dash. "Way too early for Anna to be at the Complex."

"Maybe she's here and someone in the family has her car. Let's knock."

Denny opened his door and moved toward the steps leading to Anna's side door. I followed. He went directly to the door and knocked, and I went to the window and peeked in. The table was clear of all papers. The small dining room held no sign of the mounds of copies Anna had spread everywhere earlier. "Looks like Anna's gone. And she took all the papers with her."

Denny came over to look through the window. "Man, she cleaned that mess up fast. I wonder what's she going to do with all her research."

I turned from the window, nudged Denny. "Bet I know where she is."

He moved quickly toward his truck. "No bet, 'cause I think you're right. Anna's gone to the fracking office to see if there is any evidence there."

I followed Denny, getting into the truck.

Denny turned to me, realization dawning on his face. "She doesn't know about the rattlesnakes! If she goes in snooping and opens the wrong drawer—" His face looked stricken. "We've got to get over there. Now!"

Chapter Twenty-Eight

Denny drove at a fast clip, his eyes intent on the road. "Why didn't we tell Anna there was a rattler in the desk drawer? Why did I leave it there!" He pounded the steering wheel.

"Denny, we didn't know she would go to the fracking office." I reached to touch his arm. "We can't be sure Anna's there."

"We know."

He was right, I could feel it. Anna was intent on stopping illegal fracking, and that meant getting evidence on the person at the top.

Denny tossed his phone to me. "Hit one, it goes directly to Becca's number. Tell her to call Anna." He watched me juggle the phone before hearing the ring. Becca's voicemail picked up on the fourth ring. "Hey just text. I don't check voicemail very often."

I texted. Nothing came back.

Denny stole glances my way, finally I shook my head. "She's not responding." The truck sped up.

I knew Denny was envisioning the worst scenarios, so I tried to distract him. "You know, this document proves Anna didn't kill Gerald."

"I never thought she did." He remained focused on the road. He was over the speed limit, moving as quickly as he could to get to Anna.

I nodded. "It's good to have proof Anna wasn't involved with Gerald's death. It also means she wasn't Gerald's partner trying to steal the peace medal. Anna was too busy tracking down fracking evidence."

This made him turn to me with a start of a smile. "I knew she was a guardian, like you, Mud."

"Thanks, Denny. I hope to live up to that." The words came out without thought. It was the truth; I realized that to be true to myself included sharing and saving our traditional stories . . . somehow. I pushed the thought away. Now was not the time.

My thoughts returned to hours earlier at the Complex. "If Anna was busy copying files, that means there was a second person sneaking around." Denny listened but didn't speak. I went on, "I think the second person killed Gerald—probably his partner. They planned to steal the Jefferson Peace Medal together, the plan failed, they had a falling out, and Gerald died."

"Makes sense. Who did it?"

I went on, thinking out loud, "Gerald always intended to steal the peace medal. He had access to it in the museum." I looked to Denny to remind him. "Before last night, everyone trusted Gerald. Anna said he had the alarm access code. For him, it would have been easy to copy a key. Security was pretty lax before the theft." I paused to gather my thoughts. "Gerald's partner didn't think the killing through . . . it had to be an impulse kill." Once voiced, I knew I was right.

"How do you know that?"

"The killer probably had Gerald's key to get in, but not the code to get the peace medal. The killer had to know it was the last night before the alarm code and locks get changed." I glanced out the window as thoughts formed. "Gerald had the code to get the peace medal, but the killer killed him before getting that info." We passed alfalfa fields with stems sporting new buds. First cutting was approaching. I finished my thought, "They must have had an argument and the killer lost control."

"That points to Buck. He's the only one big enough to take Gerald out in a face-to-face fight. He's got the reach to hit Gerald on the temple." Denny sounded hopeful, waited to hear confirmation.

I couldn't give it. "Remember Buck was with the Tribal Police from nine o'clock to ten. Then they let him go way over at the Pigpen." I shook my head. "Just not enough time for Buck to kill and leave a body in the maintenance office for Georgie to stumble upon."

Denny looked to me. "Seems everyone we've talked to is cleared of the murder."

I raked my fingers through my tangled curls. "Someone . . . something we're missing, I'm missing!" I knew something, but what?

"Aunt Cora says you know the solution, just gotta see it clearly."

I had no response; I was hoping Aunt Cora was right too. But sure couldn't see it at the moment.

I shifted topics, back to fracking. "We can't go marching into the office. If Anna's sneaking around, we don't want to mess her up, again." I was thinking of Georgie's scream disrupting Anna's search for evidence at the Complex.

Denny set his jaw. "I plan on driving right up to the office trailer and going in."

I tried again. "Maybe we should park a bit away and walk in. See what's going on first. We can sneak up on the frackers. The element of surprise will give us an edge."

Denny didn't look happy with my suggestion. "There's no time to sneak in and look around. If Anna's searching the office, she's going to have a rude surprise opening that drawer with an angry rattlesnake." Through clenched jaws, he added, "Mud, I gotta get to the office and stop her."

"But you don't want to expose her, Denny." I felt torn; he had a point. Not with much hope behind it, I offered, "Maybe no one's there. Gene, Wayne, and the snakes might be gone. Those two said they were leaving. Planting rattlesnakes in the office was the breaking point for them."

Denny shook his head. "Didn't believe it when Gene said it, don't now. That man's going to get his money before leaving. Gene has a plan for his future and needs money to make it happen. The snakes just made him wary and mad." Denny let out a short chuckle. "Gene's like a riled-up rattlesnake waiting for the right moment to strike."

I hated the visual, but I could see that characteristic in the smaller man. Gene was driven by greed and vengeance, but his partner wasn't. "Not sure Wayne would stay. He didn't want to be in the office even after we had the rattlesnakes captured." I had to smile a bit, thinking of the large man cowering on the desktop.

Denny kept his eyes on the road and said, "Wayne will do whatever Gene tells him to do. That's the type of guy Wayne is. Needs approval. Wayne will want to get out, but can't, he won't go against Gene—his alpha."

Denny was approaching the turn-off to the fracking office too fast. I reached across to squeeze his arm. He knew and eased on the gas; the truck slowed to turn onto the gutted acres leading to the fracking office. The truck bucked up and forward, leaving the highway for the rutted road. I bounced, grabbed the side of my seat, and held tight.

Morning light exposed the true ugliness of fracking. The road was cut with deep ruts, obvious signs of heavy loads being carried in and out. There were no crops, no life growing on the land. Denny's truck dropped and climbed, crossing the sunbaked field of red dirt ruts. My head hit the metal top of the truck and my teeth clanked together on every downward drop. My seatbelt worked overtime, squeaking in protest. Denny was pushing the truck to go as fast as possible on the uneven road.

The inactive pumps came into view first. Six giants frozen in place, each in a different pose. As I examined them, a metallic flash caught my eye. "There's Anna's SUV tucked behind that tank truck by the last pump." I pointed through the windshield.

Denny's truck bucked on. "Anna's going to be in the trailer." His gaze stayed on the office in the distance. "And that's where the rattler is."

"Let's at least look around then walk over to the office, not have the truck engine announce our arrival. Just in case Gene and Wayne are in the trailer." Thanks to yesterday's thunderstorm, the ground was too damp for the truck to provide a telltale dust trail.

"Those frackers," Denny hissed in a menacing tone, but he kept going toward the office.

I unbuckled. "Denny, let me out. I'll walk to the trailer from here. I'm looking around before charging into the office. We might find Anna or something important out here." My words came out in a rush.

"Fine, you do that."

His abrupt stop threw me forward. I scrambled to get my feet under me and jumped out the door. Before I touched the ground, the truck tires spit red dirt as Denny took off to the fracking office.

The rutted ground proved to be as hard to walk on as it was to drive across. The churned ground kept me slightly off balance; my feet kept rolling on unyielding dirt clods, forcing me to go slower than I wanted. As I approached, I eyed Anna's SUV. Although it couldn't have been left more than an hour earlier, it had an air of abandonment. A chill shook me—I was suddenly afraid to look inside the car. There were too many dead bodies showing up lately, and I really did not want Anna to be another one.

Straightening, I stumbled forward to peer through the driver's window. Nobody, and better yet, no body was inside. I stepped back, let my breath out with relief. After a moment, I moved forward to look through the passenger windows. The back seat was empty. I stepped away, thought about it, and moved to the back of the SUV. I hesitated again before forcing myself to the tailgate window.

I rubbed dust off the window, but it was tinted too dark for me to see into the back cargo area clearly. Without much hope, I pulled on the hatch's release. To my surprise the tailgate slowly rose, exposing a cargo area empty except for Anna's three-cell Maglite. I lifted the heavy flashlight and clicked it on then off again. My mind drifted to it rolling from Anna's satchel last night before she used it while sneaking into the Complex. I tucked the metal flashlight in a net bag at the hatch opening, then reached to lower the tailgate, but stopped and stared into the interior. The SUV was empty—that was wrong. Where were all the papers Anna had at her house?

On impulse, I bent low, eye level with the baggage area's carpeting. There were drag marks, as if a couple of boxes had been removed from the back. Only then did I see the tire tracks in the broken ruts behind the SUV. I bent, fingered the hard dirt. A truck or another SUV had backed rear to rear with Anna's SUV. I followed the line of the tire track from Anna's SUV toward the backside of the distant trailer office, to Gene's fancy new truck parked under the only living tree for acres. Wayne and Gene were still in the office.

My mind shot to Denny. Had he checked for the truck first? I knew the answer—he would not have taken the time to see Gene's truck behind the office. I had to admit that I'd been so focused on Anna's SUV, I'd forgotten to look for the shiny new truck until now. I pulled the SUV tailgate down. I needed to get to the office, check on Denny. As I thought it, I heard Denny shout, "What the—" and nothing more. The sudden silence rang out across the rutted field.

The abrupt end to his shout set me in motion. I sprinted toward the office. As fast as I could, up and down, breaking through hardened rut edges, tripping, getting up and running again until an unyielding edge brought me down, sprawled across the ground.

It took a moment to regain my breath and a moment longer to capture my panic-stricken mind. I stayed on the ground, hoping that Gene and Wayne hadn't seen my headlong rush toward the office. There were no movements coming from the office, no sound from Denny.

I fought the impulse to resume my run to the trailer office. Grandpa had told us that sudden moves caught the eye, while slow and steady disappeared into the background. I forced myself to crawl, slow and steady, to the back of the office. Still no movement from anyone inside the office. Maybe they hadn't seen me. Standing, I edged around to the front of the office under the window Denny and I had peeked through the night before. There were no sounds from inside the office.

On the ground, I spotted Denny's discarded branch from the night before, the one he used to camouflage the white of his eyes peering through the window. I reached for it. I needed to see what was happening inside the office.

Like Denny had, I used the branch to cover my face as I peeked into the window. I didn't need it, though; Gene and

Wayne had their backs to me. Wayne had a struggling Denny pinned to the front desk—rather, Wayne's bulk held Denny down across the desktop. Gene stood at the other desk across the office. He said something I couldn't hear but it caught Denny's attention. Then Gene lifted his arm to reveal a four-foot length of pipe. He pointed it toward Anna bound to the desk chair across from Gene. Denny went slack.

Gene laughed and tossed a coil of rope toward Wayne. I imagined him telling Denny, "Resist and Anna gets a beating." Or worse.

I needed to do something before Denny was tied up. But what? My mind stalled. I stared at the scene inside. Gene was ordering Wayne to get the rope, threatening Denny with the pipe. I needed the element of surprise—now.

Anna pushed against her bindings and shouted at Gene as he walked slowly toward Denny, tapping his hand with the pipe and smiling. I couldn't make out the words, but the intent was obvious.

Still, nothing came to mind.

Wayne got a loop on one of Denny's wrists. Anna pushed against her ropes, said something that was ignored.

Bursting in with my branch was all that came to mind. Perhaps that would be enough of a surprise. Had to be, it was all I had. I took a last look noting everyone's positions, planning how—

Hair raised on the back of my neck.

A sinister voice from behind hissed, "See anything interesting?"

Unmistakable hard metal rounds poked into my back.

Like Denny, I was caught.

Chapter Twenty-Nine

The double barrel shotgun pushed hard into my back, jerking me forward onto the trailer wall. "Hey—"

My protest was cut off by an abrupt, "Hands up."

As I stood, I turned slowly. He had his politician grin on high voltage. Only last night, just hours ago, I had placed the Jefferson Peace Medal into his hands to keep safe for the Kiowa people, he had been part of the cleansing of the medal to return the artifact to its home. Now Wyatt Walker, the Tribe's chairman, sported a wicked grin at the other end of a long black shotgun barrel pointed at me.

"You're trespassing." The barrels were aimed at my chest. I tried not to think what the shotgun blast would do to me if Wyatt pulled the trigger. I forced myself to look away from the dark muzzle.

Wyatt had dressed well for the new day. His cowboy boots were polished to a high gleam, looking like they never got dirty. Instead of jeans, he wore expensive cotton slacks with a pink button-down shirt. Wyatt's long sleeves were rolled up, as if he had work to do.

My eyes moved to his face. Wyatt's eyes were hard. I tried anyway. "I didn't mean any harm." Mustering a smile, I eased my hands down as I tried to explain. "Just looking for a friend. We wanted to see if she was making inquiries at the office."

Wyatt used the shotgun barrel to poke at my shoulder. "Yeah, I know what kind of inquiries you Sawpoles been making." He sneered, "Put your hands up." With the demand came another double-barreled shoulder jab. His index finger rested on the trigger guard.

I raised my hands. "You don't need to point that at me. I've done nothing wrong."

Wyatt stepped forward, leading with the shotgun pushing the muzzle into me, knocking me back against the trailer wall. He snarled as he asked, "Peeking through windows okay where you come from?"

Forcing me to the wall set off a spark of anger. It wasn't a smart move, but I stepped forward, pushed the gun away. "I thought I heard a scream. I needed to look at what was going on inside." I swallowed hard.

Wyatt leveled the shotgun at my head. "You're so interested in what's happening inside, let's go look." Using the shotgun, he gestured me to the office door. I didn't like him directly behind me with the shotgun; I liked less the double barrel prod he used to push me through the door. I staggered across the threshold, received another shove, and ended sprawled on the grimy floor. Wyatt followed me in and took two steps to wind up before delivering a swift kick to my midsection. I gasped, sucked in air heavy with dirty oil stench. The stink made my stomach turn. On all fours, I slowly breathed, tried to ignore the sharp pain that came with every breath.

Carefully, I shifted to a sitting position. I kept my eyes down, but looked everywhere at once—figuring distances and searching for weapons—everything, anything could be a weapon. Even the bagged rattlesnakes—especially the angry rattlers. My eyes scanned the room. The covered buckets with the snakes were nowhere in sight. The office was a junkyard of oversized nuts, bolts, and varying lengths of stacked pipes. Good weapons, but none easy to get, unless . . .

Gene had frozen at my entrance. He shot a glare at me and turned to Denny still being held by Wayne. "You said Mud wasn't with you!" Gene snarled out the accusation as he aimed a kick at the restrained Denny. Gene's pointy-toed cowboy boot connected, leaving Denny slumped across Wayne's desk.

Anna, tied to the chair by Gene's desk, screamed, "No!" Her chair legs banged on the floor as she struggled against her bonds. Gene readied another kick.

Wayne looked conflicted. "Gene, they saved us from the rattlers. This don't seem right." He still held one end of a rope. The other was looped around Denny's wrist.

Wyatt's voice rose above the cacophony of sounds. "Stop it. Now!" He marched to the center of the room in the sudden silence. "Did you get the document?" He aimed the question at Gene.

Dropping his cocked foot, Gene muttered, "Haven't had time."

Wyatt didn't look happy. "Sounds like an excuse. How much time does it take to get the info I want out of an old lady?"

"She won't talk," Wayne announced. Gene shot him a look that clearly shouted, *Shut up!*

"Won't talk. You boys willin' to settle for *won't talk*?" He walked to Anna, pulled her head back by her braid. "There's ways to get people to talk. Not always pleasant, but they get results." Wyatt jerked her head even farther back until tears of pain and frustration welled in Anna's eyes. She spit at him. He slapped her hard across the mouth. Blood trickled from one corner. She slumped back in the chair.

Denny pushed against Wayne, calling out. "Anna!"

Gene laughed and slapped Denny.

Wayne protested, "Mud and Denny saved us from those rattlesnakes." He shivered at the thought. "This just ain't right." Wayne held Denny back but released the forgotten rope.

Wyatt looked at Wayne. "Told you, those snakes were probably put here by locals." He rubbed his chin, thinking. "Wouldn't be surprised if it was James Sawpole. You said he's been causing trouble for you boys." Acting as if the thought had just occurred, Wyatt claimed, "Maybe Denny and Mud left those rattlers for you." Wyatt walked back toward me as he talked. "Then they acted the hero saving you from their rattlesnakes." Wyatt didn't realize it, but he signaled his intent. I saw the kick coming and went with it, exaggerating a roll closer to Denny and stacked pipes.

Denny lurched forward, pushing Wayne's bulk to the side. "Mu—"

Using a length of pipe, Gene shoved Denny back to Wayne.

Anna cried, "Don't hurt them! They've done nothing and know less."

Wyatt laughed. "Now we're getting somewhere."

Denny, straining against Wayne's bulk, spit out, "You believe a rattlesnake randomly crawled into your desk drawer, Gene? One you were sure to open." Denny looked pointedly at Gene.

Gene stared back. "We've worked it all out." His voice was tight.

Wayne added, "Yep, we're getting double because of the trouble you locals caused." He grinned as he repeated, "Double for trouble." When no one joined, Wayne dropped the smile.

Anna looked to Gene. "If Wyatt put rattlesnakes in here, he meant for you to get bit. Don't believe Wyatt Walker. He lies." She hissed the last at Wyatt.

I eased closer to the pile of pipes, a four-foot length in sight. A sharp jab from my injured ribs made me wince, reminded me to be careful.

Wyatt walked to where Anna was tied in the chair and slapped her. A casual, sharp backhand. "I only want to hear one thing from you."

Anna's head whipped backward with the sudden slap. She shook her head as if clearing it, set her jaw, and glared hate at Wyatt.

He looked her over then turned to consider me and smiled. "Any more outbursts and our Kiowa storyteller-wannabe gets it." The double barrels pointed directly at me, again. Every hair stood on end, but I had to act. I visibly cowered, as if moving away from the shotgun, but I slowly slid closer to the pipe stack and the pipe I wanted.

Wyatt grinned; he liked my apparent fear. He kept both barrels locked on me while he turned his head to address Anna. "I would much prefer to blow you apart, you nosy old bitch, but I need information." He swung the shotgun toward Denny before returning it to my middle. "These two are expendable. Intruders that snuck in to plant rattlesnakes on a legal fracking operation they wanted stopped. A shame they were shot and killed."

Denny started to voice a protest but was stopped by a slap from Gene. Wayne moved between the two men but said nothing. I shifted closer to the pipe. Tried to catch Denny's eye.

Wyatt's grin showed wolf-like teeth. "Up to you, Anna, if either of them lives. I plan on walking this one out first." He gave me a casual glance before continuing, "Blow her apart just outside that window there. You'll have a good view. Afterward, I'll just use one of the front loaders to cover the mess."

This time I didn't pretend to shiver in fear. Wyatt's cold voice sent a chill through me. He meant every word.

Anna's eyes opened wide, but she didn't say anything. I think she was scared speechless.

This amused Wyatt. "If you're still not talking, I'll blow the other Sawpole apart. Damn family, the only clog in my operations. Wouldn't mind you holding out, Anna. After I blow Denny in half, I'll get his grandpa." Wyatt's eyes got dreamy. "Yep, really do want to use both barrels on James." Like a switch, his eyes clicked back to cold. "Me and Strider would have had another year if James hadn't put you on to me."

Anna turned white. Her voice trembled. "I don't have anything on you. Just suspicions."

"You think I'm playing here, Anna? Huh? Think I wouldn't hear about you asking around about my business dealings?" Wyatt took three quick steps and gave me an unexpected kick, which sent me flying into the stacked pipes. Before I could think, before I could grab a weapon, Wyatt dragged me by the hair toward the front door. "Headed out with her, Anna. Got anything to say?"

Denny bucked, nearly dislodged the large Wayne. "*No!* Not Mud."

This amused Wyatt. He let my hair go but aimed the shotgun down at my face. "Anna, you know what I want."

Anna screamed at Wyatt, "You took everything I have! I don't have the lease document."

Wyatt's lips tightened, turned into thin strips as he moved back to Anna to deliver another slap. "That was all copies of nothing. Those documents can be easily explained. You know what I want.

My one little misstep before I understood the Kiowa leasing system." Wyatt took a deep breath before demanding, "Where is it?"

Wayne, holding Denny back, muttered, "I'm not liking this."

"Shut up, Wayne! The boss knows what he's doing." Gene relaxed his hold on Denny as he shouted at Wayne.

Denny shifted from under Wayne's arms and lunged toward Wyatt. Both Gene and Wayne wrestled him back to the desktop. Wyatt turned from Anna to point both barrels at Denny. Anna screamed, "*No!*"

Denny stopped resisting and glared at Wyatt coming toward him.

Wyatt poked Denny with the shotgun. "Ah, she cares for this one." His face lit up. "Boys, we got us a cougar. That it, Anna? Got something going with the young buck here."

Anna pleaded, "Wyatt, I don't have your paper. Please let us go."

"The original document," Wyatt looked over his shoulder to Anna, "the only document that ties me to illegal fracking and leases with Strider Oil is gone. You copied all my papers. Stands to reason, you've got the one I want." Shotgun still pointed at Denny, Wyatt said, "I prefer killing the Storyteller first. Just bugs me having a curly-headed Kiowa in charge of our stories." He gave an exaggerated shiver. "She's even got a feather in her hair."

Denny staring at the shotgun, protested, "Mud's more Kiowa than you will ever be. She knows our stories—feels them." He spat out, "You're a fort Indian, selling out your own people for money."

A furious Wyatt used the shotgun to club Denny, knocking him to the ground. Gene and Wayne scurried out of the way.

Wyatt, towering over Denny, shouted, "We may have the same amount of Kiowa blood, but my blend shows I'm all Indian.

I've done a lot of good for the Tribe. Got a lot of new businesses in development—"

"All positioned for you to skim from the top," Anna broke in. "I've been looking at your records—you've been getting richer with every deal made *for the Tribe*."

Wyatt shook his head and took a deep breath before replying to Anna, "Like you said, you've got nothing on me."

She answered, "It all paints a picture."

Wyatt didn't take the bait. "That could easily point to anyone else. You, even. There's nothing on me but the one document. A mistake I plan on fixing today." He turned his attention back to Denny, grabbed the rope that dangled from Denny's wrist, and jerked him to his feet. "I'm tired of the stalling—now or never, Anna." He moved to the office door with Denny being dragged behind. "Don't bother me none if this one gets blown apart first."

I screamed, "Don't hurt Denny. Let us go and I'll tell you where the paper is."

Wyatt stopped dragging Denny, and cocked his head toward me. "Why would you know where the lease doc is?"

I stood, blocked his exit. "Last night, I picked it up off your office floor."

He eyed me. "Hand it over." The shotgun rested at his side.

I took a breath and demanded, "You let us go and I'll give it to you."

Wyatt stated, "I will," with eyes that said otherwise. "Where is it?" His shotgun swung toward me.

I steadied myself. "We'll have to go outside for it."

Denny pleaded, "Mud, don't go with Wyatt, *anywhere*."

Gene came from behind, grabbed Denny's arms. "Got him, boss." But Denny shook a shoulder free. Gene turned to Wayne. "Grab his other arm. Now!" Wayne stood staring, not moving toward Denny until Wyatt's shotgun shifted from my midsection toward Wayne. Watching the shotgun move his way, Wayne went to Denny and wrestled him back to the desk.

I looked and sounded defeated as my hands flew in a silent message to Denny. Aloud, I said, "It's over, Denny. Wyatt is in control." I hoped Denny saw my hand signals, knew to doubt my words. My head dropped. "It's just a piece of paper, not worth our lives. Wyatt is going to let us go after I give it to him." I turned to face Wyatt. "You will, won't you?"

"He won't!" spat Anna. Her lip still dripped blood.

Wyatt smiled at Anna. "I'm trying to play nice here. Don't make me regret it." In a sudden move, he grabbed my arm. Twisted it and pulled me close. "Where is the lease document?" His breath smelled of stale coffee.

I tried to pull away. "I have to show you. It's stashed outside."

Wyatt tightened his grip; his eyes had a deadly spark in them. He hissed, "You better not be lying." And threw me toward the door.

Wyatt turned to look at the others in the room. His shotgun stayed at his side; a finger tapped the trigger guard as he thought. "Nobody moves until I get back." Remembering, he quickly added, "Then we'll let y'all go." A sly smile crossed his face.

Looking at Gene, Wyatt told him, "You watch these two. I'll take this one, get the paper, then we can wrap everything up." Something unsaid seemed to pass between the two. Gene nodded in agreement.

I looked to Denny, signaled my intent. Our eyes locked. I hoped it wasn't the last I would see of my cousin.

Chapter Thirty

The double barrels returned to pushing into my back. Wyatt nudged me out the door. "There's a couple steps here," I warned, "don't let that shotgun go off accidentally."

"Me and my Daisy here, been together a long time. We know each other well." Wyatt stood in the doorway admiring his shotgun. "It will be no accident if she goes off." An evil grin spread across his face.

Looking at him with his cold eyes and wicked grin, I didn't know how anyone elected him chairman of the Kiowa Tribe. Greed emoted from him. I was sure his aura was black.

As I edged off the bottom step, Wyatt shoved me hard with his Daisy. I stumbled, tangled my feet, and fell. My temper flared, I came up quickly, reached for the metal barrels before my mind overrode my raw emotions. I adjusted, reached for the trailer side to steady myself instead. Wyatt had all the advantages; he was above me and armed. I needed to wait for the right time. Surprise was my only weapon.

My steadying ploy didn't fool Wyatt. From above, he kicked me, knocked me to the red dirt. His laughter rang out across the barren land. "I can do this all day, *Koyh maton auh'-K'aut.*" He sauntered down the steps to stand above me. "Case you're not Kiowa enough to know, that means curly-headed Kiowa girl and it's not a compliment." He laughed again.

His words bounced off me as if arrows from a shield—my barrier was up. I refused to look at him, tried to rise, but Wyatt shoved me with his foot, knocking me back to my knees. "You better not be lying about that document."

Through the open door, I heard Denny struggling against Wayne. "Mud! You okay?"

"Yeah, Denny. It's okay." I got to my feet. Clenched my fists and reminded myself: I needed to seem defeated, until there was a possibility, an opening. I controlled my face, cast my eyes down. "We've got to walk to the pumps. The document is in Anna's SUV." I turned to start the trek toward the stalled pumps and Anna's empty SUV.

Wyatt followed, returning Daisy to her favorite spot between my shoulder blades. "You think I'm *mawbane*? My boys emptied Anna's SUV." The barrels prodded me, demanded an answer.

"You searched Anna's boxes. That's not where I put it." I kept walking, following in recent tire tracks. I forgot the plan to be timid and let out, "Obviously, I stashed it where you can't find it." There was too much attitude in the remark. I knew it the moment I said it. A chill came over me, I felt him coming for me. The barrels came across my shoulders like a club knocking me down, across the tracks.

Wyatt grabbed my hair, jerked my head to him. "It better be there."

I got out a choked, "It is." He let loose of my hair and pulled me up.

I stumbled forward, regained my balance, and started to walk slowly but carefully over the ruts. Wyatt followed close behind, I could feel Daisy's barrels again at my back. In a careful voice, I said, "Wyatt, you can't get away with this."

"I have. Strider and me been raking in the money for over a year. Had another year planned before time to move on. You and that grandpa of yours messed that up." The muzzle dug into my back and shoved me hard. I stayed upright, barely.

Wyatt started talking to himself more than to me. "Once I get that lease paper, Anna's got nothing on me. I can turn this mess around, put it all on to her." He chuckled.

I slowed, turned toward him to ask, "What happens to us?"

Wyatt grinned, "Like I said, y'all mind your own business, you can go on your way. If not, you were found trespassing. Unfortunately, Gene's a bit quick on the trigger since those snakes got dropped in on him. That boy don't like snakes at all." Wyatt laughed. "I did hope the rattlers would take care of my Gene and Wayne problem."

"You planted the rattlesnakes!" burst from me without thought.

"Of course. I needed to get rid of those two fools. No one would have known what was happening back here if those boys had followed orders." Realizing what he'd revealed, Wyatt quickly added, "The rattlers were meant to scare them off, not kill them."

The last line sounded like a cover story.

Wyatt's eyes narrowed. "This can all play out nicely for everyone—if you give me the document and keep your mouth shut." The shotgun nudged my middle, urged me onward.

His eyes revealed he would make sure our mouths stayed shut.

I trudged forward to the SUV that I knew didn't have the lease document, but was away from Denny, giving him a chance against Gene and Wayne, and I hoped, me an opening against Wyatt and his Daisy.

Wanting to keep him talking, I asked Wyatt, "What are you going to do with the lease document? Destroy it?"

"No, no. Can't do that. A missing document just brings up questions." Wyatt hesitated as he thought it through. "Given Anna's recent behavior—late nights alone at the Kiowa Complex and working with Gerald, a known artifact thief—maybe I'll swap out the original lease document for a copy. Yeah. A really good copy that incriminates Anna." His voice rose with excitement, "That would take care of a big problem. Set a nice stage."

Wyatt's comments started a cascade of revelations—which I had no time for. I forced myself back to the moment and stuttered, "You are going to let us go, right?" It was easy to let my voice show my fear. I knew Wyatt wasn't going to let any of us go. He wanted no witnesses. Wyatt probably intended to get the lease document, kill and bury me out here where no one would find my body—our bodies. It would be best for Wyatt if we all disappeared. He could blame the illegal fracking on Anna, who he would claim must have run off with the money after killing all witnesses. The scenarios sent a shiver down my sweating back.

We were coming to the SUV way too soon. I wasn't ready. Wyatt hadn't given me an opening, no chance to surprise him and escape. I wasn't quite sure what to do. At the rear of the SUV, I stopped and said, "You're not going to let us go, are you?" The shotgun's butt hit me before I saw the blow coming. I staggered against the SUV's tailgate, leaving finger trails in its dust as I slid to my knees.

Wyatt grabbed me, pulled me up, and threw me against the tailgate. "If you're lying to me, you won't be alive in fifteen minutes." His face came close to mine. "Get the document, now!" His coffee breath had gone sour.

I lifted my hands up as if warding off another blow. "Okay, okay. It's in the back—" I was thrown to the ground. My face pressed into the dirt. "See these truck tracks, see them right here in front of your face." Wyatt shoved my head close to the tracks. I found my voice, barely got out, "Yes. I see it."

He stopped pushing my head down, rocked back on his heels. "Those are Gene's truck tracks. Leads right to the back of Anna's SUV. We emptied everything and, I mean everything out of her vehicle and put it in his truck." He eyed me; Daisy took aim.

"The paper's in there." My chin lifted toward the SUV.

Wyatt stood, pulled me to my feet. "You want to see tomorrow, that lease better be in there. 'Cause I am in no playing mood." He leveled Daisy at me.

I stared down the dark barrels, and remembered there was something in the SUV. A surprise.

Maybe.

Watching me cower, Wyatt laughed. "Don't know why the boys were scared of you and your cousin. You two are pushovers." Wyatt kept both barrels pointed at my head. "Get the paper. Now." His finger moved off the trigger guard.

I had to play it right, get in position for a . . . chance.

I faced the SUV, fumbled with the tailgate's latch before pulling it up. The tailgate rose slowly. I stepped to the side. Wyatt moved forward, peered anxiously into the interior. He turned to me and growled, "Nothing there." His finger moved toward the trigger.

I screamed, "Wait, wait! It's underneath, with the spare!"

Wyatt cocked his head to consider. His finger returned to the trigger guard. "Get it."

I bent forward, struggled with the release for access to the spare. Wyatt pushed the barrels deeper into my back. My fingers fumbled with the cover. It dropped back into place.

Wyatt shoved me to the side. "Let me get it." Daisy wavered.

My hand snaked into the interior. My fingers walked along the side, feeling for hard metal. Finding nothing.

Wyatt pulled the cover open. A triumphant grin spread across his face, his Daisy forgotten for an instant.

My hand made contact. I grasped Anna's metal Maglite.

Wyatt somehow sensed my intent. He turned, bringing the shotgun down toward me. His finger went to the trigger, tensed for action.

I didn't hesitate. I swung with all my might.

Wyatt's eyes focused on me; glee seemed to fill them. His finger squeezed.

My blow landed, driving Wyatt's jaw upward, making a cracking sound. His eyes went flat.

Both barrels exploded.

Chapter Thirty-One

Everything was black, I could hear nothing but a high-pitched ring. It was constant and deafening. My chest hurt. I struggled to breathe, to move. A dead weight laid across me—Wyatt was out cold. Daisy rested beside us.

I shifted, jabs of pain shooting everywhere, but I was able to move Wyatt off me—able to see light and finally breathe. But no time to enjoy it. I rolled Wyatt to the side, staggered to a sitting position, and pulled the empty shotgun to me.

Wyatt hadn't had enough time to bring the barrel down level at me before I coldcocked him with the metal flashlight. Daisy's shot went high. It had been so close. *Too close.* I trembled thinking about it. Knew there wasn't time, I shook it off, for later.

Using the shotgun like a crutch, I pulled myself to a standing position. After all the kicks, hair pulling, and jabs, my body ached everywhere. I pushed the pain away. Denny and Anna were captives. They had to have heard the blast—Wayne or Gene could show up at any moment.

Wyatt's foot twitched. An eyelid fluttered, then settled and remained closed. I placed the shotgun to the side, out of Wyatt's reach, and moved to him. It was good to see he was alive, but I didn't want him awake or on the loose anytime soon. I shook my head, trying to clear the fog and the high-pitched ringing. Both stayed.

After a tug-of-war I nearly lost, I pulled Wyatt's cowboy boots, knee-high socks, and pants off him, leaving him in his tighty-whiteys. I rolled Wyatt to his stomach, pulled his arms to the back, and used a sock to bind his wrists, and with the other I tied his ankles together. Socks were not as good as rope, but it was what I had and with luck would slow him down long enough for our escape.

When the pants came off, a handful of shells rolled out of Wyatt's pockets. He had come prepared. I jammed the twelve-gauge shells into my pocket, keeping two out for Daisy. Every few minutes I looked toward the trailer. They had heard; I knew it. One would come out to check soon.

I was in a rush to get back to Denny and Anna, but I couldn't leave Wyatt yet. It would be best if his body was out of sight, not easily seen by Gene or Wayne and if Wyatt could be secured with something more than his stretchable knee-high socks.

I moved to Wyatt, bent to heft him upward and fell, nearly ending up with Wyatt's dead weight across me again. I couldn't lift him or move him far; he was too heavy . . . I eyed the SUV. But I could arrange him so he would be hard to spot.

I looked toward the office trailer. Didn't see any movement coming from there. It would take just a few minutes to hide Wyatt in plain sight.

With his hands and feet still tied, I stretched Wyatt out face down directly behind the SUV. I rushed back to the driver's seat and crossed my fingers. Luck was with me; the keys were in the ignition. I didn't want to start it, but I wanted to slide the car into neutral. It took a bit of one-legged pushing, but the SUV slowly rolled over Wyatt's unconscious body, covering him, and maybe making it harder for him to get loose when he woke up disoriented under the SUV.

I stashed his boots and pants out of sight on the floorboard, locked the SUV, and shoved the keys into my back pocket. I took a moment to shake the ringing from my head, gather my thoughts, and watch for movement from the direction of the office. Still, no one came to check about the shotgun blast.

The incessant ringing lowered to an annoying buzz. Time to move. Time to surprise Gene and Wayne. I squat-ran across the ruts as fast as I could, back to the office, Daisy at my side.

Ignoring my impulse to burst through the front door with barrels blazing, I edged to the front of the trailer and peeked around the corner at the office door. It was closed. Staying low, I eased to the front window. Before making my move, I looked back toward where I had left Wyatt under Anna's SUV. No sign of him. I peeked through the front window. Inside Denny was pinned under a mound of Wayne and Gene. It took both to keep their hold on the bucking Denny. Gene seemed to be directing Wayne to lay across Denny, giving Gene a chance to grab the rope still attached to Denny's left wrist.

Anna, still tied to a chair, was hop-walking toward Denny. She was closing in on the pile of struggling men.

I'd seen enough. Two steps and I was at the door. I burst through, letting Daisy take the lead. "Off of Denny, now!"

Gene froze, stared at the barrels. He gulped.

Wayne rolled off Denny almost immediately, whining, "I told them I didn't want to do this."

With Wayne's heft off him, Denny easily kicked free of Gene. "Mud! How—you're alive! We thought Wyatt—" He tossed Gene to the floor, put his knee in the small of Gene's back. Using his weight to hold the fracker down, Denny pulled the rope off his own wrist.

Anna leaned back in the chair and let out a heartfelt, "*Daw'kee ah ho*." Her hair stuck out everywhere. Red marks striped her face like warpaint of old. The woman had come through a battle.

Without being told, Wayne laid on his belly with his arms out to the side. He faced the floor. In a muffled voice he said, "Wyatt made us do it. You saw him with that shotgun. I didn't want to hurt y'all, he was making me d—"

His whimpering was cut off by Gene's loud, "Shut up, Wayne!" Now tied up by Denny, Gene nearly quivered with anger. He spat, "You're trespassers! You got no right tying me up in my own office!"

"We have much more reason and right to tie you up after what you did to us," Anna argued back. "You dragged me in here, you with that brute's help tied me to this chair." Still bound to the chair, Anna hopped closer to Gene. "Let me loose. Just let me loose."

Gene flopped to his side to watch the advancing Anna. He wormed back toward Denny. "Don't let her near me."

Denny grinned down at Gene. "Better make nice. Anna's the boss now."

He untied Anna, once free, she stood and pulled Denny into a hug. "I didn't want you and Mud involved. Didn't want you to get hurt; how could I explain that to Becca? And now look, y'all saved me."

Denny froze. "Y—you know."

"Of course." Anna shook her head.

I gave her a one-armed hug, keeping Daisy aimed toward Gene and Wayne. "Denny, use that rope from Anna's chair to tie Wayne up. We don't want any surprises from these two."

Denny moved to Wayne and secured the large man's wrists behind his back. He had Wayne sit up against the wall with his legs straight out in front.

I handed Anna the shotgun. "Wyatt said this shotgun's name is Daisy." I gave the shotgun an admiring pat. "I found that Daisy's a bit touchy."

Gene stopped struggling against his ropes.

Anna took the shotgun. She held it with authority. "I know just how to handle Daisy." She swung it toward Gene. "I'll keep her cocked and ready to go."

Gene's face went white. "Don't leave us with Anna. She wants to kill us."

"Like you and Wyatt planned on doing to us? Huh?" Anna aimed Daisy at the squirming man.

Gene protested, "That was Wyatt! We had to do what he said."

Wayne added, "Yeah, or be dead."

"I don't believe that BS. You two were after easy money." Anna swung Daisy toward Wayne. He cried, "No, no . . . I had to do what they said."

Anna's face showed her disgust.

Denny pulled on Gene's tied hands. "Get up against the wall." Gene wiggled to a sitting position and started butt-hopping toward Wayne.

Anna swung the shotgun toward Gene. "Stop right there. You two boys don't need to be any closer. Keep that distance between you." Both sat still, eyes on the double barrels.

Denny moved to me with a grin across his face, gave me a quick hug, then pushed me away with a shove. *He loved me.*

Smiling, I turned to Anna. "Wyatt is tied up under your car. What are you going to do with the three?"

"Oh, Wyatt is alive. After the shotgun blast, we thought . . . then . . . oh, well." Anna looked disappointed. "Guess I'll have to settle for the police." She kept her eyes on Gene.

Denny exclaimed, "Mud, how did you get away? Wyatt had the shotgun and a twitchy finger."

"Knocked him out with Anna's handy flashlight." As I thought of how close to death I had come, the smile dropped from my face. "He planned on killing me—us." I looked at Anna and Denny. I could feel the trembles coming. I shook them off, pushed them away—still no time.

Anna came to my side, the shotgun down but ready. "To answer your earlier question, I will call the police. Can't get Wyatt on the fracking, but we can charge him for assault, kidnapping, and I'm sure several other charges that will expose his cheating ways."

Gene started to protest, "We're working with the oil company. We did what Wyatt said to do."

Wayne agreed, "Yep. Wyatt made us do things we didn't want to do. Honest."

I ignored Gene and Wayne, turned to Anna. "You can get Wyatt on fracking. We've got the lease document. It's why Denny and I went back to your house."

Denny nodded. "Mud's right. We've got the original in my truck." He looked at the two trussed-up frackers and at Anna with the shotgun. "I'll be right back, my truck's right in front."

I called after him, "Denny, take your truck to Anna's SUV. Bring Wyatt back with you and the lease agreement." I grinned. "I'm sure Wyatt will appreciate seeing it."

In no time, Denny came through the office door pushing a pantless, barefoot Wyatt in first. His hands were still tied with the sock, but the other sock was in Wyatt's mouth rather than binding his feet.

Anna smiled looking at the barefoot and de-pantsed Wyatt. "You were busy, girl!" She pointed the shotgun at Wyatt. "You go sit on the floor by your buddies, but not too close. Any sudden moves—well, Daisy may just accidently go off in your direction."

Wyatt hobbled to the wall, slid down it. He looked relieved to be sitting. His jaws flexed, working on spitting out the wet wad of sock.

Denny offered a folded paper to Anna. She handed him the shotgun in exchange, and unfolded the document. At its opening, her face lit up. "This is it! We've got Wyatt connected to fracking." She waved the paper in the air. "All the other pieces will slide into place showing his trail of corruption."

Wyatt glared. Anna glanced at him and giggled. "You sitting there in your tighty-whiteys—I just can't take you seriously."

Wyatt spat the sock out but refused to speak.

I had more good news for Anna. "I think with a bit more digging, you'll find that Wyatt Walker is Strider Oil."

Denny moved to my side. "That makes perfect sense." He looked to Wyatt. "Walker—Strider, I see what you did there."

Wyatt answered with a glare. Anna shook her head. "One paper that ties it all to you, Wyatt. You're going away for a long time. Only thing you're not guilty of is murder. And that wasn't by lack of trying."

Murder echoed in my mind. There was still time . . . maybe. I took Daisy from Denny and handed the shotgun to Anna. "We've got to go."

Denny looked confused for a moment, then he remembered there was more to do.

Anna pointing Daisy downward, gave me a one-armed hug. "Mud, *saw-thaye kaul-aye thigh-gyah thaye-kope*, come and work together for the good of the people. Don't let Wyatt's bitter words keep you from being the Tribe's Storyteller."

"Anna, Wyatt only spoke aloud what others have whispered. Many don't think I'm Indian enough to be the Tribe Storyteller." I spoke the words automatically, without thought, but they didn't feel right anymore.

Anna shook her head slowly. "That's only a loud few—the people know that James made no mistake choosing his apprentice." Anna locked eyes with me. "I'm a grandparent now. I know how precious our children are. They are our future. If there is even a pinch of Kiowa blood coursing through a child's body, they are Kiowa. We need to teach our grandchildren the Kiowa Way before all is forgotten." She glanced at the three captive men, making sure they were secure before turning to me. "Mud, the Tribe needs you, your knowledge. We need our stories to be shared with our future."

I squeezed Anna's hand. "I am going to help the Kiowa people, I have to; it's in my blood." I looked at Wyatt and returned my gaze to Anna. "My whole life I've been looking for validation of my identity from others, but today I know I don't need it. I am Kiowa. I was born Kiowa, and I will die Kiowa." I smiled. "It is my responsibility to share and pass on our stories because I am a Tribe Storyteller." I took a deep breath and let it out. "Not sure how I'll do it, but something will come." I rubbed my spirit bag, feeling the truth and power of my words.

I went on, "Anna, you've got Denny." I looked to my cousin. "He's ready to help from within the Tribe's government. Together, I know you two can make a difference."

Anna nodded her agreement.

Wyatt snorted. Anna turned Daisy in his direction and narrowed her eyes. "Think I'll call the police. Get them over here to take the scum away."

"Good. Denny and I have to go." I took Denny by the shoulder and turned toward the door. "If we hurry, we can prevent a theft, and . . . possibly another death."

Chapter Thirty-Two

We bounced down the rutted dirt road, back toward the Kiowa Complex. The truck bucked getting onto the highway's blacktop. Not expecting the sudden jarring, my head bumped the side window. The ringing in my ears returned. I shook my head trying to clear the high-pitched ring and my outrageous thoughts. But if I was right—there was time if we hurried. Denny kept the speed at the legal limit, even as I silently pushed him to go faster.

"You were being a bit melodramatic back there." Denny glanced at me then returned his attention to the road. He maintained the posted speed. "Why are we going to the Kiowa Complex? Shouldn't we head for Gerald's art gallery? That's where the body is." Denny cocked his head before adding, "Where it was, anyways. Is it on the move again?"

Denny's question stopped my spinning thoughts. That's something I hadn't considered. "The body's still at the gallery as far as I know." I threw the question back: "Do you think someone moved it . . . again?" I shivered at the thought. "Why did you say that?"

"Mud, what I really want to know is why are we going to the Complex?" He let a beat pass before adding, "The dead man *is* in the other direction—as far as I know."

"We're after the murderer . . . we're stopping a theft, I think." I struggled to gather my scattered thoughts, to try and explain. "Wyatt got me thinking."

Denny nodded. "Imagine he did. Me, I was praying. Didn't see how we were going to get out of that mess. Couldn't believe it when you signaled that you were going to lead Wyatt away. Try to give me a chance to break free." He slapped the steering wheel. "Couldn't do it once Gene got me down. When I came busting into the fracking office, I saw Anna tied to the chair. I went straight across the room to untie her." Denny's jaw clenched as he continued, "And Gene took my legs out from under me with that pipe. Never saw the blow coming in my rush to Anna. She tried to warn me, but . . . I plain didn't listen."

Denny took a moment before going on. "Once down, Wayne's size kept me pinned. After you left with Wyatt, I was working my way free of Wayne when that shot went off." His voice got choked: "I thought you were . . . gone. Gene had to throw himself on the pile to keep me down. I was trying to get to you, Mud." Dark eyes melted into mine.

"I know, Denny. I did what I could to get back to you too. I got lucky." Remembering sent a shiver down my spine. "Wyatt was going to kill us; I saw it in his eyes. If it wasn't for Anna's flashlight—" *Things could have gone so wrong.*

Denny reached across to squeeze my hand. "You were saying that Wyatt got you thinking."

I smiled my thanks to Denny for moving me away from the dark thoughts. "Wyatt said he was going to create a copy of the lease document so it appeared that Anna was at the center of the illegal fracking. He said he could make a really *good* copy. That got me thinking of Brenda and really good copies. Maybe it's all about copies. . . . and the tracks may prove it." Thoughts rushed in; I let them take me away as I muttered, "The All-Seeing Owl tried to show me tracks at the creek, tried to remind me of what I saw earlier. It's in the tracks. Something off, different, but what?" I thought back, trying to see the signs written in dirt. But I couldn't.

I shook my head. "Fracking's been muddying the water. Kept me from *boen own knee,* seeing clearly. I just need to see the tracks and think."

"That was all clear as mud." Denny's frustrated tone got my attention.

My face reddened; I stared out the windshield. "Didn't mean to say that last out loud."

"Well, you did. What does it all mean?"

I didn't answer for a moment. Still thinking. *If I took fracking out of it, things became clearer, but not quite.* I felt Denny waiting. "It means, it all started with the Jefferson Peace Medal and Gerald spreading poison." I nodded to myself as my thoughts started to take form, pieces sliding into place. Could it be—the answer right in front of me the whole time? If I had paid attention to what I had heard and seen as the owl had directed . . .

"Ahem." Denny cleared his throat.

"Denny, I'm not sure, but I think I'm on the right track." I chuckled, and said it again, "Track, tracks . . . and no daisy-print Converses." My chuckle turned to a laugh. "That could be the answer."

My mind wandered back to Wyatt: his lust for money drove him to cheat his Tribe, harm the land, and want to kill—not one, but several people. I had no doubt that killing was in his heart. Yet the crooked man made me see clearer. I found myself rubbing my medicine bag in thought. Making a decision, I dropped the bundle under my shirt and said it again, "It's all about copies and tracks."

Denny slowed as we approached the town's intersection. "Enough talking in riddles. The Complex is just ahead. I don't know where you want me to go or even why we're going to the Complex."

"We need to go to the beginning . . . follow the body."

Denny sighed. "I've 'bout had enough of your cryptic comments, Mud. Where am I going?" We approached the large Compound—it appeared empty, no cars in the front parking lot and no hum of activity. It was too early for the day's business to begin.

Without hesitation, I pointed. "Go to the back of the maintenance hut. I want to see what we can see in the light of the early morning. We'll start at the back of the hut, then go through to the maintenance office and its front door. I've got no doubt the murder took place in the office where Georgie stumbled across the body."

"Now that makes sense. You should have told me; we're going back to the scene of the crime." Denny turned into a side driveway leading to the back of the converted metal Quonset hut. Tribe vehicles dotted the back parking lot. All appeared empty. Denny pulled in alongside a pickup displaying the Kiowa Nation logo.

As we exited the truck and moved toward the hut's back door, I continued, "I'm hoping to confirm the office is the scene of the crime." I said no more, but I wanted to look at the tracks outside the office door leading to the murder scene. They had something to say, I knew it.

"Whoever killed Gerald didn't want the body found in the maintenance office. That means something, doesn't it, Mud?"

The early morning air was the coolest it would be all day, and I stopped to enjoy it. I didn't answer Denny at first. A blackbird screeched as it took flight. It complained to all in earshot as it flew from sight. I watched the bird and thought some more. The bird's flight meant something; the tracks told me something . . . but what? There was the body being moved; that piece didn't fit.

Denny asked his question again, louder: "Moving the body from here to the gallery means something, right?"

I scanned the area by one of the white vans. The complaining bird had come from that direction. Nothing moved, or made a sound. A hot engine ticked in the distance. I answered slowly, "Yes . . . but I don't know what." Before Denny could protest, I added, "The office will have answers, I hope."

I eyed the ground around the parking spots nearby. "Stay off the main path to the back door. Let's look for signs of the body being moved back here before we go inside the hut." I bent low to scan the gravel walkway going toward the back door.

Nearby gravel crunched as Denny joined me. "What are you thinking, Mud?"

I bit my lip, considering. "I think Gerald arranged to meet someone in the maintenance office. It's not too far from the Complex and the museum. As Sky said, you can see the lay of the land from there. Gerald would know when the coast was clear before going to the museum, switching the copy for the real Jefferson Peace Medal, and returning to escape in a white van. Anyone seeing the van would think it's just another Tribe vehicle." I looked at the trucks and vans in the back lot. Thought of Gerald coming into the dark maintenance office. "I'm pretty sure the dead man knew his killer." I shifted, then caught sight of what I knew should be in the gravel. Tracks.

"Why?" Denny's one-word question seemed to come from far away, yet he was squatting next to me.

It took a moment to track what Denny was asking. I rocked back on my heels. "We know Gerald planned to steal the peace medal and we got in the way—kept the theft from happening. I think he intended to swap the real medal with his *exquisite* copy." I tried to imitate Brenda's high society tone.

Denny nodded, let a soft *"Haw"* slip out.

That's all the encouragement I needed. "I got a good look at the real Kiowa Jefferson Peace Medal. I had the original in my hand yesterday. If I hadn't seen it recently, Gerald's fake would have fooled me easily."

"How can you tell them apart? I mean, you're no expert."

There were no sounds on the morning breeze. I enjoyed its cool touch. "You're right, Denny. I'm not an expert and wouldn't have noticed the difference if I hadn't seen the exposed wood in the original medal only hours earlier. The copy is that good with the details, but the wood center edges were blunted, not flaked."

Denny started to respond, but I put my hand up. "Another giveaway was the sulfur smell. The fake medal had a distinct rotten egg smell. When I was using Aunt Cora's internet, I looked it up. Jewelers and forgers use hard-boiled eggs to give metal an aged look. Apparently, if you want that older-than-old look for metal jewelry, put the finished piece in a bag of hard-boiled eggs and leave it in the fridge until it reaches the desired color."

"You are kidding." Denny rolled back and forth on his heels, thinking it through. "That's not a bad plan. The theft would have gone undetected."

"I think that was the intent. Remember, Lewis and Clark had only three large four-inch Jefferson Peace Medals. Just imagine how much a private buyer would pay to own the original three. Many don't care if the treasures have to stay in hiding for a lifetime. It's their *little precious.*" I wrung my hands together, imitating Tolkien's Gollum.

Denny shook his head in obvious disgust.

"I think Gerald pulled the swap successfully with the other two medals." I thought of the framed medals at the gallery with a vacant third spot. I spoke my thoughts aloud, "Those two Jefferson Medals in the gallery are originals—not fakes. I would bet on it." Denny nodded in agreement. I went on, "Gerald met his partner in crime in the maintenance office to get the replica peace medal for the swap. I think Gerald didn't share the alarm code with his partner. He intended to be the one to do the exchange . . ." I stopped and looked at Denny.

"That's where I lose the story. We know something goes wrong—I don't know what. For some reason Gerald's partner killed him."

"That all makes sense."

"Yeah, but why move the body? That doesn't make sense." I shook my head.

Denny's eyes locked on me. "You got someone in mind? Who's the partner?"

"Is that all you heard?"

"Nope, but I'm cutting to the chase. You've got someone in mind. Who?" It was a request, not a question.

"Yeeaahhh," I drew the word out. "But the body moving doesn't work . . . maybe the tracks will make it clear."

"Because an owl told you to look at the tracks."

"Well, yeeaahhh." Again, I drew out the word. Stumbled to explain what I didn't understand . . . yet.

Denny looked thoughtful. "Okay. Some things can't be shared. Aunt Cora said the Kiowa have powerful woman medicine that can't be talked about and I should mind my own business." He smiled at me. "I understand. An owl talked to you." He said it with complete sincerity. "Let's see what this All-Seeing Owl wants you to see clearly."

Denny shifted to stand. I rested my hand on his thigh, stopped his upward motion. "The first track is here." I pointed to the walkway's gravel. There were two parallel tracks that had to be feet dragging as a body was moved to a nearby van or truck. We looked around. It could have been any of the white trucks and vans in the area.

Denny used his phone to take pictures of the tracks, moving around the area to capture different angles. "Guess this proves what we knew. Gerald was killed in the office and the dead man was moved from here."

I considered, muttered, "Probably," and considered some more. I bent low to scan the gravel in the area. Suddenly I jerked my head up to look around. I thought I heard movement. Denny returned to my side. Nothing else moved.

I gave the gravel one more scan to make sure I wasn't missing any of the story the tracks told.

Denny dropped to squat next to me. "The tracks telling you anything? They talking?" He let a grin spread across his face.

I stood, brushed my pant knees off. Realized it did no good; my jeans were dirty again. Wyatt dragging me across the red ruts had made a stained mess of my clothes. Frustrated, I said, "No, Denny, these tracks aren't talking to me."

He chuckled and moved on to the hut's back door. I followed.

At the doorway I came to an abrupt halt and looked sharply around the parking lot. Again, I thought I heard a rustling. Not the crunch of gravel underfoot, but a rustling. Yet there was no one, no movement in sight. The wind carried no sounds of life. That spoke volumes.

Denny waited, holding the door for me. He teased, "You're so jumpy. More now than last night. You afraid the dead man's spirit is hanging around?"

I surprised Denny with my quick reply, "Yes. I think terrible deeds stain the people and land . . . especially a murder. Maybe the dead man's spirit is lingering, wanting to see justice served, or it's trapped." I walked to the door. "Leave the back door open. After we're through in the hut and go to the office, I'll open the front door, give the spirit a chance to flow out with the wind." Suddenly, the hair rose on my neck. I looked everywhere for movement . . . for a spirit . . . I saw nothing, but felt a presence.

"Stop it! You're freaking me out." Denny propped the back door open and announced, "I'm going to find the hammer. It's sure to have hair or blood on it. It will prove the murder happened here." Denny purposely walked into the hut ahead of me. Like warriors of old, he boldly entered an unknown situation first. Kiowa warriors did so to shield their loved ones; they intended to be first in to confront any unseen danger within. Grandpa and his sisters talked about the dismay of the Old Ones when they watched the invading settlers step back to let their most vulnerable walk into unknown situations ahead of them. The settlers said it was what true gentlemen did. The old Kiowas thought it was what cowards did, hiding behind children and women.

I knew Denny walked into the large hut first to protect me against threats from anyone inside—alive or dead.

Chapter Thirty-Three

The old Quonset hut had several clear panels added to its cylindrical metal roof, allowing the morning sun to wash away the gloom and shadows of the night before. Inside, the hut smelled and looked like the active garage and workshop that it was. Oil and gas fumes mixed with other solvent scents. The cavernous hut was divided into various specialties, from auto care to ground blowers. There was a place for everything.

Denny moved to a nearby tool cage with a variety of tools hanging from hooks on its chain-link walls. I continued down a main walkway toward the opening into the maintenance hut's attached office—where the body had been originally. First, I bent low to examine the main walkway, but the packed dirt floor inside the maintenance hut had no story to tell. The ground was too hard to hold a track.

Denny called to me from the tool cage. "There's a few ball-peen hammers here with small round faces. Kinda like the mark on the dead man's temple." He held a small hammer and mimicked a strike to his own temple.

I walked to the tool cage.

"You think one of them coulda done it?" Denny stood back, using the hammer to point at various sizes and styles of hammers and mallets grouped on the tool wall. He watched me stare at the hammer in his hand. I raised an eyebrow at him. Denny looked at the hammer. "This hammer's way too big. I just picked it up for a visual aid." He placed the hammer down on the counter.

I examined the ball-peen hammers, especially the ones with the smallest heads. None looked like the weapon. "These aren't right. It was round but piercing." I pointed to the front of the hammers. "And smaller. It was like a puncture wound to the temple. Had to be bigger than an ice pick . . ." My eyes wandered around the cage. Nothing fit the image I had in mind, the image that fit the mark left by the killing blow.

I stepped out of the tool cage. "I'm going into the office, see if we missed anything there, then I want to look around the office's doorway where we came in last night."

Denny followed. "What are you looking for in the office? We searched it pretty good last night."

"I don't know, but I'll know it if I see it."

The walkway led to the door-size cutout linking the maintenance hut to its office. Making sure I didn't step into the walkway directly, I hugged the side, and got low to skim the surface of the office's wooden floor, looking for tracks from the night before.

The walkway flooring was cleaner than the rest of the office floor. A layer of grime had been swept away. There were no signs of a struggle, body, or even of us from the night before. A broom leaned against the office wall. "Someone swept in here."

Denny went to all fours to look across the floor. "That's strange. Sure does look like someone swept just the area in the office that mattered to us." He got up and dusted off his jeans. "Can't be absolutely sure."

Denny's words droned on in the background as I stared across the swept floor, then I saw proof. "I'm sure someone tampered with the murder scene, and I can prove it. Look at those pink slippers."

Denny bent to see the bright fuzzy slippers tucked in the desk knee well. "Not those again. I know, the slippers are right where Georgie said they would be." He rolled his eyes.

"Yeah, but not where I left them last night. I picked those slippers up and left them on top of the desk. Completely forgot to put them back where they belonged. But someone cleaning up the scene put the slippers in place."

Denny straightened. "Thought we were solving a murder, not adding more puzzles. This is giving me a headache." He pushed dark hair from his face. "Why have pink slippers here anyways?"

An image of Brenda exchanging her heels for sneakers came to mind. "So she could be comfortable." I looked up at Denny. "Someone probably wears heels to work, and these are her easy slip-on, comfortable shoes." I suddenly felt energized. The impossible was coming into focus. "I want to see the tracks coming into the office. I know I saw something yesterday that should stand out . . ." Shuffling noises came from behind us, inside the hut. I glanced toward Denny and signaled. He gave a slight nod.

I walked out the office front door then remembered and propped it open—just in case. I stepped out of the doorway, again to the side of the path, and bent down. The sparsely graveled, damp ground still held tracks from the night before.

I spoke in a loud voice, "There's Georgie's prints coming out of the office on the run. See how it's mostly toe and ends in a blur." I pointed toward another track. "You can tell it's Georgie's print by her shoe logo."

Denny peered closer. "Oh yeah, those are pricey. Gotta be Georgie. No one else has that kind of money to blow on sneakers."

I moved closer to the tracks. "Look, it shows all the traffic coming in and out of the maintenance office after the thunderstorm yesterday. There's a pointy-toed cowboy boot, probably Gerald going into the office." I thought of Gerald in his red snakeskin boots back at the gallery.

"Well, he came in upright," Denny observed.

I shook my head, continued to scan the ground. "I don't see any tracks of Gerald leaving the office."

"He was carried out the back. Those parallel marks were him being dragged out."

Denny's words were probably true, but they made me uncomfortable. I shifted to another section of the walkway, looked closer. "Here's a couple of work boots with really worn soles, but look, there's a new work boot print. Its tread left a deep impression on top of this deep circle."

Denny took pictures of the different prints in the gravel and mud. "What are the tracks telling you, Mud?"

His tone told me that Denny wasn't teasing; he wanted to know what the tracks said. "New Work Boots stepped on a Gerald print here, so New Work Boots came after Gerald went in." Shadows shifted in the office doorway. "I've seen this new work boot print before. . . ."

Denny demanded, "Where?"

Deep circular tracks caught my eye. They weren't as I had remembered. "Denny, see those round markings?" I didn't wait for a response. "I thought they were made from a cane. "Specifically, Eli's cane," I admitted.

"Don't go backward, Mud. We know it wasn't Eli that killed Gerald."

"Oh, I know it wasn't him. Eli's cane marks are much larger and flatter. These tracks are perfect rounds, and they're piercing the damp ground." I leaned back. What were the tracks telling me?

Denny answered my unspoken question. "Maybe it's a lance being stuck in the ground. Like the one Buck took from the gallery. We know that *Koitsenko* lance was used in several battles. It's tasted blood before."

I looked over to Denny standing just outside the door, safely off the tracks. There was a flicker, a shadow shift. This time I was sure there was a movement just inside the open office doorway.

"Give me a minute to think, Denny," I spoke sharply.

"What's with the attitude?" Denny demanded, his eyes watching my talking hands. He signaled confirmation while in a raised voice he announced, "Tired of your bossiness. I don't need this." Denny stomped off to the side of the hut, out of sight.

I called after him, "Fine, Denny Sawpole. I don't need your help. The tracks are telling me what I need to know." I stood, looked at the story as a whole. From the right perspective, it was obvious who had followed after others into the office. Could there be two behind it all?

Slowly, I moved back toward the open door, all the while my eyes on the tracks on the ground. Talking to myself, I announced, "Denny's idea isn't a bad one. Buck did take his family *Koitsenko* sash and lance from the gallery. The lance has an extremely sharp, round point at one end." A dark shape stood motionless just at the inside edge of the doorway.

I needed to take my time. Watch carefully, and listen before acting.

I saw a track that did tell the story. "The piercing hole print is a pair!" I spoke aloud to distract, but it helped me focus. I thought of daisy-print Converses. No Converse sneaker tracks were at the scene. I eased closer to the office doorway.

From a distance, an owl hooted: once, twice, three times quickly. Its point made, I spun suddenly and dove through the open doorway toward the dark shape within. Before I reached it, the shape ran down the office's walkway, through the cutout, and into the cavernous maintenance hut. I followed, always steps behind. The figure aimed for the opened back door, for escape. I gave a spurt of speed; the hooded figure glanced back, saw me gaining. I strained forward, reached for the fleeing figure. It shot ahead through the open back door to the parking lot and into Denny's extended foot. Denny's leg knocked the hooded figure off its feet and to the ground, sprawled out on the parking lot gravel, gasping for breath.

I was on him in an instant, straddling the unresisting figure. "Thanks for the hoots," I said to Denny. "Nice to know where you were."

"Glad it worked." Denny stood over us. "We got the killer." He bent and pulled the hood down to reveal a sputtering Buck.

"You got no right—"

"We got every right, Buck. This time you're caught. Just had to come back to clean up after the murder." Denny sounded disgusted.

"You can't blame Gerald's murder on me." Buck struggled upward. "Get off me!"

I got off Buck. He looked exhausted and lost with his hair hacked short and his once bearded face dotted with fresh shave cuts. As I watched Buck sprawled on the gravel, a missing piece fell into place. "You've been cleaning up after the killing all night."

Denny stood back, giving Buck space to stand. Instead, Buck stared up at me. There was truth in his eyes. "I didn't do it. I heard what you were saying. But I did not kill Gerald with the family warrior lance." He set his freshly shaven jaw. "That would be disrespectful."

Denny pushed, "You took the sash and lance from the gallery. Georgie said you were mad enough to want Gerald dead, and then he's killed by a strike that pierced his temple . . . like one the lance would deliver. Pretty obvious what happened."

"Buck moved the body, but he didn't kill Gerald." I spoke the words softly, but loud enough.

Denny turned a stunned face to me.

Buck looked up at me, held my eyes for a beat, then took a deep breath. "I wanted to kill him. He deserved it. Gerald poisoned the minds of everyone around him. He made me do terrible things—I am ashamed."

Denny looked to Buck. "So, you did kill Gerald?"

In answer, I shook my head.

Buck lowered his eyes, seemed to make a decision, and rolled to his feet. He took another deep breath in and out before looking at me. "It's like you figured, I moved the body. Gerald's death is my fault."

Denny looked frustrated. "Did you or did you not kill Gerald?"

Again, I shook my head. "Let him talk, Denny."

This time Denny took the deep breath. "Okay."

Buck seemed unsteady on his feet. "I did not kill Gerald. But my words led to his death." Buck moved to a nearby Tribal truck, used it for support. "Knew I got Georgie excited over Gerald's promises and money . . . all that money. She wanted the life getting the peace medal for Gerald was going to bring." He looked up at us. "I'm sure Gerald's death was an accident, but I couldn't let the mother of my child go to prison—for a mistake." He pushed off of the truck to plead: "Gerald must have hit his head on a desk corner. He was probably making a move on Georgie. I just know she didn't mean to do it. So, I took the body away to make it seem to have happened at the gallery. Figured, when the body was found cold, it would all point away from Georgie."

Buck's words were a gut punch. My first love was a thief, and probably worse.

Denny's response surprised me. He came to my side and whispered, "Mud, I am so sorry Georgie did kill Gerald. I really didn't want it to be true."

I knew Denny meant it. I turned and pulled him into a hug. We didn't have the truth yet, but I loved that Denny cared about my feelings. I released the slightly uncomfortable Denny and moved closer to Buck. "Start at the beginning and tell us what you saw."

For a moment, a spark of the old Buck flared. I prepared for battle, but the ember flickered and died. There was no sign of the bully of my childhood.

Buck leaned back against the truck. "I told you the truth. Just left out a few things."

Denny moved to the other side of Buck, facing him. "Tell us now."

Buck watched a red ant crawl across the gravel boulders at his feet. It approached the toe of his new work boot. "I knew Gerald was going to make another play for the peace medal. He had a plan in place, but I pulled out. After my grandfather's death . . ." Buck stopped for a moment, gathered himself before continuing, "I knew Gerald was poison and I was done with him. I told Georgie we were out of it, done with Gerald, his thefts, and his money. I'd get a job. Work my way through the rest of college. We'd have money again." Buck stopped there, seemed to have trouble continuing. The ant moved on to easier hills to climb.

I prompted him, "Did you meet Gerald here?"

This brought a short laugh from Buck. "You saw me, I would have killed Gerald if I had found him last night. I let my emotions control me—before." He straightened, pushed back his recently shorn hair. "I'm honoring my grandfather, walking the Kiowa Way this day forward."

Denny said, "*Haw*, that is good. I hope you can stay on the path."

Buck gave a short nod to Denny and whispered, "Me too."

I pulled Buck's attention back to the night before. "You haven't told us what you saw in the maintenance office—did you actually see Gerald get killed?"

"No. But I was walking to the Pigpen before the cop let me go, and I saw Gerald sneak into the office. When I got free of that cop, I headed for the maintenance office. Before I got there, I heard Georgie scream." Buck shook his head. "I came running." He tilted his head toward a nearby spot. "Had the van parked over there. Planned on finding Georgie and gittin' away from here before Gerald stole the peace medal and we got blamed for it. Didn't want no part of it . . . anymore." Buck let out a laugh with no humor in it. "I come in, saw Gerald's body and knew, just knew Georgie done it. She was protecting our family from the poison he spread. I knew it was my fault and I could fix it. So, I did. I took the body and left it at the gallery."

We were getting close to the truth. I asked, "Did you see anyone?"

"Nope, not here." Then Buck broke out in an unexpected grin. "Nearly got caught by that old man, Eli, at the gallery! He came for his family headdress and wasn't leaving without it."

Denny made a sound deep in his throat but didn't speak.

I pushed, "You saw Eli leave the money, and you left it there so the police would think Eli killed Gerald."

Buck leaned forward. "I was saving my family." He folded his arms. "Yeah, Gerald and me, we cheated Kiowa families. I told you, I'm ashamed of what I did for Gerald . . . for money. This time, I was protecting my wife."

"Did you ask Georgie if she did it?"

Buck seemed surprised by my question. "I haven't seen Georgie all night. You know I've been hunting for her." He pushed off the truck. "After I saw y'all earlier, I went back to the gallery. Georgie and Brenda Lee had just left. They had car trouble and had to wait a long time for a tow truck. The tow truck guy got an earful from Brenda Lee for taking so long. He didn't like her much. The guy said the girls argued about it, but were headed to Carnegie." Buck scanned the back parking lot. "Thought I would find Georgie here, getting rid of the evidence. They weren't much ahead of me."

Pieces clicked into place. My mind spun as I listened to Buck and Denny talk. My phone vibrated; I ignored the call. All was coming into focus.

Buck added, "I'd just started cleaning up—"

"Covering up," Denny corrected.

"Sweeping up when I heard y'all," Buck conceded.

"Buck, how long have you been here?" I interrupted.

Both seemed confused by my question, but Buck answered, "Got here before y'all, but had only enough time to straighten the maintenance office up a bit. About ten minutes."

I muttered, "There may be time. She would park away from the Complex and walk in. That would take time."

Denny, still with a questioning look, asked, "Time for what? You think you got time to catch Georgie?"

I grabbed his arm. "If we hurry . . . I think we can catch the killer." I turned and started running. Over my shoulder, I called, "And prevent the theft that caused Gerald's death."

Chapter Thirty-Four

Maybe that was a bit dramatic and cryptic, but I was finally seeing clearly. The All-Seeing Owl from my sweat was right: I had heard and seen everything from the start. I knew who killed Gerald. Now Grandfather Buffalo was kicking me into high gear to protect the Tribe's symbol of first contact with our conquerors. The Jefferson Peace Medal represented the friendship we offered and believed in, until we couldn't. The medal belonged to the Kiowa people, not locked away for a privileged few.

I sprinted from the back parking lot to the Complex. A steady crunch behind me confirmed that Denny followed. I stopped when I reached the Complex, and squatted by the wall, tried to settle my mind. I reached for my spirit bundle as I thought.

Denny arrived and bent at the waist. His head rested slightly above my own. He puffed out, "You think Georgie's here? She's come back for the peace medal?"

In a whisper I said, "I hope Georgie's not here." My stomach twisted. I ignored it. There was no time for emotions.

"Then why are we—" Denny started to stand as he lifted his voice.

"It's not Georgie." I grabbed a handful of his shirt and pulled him down. "Stay quiet and we might catch the thief and killer."

"Not Georgie? I thought—"

"Stop thinking so loud," I hissed.

Denny locked his jaw and lowered to his haunches. He signed; he was listening.

I whispered, "We are going in like an owl: fast and silent. We'll go through the back door and to the museum in front. I will take one direction down the hallway, you the other. That way she won't get past us."

Denny started to speak, then held his comment.

I moved to the Complex's back door, hoped I was right and she had left it unlocked for a fast getaway. Yes. I pulled the door open and slipped in, Denny slid in behind me and quietly closed the door. We moved to the interior hallway; slow and steady, I continued down the right side. I didn't look back; I knew Denny had gone left. We would meet at the front of the building.

The interior hallway was cloaked in gray—its only light source was fluorescent, and no one had flipped them on. Enough early morning light spilled from open doorways to keep the hallway in muted shadows. I wasn't worried about anyone hiding; I was sure the killer would be in the museum. There was a rich buyer waiting for the three original Jefferson Peace Medals.

I rounded the last corner and saw the museum door was open. I crawled in, stayed to the shadows within, and halted when I caught a hint of Poison on the air. Georgie's perfume—she was here. A wave of disappointment washed over me. I had held out hope she was not involved with any of it, but money was a powerful lure.

The peace medal on its pedestal stood in the center of the room. I edged closer, but a nearby voice stopped me.

"It worked! Gerald kept the code from me, but that fool could never remember anything. I knew the code would be kept with the museum's key in his desk. Good thing I had a spare key for the gallery so we could get back inside." There was delight in Brenda's voice. "After the great medal swap, we can hit the road."

Georgie emerged from the shadows. "Brenda Lee, I'm not sure we should go through with this."

"We have a buyer waiting." Brenda pulled Georgie into a hug.

Georgie slipped away from the embrace, but stayed next to Brenda, looking into the waist-high case with the Kiowa Peace Medal inside. "But after . . . after Gerald's death. The theft makes us look guilty."

Brenda turned to Georgie. She took Georgie's face in both hands. In a soft voice Brenda Lee said, "No one will ever know the original Kiowa Peace Medal is gone. The replica is that good. They have fooled two other museums." She released Georgie's face with a peck on her nose.

I rolled my eyes.

"Yeah, but . . ." Georgie wanted to be convinced.

Brenda planted a tender kiss on her lips. "No buts, with the money from this sale we have enough to start our life." A smile formed as Brenda talked. "A house with a pool for you and the baby, new cars, and a start on our own business. This is our chance to have it all, away from here."

A rustling came from the front. Neither Georgie or Brenda heard it. They were absorbed with each other and an imagined future.

Brenda gazed at the peace medal; her smile lit up the room. "I am sorry Gerald's dead." She said it with no sorrow in her voice.

Georgie seemed to stiffen but said nothing.

"Buck should never have killed him, probably fighting over the Crow family *Koitsenko* sash and lance. A jab from that lance would be deadly." She opened the casing.

A crash sounded from the front of the museum. Buck pushed through the doorway, Denny trailing. Buck was red with anger. "I did not kill Gerald!" He marched past, not noticing me crouched at the foot of a display counter. Denny faded into the shadows.

Georgie stared for a beat, letting her mind catch up with what she was seeing. "Buck, how—why?"

Buck moved toward Georgie, his hands outstretched. "You know I didn't kill Gerald. I covered it up for you. For us."

Before she could answer, Brenda stepped between the two. "We know you killed Gerald with the lance at the gallery. The *Koitsenko* warrior sash and lance are gone. And we all know they were there before Gerald ended up dead in his office." Brenda Lee had a smug look on her face.

Buck looked confused. He shifted to face Georgie. "You know Gerald wasn't killed at the gallery."

Brenda demanded, "Don't listen to him. We need to swap the medals and leave." Brenda turned back to the case, reached inside for the Jefferson Peace Medal.

My phone vibrated, emitting a slight buzz. Brenda pulled her hand out of the case without the peace medal. She looked at the case, concerned. Examined the casing door closely, apparently thinking it was the cause of the buzzing.

Denny crawled into the room. I flicked my phone off and moved low beneath a counter that held old bone tools and weapons. None of the three seemed to notice Denny or me.

Buck stepped closer to Georgie, pleading, "I took the body to the gallery, turned the AC on to mess with the time of death. For you. To protect you."

Brenda turned back to Georgie. She whispered, "Georgie, let's—"

Georgie pushed past Brenda to face Buck. "Why would you think I killed Gerald?"

Buck moved closer to her. "Going to the Pigpen, I saw Gerald head into the office. Soon as I got free of the cop, I hurried on over. I came in from the back, didn't want to be seen. Before I got to the office, I heard you scream." Buck shivered.

Georgie stared at Buck before giving a nod to continue.

"I went in the office. I saw what you did." Buck reached for Georgie's hand. "I got everything cleaned up. There's no proof. If we leave now—"

Georgie pulled away, a shocked expression on her face. "I couldn't, wouldn't kill anyone—"

Brenda Lee moved forward, took Georgie's arm. "She loves me. We're blowing this joint."

Buck grabbed Georgie's other arm. "She's my wife. Georgie's staying with me and our son."

Georgie shook free of both clinging lovers. "I want to understand. *Who killed Gerald?*" She glanced between them.

I took the opportunity to close the open display case with the original peace medal still inside. The click of the casing door broke the silence. The three turned toward me.

I stood in front of the case, blocking access. Georgie stepped back. "Mud! What are you doing here?"

"Looking for you all. We were supposed to meet at the gallery, remember?" I forced a smile. No one returned it.

Brenda reached for the peace medal replica she had placed on a nearby counter. "I don't have time for this. I have work to deal with."

"Are you going to pass the *exquisite replica* off as the original to your client, since you can't steal the real thing?" My question stopped her for a beat before Brenda, clutching the replica, stepped toward the museum's open door.

I moved in her way. "You're not leaving. You broke into the Complex. We're calling the police."

"The door was open. I came to compare the copy to the original. Something Gerald would have done, if . . ." She let the words hang in the air as she composed a sad face.

Buck whispered to Georgie.

I stood my ground.

Brenda let out an exasperated breath. "Business must go on. I'm extremely late delivering the replica Jefferson Peace Medal set to my client. Somehow, my car got two flats. We were trapped at the gallery for hours." Brenda stared at me as if I were the cause of the flats.

"I can't let the killer leave."

Georgie, hearing my words, moved closer.

Brenda's eyes hardened. "You've got the killer. Buck did it with the lance. I lied earlier to protect Georgie." Brenda lowered her voice, though we could all hear. "He's a brute. Beats her." She raised her voice, adding in a lilt, "But not anymore. Georgie and I are leaving together. We'll pick up the baby at her mother's house and hit the road." Brenda Lee turned and reached out to Georgie.

Buck growled.

Georgie shifted. Before she committed, I said, "Except Gerald's death occurred in the maintenance office, not the gallery, and not with the lance. But we *all* know that."

Buck nodded. I didn't see Denny, but I knew he was close by. Waiting.

Georgie broke the silence. "Who killed Gerald?"

Brenda Lee slipped an arm through Georgie's. "Let's go. We have a sale to close, money to collect, and a new life to start." She tucked the replica into her pocket.

Georgie turned to me. "I want to know."

Buck protested, "I didn't kill Gerald!" He pushed between Brenda and Georgie.

I raised my voice, "Buck didn't kill anyone. He moved the body because he was sure you killed Gerald." I spoke to Georgie but kept an eye on Brenda Lee. "Buck didn't know the murderer was already inside killing Gerald while Georgie was outside approaching the office. The killer had just enough time to land a single blow and slip off into the maintenance hut to hide before Georgie arrived." I shook my head, thinking of the timing of it all.

"Georgie's scream gave the cover needed for her to sneak out the back of the maintenance hut while Buck rushed into the office. Pretty smooth, Brenda Lee."

Chapter Thirty-Five

Brenda stuttered in protest, "I about fainted when we saw the body *at the gallery*. Remember?"

"I admit, that threw me off. Gerald dead at the gallery would put a lot of focus on you and the business. It made no sense that you would move the body there. And you really looked surprised to see Gerald dead, but later I realized you were shocked to see the *body there*. Not that Gerald was dead." I moved closer to Brenda. "Finally, I remembered Eli mentioned a blonde teetering around on mile-high heels—he saw you on your way to meet Gerald. And, unfortunately, you found him."

Georgie stepped back from Brenda Lee. "I was there. When Eli said that, I knew he was talking about you." She watched Brenda closely. "It was too early for our meetup. Why would you see Gerald without me?"

Brenda struggled to find an answer. She finally came up with a feeble, "For us. We deserved an equal split."

I could tell that Georgie saw through the lie. She responded, "You told me no one would be hurt. No one would ever know about the theft." Georgie turned to me. "All I did was distract you and Denny to give Brenda Lee and Gerald time to swap out the copy for the original. A victimless crime. That's what they said. And the money . . . so much money for just having you hunt for Buck with me." Georgie's eyes watered. "Instead, I find Gerald dead, the medal still in the museum, and then the body again." She wailed, "And, I got stuck in the back seat of a truck with you and Denny—all night."

I stared, couldn't believe the words spewing from the woman I had once loved. Finally, I choked out, "Good thing you were with us, or you would be getting arrested as an accomplice to murder."

Georgie protested, "I didn't know what happened, wasn't sure who killed Gerald. When Brenda Lee collapsed seeing the body, I thought Buck must have done it."

Buck shouted, "I didn't do it!"

Brenda harumphed in response.

I took a deep breath, looked directly at Georgie when I announced, "Brenda was shocked to find the body at the gallery because she knew she killed him at the maintenance office, far away from where it would incriminate her."

"I have heard enough." Brenda reached for Georgie. "We're leaving."

I raked my fingers through my tangled curls. I couldn't believe Georgie wavered, still thought of leaving with Brenda. I told them the rest. The truth—what the yellow daisy-print Converses revealed. "I can prove Brenda Lee killed Gerald. Check out her killer heels."

Brenda went white.

I continued, "Brenda was wearing her stiletto heels on the gravel at the Compound. She changed from them to her sneakers at the gallery." I looked at her in the daisy-print Converses. "The high heels are in the back of her car. One of the perfectly round heels will have blood mixed with mud and gravel. Brenda Lee used her stiletto heel to kill Gerald."

Georgie fell back. A counter covered in stone and bone artifacts stopped her from slipping to the floor.

Brenda Lee went to her. She pleaded, "It was never my intent. Gerald owed me. I wanted the medal, to go through with the sale, and he wanted to wait. All I wanted was my money—our money. Now."

Buck stared with surprise, almost shock, at Brenda. His jaw hung open.

Brenda Lee spoke only to Georgie. "Gerald laughed. Said the deal was over. The peace medal was too hot to make the switch. We had the two and needed to wait for things to cool down." Her face flushed with anger. "I told him there was no cool down for me. He promised payment, and I wanted it. That's when he said, 'We don't always get what we want, babe.' Made me so mad, I came at him." Brenda stopped to look at her hand, as if she were seeing the past. "My shoes were a mess. I had taken them off to clean them, to get that gravel and mud off my expensive heels. Had one in my hand; I forgot." Brenda Lee looked to Georgie. "It was hard walking across the gravel parking lot, then Gerald laughed at me, and I wanted my money. I needed the money to get away, to be happy. I deserve to be happy." A tear dropped down Brenda's cheek. "We were going to be happy."

Georgie backed away.

Brenda wiped the tear. She grabbed Georgie's arm. "It just *happened*. Gerald told me he needed more time and that's how it was. Then he pushed me up against that dirty wall." Brenda's face filled with disgust. "Gerald pressed into me and wiggled. Then he laughed and said, 'We can turn this into a good time.' I reacted, I hit him. I forgot I had the shoe in my hand." Brenda turned to face us. "I really did forget. I just reacted and hit him . . . hard." She stopped and looked at her hand in horror.

Georgie stared, saying, doing nothing.

A tear trailed down Brenda's nose. She rubbed it away before she spoke again, in a rush to get the words out, her tone low. "I knew right away it was bad. There was no blood, but the stiletto heel sunk into his temple like breaking through ice right into a soft center. When I pulled it out, Gerald fell, hit the back of his head on the desk, and laid there. Just laid there with that smirk. He died laughing."

Georgie turned away from Brenda.

Hurt crossed Brenda's face, quickly replaced by a sneer. She held tight to Georgie, while her other hand found a bone knife amidst the display counter. Without hesitation, the blade went to Georgie's throat. She faced the stunned Buck and me. "We're leaving now."

I stepped forward. "Brenda Lee, you don't want to do this. You're turning attempted theft and an accidental killing into grand larceny, kidnapping, and murder."

Brenda flinched when I said the last. She cried, "I didn't mean to kill Gerald, I didn't!"

Georgie stayed still in Brenda's grasp. She looked terrified.

Buck surged forward. I extended an arm to hold him back. Staying focused on Brenda, I said, "I understand."

Buck stayed in place, watched the scene unfold. Denny was nowhere in sight. Georgie's eyes begged for help.

I went on, "It sounds like Gerald's death was an accident. Don't make it worse. Give me the knife." I reached out, palm up.

Brenda pulled Georgie to her, shooting a hate-filled look toward Buck, who thankfully stayed in place. "She's mine, not his, not yours." The knife touched Georgie's throat—she stayed silent while her eyes screamed.

My voice softened. "Georgie doesn't belong to anyone, except to her son. He has first dibs on her for at least eighteen years. He needs her." I tried a shaky smile, hoped Brenda would relax her grip on the knife at Georgie's throat.

As I spoke, I stole glances at Georgie. Each time, I tried to beam comfort to her, to signal to her to stay calm, to stay in place. It didn't work.

It happened in a flash, a moment that lasted a lifetime. Georgie twisted against Brenda's hold. Buck leapt forward. Denny came from nowhere and tackled Buck midleap. Brenda pulled Georgie tight; the knife broke through flesh, bringing a thin red line of blood to the surface.

Lurching forward, I grabbed Brenda's hand with the knife at Georgie's throat, pulled it back and simply spoke her name, "Brenda." Our eyes locked. I silently pleaded.

The room went still. Time ticked on, an agonizing second at a time.

Brenda Lee released her hold on the knife and Georgie.

Chapter Thirty-Six

Denny beamed, looking around the museum. "The Kiowa's Jefferson Peace Medal is safe. Gerald's killer confessed, and the police are on their way." He squeezed my shoulder. "And our fracking worries are over."

I didn't respond, just watched Buck and Georgie in one corner whispering urgently together while across the room Brenda stared at nothing in complete silence.

Denny gave me a quizzical look. "Why aren't you happy? You can make your flight with time to spare. This muddy mess is solved." He couldn't hold back a grin.

I didn't return it. "The police are going to be questioning us for hours." I pulled my phone from my pocket, switched it on. "I'll be lucky to get back to Silicon Valley in time to see the end of my client's IPO event." My stomach tightened. "My agency will be ruined once the industry learns that I personally neglected a client right before the company's biggest event. Wasn't even there to go through the rehearsal's final changes and provide reassurances before the cameras rolled." My phone went crazy announcing calls missed and messages waiting. I silenced it without glancing at the screen. I let a deep breath out.

Denny started to speak; I raised my hand, stopping him. "It's all right, it was worth it." I felt the truth of my words. I continued, "An accidental killing was solved, Eli was saved from false accusations, the Kiowa Peace Medal is safe, and illegal fracking has been stopped." I let a smile form. "And I learned a life lesson."

Denny urged me on with "*Haw.*"

"Live life with a happy heart. It fills the world with good medicine."

Denny looked like he thought I was *mawbane.* It didn't matter; the owl feather weaved into my scalp lock hummed with satisfaction. I was listening.

Before Denny could fill the silence, I rushed on; I needed to make a confession. "Denny, you were right. I should have listened to you."

My words obviously surprised him. Denny sputtered, "I was right? What do you mean? You figured out who killed Gerald and why."

"You were right about Georgie from the start." I glanced over to Buck and Georgie huddled together. "Georgie was distracting us while Brenda and Gerald planned to swap the medals. If I had listened to you rather than think I knew the woman Georgie was . . ." I shook my head. "You were right when I was sixteen and you warned me that there was more greed than love in Georgie's heart."

Denny laughed. "Glad you've finally figured out who has the brains in the family." He snuck a glance at the three waiting for the police to arrive. "Mud, I had blinders on. I wanted Georgie or Buck guilty. I was just throwing mud to see where it stuck."

I smiled at his lame joke.

"Mud, you've got to go. Don't want to miss your flight."

"It's all right, I can't leave you with this." I looked from Buck and Georgie in a heated whispered discussion about their son to the silent Brenda Lee.

Denny's face split into a grin. "I got this handled. About the time Buck went past me into the museum, I started recording everyone and everything on my phone. I got it all. Everything the police need is right here." He held up his cell phone. Brenda's voice rang out, "I reacted, I hit him. I forgot I had the shoe in my hand." He thumbed the recording off. "You leave for your flight. I got this."

Relief flooded through me. I glanced at my phone to check. There was time. Lots of it.

Denny announced, "I told you we'd wrap this up in time for your flight."

Just as quick as my delight rose, it dropped. "Something's going on with Sky. I should . . ."

"Go catch your flight." He pointed me toward the exit. "I'll take care of Sky and Grandpa. I got them."

"Denny, are you absolutely sure I can leave?" Even as I asked, my mind was shifting into gear. I could make the flight, get back in time for final rehearsals and the IPO event.

He nodded. "Take my truck, leave it at the airport lot. I'll pick it up later."

I forced myself to not sprint for the truck. Instead, I smiled my thanks to my cousin.

"Just one thing." Denny shifted to a serious expression before he added, "You need to change clothes. You're a muddy mess, again."

I pulled Denny into a hard hug. Into my curls he said, "Mud, don't be a stranger." He added my true name, "*Ahn Tsah Hye-gyah-daw*, you know the way home."

My phone vibrated, giving me cover from the tears that started at Denny's words. I gave him a last squeeze and left the museum. Outside, the phone began another round of vibrations. I stared at it. Bernie was calling. My mind went blank; I wasn't sure what comments I had sent back early this morning. It was all a blur. My notes had felt right in the moment, but maybe my sleep-deprived mind had deceived me and the review cues made no sense. I took a deep breath and faced the buzzing phone.

"Muddy Mae, are you there?" Bernie's voice came from a distance.

I pulled the phone to my ear. "I'm here, Bernie. In fact, I'm headed to the airport. Should make my flight with time to spare." I tried to make my tone light, not betray the worry I felt.

Bernie's voice came across the air waves. It was excited, and happy. "That's great news. Though, with your notes, I don't know that we need you." I heard the smile as she continued, "Your changes were subtle, but made each piece flow so much better. The executives sense the power of the story. And if you can make engineers feel the story, we've nailed it."

I could feel her relief. I sent a smile to her as I replied, "I let the story breathe. That's all it needed. You all had everything near perfect."

Bernie let a deep breath out. "I am so glad you're coming back in time for rehearsal and the event. This is going to make everyone so happy!"

"Me too!" slipped out as I ended our call. I was happy.

I thought of *Tsi yee* Cora dancing naked around the fire. Her wise words came to me, warmed my soul, "*Live life with a happy heart. It fills the world with good medicine.*"

I headed for the plane and my Silicon Valley life—there was time. I still had time to find my way, to follow my aunt's words of wisdom, to live life happy. To spread good medicine.

In the distance, an owl hooted approval.

Glossary

Kiowa is a spoken language there is no alphabet. The following spelling of Kiowa words is a writing system to capture the sound of the words. It is for pronunciation purposes only. The spellings are not intended to represent an alphabet for the Kiowa language.

Sounds:

'k—sharp, hard K sound

K'—sharp hard K sound with touch of G at start of word

TD'—Indicates the word starts with a sharp clicking sound with cheek and tongue—like the sound used to urge a horse along.

T'—Tsk sound

To hear the sounds explained and language spoken by a Native Speaker, visit http://www.thekiowapeople.com

Words and Phrases:

A'date—Island Man. Chief of the Kiowa camp slaughtered by the United States–backed Osage in 1833. Known as Cut Throat Gap

Ah ho—Thank you

Ahn Tsah Hye-gyah-daw—She Knows The Way. Mud/Mae Sawpole's Kiowa name

Ah-T'aw-hoy—Feather headdress. Incorrectly called war bonnets.

Aim hay bay, gaw bay saw—You come in and sit down. (Greeting a single person)

Auh'K'aut—Curly hair

Aui-pah—Wrapped braids. Originally referred to the animal skin wrapping-around braids now used to reference any item used to wrap, pull back, or control long hair, including hair barrettes.

Bn'ee daw—Old Ones. Usually used to reference the last free Kiowa elders and first forced to live on reservations. The Old Ones passed oral traditions forward to their grandchildren living in two worlds.

Boen own knee—To see clearly

Daw'kee—Creator of All

Goom Maws—Dances, a gathering to celebrate a deed, person, event, or just life. Early white men called the gatherings powwows.

Hanpoko—Americans

Haw—Yes

Hawnay—No

Khoam—Friend

K'Hop'Ale—The Big Old Mountain. The Kiowa name for Mount Scott in the Wichita Wildlife Refuge.

Kohn—Water. Also, Mud's younger brother's name.

Koitsenko—Kiowa society consisting of the ten bravest warriors. Using a lance and sash, Koitsenko warriors anchored themselves to the ground, acting as the last defense between the enemy and the Kiowa people.

Kone—Grandfather

Kop-adle-gya—People of the Mountain Band of the Kiowa Tribe. Mud's band.

Kop-gya—Mountain People Band, the less formal name for *Kop-adle-gyaKoyh maton auh'-K'aut*—Curly-headed Kiowa girl

Koyh taw gee geah daw—The Kiowa Way

Mamanti—Walking above or SkyWalker

Mawbane—A nonthinking person. Said with venom and the appropriate hand signal, *mawbane* can be the worst insult given in a world dependent on each other for daily survival. Using a different tone and gesture, the word refers to someone acting crazy, not thinking or silly.

May hay bay, gaw bay saw—You all come in and sit down. (Greeting more than one person)

Ohdayhah—Enough

Ownah day aim broh—It is good to see you.

Saw-thaye kaul-aye thigh-gyah thaye-kope—Come and work together for the good of the people.

Sawpole—Owl, or when used in the right context, it could mean a silly person, a nut. Also Mud and Denny's last name.

Sawpole Gyah—Owl Talker

TD'aukoy—White people, usually those of European descent

TD'oh poat—Brush arbor

Thigh-gyah ate thoe-dayn-mah—I speak straight, tell the truth.

Tsi yee—Paternal aunt

Acknowledgments

Wow! Mud rides again! I am amazed and so very delighted with the response from readers. Thank you for reading and embracing the Mud Sawpole Mysteries. When I was twelve, my grandfather told me I was next to share our history and stories to ensure that Kiowa customs, traditions and people would not be forgotten. The Mud Sawpole Mysteries is one of the ways I try to live up to that responsibility.

I was stunned when Tristan at Once Upon a Book Club selected *Never Name the Dead* for their November selection. Thanks to OUABC, thousands more now know about the Kiowa Tribe. We are a small Tribe with a big attitude. *Ah Ho* Once Upon a Book Club for helping preserve the Kiowa culture!

Silent Are the Dead may not have made it to print if not for Carolyn Wheat, attorney, award-winning author, editor and teacher extraordinaire. I had a moment of doubt with the near-complete manuscript. Carolyn answered my call for help without hesitation. She took time to read my manuscript, provided edits, and, most important, reassured me that I had a good story that needed to be shared. Carolyn, I can *never* thank you enough!

Acknowledgments

My agent, Liz Trupin-Pulli continued to provide unflagging support to me and for the Mud Sawpole mysteries. Liz was the first to believe in my novels and concept of blending murder with a Kiowa four-day spiritual quest. I appreciate having you as my agent.

Many *Ah Hos* to the amazing Crooked Lane Books/Alcove Press for publishing the Mud Sawpole Mysteries! Thanks to Publisher Matt Martz with Editor Melissa Rechter, the marketing team of Madeline Rathle and Dulce Botello, and production expertise from Rebecca Nelson and Thaisheemarie Fantauzzi Perez, more people than I ever imagined have heard of the Kiowa Tribe. You all have helped preserve a vanishing culture! Thank you so much for getting my books out there and making me look good!

Miki Webb is the friend (really family) and cheerleader everyone should have in life. She reads all I throw at her and always provides needed insights that improves each story, article, or blurb. It is such a treat (and relief) to know Miki is just a text away!

Greg Norman never says no. The multitalented man can create anything and he does! Greg has created www.dmrowell.com, the Mud Sawpole video promos, bookmarks, postcards, information sheets, and everything of beauty surrounding my books. All he creates is wrapped in good energy, because he is full of boundless positive energy. You can see more of his creations at www.norcraftdigitalmedia.com.

Jill Norman and Amy Gorder make sure my stories are worth reading. Their opinion matters to me. As avid readers, Jill and Amy know good storytelling. Thankfully they share their thoughts on my early drafts, offering much needed insights, suggestions, and tidbits that always improves my stories.

Acknowledgments

I can't thank Dave Van Ess enough for his unending support and amazing wooden bookmarks, tessellation puzzle pieces, and slate work he makes for my book events. Dave even made a beautiful slate marker for my cat's grave site. So glad we are friends!

My family and friends are amazing! So many have read my book, come out to a reading, invited me to their book club, offered positive reviews, sent texts, and encouraged me to continue writing. Thank you all! I cannot tell you how often your kind words have given me the boost needed to write on.

Eddie Rowell scares me by coming up with great villains and unique means of killing; but I appreciate every suggestion! Diane Self is the ideal little sister; she still thinks I can do anything. Debra Rowell was my first partner in imaginary adventures, from Indians and cowboys to space exploration. Bob Price has shown a lifetime of patience enduring my daily calls while offering mumbled encouragement. Dorothy Rowell makes sure to send much needed good smoke my way daily and David Baker keeps me surrounded in good medicine with his handmade dreamcatchers and leathercrafts. *Ah Ho* and much love to you all!

Janie Rowell helped me research Kiowa traditions for years as we traveled all over Oklahoma, interviewing and videotaping Tribe elders sharing their incredible life stories, songs, dances, crafts, language, and memories of growing up Kiowa. Janie is a woman full of heart. Having her at my side made every day a fun adventure. So glad we are family!

My Mom and Dad are unending in their support and praise. There will never be enough words to thank them for a childhood that encouraged me to read and imagine possibilities. They worked hard through life to give each of their children and grandchildren better lives than they had. Thank you, Mom and Dad. I love you both!

Acknowledgments

My son, Lucas is the light of my life. I am so pleased when he reads a draft and gives me his opinions—good, bad, or indifferent. All helps! I strive to make him as proud of me as I am of him every day of his life.

Lanie and I have been together for forty years; the absolute best thirty-seven years of my life! She has pushed me when needed, pulled me along when necessary, but mostly, Lanie has been at my side urging me to live life happy, while we both strive to reach our potential, alone, together. I feel blessed to have you as my love and partner in life.

—Ah Ho!